Reviews

Book Riot — Laura Kemp's debut novel 'Evening in the Yellow Wood' is what happens when a mystery sticks comedy in its hair like flowers, frolics through a field of romance and then goes tumbling headlong down a magical hole.

Alexia Gordon, Author of the *Gethsemane Brown* Mystery Series — Laura Kemp blends folklore, the supernatural, romance, and mystery in this complex tale of a missing father, family secrets, and a killer who transforms tortured dreams into waking nightmares. The small-town setting in the backwoods of Michigan adds to the eerie suspense and throat-tightening tension of Evening in the Yellow Wood, the story of a woman's search for the father who abandoned her—and the truth for which he sacrificed everything to protect her. — Alexia Gordon Lefty Award-winning, Agatha Award-nominated author of The Gethsemane Brown Mysteries

Penni Jones, Author of *On the Bricks* and *Kricket* — Laura Kemp's debut novel 'Evening in the Yellow Wood' is an engaging and eclectic story of family bonds that surpass physical presence and friendships that survive hardships, all set against the rich backdrop of rural Michigan. It's abundant in both beauty and suspense, and I can't wait to see what Kemp delivers next.

Steph Post, Author of *A Tree Born Crooked, Lightwood,* and *Miraculum* — 'Evening in the Yellow Wood' has it all — fast pacing, deep mystery and a surprising paranormal twist, all delivered with literary finesse. A compelling story with something for everyone.

Lynda Curnyn, Author of *Killer Summer* and *Confessions of an Ex-Girlfriend* — Who do you trust in a world where nothing is what it seems, and the past is not only alive — but deadly? Laura Kemp's haunting debut novel explores how the ties that make us who we are can also be the bonds that break us.

Dedication

For Mom, who wrote down my stories when I was too little to do it myself, and Dad, who tied inner tubes together and swam with me to the middle of Klinger Lake

Evening in the
Yellow Wood

Prologue

It was Tuesday afternoon, the sun hot on my pink shoulders as I sat dangling my feet in the shallow end of the community pool. My friend Sherry was by my side when I saw Mom, her face pinched in the unforgiving light.

"We need to go," Mom said as she reached down to pull at my elbow. Instead, she came away with the strap of my blue bathing suit. I muttered under my breath, reached up to swat at her hand in pubescent embarrassment. Suppose it slipped off and revealed what God had barely given me? What would Jake Jones, my current crush who was doing backflips off the diving board, think?

I didn't move.

"Justine!" Mom hissed, and my friend made a face, rolled her eyes, and got slowly to her feet while slinging her towel over her shoulder.

"What's the rush?" I asked, annoyed, thinking I would make her pay later for being so pushy by refusing to do homework or take out the trash. Stink up the place.

"You'll see," she snapped, and something inside of me took notice.

I shut my mouth before I made things worse and grabbed my flowered terrycloth towel, keeping three paces behind as we walked towards our brown Pontiac.

I got in the back seat and slammed the door. The radio was bleating white noise as my friend gave me "The Look" that said I'd better call later with the scoop as we pulled up outside her split-level house.

I tried to smile, to apologize, but Sherry understood. Mom was a dork, but my friends put up with it because we had a ping-pong table in our basement and my Dad was cooler.

Hip.

Zen.

As his only child, I felt the same.

I looked at Mom, wondering why a man who had tied inner tubes together with fishing line and swam with me to the middle of Tamarack Lake had married someone so uptight—realizing moments later I wouldn't be here if he hadn't seen something in her that I didn't.

"Bye," Sherry called over her shoulder. And then the exaggerated wink. "Call ya later."

I knew she would, and that Mom would want to know what we talked about and that Dad would sit eating his chili supper and wonder about other things, sometimes so far away I couldn't touch him even though we sat side by side.

We pulled into our own driveway five minutes later. I sat in the backseat, sullen and staring outside at the dappled sunlight on our cracked cement until Mom finally turned to me.

"It's your Dad."

So now he belonged to me?

"What about him?" I shrugged.

"He's not here."

"I know that," I answered in a surly tone. Dad always took off for the woods when we went to the pool, said he couldn't stand the crowds or the smell of chlorine.

"I mean he's gone." She paused. "Really gone."

My eyes darted toward the garage. The door was up. Dad's spot was empty.

"Where'd he go?"

"That's just it." Mom put a hand to her face, touched her index finger to the bridge of her nose and I hated that she left me hanging.

"Mom," I asked, wanting her to answer quickly so I would know how to feel. "Where's Dad?"

"I have no idea, Justine."

I tried to make sense of what she'd said even as my breath hitched in my chest. I thought back to the last time I'd seen him: that morning before he left for his shift at the paper mill. He had bent down, ruffled the top of my head, and kissed me on the cheek.

Be good, Muffet. Give your Mom a break.

"He probably had to work overtime or something and forgot to tell you."

She shook her head and the barest of smiles touched her lips, the one I hated because it usually meant I was wrong.

"I went out to run some errands while you were at the pool and when I came home," she touched her nose again, her brown hair falling over her face in a way that made her look like a nun in prayer. "I found this."

I saw something in her clenched fist, something she was handing over the back seat, a piece of crumpled notebook paper that had been folded neatly into quarters, her name printed in the block letters I recognized.

With shaking hands, I took it, the smell of chlorine suddenly suffocating me.

I looked at Mom again.

"Read it," she said.

I did. The first line made it clear he loved us very much and always would. The second had me tearing at the car door, racing up the driveway, and into the house we'd shared for almost twelve years.

I can't tell you why I had to leave or if I'll ever be able to come back.

I made it to the front door, yanked it open, and fumbled with the hook and eye latch on our screen.

The painting in the studio just sold. Put the money toward Justine's college.

"Dad!"

It would be better if you don't try to find me.

I ran upstairs to his bedroom and threw open the closet door. Some clothes and an overnight bag he used when he went fishing were missing.

I ran down the hall to my own room—a pink and purple confection I'd just started decorating in my own style, one of Dad's forest landscapes above the bed. Had he left something for me? A note explaining what he really meant to say? A place we could meet up and ditch Mom, live the free and easy life we'd always wanted?

A package tied carefully with silver ribbon that just matched my bedspread was sitting in plain sight. A card was taped to the center.

Muffet.

I tore the card open so quickly I cut my finger.

An orange kitten with a party hat adorned the front, a ball of pink twine between his paws.

Hope your Birthday is PUUURFECT.

I clenched my teeth so hard my jaw hurt. My birthday was a month away and I sure as hell didn't care about a stupid kitten. And damn if my birthday this year would be anything close to *PUUUURFECT!*

I went to my knees, my own hair falling against my hot cheeks and sticking there. The next minute I was ripping up the card and the awful orange kitten with the party hat. I sat in the middle of the confetti pieces for a long time, sobbing, my face pressed against my bedspread.

Dad was gone.

The Zen vanished.

The magic over.

Chapter One

Webber wasn't a town that liked to surprise people. Situated about thirty miles south of Kalamazoo in the flatlands of southern Michigan, it was homespun, mellow, and meandering. People who lived there knew what to expect and whom to expect it from.

I was no different. I'd grown up in Webber, gone to school there and learned how to tee pee houses after Friday night football games within its parameters. After graduation I'd done what all the cool kids did: got the hell out and headed for college.

After four years at Western Michigan University, I surprised everyone, including myself, by moving back home and settling into a one-bedroom apartment in the bustling downtown district, a two-block radius that included the Dime a Dozen Diner and Pawsitive Pals Pet Salon.

It was a safe choice—a lame choice, I had to admit—and one that left me wondering if the quiet certainty of the town was why I decided to take a job at the local newspaper when Chicago was only three hours away.

And so I settled in, spent my free time writing poems and hanging out with the few high school friends who remained, dating some of the local guys I hadn't glanced at before, thinking that if I stayed long enough Dad would find his way back home and I would stumble upon him floating across Tamarack Lake in his silver canoe, his hair catching fire in the sun as it always had.

Whatever the reason I had decided to come home and live a mundane life, everything changed the minute I walked into work one morning and saw the latest edition of the *Webber Sentinel.*

News from the north seldom made a splash down here, but the record snowfall that buried the small village of Lantern Creek did.

The name stuck in my mind and wormed around for a bit. Aside from its poetic beauty, I was certain I'd heard Mom and Dad arguing about it one night when I stood peering around the door jam, daring them to see me and take notice and tell me to get back to my room. Why they cared about a place I'd never heard of was of no interest to me at the time, but my juvenile mind figured it was because *he* wanted to go fishing and *she* wanted him to stay home.

Like always.

So I asked to go along, but Dad had refused. Fishing was his time to be alone and contemplate whatever artists who were forced to work in paper mills thought about.

I wouldn't understand, he said. And he was right.

Yes, the name Lantern Creek struck a chord that morning at the office of the *Webber Sentinel* and so I paused, quickly scanning the article and the picture that accompanied it. It featured four men with a shovel standing beside a massive snowdrift in front of a hardware store. Measuring by the handle, it appeared that about a foot and a half of snow had fallen.

Record spring snowfall buries small Michigan town.

Then I saw it.

Inside the store, half hidden by the glare from the windowpane stood a man peering out—a man with shoulder-length blond hair—a man I hadn't seen since he told me to give Mom a break ten years before.

I felt the walls of the office go soft and rubbery.

Ten years had passed since that day at the community pool—but in some ways, it felt much longer. I remembered that first birthday without Dad and how I had refused to open the gift he'd left for me, wanting to hurt him somehow, knowing he would have no idea if I'd opened it and so I shoved it back in the far corner of my closet.

I remembered my first boyfriend later that same year, my first heartbreak—remembered wishing for a bit of Dad's common sense in the discombobulated world I shared with Mom.

I remembered ten years of whispers and stares, of piteous looks from my teachers when some activity involving a father was mentioned. It wasn't as if I was the only kid who didn't have a dad in the picture, I was just the only one who didn't know what had happened to him, and the mystery hung over my head like a giant Bermuda Triangle, drawing attention to The Great Question of "Where did Robert Cook run off to?" It seemed "The Question" was on the windward side of every encounter, along with "Did Brenda drive him to it? Was there another woman? Was he involved with the Mob? The CIA? Aliens?"

I'd heard it all—and grown up fast because of it.

And now I stood looking at a picture of him where no trace had existed before. Ten years seemed to fold like an accordion around my shoulders, the smell of chlorine coming to me as it had that day at the community pool.

I stood up quickly, stepped back from the paper, and tried to steady my breath. Momentary light-headedness was followed closely by anger, then sadness until I found myself tearing through the article again, looking for a quote or a caption or anything that would tell me who had taken the picture.

The photo was not credited.

I spun on my heel and almost ran into our receptionist.

"Sorry," I managed, a loopy smile on my face. "This article"—I hit it a couple of times with my index finger for emphasis—"is *really* great."

She nodded, looked at me like I had a lobster hanging from my earlobe, and scurried back to her desk. Scanning the office, I saw my editor and quickly made my way towards her.

She was a short woman, pleasant and plump, with a homey style and penchant for dressing in appliqued sweatshirts that made me feel comfortable. She always took a personal interest in her staff, which had never bothered me before but seemed tedious now as I endured several questions regarding the health of my cat.

"You know Joey," I shrugged. "He's up to eight and a half lives now."

She laughed in the knowing way Cat People do, then asked me what I needed.

"Who took the picture of that blizzard up north?"

She seemed to sense my uneasiness. "It was sent from Alpena. Didn't Allan caption it?"

I tried very hard not to hit her over the head with the rolled-up newspaper I held in my hand.

"He didn't. When did the snow come through?"

"I don't know," she replied, confused by my sudden interest in an obscure story about an even more obscure town. "Maybe you should read the article."

"Oh, yeah," I agreed, loopy smile in place. "Will do."

I went back to my desk, unfolded the paper as though it were one of the Dead Sea Scrolls, and discovered the record snowfall had taken place two weeks before on the fifth of May.

Five minutes later, I had the Lantern Creek Hardware Store on the telephone.

The young girl who answered was unable to tell me who had taken the picture or if a man named Robert Cook had been in that day or if he even lived in the area. After a garbled conversation with a co-worker, she handed the phone over to an older man who identified himself as the owner. He told me that he knew of some Cooks over in the Onaway area, but they didn't come into the store very often.

"They got a big Walmart goin' in over there. No need to darken our doorstep."

"Ah," I commiserated, not wanting to get involved in northern hardware store politics. "I see. Thank you for your time."

"What ya want with him?"

I considered his question. What *did* I want with a man who had ditched me in the way I'd dreamed of ditching Mom—and couldn't think of an answer. So I lied.

"He owes me some money. We thought he'd skipped the state but—"

"Come to think of it," the owner interrupted. "I can't remember anyone being in the store when that picture was taken. They all went outside, ya know. Wanted to be in the paper."

"The store was empty?" I asked, a chill as wet and heavy as the snow that had buried Lantern Creek sweeping my arms.

"Best of my knowledge."

"Who took the picture?"

He laughed, a bit of his Northern Michigan accent coming out. "One of those big newspaper people from Alpena. He was in and out lickety-split. Didn't even buy a roll of duct tape—"

"Thanks for your time," I said quickly before he got started again.

He stopped, cleared his throat. "Hope you find the SOB."

I paused, profanity never seeming so ambiguous. "Me, too."

And so I hung up, feeling full of the nothing that always seemed to follow my father. And yet the sensible side of me pulled back when I felt the uncontrollable urge to call every person in Lantern Creek and demand they tell me where Robert Cook lived.

Something like that would spook Dad, a man who had always seemed half-ghost to me anyway.

I returned to the article, looked at the picture and saw my father, plain as day, staring back at me from inside the store. I checked other copies, rummaging through our dispenser outside like a crazy woman, feeling half-crazy myself when an idea began to materialize.

The first thing I needed to do was move up north and find a cheap apartment. The next step would be to locate a reasonably sane roommate to help share expenses with. If things went well, I'd be able to track Dad down in a matter of weeks and ask him a few questions.

Like why he left the awful kitten birthday card or thought that painting would come anywhere close to covering my college expenses.

And so I set my plan in motion. I gave my editor notice, started letting my friends know I was leaving town for the summer. I even let the guy I'd gone to

Starbucks on a coffee date know, hoping it would be enough to get a rise out of him. But it didn't, and the fact that I didn't care told me all I needed to know.

When the big day finally came, I was terrified—but not enough to change course.

I got up early, ate oatmeal sprinkled with raisins for breakfast, and stared at my packed suitcases all lined up neatly by the front door before searching for Joey, an orange cat that looked suspiciously like the birthday card kitten. He usually greeted me with a figure eight swish around the legs, but today seemed to have gone AWOL. Instead of enjoying a pre-trip cuddle, I spent the morning trying to coax him out from under my bed with a can of tuna.

I looked at the clock beside my bed.

10:15 a.m.

No call from Mom yet, and she usually checked in at 10:00 a.m. to make sure I was fighting the good fight.

Instead of dwelling on what her silence meant, I tried to enjoy my last few minutes in Webber. Mom's stance on my sudden move up north was no surprise. I'd known since tenth grade that if I ever wanted to go looking for Dad, I'd have to do it on my own.

Despite the stark reality of my situation, I still wanted her to call and do the Mom Thing and say everything was going to be okay—that I would find him and he would explain why he'd chosen to leave the day I'd gone with Sherry to the community pool.

By 11:00 a.m. I'd dressed in my comfy black yoga pants and a white t-shirt. Slipping on my favorite pair of ballet flats, I wiggled my toes in search of the hollows I'd earned from months of use.

The Prodigal Daughter was leaving home for good.

Or the summer.

I hadn't decided which.

Luckily, I'd found a co-worker to sub lease the apartment. She was getting a great deal and didn't care how long I stayed in Lantern Creek as long as I left my furniture.

Donna the Editor had even promised to hold my old position if I decided to move back home. She thought I should write a story about my search, buttering me up with the assurance that it would be featured prominently in the Saturday edition beside the supermarket sales fliers. Everything had fallen into place.

It wasn't like I was leaving Webber for good.

I could always come home to more of the same.

I held that thought, wondering why it made me sad. A passing glance in the hallway mirror and I knew I was as ready as I was ever going to be. The reflection showed a petite girl with an early summer tan, wavy blonde hair that just reached the middle of her back, and large, hazel eyes.

I was short, like my Mom—and had always felt like a child compared to my taller, more voluptuous friends.

Your eyes are your best feature. And don't ever cut your hair.

Mom had given me implicit instructions on how to make myself more attractive to the opposite sex. I think she hoped I'd have better luck than her in that department, but so far that hadn't been the case.

I frowned into the mirror, wondering if my shirt was too tight and my pants were too short and how it would feel to be a semi-permanent resident of Lantern Creek. Instinctively I reached for my throat to touch my favorite silver necklace, a gift I'd given to myself by pilfering Mom's jewelry box. She seemed angry that I had taken it, but also reticent—revealing later that Dad had given it to her shortly after their wedding. The delicate circle intersected with a cross meant something to my father and since he wasn't around to yell at me for snooping, I was allowed to keep the necklace.

I touched it again, then reached for the one thing I had yet to find a place for—the old purple birthday package tied with silver ribbon.

It had faded with age, the old Scotch tape Dad had torn with his own fingers barely holding the thing together, and I still couldn't bring myself to open it.

Not after that kitten and the PUUURFECT birthday nonsense.

That didn't mean I hadn't stared at the thing a million times over the past ten years. I'd even peeled the corner back at one particularly low point—but stopped short, knowing somewhere in my juvenile heart that a Care Bear or Easy Bake Oven wasn't going to fix what Dad had broken.

I hated to think what a therapist would say about my "no opening" stance, but that didn't matter at the moment. I was packing up and heading north and maybe if I found Dad and things went good, we could open that damn thing together.

"This is it, Joey," I said once I saw him stick his nose out from under the bed. "We're really gonna do it."

One glance at the black Honda Civic parked outside my apartment and I began to have second thoughts.

We'd been in tight spots before, but never a trip of this magnitude and I offered a small prayer to the God of Automotives—a deity I imagined looked like Schneider from *One Day at a Time* reruns—before shoving Joey in his carrier and heading out the door. If the "Heap" failed me now, I'd have to fork over money for a car or bribe my new roommate to play chauffeur.

Which made me think of Holly Marchand. I'd found her through an incredible stroke of luck otherwise known as my hairdresser's boyfriend. He was originally from Cheboygan and had once dated a girl who worked at a sleepaway camp outside of Lantern Creek. He had no idea if she was still there but handed over her phone number with a strange smirk on his face that told me I was going to have an interesting summer.

I didn't ask why he still had her number.

Lucky for me, Holly still lived in Lantern Creek and still thought fondly of her time with the gentleman in question. She was in a transitional phase of her life that included spinning her wheels at Camp Menominee while living in her parents' basement. We seemed to be a match made in heaven.

We had agreed to meet at five o'clock and check out an apartment for rent in a neighborhood close to downtown. I was mildly surprised to find myself ten minutes early for our appointment after my five-and-a-half-hour drive, and so began searching the street for the blue Chevy Lumina she'd described on the phone.

Instead, I found a red Ford pickup blocking my progress into the driveway. Moments later a large, jowly man dressed in a plaid shirt stepped out. With a quick hitch of his pants, he crossed the distance between our vehicles and gave me a curious look.

This must be the landlord Holly had described as "a real ball-buster." He was also my first introduction to the local townsfolk, and so I wanted to make a good impression.

I rolled down my window, raised my hand to shade my face from the sun. "Mr. Stoddard?"

He nodded, his face impassive. "You'da flatlander?"

"Um…yeah." I had forgotten how locals referred to anyone who lived south of Grand Rapids. Although I found the term presumptuous since nothing in Lantern Creek remotely resembled a mountain.

Wiping the side of his mouth with a white hanky he'd pulled from the back pocket of his jeans, he took a step closer.

"Got any pets?"

"Um…yeah," I admitted, feeling guilty. "One cat."

"One cat?" he repeated, wiping the other side.

"Yes, sir. One cat."

"That the other girl?"

I looked down the length of Ravine Drive—an ordinary road pockmarked with rutted acne and truant gravel—and spotted Holly's car.

We watched as she rolled to a stop, the radio blaring an old ABBA tune as Holly herself stepped out.

"Holy crap," I heard her mutter. "Someone needs to seal that friggin' road!"

Even when annoyed, Holly Marchand oozed sensuality. With long, dark hair that hung in curls I wished my own would emulate and a curvaceous figure she didn't try to hide, I was reminded of Norma Jean before Marilyn took the stage.

I wondered what Mr. Stoddard would think of the bombshell standing in his driveway but he didn't speak or scold or introduce himself, he simply hitched his pants up again and made his way towards the back door.

I looked at Holly, who shrugged while extending a manicured hand.

"You must be Justine."

I nodded, hoping we would hit it off.

"You've got that cute little cheerleader thing going on," she said while emphasizing her appraisal with a clockwise swirl of her right hand.

"Oh," I started, not used to being labeled so quickly by someone I'd just met. "I guess so… I mean—"

"And I've got the dark exotic beauty thing covered," she counter-clockwised her left hand. "So we won't have to worry about competing for guys."

I laughed, unsure if she was serious. "I'm not really looking for *guys* so to speak—"

She arched an eyebrow. "Looking for girls?"

"No!" I said. "I mean…no…I like guys. I'm just not *looking* for them…so to speak."

"Speak away but they'll be looking for you." She held her hand up and coaxed me into a high five. "Most of the eligible ladies up here have seen better days. Teeth have gotten to be a rare commodity, present company excluded."

"Of course," I smiled, feeling my reserve melt away when Mr. Stoddard stuck his head out of what I hoped was our soon-to-be window, and shouted, "You girls coming up or what?"

"Prince Charming he is not." Holly jerked her thumb in his direction.

"Guess not," I agreed while turning and following her through the back door. We ascended a staircase resembling a spine wracked with scoliosis before entering a quaint kitchen with yellow walls and slanted ceilings.

Mr. Stoddard was talking about the appliances before we even had a chance to swipe the countertops for dust. I nodded like I knew what he was talking about while moving toward the window for a glimpse of our backyard. It looked perfect for sunbathing and tossing a ball with the dog we didn't have.

I smiled, wondering if Joey would like a buddy when an elderly woman in a wide-brimmed hat ambled into view. She wore slacks of an indeterminable color and gardening gloves as she bent over a patch of orange flowers.

Asclepias Tuberosa, I remembered Mom telling me as I helped her in the garden during our long summer days "Post Dad." *Otherwise known as Butterfly Weed.* Good for the Monarchs as they migrated towards South America.

Mom always wanted to make sure the butterflies got where they were going.

"Who's that?" I asked, pointing to the woman, quite clearly our downstairs neighbor.

"Her name's Iris," Mr. Stoddard came to stand beside me. "She came with the house."

I laughed before I could help myself.

He smiled. "This place has been in her family for a long time. Only catch was she got to stay downstairs."

As if she heard us, the woman turned and looked up. Something in the way her eyes met mine made me unable to look away, a gesture that would have seemed rude a moment ago but now felt natural. Suddenly embarrassed, I stepped back from the window.

She returned to her Butterfly Weed.

I made a mental note to introduce myself later, wondering if she might have information on Dad if she really had lived here that long.

Mr. Stoddard moved suddenly around the kitchen counter, barely missing a laminate bar and two wobbly stools.

Holly seized her chance to finally run her finger over the counters, asking all sorts of questions that made her seem like the next big thing in house hunting when Mr. Stoddard turned and moved to the next room.

The living area was paneled exclusively in glossy, faux-brown wood and sheathed in blue shag. Holly pivoted on her heel and made a gagging gesture. I knew exactly what she was thinking: *ski lodge, circa 1975*.

Just off the slopes was a green bathroom with turtle-trimmed wallpaper. A short hallway led to two bedrooms and a tiny porch shaded by the branches of a perfectly formed sugar maple.

Mr. Stoddard stopped mid-stride and cleared his throat. Shoving his hands in his pockets he proceeded to name his price. It was a very reasonable price—and Lord knew we needed "reasonable" with only one tenant gainfully employed.

"We'll take it," Holly said quickly.

I added my two cents with a smile while our landlord grunted out the rules, number one being the requisite speech about damages coming out of our deposit. Number two hit closer to home.

"Keep that cat under control," he looked at me and I saw a muscle twitch in his cheek. "No shitting in Iris' flowerbed."

I frowned, feeling the need to defend what had, for all practical purposes, been the only dependable man in my life. "Joey's a gentleman. He doesn't scratch or bite or pee outside of his box."

"I'm sure he's all that and a bag of chips."

I gave a half-hearted laugh, wondering if all northern men shared his charm before realizing I wasn't actually looking for a guy…so to speak.

After forking over our deposit, Ol' Sour Puss saw fit to spread his sunshine elsewhere. I listened to the heavy retreat of his footfalls with a sense of relief, seizing the opportunity to sprawl out on the blue shag. I'd only stopped once in Big Rapids to eat a bean burrito and go to the bathroom and was starting to feel the exhaustion that comes with hours on the open road.

Holly noticed my mood and came over to sprawl beside me. "This sure beats Bill and Marty's basement. Thanks for talking me into it, Squirt."

"Squirt?" I asked, puzzled.

"You're a little thing."

I frowned. I'd been looking at myself every day for the past ten years wishing for a little bit of what she had a lot of, but she didn't have to rub it in.

I rolled over onto my back, stared at the ceiling, and wondered how long I could hide the truth and if telling her would ruin my chances of finding Dad. I wasn't sure I could trust her, wasn't sure I wanted her pity, and was sure as hell certain I didn't need her questioning me every step of the way.

Despite my misgivings, I couldn't help myself. The opportunity to learn about him was so ripe, like an apple that bent the branch it hung from.

"You ever run into anyone up here named Robert Cook?"

She scrunched up her face, thinking hard for a few seconds. "How old is he?"

"Around forty-five," I tried to sound nonchalant.

She held up a hand. "You think I hang around with old guys?"

I laughed, trying to throw her off. "He's an uncle. My Dad's like, one of eight children and we heard his brother moved up here a few years ago."

Truth was my father was an only child, just like me—and his parents had died before I was born. No cousins came on Easter to hunt for colored eggs, no grandparents bounced me on their knee. Which made finding him that much harder.

"Ask the old lady downstairs, bet she knows the Founding Fathers."

I nodded, thinking I might take her advice.

"Is that what brings you up here? I mean…I wondered why you would want to come to a Podunk town like this, but I didn't wanna ask."

From what little I knew about Holly Marchand, "not wanting to ask" didn't seem like her style and so concluded her silence meant she didn't want to ruin her chances of escaping "Bill and Marty's Basement." Which meant she might be trustworthy.

In time.

"Yeah," I conceded. "Robert Cook took part of Dad's inheritance when Grandma died and we want to get it back."

"So, they sent you?" She raised an eyebrow. "You're not gonna go all 'Dog the Bounty Hunter' on me?"

I laughed nervously, trying to think of a reasonable excuse. "Heck no! He's a good guy. I was always his favorite niece, so they thought I might be able to talk him into coming home."

"Really?" the eyebrow went up again and I wondered if I'd blown it already.

"Worth a shot, right? And I needed to get out of town for a while," I coughed, fishing for the one thing I thought would intrigue her. "Man trouble."

She shook her head, a sad smile dusting her lips. "No wonder you're not looking."

"Nope," I agreed, hoping she would buy it, realizing I was going to have to get better at lying if I wanted to fly under the radar up here.

"One thing I don't understand," she asked, and my heart chirruped. "How could he be a good guy if he ran out on his whole family?"

I focused on a water stain in the pitted ceiling to keep from tearing up.

Good question.

Chapter Two

The rest of that day lingered like a wet fog over the Big Lake, blanketing everything in slippery moisture that made moving our large furniture difficult. Lucky for us the biggest load consisted of two twin beds, and even those we were able to manage with a little girl power.

More than once I found my mind wandering.

Now that I was here in Lantern Creek I felt Dad's magic surrounding me again, as though he would step from the mist at any moment and place me in the soft crook of a tree as though nothing had happened.

I knew I wasn't ready to run into him at the corner store, wasn't sure if I'd even have the courage to call his name if I saw him jogging down the sidewalk. And that was a big "if" considering Mr. Congeniality at the hardware store didn't remember anyone being inside when the picture was taken.

Holly's suggestion about our downstairs neighbor was the best advice I'd gotten yet and so I made up my mind to visit her before the week was up. Maybe she would know someone who knew someone who had somehow heard of Robert Cook.

I frowned because thoughts of Dad invariably turned towards thoughts of Mom.

She hadn't called. In fact, the last two days marked the longest breach in communication between us—an unspoken standoff that felt both strained and liberating.

I fished my cell phone from my pocket and looked at it, willing it to ring first so I wouldn't look like the sucker.

Uncomfortable moments passed—time filled with memories of that long-ago Tuesday and how my mother had cried into her pillow all night long while I listened through the back wall of my closet.

I looked at my cell phone again and dialed her number.

She answered on the third ring, breathless, no doubt having left her flower garden and all the spectacular things that seemed to happen there.

"Hey," I tried the sweet approach. "I made it."

I could almost hear her nodding, the brown hair that had once fallen across her face now a cute pixie cut. "Good."

I cleared my throat, unsure how to proceed. "The place is nice and rent's cheap."

"Will you look for a job?"

I felt guilty. "I might try the newspaper. Donna said she'd give me a reference."

She paused, and I knew she was thinking of the best way to offer up her daily dose of unsolicited advice. "Why bother, Justine? We both know you won't be up there long enough to make it worth your while."

I swallowed, my throat thickening just as it had when I was a child. "I might be here awhile. You never know."

"Going to bond with your Dad?"

I felt the edges of my eyes tingle and hated her for it. "Would that be so wrong?"

"Justine—"

"*Would* it?"

A slight pause. "Yes."

"Why?" I asked. "Tell me what you know."

She laughed. "You think I've kept some great secret from you? That I know where he's been hiding after all these years?"

I shrugged my shoulders even though she couldn't see. "Stranger things have happened."

"Not to me," she replied, and I could almost imagine her gazing out the window at her garden, checking her small wristwatch for the time.

"You hate that I'm here—that I'm looking for him."

"Your dad left us high and dry," she said, her tone dismissive. "He never wanted me or the simple life we made together in Webber. You need to let it go."

"Like you have?"

She sighed. "I had to. I had a daughter to raise."

I shook my head as if to prove a point to a woman who couldn't see me. "How could you? Let it go…I mean. He was your husband."

"And I was his wife."

I wanted to argue but couldn't. "I gotta go."

"Me, too."

I swallowed again, "I'll let you know what happens."

"Please don't."

Her words hit me like a fist, leaving me breathless.

I sat for a long time after the phone call ended, looking out our living room window, imagining her hurt and anger and frustration, wondering why she hadn't tried to find him, why she didn't want me to find him.

Dad had shown me their wedding album one night. I didn't understand it then but saw later that he was trying to paint a picture of her without his canvas and oils.

They had married on the winter solstice in a country chapel tucked so far into the woods only a chosen few were able to find it. Some brave soul must have made it through the snow with a camera because the ceremony was documented in a series of pictures that showed my mother in her best light: a bouquet of forget-me-nots in her hand, baby's breath wound into her braided hair.

Dad wore a suit, his own hair falling against the collar of his shirt, his gray eyes fastened on Mom in a way I never remembered.

The love had been there, open and raw and unspoiled.

What had happened?

I knew I couldn't answer that question, and so my melancholy stretched far into the evening until Holly came home from Camp Menominee and suggested we start the summer off with a bang and grill hot dogs for dinner.

We sat on our little porch beneath the sugar maple with a Coleman grill between us, still trying to get the feel for each other that our schedules hadn't permitted.

Holly began by diving into the deep end.

"So, how'd you meet the *jerk?*"

I should have known her curiosity would bend towards my love life. Still, talking about men was better than talking about Robert Cook. At least for now.

"Brad?"

She nodded, eager almost, as she balanced her paper plate across the top of her knees.

I shrugged, half-wishing I'd never used the "Man Trouble" excuse. The truth was there was a person I'd been hoping "get a rise out of" by coming up here. Not Starbucks, but someone I genuinely cared for and the main reason I was not looking for a summer romance…so to speak.

"I was writing for the newspaper and he was on a committee for some fundraiser I was covering. I had to interview him."

"Sounds juicy."

"Not really," I muttered, hardly ready to admit we'd waited a whopping three hours to consummate our affair, a spectacular encounter that began with a glass of white zinfandel and ended on the leather sofa in his office.

"Why aren't you with him?"

I considered the truth—that my daddy issues combined with my lousy taste in men had led me to a guy hiding a wife and two school-age sons. A man who also lived in a big Colonial at the end of a cul-de-sac and drove a Range Rover, a guy I learned the truth about when I ran into him at the Kalamazoo Target with his wife and wedding ring securely in place.

And still, I'd wanted to piss him off by running away.

These thoughts darkened my mood and so I answered Holly with a simple, "He had a lot of things going on."

She took a bite of her hot dog and said, "That's kinda weird."

"Not really."

Her laugh startled me. "You're not getting off that easy. I can smell bullshit at fifty yards."

"Oh, hey—"

"Gay?"

I looked at my hot dog.

"Drugs?"

I grabbed the ketchup and squeezed a big glob onto my plate.

"Married?"

I stopped mid-squeeze.

She sucked in her breath. "Did you know?"

I shook my head, surprised at the anger her question stirred in me.

"Don't sweat it, Squirt. Bad boys always find girls like you."

"Like me?" I questioned, a defensive flush creeping across my chest.

"You're sweet," she said.

Sweet? I had never equated that adjective with myself, just as I'd never thought about my All-American looks or penchant for unavailable men.

"But that's old news," I quickly changed the subject. "What about you? Any good stories of love in a northern town?"

She settled back into her chair and laced her fingers behind her head. "Got all night?"

"Sure."

"Well, I *don't* because I'm taking you on a little field trip."

I couldn't imagine what would be worth seeing in Presque Isle County besides my father but played along.

"That picture on your bedside table...the one of the lighthouse."

I felt embarrassed. Sure, I'd taken a picture of the painting Dad had left for my college education before the buyer took possession. Sure, I'd kept it along with a million other keepsakes, and sure, I'd brought it with me and left it amongst the clutter in my new bedroom but I still didn't want her looking at it or talking about it.

"What about it?"

"Who painted it? It's really good."

Another sore subject. But I couldn't lie. Especially if she could help me.

"My Dad. That painting helped pay for my college."

She looked at me, thoughtful. "Did he do it from memory or something?"

I felt my heart hitch in my chest. "Memory?"

"Yeah," she confirmed, still chewing her hot dog. "That lighthouse is about five miles from here. I thought you might want to see it. We could bond or something—"

I wasn't sure I'd heard her right, wasn't sure I *wanted* to hear her right, but it all made sense. If Dad had come here for the best fish in Michigan, chances are he'd also admired the local attractions and an isolated lighthouse was right up his alley.

"Are you sure it's the same one?" I asked, not wanting to hope for fear everything she said would vanish in a puff of smoke. "I mean…Dad painted a lot of lighthouses."

"Sure, I'm sure."

"Okay!" I said, a little too eager before cooling off with a casual, "Let's go. Sounds good."

"It's pretty famous around here," she paused for what I imagined was dramatic effect. "Some people say it's haunted."

"Oh?" I asked, thinking how it made sense that Dad would pick a haunted lighthouse even as I grabbed my jean jacket and slipped on my favorite pair of pink flip-flops.

Five minutes later we were heading south on Highway 23 in her Lumina. The moon was just beginning to rise, and a few clouds were obscuring it like the tattered hem of a gray gown. Passing the Big Lake at a steady clip, we swung inland between the slender fingers of Grand and Long Lakes.

Presque Isle, which means "almost an island" in French, was just that—a narrow peninsula that stuck out into Lake Huron and fattened up like a fist before slimming back down. The small village for which the county was named clung to that little strip: a few clapboard houses held together by a town hall, post office, and Lutheran Church. The lighthouse we sought was five miles from the turnoff and sat adjacent to a small restaurant known for the odd hours only places that serve outstanding food can get away with.

I felt my heart racing as we neared the lighthouse, felt like I'd gotten the first scent of my father and didn't know whether to continue the chase. If Holly noticed my apprehension, she didn't mention it. We rode in a comfortable silence I was grateful for before turning into the restaurant parking lot.

21

Perched on a rocky outcropping that vanished at high tide, I knew we couldn't reach it by foot. Still, just being this close to the subject of Dad's painting made me feel close to the man himself as I opened the car door and slid out.

"Kind of spooky out here," Holly admitted. "Why do you think your Dad painted a picture of this lighthouse? Did he come up here with your uncle or something?"

"Uncle?" I asked, realizing my misstep only moments later.

One look at Holly's face told me she was on to me.

"You don't have an uncle, do you?"

"Uh…" I stalled, feeling the wind whip around my body, wanting to rewind the clock and go back to being a mystery.

"What's going on? Tell me or you can find yourself a new roommate."

I didn't doubt she meant business, and so dug the toe of my flip-flop into the dirt in an effort to kill time. If I told her about Dad there was a good chance she could help me, and there really was no reason to think she wouldn't. Aside from my own pride.

If I wanted to get anywhere up here I was going to have to come clean about who I was: a girl who had been ditched by her father and not some cool downstate reporter sent by her family to collect a bounty on her uncle.

And so I spilled the beans about Dad's disappearance, my lonely teenage years and maladjusted mother, culminating in the fateful newspaper article that had led me to Lantern Creek.

I waited for her anger, or at least irritation, but Holly Marchand surprised me when she smiled and said, "I'm really glad you got that off your chest. I was beginning to think you were a serial killer or something."

"Oh—"

"Just kidding," she punched me in the shoulder. "I know a Thomas Cook, but he lives over in Onaway. Never heard of Robert, but like I said, that's not saying much."

"I don't want to scare him off," I said, embarrassed to be talking about my own father in that way. "Chances are he doesn't want to be found."

"That really sucks, Squirt."

I didn't know how to respond at first, and so stood silently and let the truth of what she'd just said sink in. Most of my friends in Webber had been too scared to talk to me about it, let alone empathize. When the conversation turned towards "Dads" in general, they quickly changed the subject. Sherry had asked me how I was doing a few times but after a while, it seemed like my Dad had never existed and that Mom and I had always been alone.

And here was a woman I barely knew speaking the truth…*finally*.

I felt tears well up in my eyes and fought to suppress them.

No way was I bawling now.

"Do you want to go?"

I shook my head, determined to remain at the lighthouse now that I knew it was the same one Dad had painted. The trim shafts of birch and pine had grown up a bit but there was no doubt in my mind he knew this place from memory.

I turned toward the car. The warm June wind of a moment before had suddenly grown cold. My hands were shaking, my ears numbed by a sound I didn't recognize. A strange buzzing that reminded me of the fan I had clipped to my headboard for white noise since I was a kid.

I swallowed, thinking perhaps my ears had popped, but that wasn't it.

"Holly?" I said her name, unable to hear my own voice when a flash of white caught my eye in the smudged forest behind the Lumina. I looked to the trees, looked deep within them and saw something stir between the branches—something that moved like a human where no human should have been.

"Holly?" I squeaked, pointing a finger towards what I thought I saw. A moment later the form broke from the tree line and entered open moonlight, a form that looked like a young woman in a white dressing gown.

I gulped, wondering if all upstate folks dressed like they were getting ready for Pioneer Days. "Do you see her?"

I saw Holly's mouth moving in response to my question, but I couldn't hear her, my ears were still plugged, the white noise still buzzing. Something was happening to me, that had never happened before I came to Lantern Creek.

And it was scaring the shit out of me.

I saw Holly's lips move and tried to read them. "Who?"

"The woman," I whispered, too frightened to move, knowing she couldn't be real but not able explain away her presence or why I was the only one who could see her.

"What woman?"

"Right *there*," I pointed again as the woman took another step into the open, the moonlight revealing a dark splatter on the front of her dressing gown.

My breath suspended in my throat. This woman was hurt, possibly dying…but how could she be wandering the woods in a dressing gown from over a hundred years ago?

Another step and she was only twenty yards away, her eyes glassy, but I was sure she saw me, marking me with some sort of recognition I felt but couldn't explain.

All of a sudden, the blood began to rush to my feet and legs and hands as I sprang from my spot. The buzzing sound that had reminded me of my fan stopped, and when I screamed, "Come on!" I heard my own voice, along with the welcome sounds of wind through pine trees and tossing surf.

Holly, still clueless, gave a strangled cry and hopped like a startled frog for the Lumina.

I felt the gravel crunch beneath my feet, knowing the strange woman with the bloodstained dress was there, moving too.

Twenty seconds later I reached the Lumina, my fingers slippery against the metal. The next second, I yanked open the door and jumped inside.

Holly didn't ask questions, she just threw the car into gear and peeled out of the parking lot.

"What the hell did you see?" She demanded once we had put some distance between ourselves and the lighthouse.

"I don't know," I panted, my eyes squeezed closed. "Something bad, something," I paused, "There was blood all over her."

Holly cursed—punched the gas and sent the Lumina careening down the twisting road.

I looked back, relieved to see nothing was following us and said, "I don't see anything now."

"Praise the Lord," Holly sighed, regaining some of her composure. "I never really believed the stories about the place being haunted but…" She paused. "You're not making this up, are you? Because if you are, I'm reconsidering my 'serial killer' stance."

"You didn't see her?" I asked, unwilling to believe my mind had been playing tricks on me, or worse yet—that it hadn't. "It looked like she'd been stabbed or something."

"I didn't see crap out there," Holly insisted. "And if you're trying to make me pee my pants you're doing a damn good job so just *stop it,* okay!"

"I'm not trying to scare you."

"I sure as hell hope not," she admonished. "Because I like our place and I sure don't want to go back to Bill and Marty's basement over some figment of your imagination."

I opened my mouth to argue but was cut short by a pair of headlights that seemed to be on our side of the road.

If we'd been on our side.

"Shit! *Look out!*" I cried.

Too late. Holly slammed on the brakes, leaving no choice but to swerve left—which she did—landing us squarely in the ditch.

I sat for several seconds in stunned silence, then watched as the vehicle that had run us off the road circled back in our direction. Scenes from every slasher flick where Old Hook Hand returned to finish off the surly teenagers ran through my mind.

"Holl—" I turned to see her still clenching the wheel.

"Are you okay? I never saw them coming. The curve—"

I bit back the part about staying on her own side of the road, then braced myself for the sight of a hideous monster when the driver stopped, got out, and approached her window at a brisk pace.

"Hey!" a voice cried, muffled through the glass. "You all right?"

The face that appeared behind the voice was cast in shadow, but he seemed about our age and was a far cry from the creep I'd imagined. In fact, I was certain I'd seen it splashed across the *Abercrombie and Fitch* bag I'd been using as an underwear drawer until the real thing came along.

Knowing we would have to explain ourselves for almost running him off the road, I elbowed Holly to roll down her window. She obliged, still shaking, still mumbling, "We're fine…I mean I think we're fine…who the hell knows."

He bent down then, his features illuminated by the dashboard lights. I stared but tried not to as I took in a smooth face exemplified by a strong jawline, nose, and mouth. Short, blond hair that had just enough length to curl and blue eyes completed an appealing picture I tried not to stare at.

But stare I did, hoping this wasn't going to throw me off my game…so to speak. "Dylan?"

My eyes flew to Holly. She knew this guy? Better yet, he was probably one of the conquests she didn't have time to tell me about.

"Holly?" He laughed, relieved.

"Holy cow…I haven't seen you since—"

"That night at the Deer Hunt Lounge."

She smirked. "How the heck have ya been?"

He laughed again. "Not so great considering you almost ran me off the road. "

Holly turned to me, "We're sorry. We just got a little freaked out."

"We were…uh…" I mumbled, unable to think of an explanation that wouldn't make us look like the morons we were. "Ghost hunting."

"And one got away?"

I thought of the woman with the dark splatter on her dressing gown, "You could say that."

"Let me guess," he paused, tried to suppress a smile. "Presque Isle Lighthouse?"

I nodded.

"Been there, done that," he said matter-of-factly, and I was left wondering how to introduce myself when he saved me the trouble with, "I'm Dylan Locke, by the way. The guy you almost killed." He reached across Holly to shake my hand.

I opened my mouth and answered with a fairly respectable rendition of my name.

"You sure you're okay?"

I nodded, the feeling of his hand in mine comfortable. When I let go, however, I felt a slickness that hadn't been there a moment before.

"Oh, my God," I heard him gasp. "You're bleeding!"

I looked to my hand and felt my stomach kick over.

"Justine," Holly flicked on the dome light. "Did you hit the window?"

"I don't know," I mumbled, looking for cuts on my palm, my elbows, pulling down the visor mirror and examining my hairline. It was impossible to bleed with no apparent injury, wasn't it?

"We need to get you to a doctor," Dylan said. "That looks pretty bad."

I sat, unable to find an open wound and answered, "I don't need a doctor."

He crouched down, a look of intensity on his face that matched my need for an explanation. "We don't have to report this if that's what you're worried about."

"I'm not worried about that."

"He's right," Holly said, fumbling across me to the glove box where she grabbed a handful of McDonald's napkins. "We should get it checked out."

"We will," I agreed while pressing the napkin to my palm. "When the clinic's open. I can't afford a trip to the E.R."

Dylan seemed displeased but must have realized slinging me over his shoulder and carrying me into the hospital caveman-style would be a bit presumptuous. So he turned his attention to helping us in another way.

"Can you get out of the ditch?"

Holly put the Lumina in reverse and gunned the engine. After a few moments, we were free of the brush that had entangled us and back on the open road.

"Nice to see you, Holly," Dylan said. "But next time I hope it's in passing."

She flashed him a thumbs up.

"Justine," he turned to me. "You'll take care of that hand?"

"I will," I promised, a strange warmth spreading to my chest.

"Good," he smiled. "Because I have spies in this town."

I wasn't sure how to take his humor, my fingers instinctively reaching for the silver necklace. His eyes followed, lingering for a moment before returning to my face.

"I like it," he said.

I smiled.

"Drive safe. I hear the cops are out tonight."

Holly chuckled under her breath as we watched him walk back towards his truck—an extended cab Ford F250 that would have won our little chicken contest without losing so much as a feather.

We were back on Highway 23 before Holly spoke again. "We shouldn't have gone out there."

"I'm sorry," I admitted. "But you did get to catch up with an old friend."

She glanced at me, her eyes slits. "Uh-huh."

"Were you close?"

She shrugged. "We graduated together. Hung out a few times after that."

I waited before asking more. "Did you have classes together or something?"

"Or something."

"Like Algebra or Physics or English Lit or something like that?"

I saw her hands tighten on the steering wheel. "And so, it begins," she sighed.

"So, what begins?"

"What do you *think?* Just look at him."

"I did," I smiled out the window at nothing, surprised that he could distract me from my search so quickly.

She chuckled again. "And you're his type, too."

"I am?" I didn't try to hide my delight.

"Krissy McKee was his steady bimbo back in the day. I don't need to tell you she was a blonde cheerleader with perfect tits and no depth perception, right?"

"And *I'm* his type?"

"I sure as hell wasn't," she breezed over the insult. "Although no one could say I didn't give it the old college try."

I frowned, not sure if she was making me feel better or worse. "So, what is it about me...exactly...that he would find attractive?"

"Don't get yourself all worked up, Squirt. He probably has a wife and ten kids by now."

I didn't like the sound of that, but maybe it was for the best, seeing how quickly he'd succeeded in throwing me off my game.

"And I let that stupid insurance policy lapse..." she hit her forehead. "Let's hope SuperCop keeps his word and doesn't report this. Otherwise, you can kiss our cushy digs goodbye."

"SuperCop?"

"He works for the county. Why do you think he made that stupid joke about the cops being out tonight?"

I imagined him in uniform, imagined him out of uniform, and quickly pushed that thought from my mind as we rode in silence the rest of the way home. Several times I tried to gauge Holly's mood but found it impossible. Still, the night wasn't a total bust. I'd learned that the lighthouse Dad had painted was either haunted or I was having random bouts of insanity that was kicked off by ringing in my ears.

I was still mulling things over when we arrived home. Making my way down the hall to the little room I'd acquired during a pre-dinner coin toss, I pulled my mattress from the jumbled heap of metal frame and box spring that littered the floor.

I also took the time to find a special hiding place in my closet for the birthday present I'd never opened, feeling the need to do so before Holly saw it and started asking questions.

Moments later, I heard footsteps pattering down the hallway, followed shortly by, "How's your hand?"

I looked at Holly, the bottom of her *Snoopy* sleep shirt barely covering her butt.

"Fine," I held it up, clean as a whistle after a good scrubbing.

"That was some weird shit. Ghost ladies floating around and then you bleed all over Dylan Locke." She sighed. "Hope you can keep a lid on it or this summer is gonna be off the hook."

I bit my lip, wondering the same thing while Holly, ever the gracious roommate, knelt to help me make up my bed.

"Sorry about the whole 'serial killer' thing," she said once we had finished. "And I have no right to question your depth perception."

"It's pretty good," I assured her.

"I noticed," she smiled, blowing me a mock kiss before sauntering down the hall to her own quarters. In a few minutes, Joey would be curled at my feet. My steady man.

I adjusted my pillow under my neck, settling in for what I hoped would be a peaceful night's sleep. Instead, I listened as a foghorn called from the lakeshore and imagined the lonely eye of the lighthouse watching for sailors that had drowned long ago.

Strange, rambling dreams disturbed me, ones in which a bird alighted in a tree that caught fire but never burned, and I awoke in a sweat, unnerved and homesick and wondering if this was the way it was going to be now that I'd crossed into my father's world, remembering a morning we watched cardinals eat from our winter feeders, their wings red as an open wound.

Unable to sleep, I made a mental note to take Holly out for breakfast in the morning.

I *had* scared her to death with what was most likely a figment of my imagination.

I just hoped another one didn't show up anytime soon.

Chapter Three

My first week in Lantern Creek flew by in a haze of activity as I purchased necessities that included a shower curtain with strategically placed clownfish, a used TV, and a six-dollar bottle of red wine. I also picked up a copy of the *Lantern Creek Lectern* every day and perused the classifieds.

Holly walked in after work one afternoon as I was reading the tiny section with mounting frustration.

"Did I forget to tell you we have the highest unemployment rate in the Lower Peninsula?"

I frowned. "It must have slipped your mind."

"I'd get you into camp, but Jen Reddy took the last spot." She paused. "I thought you had some money saved and were going to start a blog"—Holly stopped when she saw my wounded look—"or something."

I shook my head, wondering where she'd gotten the idea a blog would lead to anything resembling rent money.

"Newspaper?" she offered.

"They don't need any help."

She laughed out loud. "They need help but would rather die than take it. Old Miles Jenks and his sister have been running it since the last ice age. I tried for a job in high school and the jerk acted like I wanted his left kidney."

I nodded, "Apparently he thought I was after the right one."

I tried to mask my disappointment. Truth was I'd been counting on my editor in Webber to help me get a job at the *Lectern*. I had hoped it would be the edge I needed on Lantern Creek happenings, including but not limited to the whereabouts of Robert Cook. But now it seemed I was going to have to look elsewhere for a livable wage—a task that seemed impossible considering what Presque Isle County had to offer.

Holly sensed my mood and tried to cheer me up. "I've got a little money stashed away until you find something. Thank God Dylan kept his mouth shut or we'd be in Bill and Marty's basement together right now."

"I told you he'd keep his word," I said while pushing to my feet.

She smirked. "That makes one of you."

I opened the refrigerator and paused. "Huh?"

"You never went to the doctor."

I shrugged, hoping to downplay the event and how much I'd been thinking about it.

"Let me see that hand again."

I held it up as she came to inspect it under the natural light streaming through our kitchen window.

"Not a scratch."

"Maybe I have a disorder."

"Then you should go see a doctor."

"Ignorance is bliss."

"If Dylan finds out he'll hunt you down."

"Worse things could happen."

She wrinkled her nose. "What did I tell you about the wife and ten kids?"

"He wasn't wearing a ring."

She rolled her eyes. "Regardless…I've known the guy since kindergarten. His girlfriends usually end up walking around like brainless zombies after the inevitable break-up. Did I tell you about Krissy McKee?"

"You did," I shut the fridge, tired of her parenting style. "But like I said I'm not looking for a summer romance, so you don't have to worry."

"That was before you met Dylan Locke."

I sighed, stretched and tried to ignore her last comment. Next on the agenda was looking for my car keys, a daily routine Holly likened to King Richard's quest for the Holy Grail. After minutes of fruitless searching, I found them curled in my left tennis shoe and headed for the door.

"I'm just going to check out that job at the dairy farm in Posen," I called over my shoulder.

"I can't wait to see your uniform."

I laughed, ready for some space to clear my head as I walked out the door.

Moments later, I started up the Heap and headed toward downtown Lantern Creek, a place where nightlife consisted of dinner followed closely by a seven o'clock movie. Fine dining was non-existent, but a good tavern could be had for the price of a tall Bud Light and a pan of cheesy bread. Not wanting to look like an alcoholic my first week in town, I avoided the local watering hole and opted for lunch at McDonald's.

I have spies in this town…

The last thing I needed was to be thinking about him. I didn't even like zombie movies.

My Big Mac Extra Value Meal was cold comfort against that thought and so I hit the road again, weaving south, the dairy farm job forgotten as Grand Lake shimmered outside my driver's side window.

Before long I found myself at the breakwall again, staring at Dad's lighthouse, hoping that something in the light or atmosphere would explain away the woman with the dark splatter on her dress. Certainly, I shouldn't start seeing ghosts in Lantern Creek when I'd never seen them in Webber.

I sat down on a flat rock, breathed the early summer air and tried to imagine what Dad had been thinking when he set his easel up and began to paint, memories of this place flooding all the hot spots in his brain. He always wanted quiet while working, and I remembered an autumn afternoon when I ran into his studio, a wounded bird in my hands.

I'd heard it hit our front window and gone outside to investigate. The little robin was flailing but stilled when I bent to pick it up in my small hands. I knew Mom would be upset about me touching it, so went to find Dad even though I knew he didn't like to be disturbed.

I remembered him turning at the sound of my voice, putting his paintbrush down and coming towards me. He sat on a chair, invited me into his lap and unfolded my hands. I remember his clucking sound, the sound that said something was a shame, as he looked at the bird.

"Can we save it, Daddy?" I had asked.

"I don't think so, Muffet."

"But it's going to die."

Dad's eyes went soft as he kissed the top of my head. "See his wings? Even if this bird lives it will never fly again."

"I want him to live."

A pause, and then softly, "I don't."

I didn't understand it then and had no idea why the memory came to me now, on this breakwall overlooking the lighthouse. But Dad was right—there were worse things than death and so we carefully placed the bird in an old shoebox and buried it beneath the yellowing maple in our backyard.

I sat thinking about that bird until the sun hung heavy in the afternoon sky, then climbed back into the Heap and headed home, unsure if I had learned anything but feeling closer to my father than I had in a very long time.

I was near Grand Lake when I spotted something that made me start—a familiar truck pulling out of a driveway in front of an impressive log cabin. One glance and I realized it was Dylan Locke's Ford F250. My heart sped up in the slightest. I even considered pulling over to see if he wanted to chat when I saw the slender, tanned arm hanging out of his passenger window.

Was this the wife? Daughter? Soon-to-be Zombie?

A wisp of long, brown hair whipped out the side as the truck sped up and I realized it most likely belonged to the girlfriend I'd been warned about. I tried not to stare through the back window but couldn't help it. I saw their heads turn towards each other, saw him reach over and lay his arm across her shoulder and felt a wave of disappointment wash over me for the second time that day.

I have spies in this town…

Well so do I, Mister.

Yes, sir—the passenger seat of Dylan's truck was *the* place to be in Presque Isle County—and I was stuck behind in a crappy Honda Civic.

I was so full of self-pity that I almost didn't notice when he pulled into the public library.

Gorgeous, chivalrous, *and* well-read?

I couldn't win for losing, and so circled the block one last time before heading home, more discouraged than ever, knowing I was going to have to make up a story about the dairy farm job or Holly would start getting pushy.

Moments later, I pulled into the driveway and parked the Heap.

Stepping into the late afternoon sunlight, I was surprised to see my downstairs neighbor out in her flowerbed. I was even more surprised when she gave a friendly wave, followed by, "Hey, there."

I waved back, a bit shy as she straightened and wiped her hands on a pale blue apron.

"Nice day," I ventured, taking stock of her slim frame, green eyes, and the silver hair bunched neatly at the nape of her neck.

"It is," she agreed while removing her hat with a gloved hand. "Can you believe we have weeds already? It seemed like only yesterday the daffodils were pushing their way to the sunshine."

I nodded as if I spoke her language, thinking again of my mother and the particular irony of a woman who had failed to nurture a child working miracles with violets, orchids, and roses.

"Do you garden?"

I shook my head, remembering a Christmas long ago when a poinsettia, one my mother assured me I could not kill, was placed on the dining room table and into my loving care.

But murder it I did. After weeks of neglect followed by buckets of liquefied love, the poor leaves withered and curled unto themselves like a child spooning a teddy bear.

"I'm Iris," she smiled, extending her hand.

"I'm Justine."

"Nice to meet you."

"Nice to meet you, too," I motioned toward our kitchen window, perched high over the top of our heads. "My roommate and I moved in last week."

"I noticed."

I smiled to myself. "I'm not sure how long we'll be staying."

"Most people don't stay long. It's not exactly the lap of luxury up there."

"Not really," I admitted, hoping I hadn't offended her since the home had been in her family for generations.

She wiped her brow. "But sometimes new soil does a body good."

I nodded again, feeling the needle prick of her observation.

"Have you lived here long?" I began my slow approach, fancying myself quite the undercover journalist.

She laughed. "Do I look like it?"

"Well…" I began, uncomfortable.

"I'm just kidding. Yes. I've lived here all my life."

I laughed, realizing perhaps too late that Black Ops was not my calling. "I have some relatives up here. I thought I'd look them up while I was around."

'Oh?" she lifted an eyebrow. "Who would that be?"

"An uncle," I paused. "Maybe you've heard of him."

"More than likely I have."

"His name is Robert Cook." For some reason I didn't want to look into her eyes when I said the name. Still, I couldn't stare at my flip-flops forever and so bit the bullet and lifted my gaze.

To my surprise she was looking at my necklace, the delicate silver circle intersected with a cross that had never seemed interesting to anyone before.

"Uncle, you say?"

I nodded. "My dad's brother."

Her eyes met mine, reflecting something so subtle I felt she must know something. It gave me hope—a small ember in a cold room.

"That name is common to folks that live out past the Falls."

"The Falls?"

"Ocqueoc—you must have passed the signs when you came into town."

I shook my head, not remembering much about my grand entrance into Lantern Creek besides my need to use the bathroom.

"Long story short, the Cook Family had a homestead out that way. Some of their children settled around Onaway and in the country beside the waterfall. Maybe your uncle is out there."

I smiled to myself. It wasn't much—but it was enough to steer me in the right direction.

"Have you found a job yet?" She asked while peeling off her gloves.

I felt almost embarrassed when I answered, "Not yet."

"Think you'll be staying here long enough to need one?"

I shrugged. "I hope so."

Iris looked down, worked the dirt from beneath her thumbnails. "My daughter runs Three Fires Lodge out on Ocqueoc Lake. That's near the Falls. They always need help getting the place ready for the season." She stopped short. "I'll give her a call."

"Wow," I began, suddenly energized. "That's really nice of you."

"If you don't like housekeeping the lodge has a tavern you can barmaid at. Pam says it's pretty busy most of the year. Tips are good, too."

I felt the ember of hope swell to a full-blown flame. If the Cook family had settled past the Falls and I was working at Three Fires Lodge, I was sure to run into someone who had heard of Dad.

"I'll go inside and make a call, then," She turned, glancing at me over her shoulder. "Enjoy the rest of your afternoon, Justine. And rest easy."

I nodded before I knew what I was doing.

Rest easy...

Was it that obvious? Or did I possess a certain look wise old women mistook as that of the perpetually stressed? Whatever the reason, I caught myself smiling as sunshine washed over the side of my neck. I closed my eyes and smelled the breeze- pine mixed with water and well-worked earth.

Rest easy...

If only I could.

Chapter Four

True to her word, Iris phoned her daughter and secured my first official job interview of the summer. Choosing a conservative, *"I mean to be taken seriously"* outfit, I came out to model the ensemble for Holly.

My roommate was not impressed. "Is that lace on your collar? You're trying for a job at a fishing lodge, not a church."

I glanced down at my blouse just as Holly took my hand and dragged me to the threshold of her closet. "Your mom should've done this a long time ago."

I cringed, thinking that my Mom's fashion sense might have gotten me killed in high school when Holly held up an aquamarine T-shirt with a scooped neckline.

"What were you wearing when we wound up in the ditch?" she asked and I looked away, hating how my face caught fire. "You're lucky Dylan didn't haul you in for a fashion emergency."

"I get it," I muttered. "And while we're on the subject—he has a girlfriend, so it wouldn't have mattered what I was wearing."

She shrugged, "I figured."

Angry, frustrated, and still saddened by the fact that he had a significant other, I pulled the offensive blouse over my head and tossed it in the corner.

"How'd you find out?" she asked.

I didn't answer, just reached for the blue shirt, but before I could grab it Holly snatched it away and I was left standing in my skivvies with a job interview less than twenty minutes away.

"I went for a drive out by Grand Lake."

She wrinkled her nose and handed me the blouse. "Were you *stalking* him?"

"No! I went out to the lighthouse again and they just happened to pull out of his driveway. Come on—I would never—"

"Never say never, Squirt." She took a step closer and adjusted the bottom of the borrowed shirt. "I just don't want to see you get hurt."

"He has a girlfriend, Holl. It's never going to happen."

"Like that matters."

If I'd had more time I would have asked her what she meant, but I didn't, and so headed for the door and Three Fires Lodge—a small resort situated on Ocqueoc Lake, ten miles northwest of Lantern Creek.

The drive was beautiful and wild and lonely as I hugged the lakeshore, praying the Heap wouldn't choose this remote location to finally call it a day.

A dirt road veered left and I took the right fork because it was paved, thinking I'd mistaken Pam's directions for the nearest route to nowhere. Moments later I saw the sign for Three Fires Lodge. A long gravel driveway broke from the paved road and wound into the face of dense woodland. A quarter mile later and I pulled up beside a large A-frame log cabin.

My heart beating just a bit faster than usual, I stepped out of the car and climbed the steps. Not watching my feet, I almost tripped over a slumbering black Labrador who snorted at the inconvenience.

I raised my hand to knock when the door opened and a woman stepped into the space between us. She was short and slim and wore faded jeans paired with a yellow shirt. Her hair was red and curly and tied back with a handkerchief of the same color. Shading her eyes, she looked me up and down.

I gave a little wave, then let my hand drop to my side, feeling like a dork.

"Rocky!" she nudged him with her foot. "You are no gentleman."

I smiled as he rolled over onto his side, leaving me just enough room to squeeze into the front lobby of Three Fires Lodge. If this dog greeted everyone, I was surprised the place had any guests.

I had a change of heart when I saw the front room. Doorstop or no, the space was homey and charming with an 'Up North' feel that made flatlanders like myself feel like we were really rustic adventurers.

An impressive fieldstone fireplace dominated the far wall, an elk head hanging above the mantle and I could picture the Lodge on winter nights with the snow blowing outside. People would be gathered around the fire, playing checkers or telling ghost stories. The cold would make this room seem welcoming, a refuge from the elements.

"I'm Pam Mallory," the woman in front of me spoke and I snapped back into the present moment, hoping she didn't think I was flighty.

"Hello," I reached out and shook her hand. "I'm Justine."

"Mom doesn't ever call me."

"Oh," I said. "She doesn't?"

"You must have impressed her."

"She…uh," I paused, thinking of the woman I knew nothing about, "Likes to dig in the dirt."

Pam chuckled, then reached up to tighten her yellow handkerchief. "Let me show you around."

I nodded, more nervous than I cared to admit as we made our way through the lobby.

"This is the main lodge." She explained. "Next week this room will be full."

"I can imagine," I said. This was just the sort of place I'd dreamed of when I spent hours wishing away the cornfields and lame human-interest stories.

"See that place?" She pointed out the nearest window to a white cottage partially hidden by a massive oak tree. It was quaint and charming, just like the rest of the property, with a split rail fence I imagined she had put in herself. "I live there with my son."

I nodded again, not wanting to ask questions so soon, and came up with the neutral, "How old is he?"

"Ten going on thirty-seven."

I gave a polite laugh, wondering when I would get to meet this boy and if he would be annoying or cool when she reached over and opened a sliding glass door. A small porch led to some steps and a gravel road that wound into the woods. Framing either side of the path and separated by several large trees were red clapboard buildings that resembled my bunkhouse from fifth-grade camp.

"All the cabins look pretty much the same," Pam said while we walked. Stopping in front of the first one, she ascended the steps and opened the front door. "I need help with spring cleaning but after that only on Saturdays."

I looked down, disappointed. If I didn't start pulling my weight back home I wasn't sure how long I could stay in Holly's good graces. Catching my look, Pam added, "We have a tavern that stays open year-round. I have one good barmaid, but she just gave her notice."

I twisted my face into something cheery, scared she might suspect I didn't know crap about mixing drinks.

Still, a barmaid uniform had to be better than a milkmaid's.

"I could do that."

"Good," she smiled. "Now for the grand tour."

The cabin was simple and rustic. One large room with a floral print couch and two wicker chairs overlooked Ocqueoc Lake. An adjoining kitchen, bathroom, and bedroom completed the tour in about twenty-two seconds.

"We have ten cabins. The last two are out on the point and more secluded."

"They look nice," I said, hoping to segue into the question I'd wanted to ask when I first entered the main lodge. "My uncle would love this place."

"Your uncle?" she asked.

"He likes to fish and these cabins are right up his alley. I can't believe he's never been out here."

She was about to take the bait and ask his name when someone entered the cabin behind us. Turning, I saw a young man dressed in jeans and a plaid work shirt. He stood about six-foot and was lean-muscled with a pleasant face, amber eyes, and a generous amount of brown hair.

"Sorry to bother you," he said. "Just finished with the porch on Cabin Seven and thought I'd take a breather."

"Jamie," Pam smiled, her eyes searching behind him for a moment. Then, with added tension, "Where's Adam?"

He waited for a beat before answering, "Out front."

"Oh," she breathed, and I wondered at her caution. Turning to me, she said, "Jamie, this is Justine. I just hired her."

I felt my eyes go wide with delight and Jamie laughed. "I think that's news to her."

"Shouldn't be. Lord knows I'm desperate this time of year."

"Don't let her fool you," Jamie chuckled, his crooked smile breaking through. "She runs a tight ship."

"So he thinks," Pam gave him a playful punch on the arm and I wondered how long these two had known each other and if either of them had heard of Dad. "This guy doesn't know how good he has it. "

"I know," Jamie laughed. "Where else can I get paid for hanging out in the woods and chatting with pretty ladies?"

I looked up quickly.

"Come meet Adam," Pam said, breezing over what could have turned into an awkward moment. I followed her outside.

A boy sat with his back to us in a lawn chair on the front porch. His hair was curly like Pam's, but of a darker, richer color that held no hint of red.

"Adam?" Pam asked, and for a moment his eyes met hers—large eyes that just matched his hair. "This is Justine."

He didn't answer, just sat with the wind ruffling those dark curls before his eyes found mine.

I smiled.

It took a moment to realize something was wrong. Maybe it was the way his gaze flickered over me and never really caught, or the way his fingers went to his ears, or the soft sound he began to make.

I looked to Pam, who was watching her son with a mixture of affection and resignation, perhaps hoping those eyes would linger and stay and catch hold of something. Anything.

"My son is autistic."

I searched my memory for something that would hold resonance for me and came up empty.

"He doesn't talk but he's very bright," she went on. "Jamie sometimes takes him along when he has projects but most of the time he's with me or Rocky."

"I see," I said, searching for the right thing to say. Feeling dumb. Every mother wanted a person to make a fuss over their kid, and here I stood acting like he had the plague.

"He won't bother you."

"Oh," I began, "I didn't—"

"I know you didn't."

I smiled, feeling like she understood my embarrassment. Like it hadn't been the first time.

"We'll see you on Saturday morning, then. Nine o'clock."

"Okay," I said. "Thanks, again. This really means a lot."

"No problem," she said while touching Adam's elbow. The boy stood up and followed his mother, turning once more to look at me before walking up the driveway towards his house. I felt his brown eyes on me, lingering longer than the last time and wondered what he was thinking and how it would feel to be unable to speak what was in my heart.

He's very bright...

All the worse.

"Oh, Justine," Pam turned at the bottom of the steps. "Who was that uncle you were talking about?"

I paused, adrenaline kicking up.

"Robert Cook."

Pam's face tightened and I thought I saw her swallow. One moment turned into several before I had the courage to ask her if she was all right.

"Sure," she nodded. "I just haven't heard that name in a while."

My chest ignited and I took a deep breath to steady myself. Would she finally tell me my father was living in some little shack past Ocqueoc Falls, waiting for the daughter he'd left behind in Webber? Painting? Putting lost birds back in their nests?

"Where is he?" I asked, surprised that my voice was steady. "We heard he lived up here but my Dad hasn't seen him in ten years."

She shrugged, her face softer now. "I wish I knew."

I felt my hope flee and reached out to grab it by the scruff of the neck. "But you did know him?"

"Oh, yes," she smiled, fondly even, and for the first time, I felt fear creep into my heart, fear for what I might learn about the father I loved.

"How did you know him?"

She smiled again, looked down at her son and touched the topmost of his windblown curls.

"He's Adam's father."

Chapter Five

Had it not been for the porch railing I'm sure I would have sunk to the ground and began to hyperventilate. Or laugh or cry out to the sky in some sort of primal awakening that only takes place in forests like these, but I just stood there, too dumbstruck to speak until Pam cocked her head and said, "Guess we're related, then. All the better. Keep the good jobs in the family."

Jamie chuckled behind me and I wanted to turn and speak my grief, wanted to run into the woods where no one could see me and try to wrap my head around how Dad could have a son.

How I could have a brother.

Had Mom known? Or Iris—when she felt "compelled" to speak to her daughter after I mentioned Robert Cook's name?

Mom never calls me...

I looked at Adam Mallory, feeling a strange mixture of hatred and love swell within me for the sibling I'd always wanted. I wondered who he looked like, why he was so dark when I was fair and if Dad had loved him as much as he loved me. Had he sat him in the crook of a soft tree or paddled to the middle of the lake in an old inner tube?

He was ten years old, which meant Dad might have abandoned us about the time he found out Pam was pregnant.

Anger surged beneath my controlled exterior.

This boy had gotten the father I'd wanted, the man I'd needed during my years of teenage angst. I touched my forehead, suddenly dizzy, wondering how long I could stand here gripping the porch railing on Cabin One before they got suspicious and asked me what was wrong.

"You okay?" Jamie finally said, his hand on my shoulder.

"Oh, sure. We just didn't know Uncle Rob had any kids. It's kind of a—"

"Surprise?" Pam asked. "It was for me, too."

"I'm sorry," I stammered, wanting to get to the Heap and call Mom even though she'd told me not to. "I didn't mean to stir up bad memories."

Pam smiled again. "No bad memories here. "

I wanted to ask her what sort of memories she had, exactly, and if she'd known about Robert's wife and daughter and how many Christmases we'd spent by ourselves, but she was turning and moving down the pathway with Adam. I was grateful for the silence and didn't stop her. I let her go, watching as the two of them grasped hands, two peas in a pod that had made their way all on their own.

Like Mom and me.

And for the first time in my life, I hated my father.

"You sure you're okay?" I heard Jamie say again. "Maybe I should walk you to the lodge."

I didn't want him to walk me to the lodge, but I did want information and so put on a fake happy face and accepted his offer. Before long we were standing beside the Heap, my horrible mood complete when he let out a low whistle.

"Don't take this the wrong way, but did you drive here in that?"

"I know it's bad," I snapped, unable to hide my impatience. "That's why I need a job."

"Sorry." He paused, leaned up against the Heap and crossed his arms across his chest. "We didn't think you'd take the news about your uncle so hard."

"It's okay." I tried to steady my voice, wishing I'd majored in theatre instead of English. "Dad may have a thing or two to say to him if we ever track him down."

"Good luck on that one."

I paused, unsure if I should press him. "What happened between the two of them?"

He sighed and adjusted his position against the Heap. I looked at his arms, nicely displayed in rolled sleeves and saw that they were strong and used to heavy labor. His face held traces of sunburn and the jeans he wore were thin at the knees as though he spent a lot of time getting out of tight spots. "Pam doesn't say much."

I nodded, unable to think of another question when millions were floating like fireflies just within reach.

"He came up here to fish. I think that's how they met."

"Did she know anything about him?"

Jamie shrugged. "Only what he told her. And I have a feeling he didn't come clean. Why else would he take off just after Adam was born?"

I gritted my teeth. "He left them?"

"She's been on her own for years." He paused. Looked closer at me. "What kind of guy was he? I mean…you said you were surprised he had kids. I always thought maybe he was married or something."

"No kids," I said quickly. "Uncle Rob was always kind of a loner. That's why we never thought anything of it when he packed up and moved here."

"Makes sense," Jamie nodded, his face as placid and I was grateful for it.

"She never remarried?"

"Nope," Jamie smiled, a hint of amusement playing across his mouth. "You ask me, I think she's still in love with him."

I reached for the handle of the Heap, hoping that would be enough to tell him I was done talking when he said, "Pop says you're staying in the old two-story out on Ravine."

"Pop?" I repeated.

"Big guy. Red truck. Hates cats."

It took me a moment to connect the dots, but when I did I felt my mouth fall open in a caricature of surprise. "*You're* Mr. Stoddard's son?"

His laughter affirmed my guess as I studied his face, looking for any sign that would link him to his father. As the moment stretched into several I saw it in the way the two men carried themselves—the easy slouch to their shoulders—as though the world were a place that would wait for them.

And while the look made Mr. Stoddard seen arrogant, it fit his son well.

"You're taking your life in your hands rooming with Holly Would."

I giggled, amused at how quickly he could distract me. "Holly Would?"

"We used to call her that in high school." He shook his head, rubbed a hand along the back of his sunburned neck. "Not very nice, huh?"

I shrugged. "Was it true?"

"We sure didn't call her Holly Wouldn't."

I laughed and he grinned while looking down at his work boots. I couldn't help but compare his smile to Dylan's. One so startling—and the other pleasing in a way that could sneak up on a girl and pull the rug out from under her.

"Your uncle give you that necklace?"

I looked into his eyes, my fingers seeking the pendant as they had a hundred times in the past.

"Yes."

"Figures. Adam has one just like it."

I tensed, anger rising within me again as I remembered the way I'd begged Mom to give it to me.

And now some kid I didn't even know had one just like it.

43

I was bitter, and angry and feeling a little less like the adored only child I had been twenty minutes before and so welcomed the reprieve when Jamie finally walked away.

I climbed into the Heap and sat for several seconds before starting her up. Back on the road and more confused than ever, I tried my best to keep a level head even as Pam's story stirred the pot.

Not only had Dad been to Lantern Creek, he'd fathered a child with some woman he'd met at a backwoods fishing lodge—a pretty woman with a down-to-earth personality that was a far cry from my mother's.

And yet both women had raised their children on their own, perhaps waiting for the day he would return.

Just as I was.

I imagined Dad and the life he'd created in this place with the woman I'd met on the steps of Three Fires. Did they enjoy a few months together, walking in the woods near the waterfall while they waited for their son to be born? And how long afterward did he stick around? A week, perhaps, before he realized he couldn't hack being a dad and took off.

I looked out the window at the birch and pine and a lowland meadow patched together by strips of sunlight and knew why Dad had been drawn to this place.

And I couldn't hate him.

I could only wonder why he'd chosen to leave.

* * *

That night I dreamt of a creek I used to swim in as a child, one on the south side of Webber that meandered between a forest of cattails and burnt rushes. Standing on a wooded bank, I watched a silver canoe navigate a sharp bend.

Dad was sitting upright in the stern, his paddle firmly in hand as I always remembered it to be. He paused mid-stroke when he saw me standing barefoot in my pajamas. Drawing up his paddle, he laid it across the gunwales.

No movement. No moon. Nothing except the secret we now shared.

"Why didn't you tell Mom?"

"Who says I didn't?"

I wanted to protest but felt the cool intrusion of water mixed with sand between my toes. To my right, a willow kissed its mirror image as a sudden breeze pushed the canoe away from shore.

My father was leaving and I couldn't stop him. Didn't want to stop him.

"Watch for the red bird, Muffet."

I stood still, thinking of our winter feeders.

"And a tree that catches fire but never burns."

"Why?"

But there was no answer, just a whisper of wind as it startled the willow, pushing him away, and still he sat, back straight, staring ahead as the woman I'd seen at the lighthouse stepped from the darkness, her chest a bloom of crimson.

I awoke in a sweat and sat upright in bed. Heart pounding, I swung my legs off the side and stumbled down the hallway. Entering Holly's room, I plopped down on top of her empty bed.

Her digital clock read 3:27 a.m.

Holly Would?

I wondered if this was the way it would be all summer and felt a lonely knot creep into my throat.

Exhausted, I curled up in a ball and fell asleep.

A sleep without dreams.

Chapter Six

It was almost noon the next day when Holly waltzed back into the house, fresh from an overnight stay I had no idea she'd been contemplating. I shot her my "disappointed" face, but she gave no indication of remorse, just threw her purse on the counter and ran a hand through her hair.

"What's up?"

I shook my head. "No note?"

She sighed while making her way to our mustard yellow La-Z-Boy. Once seated, she began drumming her fingers on the armrest. "Jen Reddy and I went out for a few drinks after work. I met a guy and made a spur-of-the-moment decision."

"Who is he?" I asked, hoping to divert my thoughts from their true course—my strange dream and how the hell I was supposed to find a tree that caught fire but never burned.

"No one you'd know."

"I figured."

She smiled, tapped her chin with the end of her index finger and swiveled my way. "He *does* happen to be pals with a certain Deputy Locke."

My already frayed nerves unraveled upon impact. "Are you trying to torture me?"

She rolled her eyes. "I'm trying to cheer you up because girlfriend or not, it was obvious he had the hots for you that night."

My ego did a little chin up and flexed her biceps.

"I'm flattered."

"You should be. Turning Dylan Locke's head isn't easy. Jen's been trying for months. She has one of those police scanners. Speeds on purpose."

But I didn't want to talk about Jen or Dylan or the guy she'd just met. I wanted to spill my guts about what had happened at Three Fires, including my possible run-in with the extended family I didn't know I had. But I couldn't, and so I asked a question I knew would distract her. "What's this guy's name?"

She gave a half smile and sighed in a way that told me I might be spending tonight alone as well. "His name is Dave and he works on the marina docks, so it goes without saying he's got a killer tan *and* body."

"Good to know."

She got up from her chair and circled the kitchen counter. "That's how he met Dylan."

"Oh?" I asked, unable to kick my confounded curiosity where Mr. Locke was concerned.

"He runs for Marine Patrol on the weekends. Dave said he rescued a kid caught in a riptide two weeks ago. Dove off his jet ski and everything."

The image of Dylan diving off a jet ski to save a child dealt a serious blow to my tenuous 'no summer romance' policy and so I squished the image by saying, "I ran into another old classmate of yours yesterday."

She raised an eyebrow. "Who?"

"Jamie Stoddard."

"Where?" she asked.

"He works out at the Lodge."

She made a face, grabbed a banana from our laminate bar and commenced to peel. "Did he seem…*okay?*"

Warning bells went off in my head. "Why wouldn't he?"

"No reason," she took a bite, trying to downplay her question.

"Now *my* bullshit meter is going off and I'm only five feet away."

She looked uncomfortable. "You're new to town and I don't want you to say anything to him—"

"I don't even know him."

"Well," she began slowly. "It's just that his fiancée was killed last year in a car accident."

"Oh, geez—"

"We all thought he'd gone off the deep end but…I guess not."

"Guess not," I echoed, leaning against the counter. "He never mentioned a fiancée,"

"And he probably won't. Her name was Karen and he was driving when they crashed." She took another bite of banana and shook her head. "It was a really big deal. Her parents flipped out, tried to sue him for manslaughter or something stupid like that."

"Was it his fault?" I asked, wondering how her response would affect the way I viewed the young man who'd been so nice to me.

"Far as anyone knows he just lost control when a deer jumped out in front of them. Karen's parents dropped the charges, but the families don't speak anymore. It kind of tore the town in two."

I frowned, feeling for Jamie and what he must have gone through when I saw Holly's mouth move. That in and of itself was not strange, but the fact that no sound came out made me think of the lighthouse and the woman with the red stain on her nightdress. I turned away, hoping to focus my attention on the four senses I had left and heard the familiar sound of white noise humming in my ears, cushioning them in a cocoon as it had before. Which meant something was happening again.

I felt sleepy, heavy, as though I were being sucked into a huge feather bed after running a marathon.

I glanced back but Holly seemed oblivious to my condition as she busied herself with some dishes in the sink. I turned, sat down on one of our wobbly stools as the afternoon sunlight extinguished itself and I was engulfed by the vision.

I was crouched beside a wooded roadway at dusk.

A black Jetta was coming my way, kicking up dust, the occupants engaged in a heated argument. A moment later the driver took his eyes off the road and the car swerved. I covered my head as it fishtailed around me, rolling end over end before finally hitting a tree.

The next instant I was running, dropping to my knees beside the passenger door of the Jetta. Yanking it open, I saw a young woman bleeding from the mouth and choking on it—her blonde hair a tangle of tissue that seemed to be seeping from her ears.

I choked on my scream, tried to reach into my pocket for my cell phone before I realized I was in some alternate universe where things like that didn't exist.

I reached in for the girl, not wanting to touch her but wanting to help and saw Jamie Stoddard strapped in beside her, his amber eyes watching me.

I tried to say his name but couldn't.

"Hello, Muffet," he said, blood running from his nose and between his lips. One drop hung there, suspended before dropping to the earth and blooming against the brown dirt.

I screamed—my voice wet and heavy—my lungs full. Like a struggling swimmer, I fought for the surface, sunlight piercing the sky in patchwork places and I climbed it like a ladder as if my life depended on it and the forest began to melt away and our kitchen reappeared.

Holly had her back to me, digging in the fridge for more food.

Had an hour passed? A minute? A second?

I had no idea how long I'd been in a comatose state or why it had happened, but I knew it had nothing to do with the normal girl from Webber and everything to do with Dad.

Blinking, I looked around and touched my forehead just as Holly turned to face me with a carton of yogurt in her hand. Her face went slack when she saw me and she put the yogurt down in a hurry.

"You feel sick or something?"

I shook my head and tried to get my bearings but the vision of the crash that had taken Karen's life was too vivid to ignore. And Jamie had seen me—spoken as though I were there beside him.

"Hot flash," I lied while wiping my brow with the back of my hand.

"At twenty-two?"

I laughed and the sound scratched my throat. Had I been screaming? And did screaming in an alternate universe equate to screaming here, in Lantern Creek?

I took a quick drink of a can of Coke that had been sitting on the counter for an indeterminable amount of time.

"Maybe you should go to the doctor."

"Nothing's wrong with me."

"The blood," she persisted. "We never figured out where it came from."

"So what?" I said, trying to sound confident.

"I don't know—it just seems weird."

"There's nothing weird about bleeding when you've just been in a car accident. You're overreacting."

"I don't think—"

"Good," I interrupted. "That's what I want you to do."

Defeated, Holly pulled open our silverware drawer and looked for a spoon. "Dave and I are going out again on Friday night. You should come along. Bring a date."

I made a face, hating how my thoughts flew to Dylan and that tanned arm hanging from his passenger window, wisps of long, brown hair dancing around the two of them like a lightning storm.

"Where would I find my unsuspecting victim?"

Holly smiled. "Leave that to me."

* * *

Miracles were in short supply when Friday night rolled around. Not that I hadn't tried to snag a man, but solo lunches at Dairy Queen and lonely trips to the Dollar General weren't exactly prime opportunities for pick-ups.

And I had other things on my mind…like figuring out what the hell was happening to me.

Nothing logical had come to mind aside from the possibility that I'd fallen down Alice's rabbit hole, and even that would have been reassuring in its constant, measured absurdity. But these random trips to the Twilight Zone sandwiched between mundane tasks like folding laundry were beginning to make me feel like the girl from Webber had never existed.

I was contemplating how to get around Holly when she emerged from her room wearing a crushed velvet blouse I thought a church secretary might like.

"You coming or what?"

I frowned, knowing a night out would do me good but not wanting to be a third wheel.

"Couldn't find a date?"

"Didn't look too hard."

"Come out anyway," she said. "You never know who you might run into."

That was true, and I certainly didn't need an excuse not to call Mom and act like I hadn't found anything of interest at Three Fires Lodge aside from a job.

Still, a part of me wondered if she had known about Pam and Adam—and if she had, what that would mean.

I knew I didn't want to spend another evening sitting alone, and so resigned myself to a playing tag along with Holly and Dave.

Downstate, I may have called up a couple of friends and gone to the mall in Kalamazoo, but up here our choices were limited to either hanging out at the marina with the potheads or springing for a dimly lit karaoke bar that served dollar jello shots until midnight.

We chose the latter.

I knew I was overdressed when the people at the next table stood up and unknowingly modeled the latest in pajama bottoms. Still, a sheer white blouse, cami, and blue jeans didn't seem over-the-top.

"Thanks for coming out, J—" Holly giggled between nuzzles from her date, a dead ringer for some Hollywood actor with eyes the color of galvanized smoke.

"Sure," I mumbled through the lime-green Jello that had coagulated between my front teeth. "You come here often?"

Dave leaned back in his chair. "Me and some friends try to catch Ned's Belly when they play."

"Ned's Belly?" I laughed, liking the way I was beginning to feel.

"The bass player was a year ahead of me in school. We used to jam together."

"Yeah?" I tried to sound interested, the third wheels in my mind trying to catch some traction. "How'd they come up with that name?"

"Ready for this one?" Dave asked, leaning forward and I had to admit, Holly could pick them. "He used to have a cat named Ned that would paw at the front door. All he saw was that fat belly every morning and I guess it inspired him."

I laughed again, ran a hand through my hair and glanced around. No one even close to our age was seated anywhere near us. This place wasn't cheering me up. In fact, it was reminding me of what I had to look forward to when the social security checks started pouring in.

So, I had another drink.

And then another.

Halfway through the evening I was feeling as tipsy as the table and was about to excuse myself when I spotted someone entering the bar. Through the dim lighting, I was able to place a familiarity in the way he carried himself, the casual slope of his shoulders and the cloud of brown hair that seemed always out of place.

Holly noticed my interest, followed my gaze and giggled, "Better late than never."

I turned on her at once, "What does that mean?"

"He's our handyman, Squirt. Mr. Stoddard left his number and—"

"So?"

"Maybe I just happened to ask him to join us when he fixed our toilet."

I raised an eyebrow. "I didn't know it was broken."

Holly smiled, her eyes squinty. "Funny what two rolls of Charmin will do."

My eyes flew to Dave, who was looking at me with what I could only assume was pity.

"I don't need help getting *dates* if that's what you think!"

Holly leaned closer, an amused look on her face that mirrored Dave's. "You told me not to think, remember?"

She had a point.

"Come on," she interrupted. "Jamie's a good guy...apart from the whole *'the love of my life was killed in an accident I caused'* thing. It's time he got back in the saddle."

"I'm not a horse!"

"It's just an idiom...or whatever you call it. Dylan has a girlfriend so—"

"Shh!" I said, afraid Dave would catch on but he was too busy waving Jamie over to our table.

"My point is..." she leaned closer, whispered, "Jamie's a nice guy. And not that bad to look at if you don't compare him to...well, you know."

I thought of my vision—or whatever the hell it was—thought of the single band of blood running between Jamie's nose and lips. "You just don't get it. I don't want—"

I saw her gaze hovering above my head and turned to find Jamie standing over me, an easy-going smile on his face. He looked good in a green shirt that complimented his skin and blue jeans that did the same for his legs.

Maybe I could get through this if I didn't think about what I'd seen in the driver's seat of that black Jetta.

"Hey," I laugh-talked. "What're you doing here?"

I felt Holly kick me under the table as Dave spun around, karaoke book in hand. "Have a seat. We were just ready to order another round."

"We were?" I asked. Holly kicked me again, and so I shut my mouth as Jamie sunk into the chair beside me.

Laboratory conditions aside, I found his presence slightly comforting as we sat in a silence smothered by an off-key rendition of *Islands in the Stream*. Another Jello-shot and I was ready for small talk, or whatever I could manage without revealing too much.

"You come here often?"

He nodded. "Just to hear Ned's Belly."

At this revelation, Dave leaned over us and gave him a high five. "They rock, Bro!"

Jamie nodded, seemingly bored by Dave or perhaps not buzzed enough to share his enthusiasm.

"You gonna sing?" He turned to me.

"I'm only good at one thing and even that's negotiable."

Holly, half in the bag by this time, leaned over and hit his shoulder. "She means *writing!*"

"She serious?" Jamie asked with what I thought might be genuine interest.

"I used to work for a newspaper," I shrugged. "No big deal."

"That's cool," Jamie said, pushing his brown hair out of his eyes. "What sort of articles did you write?"

I shrugged again, hating how I felt like a misfit when I should be proud of my accomplishments. "Human interest. You know…*woman runs antique store for fifty-seven years without a bathroom break*…that sort of thing."

"She's just being modest," Holly piped up. "What she really wants to do is start a blog…or something."

I gritted my teeth and looked away as our drinks arrived, plopped unceremoniously on the table by a cocktail waitress with a shirt that read *'If it wasn't for Presque Isle County, Michigan would be flipping you off.'* I was spared further career inquiries when Holly stood and made her way to the microphone, intent on nailing *Barracuda* via the B-52s. Four minutes and twenty-one seconds later she accomplished her mission to a smattering of applause. Sitting down with a heavy sigh, she began what I was hoping she wouldn't.

"So, Jamie…how've ya been?"

I felt the man beside me tense. "Fine."

"You sure?"

"Yeah," he said, his tone abrupt. "Why wouldn't I be?"

"Because I haven't talked to you since"—Holly looked at Dave as though unsure whether to continue with her line of questioning—"it happened."

I looked at Jamie, a little horrified by what my roommate had said, and saw something in him change—something that reminded me of his father. "So, you filled Justine in, eh?"

"I guess you could say that," Holly simpered, too drunk for shame.

"I wish you hadn't done that."

I reached out and touched his arm, wondering why I felt the need to comfort him. "It's okay."

He turned to me, "No, it's not."

I looked at Holly, unsure of his meaning, and was saved once again by the waitress who arrived bearing a Long Island iced tea.

"I ordered for you," Jamie offered. "Someone told me it was your favorite."

Holly looked ready to crawl in a hole as I grabbed the drink and took a gulp. Usually, I was too level-headed to cure my troubles with alcohol, but this was a special occasion.

Four swallows later and I was ready to crawl in a hole myself.

The room grew watery around the edges and I felt myself leaning on Jamie, who was becoming increasingly attentive. Remembering that I had to use the bathroom, I excused myself and found Holly not far behind, chattering in my ear about how Jamie seemed to like me and she sure hoped she hadn't screwed anything up by mentioning the accident.

Bladders emptied, my companions seemed ready to call it a night. I sat waiting for Jamie to offer me a ride, but he seemed hesitant, as though the simple gesture might upend something unspoken.

Looking around, I saw Dave and Holly waiting and felt a wave of humiliation wash over me—poor inebriated girl who couldn't even get the guy who'd gotten her buzzed to drive her home.

And still, Jamie didn't make a move as I felt the pounding music in my bones, felt the room gather heat and closed my eyes. The others were talking but I couldn't make out what they were saying and I didn't know it if was my own mind or the Long Island that had caused it.

I've been waiting…

I saw the girl slumped across the dashboard, her face peppered with pieces of glass and blood and the hazel eyes, which looked an awful lot like my own, were open and unseeing.

Which looked an awful lot like my own…

I recoiled from the sight, felt my butt rock in the chair and opened my eyes. The other three were gathered at loose ends and didn't seem to notice when I pushed to my feet, gripping the back of a chair for support.

"I'm ready," I managed.

"I'll drive you home," Jamie put a hand to my wrist.

"No," I began. "I don't want you to go out of your way."

"It's not out of my way."

"See, J," Holly said, "It's not out of his way."

I turned on her, "Thanks for pointing that out."

She flashed me a thumbs-up.

A few moments later we were standing in front of his truck, a jacked-up blue Chevy with a bumper sticker that read *Arctic Cat Kicks Ass*. Taking a breath, I climbed inside and buckled my seatbelt.

No one had told me not to, but sitting alone in a truck with a man who may or may not have killed his fiancée didn't seem like a good idea. Glancing out the window, I saw him pull out of the parking lot and onto the highway, saw the ever-present birch, pine, and cedar whiz by in the arc of our headlights.

"Thanks for driving me home," I finally spoke.

"No prob," he answered. "I think those two want to be alone."

I laughed lightly, looked back out the window as we picked up speed.

Several minutes passed and I wondered how we could have been so comfortable at Three Fires and so awkward here.

It's not like Jamie knew I had a vision about the accident or had seen what type of car they'd been driving because it all could have been a stupid daydream. But if I was right, and the car really had been a black Jetta…

But how could I ask him?

I was just gathering the courage to put my reporter cap back on when he spoke.

"If I tell you something do you promise not to freak out?"

As if I wasn't freaked out enough.

"You look like Karen." He paused, unsure. "My fiancée."

"I do?" All the worse for me.

"Yeah. It's kind of weird to be driving you home. But kind of familiar, too."

"Is that why you wanted to do it?" I asked.

He didn't answer, but one sideways glance told me I'd insulted him.

"Jamie—"

"It's okay." He shrugged. "Fair question."

"No, it isn't," I looked down. "It isn't fair at all."

He didn't answer, just reached over and turned the radio up and I was left thinking about Karen and what part of me resembled her. Was it the wavy blonde hair? The hazel eyes? The way I dressed or talked or moved?

Was it driving Jamie crazy right now, having someone who looked like her sitting beside him? Was he going off the deep end? Driving me into the woods to abandon me...or worse. The roads didn't seem familiar. Not that that said much.

"Are you taking me back to Lantern Creek?"

He nodded, fiddling with the radio again until he settled on a song by the Eagles. "This is a good one," he said. "Nothin' like an Ol' 55."

I nodded. It was good. And eerie. And I wanted to go home. "Why didn't you take the road we came in on?"

"I know a shortcut."

"Oh," I said lamely, feeling quite helpless as I watched the speedometer creep past seventy. Reaching across my shoulder, I tightened my seat belt.

"Sorry," he took his foot off the gas and glanced my way, "I'm not really myself tonight. I probably should have stayed home to tell you the truth. It's been a year. Exactly."

"Oh, geez," I began, the talk-laugh there again. "I had no idea—"

"It's not something I like to bring up on a first date."

I didn't say anything, but dropped my hands and fingered my bracelet, a string of green beads Mom had given me last Christmas.

"Karen's folks didn't like me," he began, and I thought I would let him vent. Get it all out of his system and then maybe the creepy feeling would go away. "They thought a guy who rakes leaves for a living wasn't good enough for their princess."

"I'm sorry," I said, looking out the window again for something, anything, that was familiar.

"Took them a long time to warm up. But not Karen—we knew right away it was the real deal. You ever feel that way?"

I thought about my lousy taste in men and wondered if I had ever really been in love since Dad skipped town.

"Sorry. I shouldn't be talking about her."

56

"Jamie—"

"I know it's weird."

"It's okay."

He seemed to consider my words, lost in thought as we sped through an intersection without stopping. "Shit," he cursed under his breath. "I think I saw a bear in the woods."

"What?" I asked, unsure if he was serious or using some form of northern lingo when I saw the flashing lights of a police cruiser closing in on us from behind.

"Is that the bear?"

Jamie nodded. "How fast was I going?"

"Eighty," I said, an odd sort of relief sweeping through me as he pulled off on a wide stretch of road just this side of nowhere.

We waited in strained silence as the cop switched on his searchlight and stepped from his cruiser. Moments later the officer was at the window.

"Stoddard?"

And the curt reply.

"Locke."

I looked closer and felt the wind leave my lungs.

I'd dreamed him up a thousand times since our first meeting, imagining what I'd say if he ever asked about the doctor and here he stood in the middle of the woods giving my date a speeding ticket.

"Dylan?"

Jamie turned to me, his face marked with confusion. "You know each other?"

Dylan's smile did not reach his eyes. "She ran me off the road."

"Holly ran you off the road."

"But you got the worst of it," he paused, and I noticed how good he looked in uniform, just as I'd imagined, and how he seemed to be holding his emotions in check with some degree of effort.

"Were you hurt?" Jamie asked while reaching up to squeeze my shoulder, a gesture I found suspect and infuriating.

"She was bleeding," Dylan answered for me. "Ever get to the doctor?"

I averted my eyes from the reproach I was certain I'd see.

"So, you don't keep your promises."

"Usually I do," I found myself stammering. "But money's tight and I couldn't afford—"

"A trip to the E.R."

I looked up and caught his gaze again, one second turning into several before I had the strength to break what we'd started.

57

"Guess I should pay my spies more."

I laughed, then put a hand to my face to hide the color that had risen there, jerking spontaneously when I heard Jamie snap, "Gonna give me the fucking ticket or what?"

I glanced at Dylan, suddenly embarrassed by the company I kept and saw his face harden.

"Knock over a few tonight?"

"None of your business."

I wanted to laugh at the irony but refrained when Dylan repeated his question.

Jamie smirked. "Calm down, Do-Right, I just had a couple of beers. I'm perfectly capable of driving her home."

"Think so?"

I sat, watching Dylan watch Jamie, then shifted my gaze to the latter. He seemed more inebriated than I remembered. But what did I remember after seven jello-shots and a Long Island?

"I'm a careful guy," Jamie continued. "No matter what people seem to think."

"Never said you weren't."

"You didn't have to."

Dylan didn't respond, just shifted to his other foot and I was left wondering what had happened between these two.

"Where were you headed?"

"Back to Lantern Creek."

"By way of Chicago?"

I stifled a giggle, reached up to cover my mouth and was surprised to find my upper lip slick with something I prayed wasn't what I thought it was.

I tried to cover it, tried not to let Dylan see but it was too late because Jamie was nudging me. "Your nose is bleeding."

"My nose?" I asked, unable to understand why it would start up again when Dylan was around. At this rate, he was going to think I couldn't control my bodily functions.

"Mystery solved," he said.

"What mystery?" I asked, digging in my purse for a Kleenex.

"The blood on your hand that night. You must get nosebleeds."

I squeezed my nostrils together as Alvin the Chipmunk answered, "No, I don't!"

58

Dylan turned to Jamie, civil for the first time since our encounter began, "How much did she drink tonight?"

Jamie shrugged. "Not much."

I wasn't sure what sort of girls he was used to, but seven jello-shots and a Long Island seemed respectable enough.

"How much is that?"

The two of them talking over me as though I didn't exist made me furious and frustrated and just this close to flipping them off and walking home. "I'm perfectly capable of answering for myself, thank you very much!"

I saw Dylan's eyes crinkle at the corners. "I don't doubt that, but I'm still waiting for Stoddard to tell me where you're headed."

"One guess," he answered. "And I'll even give you a hint."

"You don't have to."

"Then why'd you ask?"

I saw Dylan's hand grip and release the windowsill before he said, "Whatever you had planned for tonight is officially off. Head to town and I won't give you a ticket."

"Jealous?" Jamie snickered, and I felt my throat tighten even as the blood died at the back of it.

"Don't flatter yourself."

I would have been insulted if I hadn't felt his comment was meant for Jamie alone. He seemed to think the same, silently fuming as I sat holding the Kleenex to my nose, wondering if I was making the biggest mistake of my life by not opening the door and jumping out.

"Take her home," Dylan's voice cut my thoughts in half. "Now."

"Looking forward to it," Jamie said, his tone speaking to my instincts as he rolled up his window and started the Chevy, tires crushing gravel before I had the guts to scream, "Wait!"

Jamie slammed on the brakes and in an instant, I threw the door open and jumped out.

I saw Dylan pivot as Jamie turned in his seat, idling for a moment as our eyes met and in them, I saw anger and disbelief and for just an instant, relief.

"Go on, then," he said, his words slow as he sat a moment longer, letting the implication settle before shutting his door and pulling back onto the road.

I stood watching his taillights until distance reduced them to embers burning in the forest, wondering where my fear had come from and how I would explain myself to Dylan, who was now standing in front of me.

"What's going on?"

I looked down, embarrassed, and crumpled the bloody napkin in my hand.

"Justine?" he took a step closer. "You can tell me."

But I couldn't explain. Not here, in the middle of the road with the wind picking up and gooseflesh rising on my arms.

"We can talk in the car."

I nodded, followed him to the cruiser, and climbed in. I was just thinking how surreal my situation was when he asked, "Been dating Stoddard long?"

"We're not dating."

Another chuckle, "That's not what he thinks."

"I don't care what he thinks."

"He try something?"

I shook my head.

"Intuition?"

I sat silently.

"Good enough for me," he shifted in the seat, his arm grazing mine as he reached to adjust the radio, and an image of his girlfriend popped into my mind.

"Thanks for the ride but I can call my roommate and have her meet us somewhere."

"Holly Would?"

I scowled, realizing she was probably in no condition to pick me up.

"It's my job," he smiled while pulling back onto the road. "Rescuing damsels in distress."

"I'm not in *distress*."

"Could've fooled me."

"Listen," I began, hating the defensiveness in my voice. "I don't need your help. I can walk."

"In those shoes?"

I glanced down at my pink flip-flops and felt my anger rising.

"Don't get mad," he said. "I had a bad feeling when I walked up."

"You did?"

"And then I see you sitting there," he paused, and I saw him glance at my necklace.

I felt my fingers reach for it and blurted out, "Jamie started talking about his fiancée—"

Dylan nodded as though he knew the story. "Karen?"

"I have the feeling he's not over her."

"Can't say I blame him."

I touched my forehead, willing away anything that had to do with northern soap operas, wishing for my bed and Joey cuddled up beside me when I saw the lights of Lantern Creek glittering across the bay.

"What was going on back there?" I asked, knowing I'd better get it over with before we got home.

Dylan looked straight ahead and I studied his profile, the straight line of his nose, the swell of his lips and the way he swallowed, his Adam's apple bobbing.

"Stoddard's always had a chip on his shoulder."

I looked ahead again, "He said Karen's parents didn't think he was good enough for her."

"He wasn't."

Wow, this guy was tough to crack.

"If you don't want to tell me—"

"There's nothing to tell. We just didn't get along in school."

I stopped talking, mystified by his brusque manner as he pulled into my driveway. I sat for a moment in silence. The only sound I could hear was my heart in my ears, the only question on my mind was whether I had the strength to get out of the cruiser, feeling the anxiety I always did when faced with a choice I did not want to make.

"About Stoddard," he turned to me, clearly struggling with something. "You were right to get out of the truck."

I looked down, fiddled with the bracelet again.

"I was going to follow you," Dylan said. "Make sure he took you home."

I opened my mouth, searching for the right words that would make me seem mysterious and alluring and unattainable and came up with, "I was *really* hoping you would."

He paused, startled by my confession and I looked away, my mortification complete when he said, "Things are kind of complicated right now."

"Oh, sure," I mumbled while reaching for the door handle. It's not like I didn't know about his supermodel girlfriend. "Forget I said anything."

"Justine—"

"I understand. Thanks for the ride."

"Wait."

Something about his tone made me stop. I turned and looked at him, really seeing him for the first time and noticed how intently he was watching me, how his eyes skimmed the line between blue and gray—a sky that couldn't decide—and how his hair held tints of gold that would curl around his ears if he ever grew it out.

I imagined putting a hand to that face and bringing it to my own, imagined what it would feel like to have his mouth move against mine and remembered the girl with the lightning storm hair.

The girl who was probably waiting for him at home.

I let my mind wander to the beautiful house I'd seen on the shores of Grand Lake and imagined him removing his clothes and crawling into a large bed where he would touch her shoulder and roll her towards him.

I imagined myself in her place.

I wanted him now—just as I'd wanted Dad to stay and Mom to grow a heart. I wanted it and I couldn't explain why it scared me.

"I heard you were hired on at Three Fires," His voice interrupted my thoughts and I smiled, thinking he might have been talking to Dave about me. "I want to know if Stoddard gives you any trouble."

As in call him? On the phone?

"I don't... I mean... I don't have—"

"I'll give you my number."

"Sure," was all I could say. I hadn't felt this way since Jake Jones and I were paired up in middle school science lab.

"I said things were complicated, but I didn't mean impossible."

I sat dumbfounded, thinking again of the pretty girl he'd driven all the way to the library, the girl who worried about him when he worked the night shift. Just like I would.

"Dylan," I began. "I don't think—"

"I've got other commitments, but nothing we couldn't work around."

My eyes widened as he leaned towards me.

"You're on duty," I reminded him—not believing I was reminding him.

He smiled, checked the clock on the dash. "Not anymore."

Fast as lightening my hand shot out and I smacked his face. Immediately I felt better, then sick to my stomach when I saw how shocked he looked, as though he'd honestly expected me to shut up and pucker.

I drew my hand back while muttering, "Does your girlfriend know you troll the streets looking for damsels in distress?"

"*Girlfriend?*" He rubbed his cheek, and to my horror, I saw a red mark appearing.

"The one you took to the library," I muttered.

He shook his head, tried to grin but grimaced instead. "My sister needed a ride to work."

I felt like throwing up, literally, right in the middle of my driveway at one o'clock in the morning. "*Sister?*"

He rubbed his face again. "Damn, you got me good."

I thought of the way he'd put his arm around her shoulder, the way it had appeared romantic but could have been nothing more than brotherly affection.

And now I was seriously screwed.

"Oh, Dylan," I stammered. "I thought—"

"How did you know I gave her a ride to the library?"

I wanted to lie and tell him I'd recognized his truck while picking up Chinese takeout, that I'd never stalked him in broad daylight or been close to his lake house.

"I was driving by the lighthouse the other day."

"The lighthouse again?"

I nodded.

"Listen," he shifted in his seat, anxious to wrap things up with the only girl in Presque Isle who'd ever rebuffed his advances. "It's getting late."

My nose began to tingle.

"I'll see you around."

I nodded again, feeling exquisitely miserable before reaching for the door handle.

"Justine."

I turned to his voice as he reached up slowly and touched my cheek.

"Is it safe?"

I nodded, every stringed instrument I'd ever heard playing in my mind.

"Just the same," he smiled again, "I think I'll keep my distance."

"That might be for the best," I said, not meaning it but feeling something in his restraint that was different—and good.

He chuckled, left me wondering when I would see him again when he took a piece of paper out of his pocket and wrote his number down. One look and I knew I would not be dialing up the sheriff's office.

"Sleep tight," he said while placing the piece of paper in my hand, his fingers lingering for a moment against my own.

I imagined him doing just that. Imagined what it would be like to be the girl he came home to.

"Thanks," I managed while opening my door and stepping out into the arms of an early morning. "But I don't think I will."

He smiled briefly before backing out of the driveway and I stood for several minutes after he'd left, listening to the sounds a small town makes past its bedtime—then slowly made my way inside.

Chapter Seven

I was standing in the middle of Cabin Five on my first day at Three Fires with vacuum in hand, ready to tackle the main rug when Pam laid a hand on my shoulder.

I jumped, my nerves frayed from the night before, and turned to face her.

"Can you start at the tavern tonight? I know it's short notice, but Nat called in sick and Saturday's our big night."

"Gee…"

"Our manager's there and you can train on the job." She stopped and smiled at me in a way that must have captivated dear old Dad. "Best way to learn if you ask me."

I frowned, trying to be brave in the face of this new challenge, but just showing up this morning had been a monumental feat. The possibility that Jamie might harass me seemed promising only in the respect that I would have an excuse to call Dylan. But Pam had sent him out to clear trails, a task that would keep him in the woods and out of my hair for most of the day.

"I'd do it myself but I'm taking Adam up to Mackinaw City tonight."

"You are?" I asked while bending to scoot an ancient end table that supported exactly four copies of *Good Housekeeping* off the rug. The smell of dust and mildew and traces of Pine-Sol met my nose when I did so.

"A guy I dated lives up there and he likes to see Adam every now and again."

A guy she dated?

I stopped, stood back up and wiped my sweaty forehead with the back of my hand. I had dressed the part in a pair of cut off jean shorts and a gray Detroit Tigers shirt. Not that I cared about sports, but Brad had been sweet enough to pick it up for me when he took the boys to a game.

Which made it perfect for scrubbing toilets.

"So you'll do it?" Pam asked.

"Yeah," I answered, forgetting about the bartending gig, wanting to know what sort of guys she'd dated and if Dad had ever called or written or sent paintings to pay for what he couldn't give his son.

"About Uncle Rob," I said hesitantly, sticking my toe in the bathwater to see if it was warm. "What happened between you two?"

She wiped her own forehead and shook her head. "Isn't it obvious?"

I didn't really want to think of that, but she'd cracked the door and I was going in.

"You said there were no bad memories."

Pam looked at me, scrutinizing at first before her face softened into the person my Dad must have loved.

"I met Robert while canoeing the Ocqueoc River. Came around the bend and there he was, standing in the middle of my current with a fly rod in his hand." She paused, wiped her face again and I saw the flush wasn't from heat alone. "Ran right into him!"

I imagined Dad, his khaki waders protecting him, his flies tied to his vest, his shoulder-length hair pulled back in a ponytail and wondered if Pam had loved him at first sight, and if he had pushed the memory of the girl he'd married in the country chapel out of his mind.

"We dated for a few months and I got pregnant. Robert had a job downstate and spent a lot of time there, but he made it back for Adam's birth. We lived together for a while, but he never asked me to marry him."

I felt my jaw tighten. "Did you want him to?"

She nodded, the color in her cheeks again. "I loved him."

Of *course* she loved him. Everyone loved him—Mom and I included.

"He left for good not long after Adam was born."

A terrible thought formed in my mind, and I opened my mouth, shut it again before I had the guts to mumble, "Did he know? About Adam?"

Pam shook her head, and I could tell the subject bothered her, which meant she'd thought about it. "Adam didn't show any signs until he was two."

"You never saw him again?"

"No."

"No note or anything?"

She looked at me, her green eyes seeming to go deeper than I was comfortable with, and answered, "He left nothing."

"I'm sorry—"

She shrugged. "I'm assuming you don't know where he is."

"No," I said quickly. "Of course not."

"Of course not."

"Can I take a break?" I asked, feeling strange, lightheaded, and heavy.

"Sure thing," she answered. "If you need to cool off go out on the porch."

"I will," I said while moving off to do just that. Once seated in a white plastic chair, I stared out at Ocqueoc Lake while a memory from my childhood took root and found a place in the present. Dad and I were sitting at the breakfast nook in our house on Harbrooke Street, the one with the bay windows. He was holding a cup of coffee and I had my coloring book.

I had just finished a picture and Dad had leaned closer to see.

"What is it, Muffet?"

Laying my crayons aside, I held the picture up. I'd drawn a man with a long riding coat and high leather boots. A man with no face.

"Is that a cowboy?" my father asked, his tone tender, hoping.

"No," I answered, certain he was no such thing.

"Does he scare you?"

I nodded, "Sometimes I see him in my dreams."

Dad had come closer then, leaning down, his hair just brushing the side of my cheek and I touched his face. He turned so I could look into his eyes.

They were worried.

"He can't hurt you, Muffet."

I looked up at him, unsure. "Does he scare you, Daddy?"

He nodded. "Very much."

"Feel better?" Another voice coated my memory, dissolving it as water would a chalk drawing on the sidewalk and I was left with Pam at my left ear, coaxing me back to the present moment as gently as a warm wind.

"Yep," I said while standing up and turning towards the cabin.

Just then the screen door opened and Jamie Stoddard walked out looking every bit the backwoodsman with a chip on his shoulder. Gunning for me, no doubt. Wanting to bend my ear for ditching him in the early morning hours. But he didn't say anything, just stood with his arms crossed and waited.

Pam turned as Adam entered behind Jamie, his dark eyes searching the room for me.

I KNOW WHO YOU ARE.

I heard it as surely as I'd heard Pam speak a moment ago, only stronger, as though the voice trapped inside this boy had been rattling the cage that imprisoned it. And while this should have been the strangest thing to ever happen to me, it didn't surprise me as much as it would have two weeks ago.

Holding his gaze with my own, I tried to direct my response in a way he might hear and tossed my thought towards him like a baseball toward a catcher's mitt.

WHO AM I?

Adam moved closer, put a hand to his left ear.

YOU'RE MY SISTER

I felt his words like a bucket of ice water to the face—which soon passed into the warm feeling of an expectation realized. Wanted. Hoped for.

"How's your first day going?" Jamie asked, his voice a rude reminder of where I was and who I shouldn't be able to hear inside my head.

"Fine."

"Not too tired, I hope."

I wondered what he thought I'd done after he drove off then gave a quick shake of my head.

"She's doing great," Pam offered. "And she's gonna switch hit for me tonight."

Jamie's gaze shifted to me again. "Starting at the tavern?"

I nodded.

"Maybe I'll swing by and give you a hand."

"Mallard'll be there. Nothing to worry about," Pam stepped in, leading Jamie back towards the side of the cabin to talk about which trails he'd cleared—and I was grateful.

But who the hell was Mallard?

YOU'LL SEE

I turned to see Adam smiling.

Was I imagining this, too, or was it time to let go and surrender?

STAY OUT OF MY HEAD, LITTLE BROTHER

MAKE ME.

Chapter Eight

"Hey!" I tried to sound chipper when Mom answered the phone. It had been just over a week and a half since we had talked, the new pattern establishing itself in our lives as other patterns had before.

"Justine?"

"Yep."

"I was out in my garden."

I felt the familiar sinking in my chest, an excuse she'd used a hundred times for a million things she didn't want to say to me. "I'm sorry to interrupt."

"You're not interrupting. I'm glad to hear from you."

I bit my lip and said, "Phone works both ways."

Silence—extended and anything but golden—followed my remark.

"I have a question."

"Of course you do," she began, and I heard her draw up a chair and sit down in it. I imagined she was in the dining room, looking out at the backyard I used to play alone in.

"Tell me what happened to Dad. And I don't want the story you've reheated since I was old enough to understand."

The air seemed static between us and I imagined her putting a hand to her face as she often did.

"And the necklace," I continued, unwilling to stop now that I'd unearthed some courage. "Does it mean something?"

"Is this a joke?"

When I didn't respond, she sighed, obviously annoyed at having to abandon her hobby for such nonsense. "You read the note yourself, Justine. I haven't been hiding anything from you. The painting paid for your college like Robert wanted—"

"Like Robert wanted," I echoed.

She sighed again, and I could sense her growing irritation "What are you getting at?"

"He was my Dad, not just some guy named Robert."

"And he was my husband, in case you've forgotten."

"I haven't forgotten."

"Neither have I," she said, her voice cool and I realized the conversation might be over before it had begun.

"Tell me about the necklace. People up here keep looking at it like…I don't know…like it has some kind of special meaning."

"Robert bought it at the jewelry store downtown. He gave it to me the first year we were married."

I wished I could see her face, to look for the tell-tale signs that she was lying or just making something up because she didn't have the answer and was too tired to go looking for it. Like she'd been too tired to look for him, the husband she raved about.

"If you don't believe me, feel free to ask your Dad if you find him."

"*If* I find him?"

"Yes."

I pushed to my feet and walked to the kitchen window. Iris was outside, dog leash in hand, a tiny mutt of the terrier persuasion at the other end of it.

"At least I'm looking."

Her laughter was light. "At the very least."

I bit my lip, realizing seconds later that calling her had been a very bad decision. One I would not repeat.

"I'll let you get back to your work."

"That would be nice."

I opened my mouth to tell her I loved her but couldn't. Instead, I muttered something about needing to take a shower and hung up quickly. A few shuffling steps carried me to my bedroom where I shut the door and sank to the floor. A low purr to my left and I scooped up Joey and nuzzled his soft, orange fur as tears began to squeeze out of the corner of my eyelids.

Wiping my cheeks with the back of my hand, I went to the closet and shoved the shoes I kept on my high shelf aside. Beside my black flats, I spied the purple package that had yellowed with time, thinking again of that stupid card and how it had made me feel like less than nothing.

If you find him…

He'd done a damn good job making me believe he never wanted to see me again.

I pushed the present back further and grabbed a pair of blue jeans. Paired with a tight black shirt, I was sure to get plenty of tips.

Might as well start saving for my new life now.

I was never going back to Webber again.

Chapter Nine

I walked into Huff and Puff's, the tavern that supplemented Adam and Pam through the winter months on a gorgeous evening in mid-June, having driven around the block three times before I decided it was safe to stop. The structure looked condemned, but the tiny "Open" sign placed beside a swinging placard featuring the Big Bad Wolf blowing down a straw house as a curly-tailed pig ran for the hills finally convinced me I'd found the right place.

A wiry fellow with tanned skin and cut-off jean shorts was sitting on a bench near the front door. He waved cheerfully as I parked next to what had once been an attached garage but was now nothing more than a ramshackle lean-to.

I locked my car and pulled the handle just to be sure.

The friendly guy on the bench smiled widely as I approached. His large, white teeth were a stark contrast to his dark face and the wrinkles that lined it told me he might be older than he looked.

"Hello," I ventured while climbing the steps to the porch.

"Hey," he stuck his hand out. "You the new barmaid?"

"Yep."

"I'm Mallard Brauski."

I looked him up and down, wondering if I'd caught the right name, realizing I had and that this guy was calling the shots.

"Nice to meet you…Mallard."

He nodded, showing his pearly whites, then turned so I could follow him inside.

The interior of Huff and Puff's was a lot better looking that the outside and featured a pool table, jukebox, and smattering of tables. Multi-colored Christmas lights were strung over the doorway I'd just walked through, and a worn-out woman I could only assume was the town drunk sat hunched at the far end of the bar, a cigarette dangling loosely from her lips.

"How'd Pam talk you into it?"

I turned to find Mallard standing with his hands on his hips. The jean shorts gave him the appearance of Jane Fonda on steroids, and I had to cover my mouth to stifle the laughter I felt sure would infuriate him.

"She told me the tips were good."

Mallard looked me up and down. Shaking his shaggy head once the inspection was over, he nodded. "You'll get tips all right, but I'm gonna have to keep my fuckin' eye on you. Pam may own the joint, but I call the shots."

"Be nice," I heard the woman say from her barstool. "Don't scare her off like ya did the last barmaid."

I felt myself stiffen. "What'd you do?"

Mallard shook his head, then stepped forward, smiled widely and became a dead-ringer for the Cheshire Cat.

"I waylaid her. And now she's my old lady."

I didn't have to time reflect on that disturbing thought because he was moving through the alcove, waving his arms while explaining the finer points of northern bartending.

"Up here we ain't got no blenders, so if they want one o' those froufrou drinks they can take themselves to the Red Lobster in Alpena. Got it?"

I nodded, watching intently as he ran the tip of his index finger along a row of glistening liquor bottles. "Up here all you gotta do is know how to count a shot and pop the top off a beer. Can ya do that, Flatlander?"

I nodded. "The beer I can do."

He grabbed a shot glass out of the sink and set it up on the bar, then turned and selected a bottle of Ol' Granddad Whiskey.

"All these bottles has got a stopper, see? All you do is count down one…two…three—and then lift it up again. See? Then you put it back down and count to six… Nine altogether."

Ten minutes later I was pouring a drink to my first customer, still knowing next-to-nothing about tending bar, hoping that my sparkling personality and tight black shirt would make up for it.

More than once I checked my cell phone, hoping Dylan had called, realizing later that I'd never given him my number and that if I wanted to hear his voice I was going to have to make the first move.

I thought about how close we had come to kissing, thought about him kissing me in other places and realized I stunk at being aloof because what I wanted was to call him up for a good old-fashioned make-out session.

I bit the inside of my lip, wondering what he would think if he accepted my invitation and came back to my place. Had I scooped the litter? Picked up my dirty laundry? "Listen up, Flats!"

I turned to find Mallard pouring a draft with the dexterity of Da Vinci. "This here's Shaw an' he'll shoot you if you don't pull a good head."

Shaw, a fat fellow with and handlebar mustache that had whitened with age, shifted his weight on a barstool that had no choice but to protest.

By eight o'clock the regulars had started to filter in, and by ten I had fried my first burger and kept a steady eight customers satisfied. Pam's busy night was starting to pan out for me when Mallard called for everyone to shut the fuck up. I glanced up as he adjusted the volume on the television—an exhausted device that teetered on a metal stand someone had duct taped to the wall.

A hush fell over the patrons as a local reporter appeared on screen in front of flashing police lights. Obviously, a crime scene had been established and I immediately thought about Dylan, wondering if he was working, if he was safe and knew this guy was getting to be a major distraction.

I was staring into space when the reporter finally spoke.

The body of a Lantern Creek girl reported missing last night was found on County Road 449 at about seven o'clock a.m. local time. Cause of death is still undetermined. Homicide detectives and police have sealed off the area...

"Fuck me!" Mallard cried. "That's just up the road."

Authorities have identified the body as that of Suzy Marsh, a young Onaway woman who was last seen leaving a friend's house in the early morning hours.

"Think she was on drugs?" Shaw asked. "Kids go out there to get high."

"How would you know, you old fucker?" Mallard asked while popping the top off a Busch Light.

I barely heard their banter because as I looked closer at the reporter and the trees behind her I remembered the lonely stretch of gravel I'd seen a black Jetta spin out on, a blonde girl bleeding to death inside of it while Jamie looked on.

I saw his face plainly now, his eyes wide with the same relief I'd seen while jumping from his truck.

"Flats!" Mallard grabbed my wrist. "Answer your goddamn phone!"

"Oh..." I managed, hearing the familiar ringtone, finding it just before voicemail kicked in.

"Justine?"

I smiled into the phone, suddenly giddy. "Dylan?"

"Turn on the news."

Boy, was he bossy for a first phone call. "Already did."

"You bartending at Huff's?"

"Yeah, but how did you—"

"Can you sit tight for a while?"

"Sure," I answered. "My shift ends at two."

"Good," he said. "I'll be out then. I just need to ask you a few questions."

A few *questions*?

My heart did a nosedive into my black flats.

"Keep someone with you until I get there."

I thought about telling him I could take care of myself but answered with a lukewarm version of, "Sure thing."

Once I hung up I couldn't shake my disappointment. Mallard, on the other hand, just wanted the scoop.

"Who the fuck was that?"

"A friend."

"Why'd you tell him when you get off work?"

"He's a cop. I had to tell him."

Mallard chuckled, took a drag off the cigarette that had been burning in the trough. "A cop, eh?" He turned to Shaw. "Same one what flunked outta that big college and had to ask his Daddy for more money so he could go to the dickhead academy?"

I shrugged my shoulders. I knew next to nothing about Dylan besides the fact that he was hot.

"Same one what every female over fourteen and under fifty wants to fuck?"

"Leave her alone," Shaw grunted.

"I'll leave her alone when she grows a brain," he came closer, shaking one finger so close to my nose that he actually touched it. "Don't you ever tell no one when your shift ends. I gotta lot of money in that till and it needs to stay right where I put it."

I stood and stewed and thought about the choice words I was going to have with Pam—like why she thought learning the ropes under this guy came anywhere close to a good idea.

"Lots of pricks with one thing on their mind hang around after hours an' I won't always be here to save your ass."

I thought about telling him I didn't need anyone named Mallard saving anything remotely close to my ass but realized it wasn't worth it and grabbed a rag to wash down the bar.

The time seemed to creep by as my steady eight turned to six, then five, then two when Shaw finally paid his tab and called it a night. Mallard kept to himself while washing the bar glasses, breaking his silence only when I started sweeping the floor.

"Didn't mean to rattle your chain."

"You didn't," I lied.

He leaned against the bar, one hand resting at the nape of his neck, the other reaching for a fresh cigarette from his already-exhausted pack. "Where that girl was found tonight—I may joke about it when Ol' Fat Ass is around but it ain't no laughin' matter."

I sensed a story and took a seat on the nearest stool.

Finally, someone was talking.

"That road runs right through what used to be Back Forty Farm," he paused, waiting for the name to register and when it didn't he seemed irritated. "Forgot you don't know your head from your asshole."

"I was just going to say the same about you."

He chuckled, then took a long drag. "A married couple what went by the name of Ebersole was murdered out there back in the 1880s. Never found the killer but he must not have liked the husband none because he stripped him naked an' threw his drawers on an ol' manure pile in the barn. Took the best fuckin' horse and split. Hired girl was sleepin' upstairs and didn't hear a thing."

I looked down, tracing a groove in the bar with my fingernail. "Sounds suspicious."

"And that ain't even the fucked-up part. Seems after the Mrs. was buried a few of her folks went back to the graveyard and found her body had been disturbed."

I scrunched up my nose, disgusted. "As in '*I'm Igor and I'm looking for body parts*' disturbed?"

Mallard shrugged. "Sheriff must've wondered the same thing because when all the fuckin' leads ran dry he started workin' with a gal what everyone thought had the Sight."

"The Sight?"

"Holy Hell, Flats! Ain't ya ever seen *The Sixth Sense?*'"

I smiled at him and asked, "Did she find the killer?"

My companion took another long drag, trying to draw out the suspense. "She coughed up a name all right."

"And?" I was finding it hard to hide my impatience.

"They lynched him on it."

My finger stopped mid-stroke as his voice became muffled in the familiar envelope of white noise. Looking up, I saw him talking and knew he didn't realize what was happening. I took a steadying breath and stared at the groove in the wooden bar, continuing to trace as images flashed before my eyes—pictures I was beginning to accept as part of my new reality.

A woman lay dead in her bed, her black hair plaited into two braids that hung below her waist. Her chest was a blossom of red and I realized I'd seen her before, on the waterfront as I stood watching the lighthouse. Turning from her I noticed the man, naked from the waist down and lying on top of her while the hired girl shivered in her bed upstairs, hoping no one would search the house because it was obvious the killer was just after the Mrs. and it served her right for being such a hussy.

Moments later I fled the bedroom and ran down the porch steps, saw the killer standing in the open yard, his riding coat unbuttoned, his hat low on his head.

Does he scare you, Muffet?

"Very much," I heard myself say, thinking of my father and his coffee, the red birds watching as snow electrified the air.

I turned from the scene, listened as the wind held its breath and then heard the jukebox, recognized Reba McEntire and turned my head just in time to catch Mallard's second-hand smoke.

"You gonna wipe that ashtray or just stare at it?"

I looked up, saw his face and knew mine must have given me away.

"My story scare you some?"

I nodded, then carefully set the ashtray down. "What was the killer's name?"

Mallard smiled, pleased that his story had hooked me. "Jonas Younts."

I set the ashtray aside. "And the woman with the Sight?"

He took another long drag. Let the smoke out slowly.

"Went by Odessa Cook."

* * *

I was sitting on the front steps, feeling as though I'd fallen in with Alice's rabbit again when Dylan pulled up. Waving once, I stood and waited while he exited his truck.

"You alone?"

I shook my head. "Mallard's inside counting down the till."

"Free to leave?"

I nodded, thinking Mr. Locke looked mighty fine in a white T-shirt that accentuated his chest and khaki cargo shorts that just reached his tanned kneecaps. I'd always imagined cops to be pasty and pudgy from spending so much time indoors eating donuts, but Dylan ran for Marine Patrol, which meant he spent plenty of time soaking up the sun.

I was trying to decide if I should tell him about Mallard's story when he reminded me of why he'd come.

"Can we talk?"

"Sure."

"Off the record?"

I shoved my hands into the front pocket of my hoodie, thinking that gesture would be enough to let him know he'd hurt my feelings. "I guess…but I really don't know what this is about."

He motioned for me to get in the truck, and I threw a glance over my shoulder. Sure enough, Mallard was watching from the window.

"My car—" I pointed at the Heap.

"Would probably thank me."

A moment later he was opening his passenger door, ever the gracious gentleman to the woman he was about to interrogate. Once inside, he settled back against the seat and ran a hand over the back of his head.

"I didn't want to make this about business."

I didn't either and was feeling kind of lousy about possibly being related to a woman who had lynched a man on a silly little vision. Wanting some admiration, I looked his way and then unzipped my hoodie for full black-shirt effect. It must have worked because his eyes went straight to my chest in an appreciative sweep.

"You make decent tips tonight?"

I nodded. "Mallard helped me out."

"I'll bet he did." Then, with more gentleness. "You heard about the body?"

I nodded. I'd heard about a lot of bodies.

"It was found in the area where I pulled you over last night."

"You pulled me over?"

My joke broke the mood and he laughed, settled back and reached across the seat, his arm resting just behind my shoulders. "I must have made an impression."

I smiled, thinking of the mark on his face. "I think that was me."

"Can you tell me what you were doing before I stopped you?"

I shrugged—not wanting to talk about Holly's *Barracuda* cover or the Jello-shots or how lame I felt for not being able to get a date on my own. "We went out to the bar on 68."

He nodded. "Notice anything strange about Stoddard?"

I shrugged, unsure how to proceed. "Jamie was upset. It'd been a year since—"

"I know."

I fiddled with my necklace, remembering the day I'd followed him into town, wishing I could crawl into the passenger seat and here I sat, living the dream with absolutely nothing to say. Still, I knew silence was the best policy because if I opened my mouth the truth about my father would come out followed shortly by what I'd learned about Pam and Odessa Cook.

And why stop there? Why not fill him in on my dysfunctional childhood and neurotic mother? Tell him about Brad and the crappy Detroit Tigers T-shirt.

"Forensics puts the time of death around one o'clock."

His words broke into my thoughts and stopped them cold.

"Right after you pulled us over?"

He nodded.

"And County Road 449?"

"I think Stoddard was taking you there."

I swallowed, suddenly weak with fear. "Why?"

Dylan turned towards me, and I noticed the intensity in his eyes, the same way he'd looked at the lighthouse like he was trying to figure out something that didn't make sense.

"You tell me."

I shook my head. "He said he knew a shortcut to Lantern Creek... I believed him," I paused, ran a hand over my mouth. "You don't think—"

"I don't know what to think, but if the homicide detective knew where you were last night he'd be interviewing you down at the station right now."

"Instead of you?" I asked, impressed that he didn't want to see me interrogated, wanting him to get to the point and ask me if Jamie had mentioned anything about wanting to murder me or anyone else on our so-called karaoke date.

"Isn't that a better option?"

I shrugged, "It could get you in trouble."

"I don't care."

I looked down at my hands and smiled.

"So, you're willing to forget everything?"

He didn't answer right away, just slowed the truck and pulled over on a wide spot that overlooked Lantern Creek's pride and joy: an enormous limestone quarry that employed half the men in town.

"If you tell me you don't know anything then I believe you."

I looked him, held his gaze. "I don't know anything."

He smiled, and the effect was startling, hurling me headlong into a mixture of emotions I had no idea how to deal with. "If it had been any other guy with you last night—"

"Why does it matter?"

He looked out the window at the lights of the quarry sparkling far below us. "I told you we didn't get along."

I put my hand to the side of his face, not knowing why I was doing it but wanting to comfort him.

"Was it because of Karen?"

He looked over quickly. "I never bought that bullshit story about a deer running in front of them. None of her friends did either—or her parents. I played ball with her older brother in school. We grew up together. She was like a sister."

He stopped abruptly and I felt my heart warm to him.

"Why would he hurt her? I mean—they were engaged—he obviously loved her."

Dylan shook his head, brought his hand over to cup mine as it rested between us. "I don't know what went on behind closed doors. I just know Stoddard."

"Let it go, Dylan," I whispered, feeling the pull of his presence, the wanting deep within my belly that went far beyond the physical. "There's nothing you or her family could have done."

"I keep telling myself that."

I smiled, my lips inches from his. "Start believing it."

He closed the distance between us in an instant. I felt his mouth cover mine, the sensation of dizziness and static playing heavy against my rapid heartbeat.

His breath fanned my ear, my lips found his cheek, kissing the spot where I'd struck him the night before. He said my name, carried away by the same thing I was experiencing as his mouth travelled down my throat. "I don't know what it is about you."

All rational thoughts left me as his hand found my breast, kneading its way under the tight black shirt.

"Dylan—" I touched his arm, felt him tense.

"Don't," he sighed against my neck. "I want you."

I wanted him, too, but not in the front seat of his truck overlooking the quarry where the vast majority of Lantern Creek teenagers had lost their virginity.

"Dylan," I pushed at him again.

"What?" he asked, raising his eyes to mine and in that moment, he came to his senses, pulled away and muttered, "Justine, I'm so sorry."

"Don't be," I breathed, still trying to get my bearings as he flopped back into his own seat.

"I'm usually not like this."

I thought about Jen Reddy and her penchant for police scanners. "It's okay."

"No, it's not." He swallowed, visibly upset. "I'll take you back to Huff's."

I didn't look at him as I pulled my shirt down, smoothing the wrinkles like a Victorian lady after a good romp in the boudoir.

He didn't speak again until we reached the bar.

"I have a bad feeling about Suzy Marsh."

I chuckled, trying to put him at ease. "Don't most people have bad feelings about murder?"

"I think it's pretty obvious that I've taken a personal interest in your"—he paused, searching for the words—"well-being."

I smiled, looked down at my lap. "Pretty obvious."

"Please call if you remember anything else about last night."

I bit my lip, suddenly shy when he'd had his hand up my shirt only ten minutes before. "Can I just call?"

He smiled softly, touched the side of my face.

"How about when you get home. Your car gives me the creeps."

"That makes two of us."

He got out of the truck and circled to my side. Opening the door, he helped me out and then stood holding me, his arms tightening around my back as we stood in the darkness.

"Don't forget."

Did he think I was a lunatic?

"I won't."

He leaned down, kissed me lightly on the lips—his touch igniting the memory of what had happened inside the truck.

Somehow, I found the strength to pull away and crawl into the Heap.

For the first time, I was disappointed when she kicked to life on the first try. Waving through the window, I was able to get a good head start—dreaming of what I would say to him as I lay in bed that night.

Humming to myself like a schoolgirl, I thought of Dad, wondering if I could ever get my mind back on track with Dylan in the picture.

But I liked him in the picture—liked feeling that someone wondered and worried and had my back, so if I wanted to indulge in something that made me feel good, why not?

I knew why…

Because of Robert Cook.

If I did luck out and find him, or give up when the trail ran cold—could I stay in Lantern Creek just because Dylan was here? Would he pack up and follow me wherever it was I wanted to go?

Considering we ever got that far.

A kiss was not a commitment, and I had the feeling I could get some serious competition where his affection was concerned.

The humming stopped, the schoolgirl now a sober realist. I'd always wanted to be swept off my feet by a decent guy—but now found the scenario just as complicated as being ignored by a bad one.

I was lost in thought when I pulled into my driveway and found Holly's Lumina missing from its customary spot. Girl talk would have been nice but Dave the dock boy had entered the equation and she'd have her own conundrum to figure out soon enough.

Climbing the stairs, I was surprised to find the kitchen door slightly ajar.

Holly probably forgot to lock it...

That was it...she was in such a hurry to get to her man that she forgot to pull it shut.

Entering the darkened kitchen, I felt something brush against my pant legs and almost screamed before I heard Joey greet me with a high-pitched "meow." Scooping him up, I groped for the light switch.

The living room suddenly sprang to life under the bright glare of the kitchen's fluorescents and I was relieved to see everything in its proper place—or whatever that meant to two girls who lived on the sloppy side.

Not that I hadn't tried to reign Holly in, but all her years living from one escapade to the next left little time for housekeeping. Which left me wondering what my excuse was.

I was just picking up my cell phone when I heard a faint noise from the direction of our porch. Joey arched his back and I had no choice but to drop him. Scampering away, I hoped he'd flush out whatever I imagined to be hiding in the darkness as long as that something was no bigger than a mouse.

But nothing happened. Minutes passed as I considered calling Dylan and asking him to once again rush to my rescue.

No—I would just do a quick sweep of the house and save myself the trouble of looking like a fool. Setting my cell phone down on the kitchen counter, I searched for a suitable weapon. The butcher knife seemed grandiose, but it was better than a cheese grater, so I grabbed it and tiptoed down the hall, intent on confronting the worst figment my imagination had ever created.

The fifteen feet to my bedroom had never seemed so long as I made my way down the paneled hallway, listening for any sound that might alert me to danger.

When I finally reached my room, I hit the light switch, not daring to drop the butcher knife for fear the man in the long riding coat would be waiting. The man who had somehow been involved in the Ebersole murders if my visions were to be trusted.

My story scare you some?

The room lit up and I was faced with a purring Joey, who was sitting in the middle of my unmade bed cleaning his left paw.

Exhaling for the first time since I grabbed the butcher knife, I slumped against the wall and slid into a seated position while my eyes focused on my closet door. It was wide open, the *Abercrombie and Fitch* bag toppled to the side when I knew I'd left it upright.

I scooted over, stood up, and reached towards my high shelf while pushing my shoes aside.

Nothing…

Frantically I swept the shelf, knocking purses to the floor before dropping to my knees and looking under my bed.

Nothing…

I would never have misplaced Dad's present. And Holly didn't know about it, wouldn't have touched it if she did.

I was just about the cuss and break something when I heard a board creak on our back porch.

Weak with fear, I crawled to the window, gripped the sill, and peered out.

A man was staring back.

Chapter Ten

Reeling backward, I fell on my backside.

I tried not to scream, tried not to imagine what Dylan or Holly or Mom would do when news of my brutal murder hit the morning news.

I just needed to get out before he got back in.

Seconds later I grabbed my cell phone as my watery kneecaps found the front door and then the staircase. Twenty seconds and I was dashing across our driveway towards the Heap. Locking myself inside, I started it up and dialed Holly's number.

Four rings and her voicemail kicked in: *This is Holly... You know the drill...*

"Holl," I began, my voice bending like a joint. "Wherever you are, I need you to stay put. Don't come home. I think someone might have broken in and—"

My phone went dead.

"Dammit!" I cursed myself for not sending a text first. My one and only charger was somewhere in the vicinity of our laminate counter and I sure as hell wasn't going back inside to get it.

Now I couldn't call Dylan. Or the police.

The Sheriff's Department didn't seem half as appealing as his big lake house and so I peeled off towards Grand Lake. Maybe he could call dispatch, send someone out to check the place while I curled up in a chair, sipping something warm that he'd prepared for me.

Yes, this whole "taking a personal interest in my well-being" was quite intoxicating considering my track record.

Even that delightful thought couldn't distract me from the fact that all was dead in Presque Isle County this time of night, including a girl named Suzy Marsh who may have wound up on the wrong side of the guy I'd been on a date with the night before.

But the man on my balcony didn't carry himself the way Jamie did.

And why the hell would he want my old birthday present?

I cursed myself for never opening it, for never getting past that hideous kitten because now I would never know what Dad had wanted to give me.

I was driving so fast that I almost missed the turnoff to Dylan's road. Slamming on my brakes, I skidded to a halt before the Heap finally gave in, belched and called it a night. I turned the key once, twice, three times and still, she refused to comply.

"Dammit!" I cursed again. No phone. No car. No charger. No Dylan.

But I did have two legs.

Five minutes later and the lake house was in sight. I stopped, listened to the night sounds. Crickets were calling from the forest crevices, and somewhere deeper the eerie sound of a barred owl pierced the rhythm they created.

HIS NAME IS RED ROVER

I stopped walking, hugged myself to keep warm.

ADAM?

It seemed natural that I could hear him, as though it had always been.

DID HE KILL SUZY MARSH?

WHAT DO YOU THINK?

I swallowed hard, not wanting to believe that a murderer was inside my apartment messing with my things, wondering how I could present this particular piece of evidence to Dylan without sounding nuts.

I couldn't.

His house was now in view. A light was on upstairs and I hurried towards it like a beacon in a November gale.

Laying my forehead against the wooden surface of his front door, I pounded with the flat of my hand as hard as I could. Several seconds passed with no response and so I pounded again.

A shadow flickered across the upstairs window and I took this as my cue to call his name. I was rewarded with the sound of someone running down the stairs and fumbling with the lock on the front door. Seconds later he yanked it open and stood before me, bare-chested and in red boxer shorts.

"Justine?" he asked, taking me inside with one swoop of his arm. "What's going on?" Then, after a glance outside, "Where's your car?"

"I walked," I began, my voice unraveling with relief. "My car died out on the turnoff and I tried to call you, but the phone charger was up in my apartment and I was scared to go back in and I didn't know where else to go and I'm really sorry—"

"Hold up," he said while shutting the door behind us and I could tell calling me stupid was the last thing on his mind. "You need to sit down and tell me what happened."

The living room was off the main entry, a huge space with vaulted ceilings and wooden beams that created an atmosphere not unlike the lobby at Three Fires. A lamp was burning at the far end of the room and he led me to a chair beside it.

"Need something to drink?"

I shook my head, my gaze travelling over the smooth expanse of his chest.

"Let me throw on some clothes."

I wanted to tell him not to bother, that the sight of his half-naked body was calming me considerably but refrained while he ran back upstairs only to appear moments later in a gray hooded sweatshirt. Sitting down beside me, he waited while I tried to collect myself.

"I'm sorry."

"Stop saying that and tell me what happened. You said you'd call—"

"I know. I should have but I called Holly first and then the phone went dead," I looked up and blurted, "Someone broke into my apartment."

His eyes widened. "While you were home?"

"Before I got there," I explained. "I saw him on the back porch."

"Shit," he cursed under his breath. "Did he see you?"

I thought back to the moment I'd seen his face, or what I'd thought was his face but there hadn't been anything but darkness where the nose and eyes and mouth should have been. Nothing but a tall figure with a wide-brimmed hat.

I felt myself sliding lower in the chair. "Yes."

"Shit, Justine," he paused in front of me, put a hand to the side of my face. "I'm calling Dispatch."

"You don't have to," I began, thinking of my room and how I'd left my underwear on the floor and how silly it was to be worrying about what a patrol officer would think of my housekeeping skills at a time like this. "I'm sure he's gone."

"I'm making the call."

I slunk lower in the chair and looked at myself, still wearing the clothes I'd bartended in, feet aching from hiking a mile in black flats, phantom voices ringing in my head and knew he was right.

I wasn't going anywhere and I sure as hell needed him.

More than needed. Wanted.

After a few minutes, he returned with a glass of water. I sat holding it for a long time, the cool surface giving me something to focus on.

"Tell me what happened."

I shrugged, feeling sheepish. Did I really think I could knock on his door at three o'clock in the morning and come away with my secrets intact? What was wrong with opening up? Letting go?

Like I'd told him to do.

"Tell me."

I closed my eyes, remembering that day at the pool and the smell of chlorine burning my nose. "The guy who broke in stole something from me."

"What was it?"

I drew a silent breath, feeling like I was about to jump off a cliff with this guy, hoping we wouldn't land in the shallow end and break our necks.

"A birthday present my Dad gave me. I've never opened it."

"Why?" he asked.

I shrugged, more embarrassed than I cared to admit. "He took off on Mom and me. Didn't leave a thing behind but that stupid present and I guess…I wanted to teach him a lesson."

"You've never wondered what was inside?" he asked, and I felt my annoyance rise.

"Of course I did, but if I opened it, I knew it would be the end."

"The end?" he echoed, clearly confused. "Of what?"

"Of Dad and me."

He seemed to understand, which was more than I could say for myself.

"I don't even care anymore. He left a note. That should be enough."

Dylan's voice was soft when he asked, "What did it say?"

I shrugged again. "Not to look for him."

"So, you didn't?"

"Not then."

He drew back, awareness sinking in. "Is that why you came up here?"

"He used to fish the Ocqueoc River. I saw a picture of him in the paper when you got that heavy snow." I shook my head, unwilling to go any farther. "I don't know what I thought."

"I'm sorry," he kneeled in front of me, taking my hands in his. "You didn't deserve that."

I looked down, tears forming in the corners of my eyes and it seemed to throw him off. So, he started asking questions. Cop questions.

"Why do you think he wanted the present?"

"I don't know."

"Any sign of forced entry?"

"No. The door was open when I came home and Holly was gone."

"Why didn't you call me?"

I felt embarrassed. I'd been on my own for so long, it was second nature to handle things myself. "I tried Holly first. I didn't want her to come home."

"I was worried about you."

I looked into his eyes, knew he was telling the truth. "I'm sorry."

He softened a little, sat down on a sofa adjacent to my chair and let out a sigh. "I don't mean to be a hardass, but you have no idea what I've seen."

I wanted to tell him the same thing but nodded instead while he continued to rattle off questions.

"Think you could spot this guy in a lineup?"

"No."

"Why not?"

I paused, thinking of the man in the wide-brimmed hat, the man I'd colored while sitting beside Dad in our breakfast nook. "He didn't have a face."

Dylan's eyes darkened.

The phone rang. He moved off to answer it and after a few minutes returned to the living room, confusion marking his features.

"One of the guys on patrol checked the place out," he sat down opposite me. "Said everything was in place."

I felt sick to my stomach. "The package—"

"Was on the back porch."

I released my breath, a stab of relief piercing my chest. "He must have dropped it when he saw me looking out the window."

Dylan nodded. "Not surprised. It's not the kind of thing a thief would risk jail time over."

"What was he after then?"

"No idea. But you need to keep your doors locked."

I looked away, feeling like a naughty child.

"Justine—"

"I know," I turned back, my throat catching when I saw how serious he was. "Sorry I bothered you."

"You really think you bothered me? I just made out with you in my truck."

"Well," I began, slightly embarrassed.

Dylan chuckled under his breath, then moved away from me, gathering blankets and pillows while making up a bed on the couch.

"I can go home."

"Not tonight."

I opened my mouth to call his bluff but the look on his face silenced me. He really cared and there was no way I was going to mess with that.

"That guy could have hurt you."

I laughed, uncomfortable with the damp smother of infatuation that was suffocating me. "I can run pretty fast."

He smiled again. "I hope so."

A moment passed in silence, both of us unsure how to label what we were and why I was staying overnight but sleeping downstairs.

"I'll be gone before you get up." He came closer and touched the side of my face in the way an artist might move his subject to better light. "The keys to the Jeep will be on the table."

"Wow, Dylan- you don't have to—"

"Yes, I do."

I smiled my thanks, trying hard not to question his motives, wanting to sink into the startling possibility that he might have a desire to watch over me.

"Justine," his thumb worked my jawbone. "I'm sorry again about what happened in the truck."

"Oh," I felt the wind leave my lungs like the huff of a bellows, followed shortly by a flash of heat that radiated up my face. "Don't be. I just thought—"

"You were right. I like you too much to have it happen that way."

My stomach did a little flip-flop and landed on two feet. What if I really fell for this guy and he took off like Dad. How could I deal with that?

Maybe I was the one who needed to let go. Fall backwards into the water and trust that something bigger than myself would pull me to the surface in one piece.

I smiled, drew his face to mine, kissed his lips in the soft way he had only an hour before. The next instant his arms were around my back, pulling me against him and I thought how wonderful he felt, how naturally our bodies fit and if I was just imagining it because I wanted it so badly.

"You're torturing me," he whispered against my mouth as his tongue traced my bottom lip.

"Same here," I said. "Now go to sleep before I ask you to keep me company downstairs."

"Justine—"

"Sleep tight," I pulled away while sprawling out on the nest he'd made for me on the couch.

"Thanks anyway," he grinned while moving towards the stairs. "But I don't think I will."

Chapter Eleven

It was early morning when I dreamt of the silver canoe.

Standing where the willows kissed their mirror image, I called Dad's name. It took a moment before he appeared on the shore, his hair long and golden, his hands gripping the low branch to keep from floating away.

"Do you remember when you cut your knee?"

I'd cut my knee dozens of times in the course of my rough and rowdy childhood, but I knew what Dad was talking about.

When I was ten we had decided to climb to the top of an old grain silo. Mom had disapproved but Dad was eager, impatient even, to see the view from the top. Halfway up the side, I'd sliced my left kneecap on a rusty nail.

The blood had come quickly over my panicked screams as Dad carried me home, repentance on his face while Mom rushed me to the doctor for a tetanus shot.

"I remember," I said, feeling a slight tug on the blanket that covered me, the blanket that connected me to the fixed world in which I normally lived. Unable to pull myself from my hard-earned slumber, I turned over and dreamed on.

"I was afraid when the cut didn't heal."

"Why?" I asked, wandering ahead, watching moonlight stitch one side of the river to the other. Imagining a faun or satyr watching from a clearing of the wood. Shakespeare's fairies waiting to flee.

"It meant you would keep the scar."

I felt my fear rise like the river as the water reached up to cradle the canoe, pulling it away from shore. "Stay close to your brother."

"Dad—" I put a hand out, the sound of the falls drowning his voice.

"You're stronger together."

I sat up suddenly, his words ringing in my ears and fumbled from beneath the blanket. Morning streamed through the eastern windows while I tried to get my bearings.

Shaking my hair out from the ponytail that had imprisoned it, I ran a hand through the tangled mess. Looking around, I stretched and yawned, my blurry eyes finally coming into focus.

Big room. Comfy couch. No Dylan.

But he'd left a note on the nearby table and my cell phone charging next to it.

J—Didn't want to wake you. Keys are on the counter. I'll be home at six.

I smiled again. The note was brief and concise—like Dylan himself—but with so much lying just beneath the surface. *Didn't want to wake you.* Considerate of my needs. *Keys are on the counter.* Generous to a fault. *I'll be home at six.* Calling this place "home" even though I had my own cushy digs.

That last one had my mind spinning when my cell phone sprang to life.

I made a mad dash before answering with a timid, "Hello?"

"What's the big idea leaving a message like that and then dropping off the side of the mitten! I called your cell, like, *fifty-seven* times!"

I rolled my eyes while wandering to the kitchen to pour myself a cup of coffee. "I stayed with Dylan last night."

"I figured." She huffed as though in awe of my magnificent fortune. "And I can't friggin' believe you scored him. Jen's been trying for months. *I've* been trying since eighth grade."

"*Holl—*"

"It's like a third chair clarinet getting into the Philharmonic."

I frowned into the phone. "I get it."

Ever the pragmatist, she changed the subject. "You coming home today? Dave called Dylan and he said a cop checked the place out and didn't find anything. I swear I locked the door when I left."

"You swear a lot of things, Holl."

"Maybe I didn't pull it shut all the way. I was kind of in a hurry."

"Check next time."

"Ooo," she giggled. "Did Dylan give you crap about it? Did he get out the cuffs?"

I smiled. Having located a mug with a picture of a moose smoking a cigar on the side, I poured myself a cup. "None of your damn business."

"You're not coming home?"

I looked at Dylan's note.

"Would you?"

She giggled again and hung up.

Coffee cup and cell phone in hand, I turned to examine my surroundings. Being alone in Dylan's house held so many interesting possibilities, not the least of which involved a little snooping. The angel on my right shoulder told me that honesty was always the best policy where new relationships were concerned, and for a while, she won out when I flipped on the TV and stumbled across a documentary featuring the six wives of King Henry the Eighth.

Two beheadings later, I was starting to rethink my strategy. The devil on my left shoulder told me it was only natural to want to know something about the guy I lusted after, the guy who had practically saved my life two nights in a row.

I stood and went upstairs, intent on raiding his closet for some comfy clothes to lounge around in, and found myself staring at the framed pictures on his bedside bureau. One 5x7 featured a couple who were probably members in good standing at the Presque Isle Country Club.

His parents?

Anxiety nibbled at my nerves. What would people like this make of a barmaid who scrubbed toilets on the weekend? A college graduate who had never quite kicked off her career? Would they dismiss me as they had so many others while waiting for the moment he came to his senses and married the debutante next door?

My jitters moved me down the line to a small 4x6 of the girl I'd smacked him across the face over. Another picture of the entire family at a ski resort finally convinced me the sister existed in the format he'd described.

That done, I spared a glance at the bed.

It was large—with a manly comforter that held tints of brown and black and gold. I imagined him sleeping in it, imagined myself curled up beside him and had to try it out. The mattress was firm, the sheets soft and the pillows delectably indented with the shape of his head.

Rolling over, I breathed deeply, smelling the scent I'd come to recognize.

Yes…it could definitely happen here.

Ten minutes later I decided it was time to get dressed and perhaps check out the Jeep he'd put on ice for me. But the bed was so inviting, the images of what might be so intoxicating, that I couldn't leave. Trailing my hand along the side of the mattress, I felt my fingertips brush against a piece of paper.

My first thought was that he'd forgotten to remove the tags and so I gave it a tug.

A letter. Or more appropriately…a hidden letter. That I wasn't supposed to read. Another swipe beneath the mattress and I drew out a picture. It was a candid shot of a petite blonde laughing on the beach, the sun against her back, the wind blowing a stray piece of hair over her face.

The angel on my right shoulder told me that only a fool who wanted her heart broken would go farther.

The devil just wanted the dirt.

Thanks for not waking me.

Oh, crap…

Having you beside me all night was the closest I've been to happy in a very long time.

I put the letter aside, my heart fluttering away like a caffeinated hummingbird. I shouldn't be reading this. He'd hidden it for a reason. The reason being it was meaningful and he didn't want anyone to see it.

Jamie asked me about you the other day and I couldn't lie.

I stopped again. Went back for more like an addict with a new stash.

I can't go through with a wedding when all I think about is you. Please tell me you feel the same and that last night meant as much to you as it did to me.

My stomach felt queasy as the coffee I'd drank came back into my throat.

He's taking me out for dinner but I'll call you when I get home. Promise. Love, Karen

And like a schoolgirl with an eye for posterity, she'd scribbled the date in the upper right-hand corner.

The day before yesterday.

I quickly folded the letter and stuffed it back in place, jealousy unlike anything I'd ever experienced turning my guts to jelly.

I didn't want to wake you… Had he left a love note for her as well? Telling her she was too beautiful to wake? Asking her to please wait for him? That he'd leave the keys to the Jeep on the table?

She was like a sister… If he was into that sort of thing.

I scowled, tried to talk myself into a better mood, tried to tell myself he hadn't done anything wrong by keeping the letter, by loving her. It wasn't like he'd cheated on me.

More like he'd cheated on her.

Yes, I definitely needed to protect myself from the guy who was probably seeing his dead lover every time he looked at me.

I was just about to curse and break something when my cell phone rang again.

"Yeah?" I answered with uncharacteristic brevity.

"Hey," Dylan's voice was thick with oblivious affection. "How'd you sleep?"

"Great. Thanks for not waking me."

He paused. "Did you get my note?"

"Oh, yeah," I laughed. "That was great. Really super."

He seemed to sense something was off. "Sure you're all right?"

I put a hand to my forehead, my stomach rolling when I thought of what she'd written—how much she obviously loved him. I thought of the crumpled black car and how she'd died with her eyes open, perhaps remembering his face in the last moments.

Drawing a nonexistent breath, I asked, "Do I remind you of someone?"

He was silent for a moment, obviously trying to formulate the best way around my very pointed question. "Did Stoddard say something about that?"

"Just answer my question."

"Did you find the note?" he asked, cutting to the chase and I felt ashamed to admit I'd been snooping.

"Yes."

"I know what you're thinking and it has nothing to do with how I feel about you."

"I find that hard to believe."

"You shouldn't."

I scrunched up my brow. "I don't even know you, Dylan."

"Yes, you do," he said, pausing, and I could sense his discomfort. "There's a lot I want to tell you, but I don't want to do it over the phone. Do you work tonight? Can you come back after?"

"Mallard said he might need me."

He sighed, "I'm not sure what's worse, a burglar or Butt-head Brauski. I can't tell you how many times we've hauled him in to sleep it off."

I smiled at the image of Mallard curled up in the drunk tank, jean shorts and all.

"And don't get on the wrong side of his old lady. She's got bigger arms than he does. More facial hair, too."

His plot to lift my spirits worked. I laughed outright, Karen and the letter temporarily forgotten.

"I'll see you tonight," I offered.

"I'll be there," he finished.

After hanging up, I began a tentative plan for the rest of my day, which included clothing myself in something of Dylan's and lounging around his house until my shift at Huff's began.

I had just grabbed a red-hooded sweatshirt and a pair of athletic shorts when my ears began to ring. Gripping the banister, I tried to sit down but felt my body twist on the staircase as I fought for balance—the sound of the crash that ended Karen's life and forever changed the men who loved her fresh in my ears.

FIGHTING MAKES IT WORSE

HOW DO YOU KNOW THAT?

I LEARNED THE HARD WAY

"What?" I asked, but I had no idea if Adam heard me, no idea if I was speaking at all or if my brother had the same kind of visions I did as a picture of Dylan flashed before me.

He was in the same sweatshirt I was wearing now, walking between the window and the bed, pausing once to pull back the curtain and look out, the letter from Karen in his hand. And then he moved, picked up his cell phone and answered it.

I tried to close my eyes but couldn't.

Shoulders hunched, face covered, I saw Dylan go to his knees, the phone falling from his hand. I'd never seen a man cry, never been privy to such emotion from my father or Brad but I didn't look away. Instead, I let it flow over me as light passes through a leaf and shades the ground beneath. I watched as Dylan mourned the death of the woman he loved, absorbed the graphic beauty of his grief.

And like a silent deer passes through the woods unseen, the vision left and I found myself bunched in a graceless heap at the top of the staircase.

"Geez," I mumbled while trying to sit up. A headache was beginning to pulse just between my eyes. This was going to get old real fast. But Adam was right, fighting had made it worse.

You're stronger together…

My legs were weak as I stumbled to the kitchen, intent on making myself another cup of coffee. After witnessing what he'd gone through the night Karen died, a babbling basket case was the last thing Dylan needed when he came home. And I needed to start locking my doors. And charging my phone. And calling when I said I would.

Stick with your brother…

That seemed like a damn good idea.

Chapter Twelve

"Hey, Pam."

I was standing on the threshold of the house she shared with her son, early afternoon sunbathing my neck, feeling twisted in a million directions, wanting to jump in the lake and drift down the stream to wherever my father had gone in his silver canoe.

"Come in," she offered, stepping aside and I saw her house was plain and comfortable, a brown sofa just to my right. "What's up?"

"I need to talk with my brother."

I saw her face stiffen, saw her step back.

"You're his daughter," she finally said. "I could tell by your cheekbones. And your nose. He said you took after him in that way."

I felt my own face stiffen. "He told you about me?"

"Of course."

"And Mom?" I continued.

Pam's eyes went to her shoes. "He said they were having some problems."

It took a moment to process her words, to come to terms with the fact that she'd known about us, but once done I had to fight the instinct to flee as quickly as I'd come.

"I can't tell you how many times I've thought about you." She moved aside, motioned for me to sit on the couch.

I did as she asked, then took a closer look at the room. Pictures of Adam as a baby lined the walls and spider plants decorated the windowsill, thriving in the sunlight and I imagined she had a green thumb herself, like all the women Dad loved.

"We never meant to hurt you or your mother," she began—twisting the fingers on her right hand.

"Dad loved her, you know."

"I know."

"We were a family."

She smiled. "Why wouldn't you be?"

Because Robert Cook hadn't wanted to settle down. He'd wanted to paint pictures and tame horses and maybe steal a car or two. Float from town to town like dust seen only in the sunshine.

And maybe he'd begun planning his escape the moment he found out Mom was pregnant with me.

STOP IT!

I looked up, unaccustomed to being yelled at by someone who couldn't speak and saw my brother staring at me from the open doorway, Jamie close behind.

"Adam?" I asked.

"Justine," Jamie said. "What a surprise."

"A good one, I hope," I tried to laugh, but the sound died in my throat.

"That goes without saying."

Adam started humming, rocking back and forth as his fingertips went to his ears. Jamie turned to Pam, asking about some canoes that needed to be cleaned out and I took my opportunity.

WHERE IS DAD?

I DON'T KNOW

SO, YOU CAN TALK TO ME IN MY HEAD BUT YOU CAN'T SEE WHERE OUR FATHER IS?

YOU'RE TALKING TO ME. DO YOU SEE HIM ANYWHERE?

WHO WAS IN MY APARTMENT?

SOMEONE WHO WANTS US DEAD

WHY?

BECAUSE WE'RE SPECIAL

NO SHIT!

I put a hand to my mouth, ashamed to be talking to a ten-year-old like that, but Adam just smiled.

PLEASE JUST TELL ME WHAT'S GOING ON

I'M TELLING YOU WHAT I KNOW. YOU HAVE TO DO THE REST

I CAN'T DO SHIT, ADAM…I'M JUST SOME STUPID GIRL FROM DOWNSTATE

He began making noise, the hum of an engine set to low speed, and Pam was instantly at his side. "He's upset about something."

Jamie's eyes flew to mine, and I couldn't hide from the accusation I saw in them.

HE DOESN'T HAVE A FACE

I wanted to scream at him, tell him to stop talking in riddles but his voice stopped me cold.

ODESSA TOOK IT AWAY

I couldn't walk out now, not with her name hovering between us and Jamie watching as though he could listen in.

WHY?

Adam's gaze didn't waver.

SHE WANTED HIM TO DIE. SHE WANTED THEM BOTH TO DIE.

The air seemed wet and heavy as I waited for Adam to explain himself. Instead, he retreated to his bedroom and shut the door. I took a step as if to follow but felt Pam at my elbow.

"I have to check on him." She muttered, lightly touching me as she maneuvered around. "This isn't normal."

"Sure," I said. "I'll go."

She didn't try to stop me, didn't beg me to stay so she could explain what had happened between her and my father, so I opened the door, walked down the steps and across the yard without looking back to see if Jamie was following.

I should have known better.

"Justine—"

I spun around and found him behind me.

"I can't talk to you."

"Just hear me out."

We were in front of the Jeep now, and I wondered if he recognized it from a stolen moment from his past. Karen climbing inside, another man at the wheel. "I'm sorry about the other night."

I gripped the door handle, ready to yank it open if things got hairy.

"Locke and I go way back," he began, searching my face for any kind of reaction. "Do you know I pulled him out of the river once? Back when the current was fast after spring thaw? Stupid lug reached over to unhook a fish and fell right in."

I tried not to let my emotions show, the thought of Dylan almost drowning as disturbing as the thought that Jamie had saved him.

"They wrote it up in the paper and everything."

I looked away. "I guess I should thank you, then."

"No need," he paused. "Think of all the cats that would be stuck up in trees if he hadn't made it out."

I tightened my grip on the handle.

"Nowadays Do-Right won't give me the time of day unless it's one o'clock in the morning and I've got you in my truck." He shoved his hands in his pockets. "Ingrate."

One motion and I was inside the Jeep. "I've gotta go."

Jamie continued as if I'd never spoken. "He knew what day it was, knew I'd be out of it and he went ahead and pulled that little stunt just to show off in front of you."

"Jamie—"

"Did he mention you look like her?"

I felt my eyes narrow, unable to fight the cauldron of emotions his words stirred in me. The pictures it painted in my head of Dylan's hand sliding over mine for the first time, wet with blood. And his blue eyes, wide with surprise, thinking he'd seen a ghost.

"I knew she was into him. Knew she was planning her getaway but I took care of that, didn't I?"

I flinched, tried to pull the door closed but Jamie held it fast, his knuckles white.

"But he doesn't know how hard I fought to save her—how much I wanted her to live, even if it meant giving her up."

My eyes met his for the first time. "It was an accident."

He laughed hard, his mouth open and suddenly I noticed how strong he was, how he could break my neck out here in the middle of the woods where no one could see.

As if to prove me right, he reached over and took my wrist. Turning it, he examined the blue veins on the underside of my arm. "Sometimes it doesn't seem like you're real."

I tried to pull away but he wouldn't let go.

"And I feel like it's happening all over again." He reached inside the Jeep, put his other hand on the steering wheel and my eyes flew to the main lodge, praying that someone would come outside.

"I should've let him drown."

I didn't hear another word because one moment he had me trapped in the Jeep and the next I had him pinned, face down against the hood. Only the barest of ties to my former self kept me from beating his head into a bloody pulp.

"Shit," he mumbled, his face smashed against the metal. "What the—"

"Shut up," I whispered, more to myself than to him, unable to understand how I'd gotten out of the Jeep and into my current position. And I felt the power seep into me, the awe at being able to make things exactly how I wanted them when I wanted them.

"Let go and back away," he instructed, quite calm, and I waited, feeling his pulse on either side of my grip, wanting to squeeze and end the beating.

"Justine," he began again. "I want you to let go and back away. If Pam sees you she'll fire you."

I thought about what he said, knew it made sense and released him.

Standing up, he shook free as if to remove all traces of my touch, his amber eyes holding mine with new appreciation. Then they dropped, took in the scar that split my left kneecap.

"What just happened?"

"I don't know," I whispered, my hands shaking. "I was mad."

"I'll say."

Five minutes ago, I'd been a girl who'd never won an arm-wrestling match, and now I was pinning a man against the side of a Jeep. But things had changed, and I needed to get away before my head exploded.

"I've gotta go," I muttered. And Jamie didn't protest, didn't say another word as I climbed back into the Jeep and started the engine. He simply took another step back and watched me from a distance.

I was lost in troubled thought when I saw the sign for County Road 449.

The angel on my right shoulder told me it might not be a good idea to visit the scene of a gruesome, unsolved homicide.

The devil reminded me that it didn't really matter at this point.

I tried to remember if Dylan had told me specifically not to come out here, feeling guilty the next because my actions would cause him to worry.

Not that he needed to if that little stunt at Three Fires meant anything.

I smiled when I thought of all the times I'd wanted to throw Brad over my shoulder and beat his head against something hard and inanimate.

If only I'd known.

The road was widening now, the forest thinning when I came upon the lawn of what used to be Back Forty Farm. The tilting remains of a weathered homestead stood front and center, and behind—a field of overgrown lavender that stretched towards the horizon.

I imagined Mrs. Ebersole tending the garden, her black hair tied back with a white handkerchief and her husband coming in from a long day in the fields atop the horse his murderer had stolen.

I stopped the Jeep, got out and listened. Everything was silent, and so I spoke my own name and heard nothing and knew it was happening. Knew I could make it happen if I wanted to. And I wanted to.

I circled my way towards the back of the house. A lawn patched with weeds stretched before me, reaching for the lavender and I did not doubt it would eventually have its way. I took another step, saw the murdered woman pin her collar with a cameo brooch only to have it removed by the hand of the man who loved her. A man who was not her husband.

They were in the lavender now, hidden amongst the flowers, her pale skin glowing in the sunlight as he slowly undressed her.

I could almost smell the adrenaline as they fell to the ground together, their naked bodies entangled, watching every moment for the hired girl who had a loose tongue and would spread gossip in town. Gossip they couldn't afford.

I listened as a sharp whistle met my ear and the breeze caught flight, scattering my hair.

Turning slowly, I caught sight of an ancient oak standing tall against the edge of the lawn and knew Jonas Younts had been hanged from it. My gaze travelled the length of the thick trunk, followed the path of branches as they held the summer sky—autumn leaves still clinging—fresh and red.

Caught fire but never burned.

My father had been right. And if I wanted to find out what was happening to me, I needed to start here.

Chapter Thirteen

"Gonna give it another go, Flats?" Mallard asked as I walked in and threw my purse under the till.

I shrugged, my mood contemplative. "I made good tips last night."

Mallard's gaze dropped to my chest, obscured behind the red sweatshirt I had yet to part with, and laughed. "Don't get your hopes up."

After discovering the oak tree behind Back Forty Farm, I'd quickly left for the apartment, wondering why my father had warned me about it.

Was treasure buried beneath? A doorway to another dimension? Jimmy Hoffa?

Holly hadn't been home and that made things easier. Joey was AWOL too…but obviously had used the litter box.

Pet care aside, I charged my phone and made my way to my bedroom. Nothing was out of place save the covers I'd thrown aside two mornings before and my present, placed nicely on the bed by whatever cop Dylan had asked to swing by the place.

Nothing indicated that it had been tampered with, but the thought was enough to ignite a protective inferno in me, and so I carefully picked up the box and held it against my chest.

"Flats!"

I snapped to attention, the memory gone.

"I'm callin' it a night."

"Huh?"

"Gotta learn to fly sometime, little bird," he grinned, his gaze seeking that of a young woman who had just taken a seat in front of us. "Besides, it's my old lady's birthday," stealing another glance, he caught the girl's attention and extinguished his cigarette. "Might be her last for all I know."

"Oh, but—"

"Don't let any assholes in after two o'clock," he ordered while grabbing his black leather jacket. "Including me."

He walked out seconds later, not bothering to ask if I had any questions and the place seemed desolate without him. One by one the customers thinned out as I worked on automatic, hoping no one would order a drink I couldn't deliver.

An hour passed with no new bodies to fill the barstools. Then two. I was just starting to consider closing shop early when the door opened and an old woman sauntered in. I did a double take as she sat down and ordered a Bud Light with tomato juice.

"Iris?" I asked, unable to figure out why she'd driven to a dive bar so late at night when she should be home knitting afghans and baking apple pies. "How did you get here?"

"Horse and buggy."

She was laughing at me, along with a couple of other regulars who seemed to know her quite well. Small talk kept her occupied for some time while I stayed busy behind the bar, pausing once to pour her a fresh draft.

Finally, the regulars began to filter out, save Shaw, who had scooted down to get closer to Iris. I sensed a connection but tried not to eavesdrop while catching choice phrases like "Thanks for watching my dog," "Like to keep the home fires burning," and "Drop by the Methodist Bazaar on Monday night."

I was just wondering what a hot date on the senior citizen circuit looked like when she called out, "Jack on the rocks."

"Oh," I muttered, surprised to find us alone in the bar. "You sure? That's kind of a strong drink."

"I was born sure," she smiled, reminding me of the woman I'd met in the perennial garden, a woman who seemed as far from this antiquated barfly as was humanly possible. "Mr. Jack Daniels and I go way back, and I can assure you he's always been a gentleman."

"I hope you're right or I may have to drive your buggy home."

She smiled, watching as I mixed her drink, then curled three long fingers around the glass and took a demure sip. Moments later she went to check out the jukebox. Her selection made, she returned to her stool, stopping once to draw a finger down the side of a pool table as though looking for dust.

"So," I said, thinking I'd take a shot at small talk since the bar was empty and looked to remain so for the rest of my shift. "Did you run this place before your daughter bought it?"

"Place wasn't here," she took another drink, staring at me over the top of her glass. "Wasn't much of anything out this way save for Back Forty Farm."

"I went there today."

I had no idea why I said that, but Iris did not react to my admission. She simply set her glass down and smoothed the napkin beneath it. I noticed her fingers, how straight and slim they were, how the nails were painted with pink polish.

"Look under the till."

I wanted to ask why but went to the drawer instead and gave it a little tug. Sitting on top of a pile of burger baskets was a book with a glossy cover.

I opened the front page and sneezed as a cloud of dust kissed my nose.

Iris laughed. "Mallard's not much for reading. I try not to take offense."

I shut the cover, saw her name printed under the title *A Brief History of Presque Isle County* and felt my heart warm.

"You wrote this," I said, my voice belying the awe I felt.

She shrugged. "It was on my Bucket List. Look at the chapter on Back Forty Farm."

Thumbing to the section, I was surprised to find several photographs.

"Mr. and Mrs. Ebersole were the only owners. Wasn't a lovelier bit of acreage west of the Big Lake when they bought it. Such a shame they had to die the way they did and the place had to get so run down. I suppose no one wanted to live there after all the terrible things that happened."

I didn't answer because staring back at me from the pages was a picture of the most beautiful woman I had ever seen.

I shouldn't have been surprised by the black hair plaited into a heavy mass her slender neck was hard pressed to support. Clear eyes complimented a smooth face. Lips slightly parted, she seemed every bit the Victorian housewife right down to the cameo that secured her collar.

The same cameo I'd seen her lover unclasp in my vision.

Turning the page, I found a picture of Mr. Ebersole.

Not nearly as attractive as his wife, I could understand why she'd found comfort in the arms of another. Sunken cheekbones and a weak chin were his most prominent features, followed closely by a comb-over that seemed to stretch his sparse hair to the limit.

"No one understood the pairing."

I nodded without looking up.

"Abraham was a lumber baron, so it must have been the money."

I traced the lines of Esther's face, trying to imagine my own father selling me into a loveless marriage, then skipped to the next page.

"That's Odessa Cook," Iris pointed to a group of homesteaders poised in their work. "Had one boy by the name of Calvert. Folks just called him Cal."

I leaned closer, followed the line of her finger as it settled on a kneeling woman in a worn gingham dress and sunbonnet. Standing to her left, no higher than her shoulder was the boy named Cal.

I squinted, trying to make out her features when my eyes focused on the person standing behind her, his hand cupping her elbow. Smooth, dark skin and prominent cheekbones set him apart from the other homesteaders, as did his long hair.

Iris followed my gaze. "Odessa and the Indian were very close."

"Indian?"

"Went by Butler. No one knew his Ojibwa name."

My eyes flew to Iris' as she sat her drink aside. "Butler was the last in a long line of Shamans. Legend was he gave his medicine—his magic—to Odessa as a special gift."

"Medicine?" I repeated.

"A bag filled with totems from the Elk, Turtle, Wolf, and Raven. Each gave special powers and Butler wanted to make sure Odessa and Cal were always protected. He left this medicine bag in their care and word got around soon after." She took another drink, shook her head. "Small towns."

"I don't understand. How could a bag full of totems protect Odessa and Cal?" But I did understand because Mallard had told me she had the Sight. Maybe this was why.

"Shamans believe in more than what you or I can see. They believe that each animal carries a special medicine that can enter the body of a human."

I laughed, not meaning to. "Like Spiderman or something?"

Iris looked at me over the top of her drink. "Or something."

I quickly collected myself. "What does this have to do with Back Forty Farm and the Ebersoles?"

"I think you already know."

"What do you mean?" I asked, setting the book aside.

"No one understood the pairing," she repeated. "But Jonas Younts was young and strong and full of potential. Not rich like Abraham, but Esther loved him."

"Esther loved him?" I echoed, thinking of the man without a face, the man I'd seen standing in the darkness outside my bedroom window and felt my muscles tighten.

Was this man Jonas Younts? Hanged because my grandmother had a vision and the lynch mob needed a body?

"Why did Odessa accuse Jonas Younts?"

For an instant, my unflappable friend seemed surprised. "She saw it in a vision."

"But if he loved Esther Ebersole why would he kill her?"

Iris looked at me closely, perhaps wondering what I knew and why I felt so strongly about a man who had died over a hundred years before. "There's no telling what someone would do if pushed to their limits."

I didn't know if her words held some secret meaning for me, so I looked away and glanced at the clock. It was already half past one. One more hour until I returned to the lake house, where Dylan would be waiting. I imagined his arms closing around me, imagined sleeping in the strong nest they provided and would have kicked her out right then and there had her story not intrigued me.

Elk, Wolf, Raven, and Turtle.

Maybe the medicine had been passed down to her descendants through Calvert, who could have been related to my father. I thought back on our eleven years spent together, trying to piece together a family history he'd never shared—a legacy he'd hidden for reasons known only to him.

Or maybe I'd wake up the next morning with tail feathers, antlers, and dry, scaly skin. Then I could kiss my little romance with the hottest guy in Presque Isle goodbye.

A commotion on the porch caught my attention. I was just getting ready to heed Mallard's advice and lock the door when three burly men stomped in. One was short and wore a John Deere trucker's hat, the other two were big and ugly and wore gray shirts stained with a strange substance that looked like a mixture of grease, chewing tobacco, and sweat.

The biggest one took a seat on the corner stool and ordered a beer. The other two waited until he'd gotten it before ordering their own, making it clear who wore the pants in their dysfunctional family.

"You the new barmaid?" the big one asked while spreading his hands on the bar and I was shocked to see eight full fingers and two stumps.

"Yep," I tried to sound confident, cheery even, and failed in that regard.

"I've heard about you, Tootsie." Following my stare, he said, "Pulled 'em off in an oil drill." Then, his gaze sweeping to Iris. "Shouldn't you be in bed by now?"

She only smiled. "What I do in bed is none of your business."

I grimaced, but John Deere just laughed, adjusting his hat as he did so. "That so, Grandma?"

Iris smiled again, her face a mask of complacency. "That's so."

He shrugged, perhaps impressed with her pluck, and ordered another beer. I jumped up and immediately honored his request, all the while searching Iris' eyes for some sort of assurance that I'd end my shift in one piece, but she wouldn't meet my gaze.

I thought about calling Mallard. These three certainly fit the bill where "assholes" were concerned, but I wasn't sure how to get away without attracting attention. And they wanted lots of it.

Their first round gone, the trio seemed in no hurry to leave. They lit up, ordered Pabst Blue Ribbon like it was going out of style and told dirty jokes that featured a bevy of dumb blondes. As the second-hand inched past two, I began to feel the first stab of fear.

"Last call, guys," I said while eyeing the clock.

"Give me a fuckin' break," Stumpy grumbled while getting up to saunter towards the jukebox. Once there he made his selection and shuffled back via Gordon Lightfoot. "I know you've got that clock set to bar time."

"Name one place that doesn't?" I scowled, wondering where I had gotten the courage, remembering where my anger had taken me that afternoon.

"You've got quite a mouth on ya, Tootsie," Stumpy smiled, his teeth just as bad as his shirt. "I'd like to see it wrapped around my—"

"Last call," I blurted, blood pounding in my ears, the sweatshirt making me hot. "Give me your order or get the hell out."

Stumpy just grinned, his eyes darting between me and Iris while the latter sat with her hands folded as though waiting out bingo calls at the grange hall.

The legend lives on from the Chippewa on down to the big lake they call Gitchee Gumee.

I heard the song, knew it by heart as one of Dad's favorites and felt in some strange way that it would become a part of what was going to happen.

It was now quarter past two. I should have been closed up, counting down the till, and heading for Dylan's house.

"All right, boys," Iris said while straightening on her stool. "Time to wrap it up."

"What for?" Stumpy belched. "Tootsie got a hot date?"

I didn't answer, but the blood continued to pump in my ears, making it hard to hear and harder to concentrate. The room felt hot, stuffy, and I yanked on the collar of Dylan's sweatshirt in an effort to cool myself. Meanwhile, Iris' eyes sought mine and held them until I thought I'd go mad.

My cell phone rang. I knew Dylan must be wondering where I was for the second night in a row and I wanted to answer and tell him I'd charged my phone and locked my front door but I sure as hell didn't want him mixed up in what I felt sure was about to happen.

"Why didn't you answer it?" John Deere asked.

"Shut up," I whispered, pulling on my collar again.

"Think we hit a nerve," No Name said. "Answer the call and maybe we can have us a party. See what makes Tootsie twitch."

"You're an asshole, you know that," I spat, so angry I could hardly see, feeling the soft pulp of Jamie's neck between my fingers. Wanting that feeling again.

Does anyone know where the love of God goes when the waves turn the minutes to hours...

"And you're gonna get an ass-kickin', you know that?" Stumpy spoke up.

"Boys," Iris began, but in an instant Stumpy reached across the bar, one meaty hand going for my wrist.

Shit! My brain screamed as my body went into automatic overdrive. Leaping across the bar in a single bound, I hit him square in the jaw before he had time to get off his stool. He howled in pain, stumbled towards the door only to hit the screen and ricochet out onto the porch. I heard him hit the wooden floor and roll away like the proverbial sack of potatoes.

No Name was looking for his chance before I'd finished. Coming from behind, he got a grip on my neck that felt impossible to break. Stars danced before my eyes as I thought about Dylan, waiting at the lake house for a girl who had picked a bar fight.

Frenzied heat rushed through my body, followed by a surge of adrenaline I felt powerless over. Reaching behind me, I took hold of No Name's throat and dug my thumbs into the soft spot on either side of his windpipe.

He immediately began to gag, then sputter, but his grip loosened and I was able to slip from beneath his hold. Slumping to the ground, he began to crawl for the door when I turned to Iris.

Fearing she might already be injured, I berated myself for not tackling John Deere first when I saw her against the wall, his elbow pinning her just beneath the shoulder blades. Still, she didn't seem alarmed as she looked at me and said, "Take him."

Rushing from behind, I grabbed beneath the armpits and pulled him off of her. Spinning, he took a swing at my face that I was able to duck under. Instinct told me to act fast before he struck again and so I pulled back, slamming my fist into his belly with all the strength I couldn't believe I possessed.

John Deere gurgled, fell to his knees and hit the floor face first. Rolling over onto his back, I saw his eyes wide with terror as he scooted towards the door.

"Get out," I growled, feeling more powerful than I ever had in my life.

John Deere nodded, his mouth full of blood, then rolled over and scurried out the front door on all fours.

I stood still, suspended in a cocoon of static, my hands balled into fists at my sides, my hair a matted mess of sweat that was plastered against my neck and forehead.

The Lake it is said never gives up her dead when the skies of November turn gloomy...

All was silent, too silent—as I sat listening to the song and the sound of my breath, my heartbeat stilling—the anger that had propelled me dissipating like Mallard's cigarette smoke.

I touched my throat, felt the ache where No Name had put his hands and groaned.

"That was beautiful," Iris took a step closer, her eyes shining, "Better than I ever expected."

I put my head in my hands and sat down on the nearest stool, my knuckles blazing as though I'd dragged them across sandpaper.

"Expected?"

"You've got it, my dear. And in spades."

"What have I got?" I whispered, my voice hurting. "Tell me because I feel like I'm going crazy."

She chuckled and sat down beside me. "You're not crazy, you're a Cook."

I couldn't look at her. Pam must have told her and now she was dragging me into the middle of this stupid Medicine Man meets Single Pioneer Mom story, believing I had some sort of superpowers when obviously…

Well…I couldn't argue that point at the moment.

"Was it the Elk that gave Odessa strength? Or the wolf? Sure wasn't the damn turtle."

"So, you think you've inherited the medicine from your ancestors, eh?"

"I don't know, Iris," I said, careful to control my emotions. "I don't know who I am or why I just did what I did but I know it doesn't make any sense."

"It does to me," she said, one hand reaching up to clap me on the shoulder. "You're Odessa's all right—a few generations removed but it's only made the medicine stronger."

I looked over, put my hand on top of hers and knew she knew everything.

"What about Adam?"

"He has his own gifts."

I didn't understand at first, but soon realized there was a reason Dad had said we were stronger together.

"Are you saying the powers are divided between us?"

She smiled.

And nodded.

Chapter Fourteen

I called Dylan soon after. He seemed relieved that I'd ended my shift in one piece, but also angry that Mallard had left me alone with the Presque Isle Mafia on the loose.

"Presque Isle Mafia?" I asked.

"Last weekend of every month they raise hell when the oil rigs shut down. Butt-head Brauski should've warned you."

"He didn't."

I heard him chuckle and knew he was faking it for my sake. "You're gonna give me a heart attack, you know that? Dead at twenty-four because of some barmaid I didn't know three weeks ago. I was jumping in the truck to come down there."

I smiled into my phone even as I made my way to the Jeep. "I'm sorry…again."

"Don't be sorry," he said softly. "Just be here."

He was waiting when I pulled up outside the lake house, his delectable silhouette blocking the light just behind the front door. I felt the warmth and love and safety swirl in an intoxicating mix, making the space between us vibrant.

Parking next to the truck, I jumped out and almost tripped in my haste to get to him. He had me in his arms before I reached the doorstep, squeezing tightly while his mouth sought my own.

"Can we talk?"

I nodded.

"Upstairs?"

I knew what he wanted and nodded again.

Now was the time. Before I killed someone and went to jail forever.

He took my hand, led me up the staircase and into his room where I saw a small lamp burning on his bedside table, a book opened beneath it. I wanted to see the cover, hoping it was something terribly intellectual like *Quantum Physics for*

Dummies, but he gave me no chance, his arms encircling me once again in an attempt to get the sweatshirt over my head.

"Dylan," I tried to speak as the sweatshirt finally gave way. A moment later he had my shorts down around my ankles and I stood in my bra and panties before him.

"Justine," he whispered. "You're beautiful."

I wanted to argue, as I always had in my mind whenever a man complimented me.

He must have noticed my embarrassment because he took my face in his hands and kissed me as though he had nothing better to do for the next twelve hours than explore my mouth with his own.

I felt my knees beginning to give way, but he grasped me around the waist, letting his hands slide down to caress the small of my back while his mouth moved to my throat. I winced as he moved over the spot No Name had gotten his hands on, then tried to cover it with a seductive moan.

"What's wrong?" He took my hand in his and brought it to his lips, his tongue lingering over each knuckle until I thought I'd go insane.

A moment later he was examining it under the low light of the bedside lamp.

"Hey," I tried to pull away, uncomfortable with the turn our interlude had taken.

"Why are your knuckles raw?"

I looked down, wanting to prove him wrong but knowing I couldn't because smashing Stumpy in the face was going to leave a mark no matter what Butler had stuffed into his little bag.

And so I laughed, so nervous I thought I might shatter. "I told you I had a hard time getting those guys to leave."

"So, you punched one of them?" he asked, his face a mixture of anger and apprehension, and all I wanted to do was take him in my arms and tell him not to worry. That I really could take care of myself and probably all of Lantern Creek, too. That I wasn't like Karen. That I would survive whatever was thrown at me. "Why didn't you tell me?"

"I didn't want to upset you," I tried to explain while sitting down on the bed.

He sat down beside me, let out a sigh that told me more than I wanted to know. "If I can't trust you then we should end this now."

He was right—I had no reason to lie aside from the fear that he might call me a psycho and kick me out of his house.

Better to let go.

And so, I spilled the story about Iris and Odessa and how I believed myself to be the latter's long-lost granddaughter, how just that afternoon I'd thrown Jamie over my shoulder and how the three roughnecks had really never stood a chance.

I told him about Butler and his medicine bag and the cut my father had looked for when I was a child and how it had left a scar I'd always been self-conscious about. Finally, I told him about Adam and my trip to Back Forty Farm and the visions that had begun to haunt my waking hours.

I told him everything in my bra and panties while sitting on the side of his bed, praying he wouldn't send me packing and break my heart.

Because I'd fallen hard.

I waited while he took it all in, while he ran his hands over his face, his eyes darkening to a musky gray.

I was just about to get up and retrieve the sweatshirt when he reached over and took my hand. Squeezing lightly so as not to hurt me, he brought his hand to my cheek while rubbing my bottom lip with his thumb.

"Do you have any idea what you've just said?"

I looked at him, unsure.

"Now I know who you are," he began, his hands travelling to my shoulders as he lowered me back onto the bed. Sprawling beside me, he caressed my face with the dexterity of a potter sculpting clay. "I've had the same dream since I was a kid, over and over and there was this girl who looked like Karen. In the dream I was supposed to protect her," he paused, his hands dropping to my bra and in a moment, he'd unclasped it, removed it. "And when she died...I thought I'd failed."

I closed my eyes, my back arching under his caress and in an instant, his mouth was on the skin he'd just exposed. My lips formed the next question, but no sound came. I could only wait until he chose to answer, however long that may be.

"I couldn't protect her. And I thought I loved her but—" he turned me over, his hands sliding to my panties as he rolled them down my thighs. "She didn't have this." His hand stopped on my knee, his index finger tracing the scar. "I kept seeing this, but she didn't have it. And I couldn't—" he stopped, lowered his head and kissed it. "I couldn't make it make sense but now it does."

I tried to speak again, words gone in the texture of his open mouth against my knee, a moan escaping as he moved to my thigh.

What does it mean?

I wanted to know but couldn't ask, couldn't do anything but lay there while he did things to me no other lover had, telling me things I never would have believed possible. Moments later he moved upwards so our faces were inches apart, his hands tangling in my hair.

"What happened in your dream?" I just managed as he positioned himself on top of me.

"You were following a bird. A red bird that flew through the forest and I was chasing you, trying to catch up when you cut your wrist with a knife. There was blood everywhere," he paused, pulled back, and for an instant I feared he might change his mind. "I tried to stop it, to put my hands on it but—"

I put my palms on his chest. "What happened?"

111

"I woke up," he touched my temple, combing my hair back but something in me knew he was lying. That he couldn't stop the blood. That it kept coming. "I promise I won't let anything happen to you."

I smiled, his words opening a world for me I didn't believe was possible. "Dylan,"

"I'll do whatever it takes."

I looked into his eyes, knew he was telling the truth, and felt a chord of anxiety tighten around my chest.

"As long as you stop beating up guys twice your size."

"No promises."

He laughed, and the feel of his mouth and hands and body all but numbed my fear as I turned my face to the side, looking at the window and the darkness pressed against it.

I felt Dylan's breath, felt the bed shift beneath us as my ears began to fill with familiar silence. I saw the red bird, saw Dylan chasing it through the woods and then Butler's eyes, black as the ice that gripped the Big Lake in winter, came between me and the man I loved.

I saw him bend at the waist and pick up a black feather, white antler, and broken jawbone. I saw him with a turtle's shell, drawing a wheel with four spokes in the soft earth that moistened the swamp by Ocqueoc Falls. A wheel that looked like my necklace.

This done, he placed the totems inside and lit a fire.

I saw these things even as my body moved with Dylan's. I saw them and wanted to know why my father had searched so hard for a cut Dylan had dreamed of.

"J—" I heard him above me, knew the vision had passed and felt myself letting go.

Now I know who you are...

I closed my eyes, his name on my lips, lost for a moment in the way he made love, the tender movements and whispered endearments. Wrapping my arms around his neck, I let the present surround me before the past swallowed me.

Don't fight it...

And I didn't.

* * *

I lay with my head resting on his chest for a long time without speaking. I listened to his heartbeat, felt his fingers as they worked tiny circles at the nape of my neck.

He'd dreamed of me since he was a boy—the girl who had scraped her knee on a rusty nail, leaving a scar I never knew I'd be grateful for.

"What're you thinking?" he asked, his voice as lazy as we felt.

I turned my lips to his skin, kissing the smooth flesh that stretched over his collarbone, still unable to believe I was lying in his bed. "I'm wondering why a guy like you isn't married with fourteen kids."

He didn't answer at first, his silence reminding me of Karen and the dreams they may have shared.

"Did you love her?" I couldn't look at him after I asked it but stared at a knot in the ceiling that resembled a miniature Mr. Potato Head.

"J—"

I sat up in bed, pulled the sheet to my chest. "Because I look so much like her…if you've just sort of replaced her with me."

"That's not what I've done."

"I know," I said, hating myself.

"If anything, it's the other way around," He paused, his hand grazing my chin. "And it scares the hell out of me."

I looked at him. "Why?"

"Because I don't want to lose you."

I laughed, thinking again of John Deere and his mouthful of blood. "I think it's pretty obvious I can take care of myself."

"Stop, Justine."

"So maybe you should put the whole 'damsel in distress' thing aside and enjoy the moment."

It was his turn to smile. "Oh, I've enjoyed the moment."

I turned my lips to his.

"But maybe I'm thinking the dreams where you bleed to death are bad enough and I should walk away right now."

I forgot to breathe, hoping he was making some sort of joke, thinking his timing was lousy.

"Maybe I was never meant to have you if I can't save you."

"It's just a dream."

"Like your visions? And the cut on your knee? It's all coming true, J—"

"Please, don't," I begged, hating myself even more. "If you walk away—"

"You just said you can take care of yourself."

Damn him! Sure, I could pretend to be cool and independent and sure my newfound super strength came in handy during bar brawls, but deep down I knew I needed him.

"Maybe I'm thinking none of that matters and what I want more than anything is lying beside me."

I dared a glance as he sat propped amongst the pillows and saw he wasn't looking at me, but at the ceiling and perhaps the same wooden knothole.

"What does that mean?"

He turned, taking me into his arms again. "I don't know. And that's okay."

I smiled. Uncertainty had never been my favorite setting on the emotional barometer. But all thoughts fled as he kissed me again, his touch playful, ticklish.

"Tell me about Webber and what you did down there."

"Ugh," I sighed. Bore him with stories about city council meetings and cornfields and Donna the Editor asking me to cover the grand opening of her sister's beauty salon? No thanks.

"Were you seeing anyone?"

I made another face because talking about Brad wasn't high on my to-do list, but I figured I owed him at least a rough draft of the most awkward chapter in my life.

"There was a guy downstate but it didn't work out."

"What happened?" he asked, his tone casual.

"He had a lot on his plate," I muttered. "You know the drill."

"Oh, I know the drill," he teased, rolling me over so I was beneath him again, his kisses travelling down my chest to my stomach where he seemed to linger.

I sighed, my mind turning to the lavender fields behind Back Forty Farm—to Esther Ebersole and Jonas Younts hidden amongst the blooms and wondered if she had loved him and how he had come to be blamed for her murder.

I thought of her beautiful skin, of the cameo on her collar, as Dylan returned to my face, one hand falling to my breast, his kisses more insistent.

"Stop," I whispered and at once he pulled away.

"What?"

I looked at him, traced his bottom lip with the tip of my index finger. "Whatever happens I want you to know that this was enough."

He dipped his head again, kissed my mouth lightly. "I know it."

I smiled, put a hand to his chest, the steady staccato of his heartbeat lulling me into the belief that he would always be here, and knew I had to tell him how I felt before I racked up any more regrets.

"I love you."

He tensed, his hands tightening on my shoulder as his thumbs worked the soft skin of my upper arm.

"I know that, too."

Chapter Fifteen

I'd never been superstitious, but the next day I found myself avoiding black cats, throwing salt over my left shoulder and knocking on wood in a feeble attempt to preserve my glorious bubble.

As the afternoon approached, I reluctantly left Dylan's bed and his house even more so.

Holly was watching TV when I opened the door, some soap opera she'd had a soft spot for since puberty playing across the screen like a B-List production of *Antigone.*

"How was it?" She asked, spinning slowly in the La-Z-Boy while twirling her long hair around her index finger.

"How was what?" I asked, wondering if I looked as different as I felt.

"I can almost hear 'Like a Virgin' playing in the background so spare me the innocent act."

"Knock it off," I scolded. "I kinda like this guy."

"No one kinda 'likes' Dylan Locke, Squirt," she explained.

I frowned.

"You just bagged the hottest guy up here—aside from Dave, of course, so lighten up and enjoy the afterglow."

I looked at her, wanting to be cheerful but already feeling his absence in the pit of my belly.

"You don't look so good."

"I'm fine," I lied. "I'm just having a few doubts."

She grabbed the remote and turned the drama down. "Women are constitutionally incapable of confidence after sex."

I looked at my hands, remembering the moment he'd kissed my knuckles, the moment he'd kissed me other places, memories that should have left no uncertainty in their wake, and still, I'd gotten the hint—he wasn't ready to say he loved me.

"Dave wants to double for Salmon Fest."

"Salmon Fest? That little festival I keep seeing fliers for in Dollar General?"

"We can all hang out together."

"As in a foursome?"

"Uh…sure," she replied. "Not that I wouldn't find that interesting. You excluded, of course."

"Of course," I muttered.

"It's coming up next weekend, but if you're gonna mope around, I'll tell him to forget it."

"No," I began, my thoughts flying to a darkened beach, fireworks and Dylan's hand in mine. "That sounds great."

She didn't answer, her eyes searching mine with more perception than I liked. "He called here last night looking for you."

"Oh," I asked, unprepared for the warm rush that glazed my skin. "He never said anything."

"Not his style to let a girl know she's worked him over."

I twirled a piece of my hair around my finger thinking how little she really knew about him, when she pushed to her feet and headed towards the kitchen. I heard her rummaging through a box of leftover pizza, listened while she opened a can of Diet Coke and poured it into a *Scooby-Doo* cup she'd pilfered from camp.

"Said he was driving out to the bar if you didn't show up in the next five minutes."

I scowled, thinking of the sight that would have greeted my would-be rescuer when my cell phone rang.

"Hello?" I answered, hoping he'd missed me enough to call first.

"Babe?"

It took me a moment to recognize his voice. Buried so long in my subconscious, it felt like a call from the dead.

"Brad?"

Holly spun on her heel, a slice of pepperoni pizza hanging from her mouth. "Yeppers."

An image of the riverboat he'd borrowed from a friend flashed before my eyes and I wondered if he was thinking about us in the bow, a bottle of wine between us. Right before I found out about the wife and kids.

"J?" he asked. "You there?"

I drew my finger across my throat and Holly gave me a sad face before slinking out of the room.

"I'm here."

I heard him shuffle some papers and glanced at the clock.
11:45 a.m.

He'd be ready to break for lunch. Turkey club on wheat. Hold the mayo. Water and a hot cup of coffee to get him through the afternoon.

"Haven't heard from you in a while."

"Yep," I said, "That was kind of the point."

"Ooo, Babe," he let out a low whistle. "You're *kind of* harsh."

I didn't want to play games now. So I kept my mouth shut.

"Blowing me off?"

"I didn't blow you off," I answered. "You have a wife and kids. I needed some time to think."

He sighed again, shuffled some more papers while a woman's voice I recognized as his secretary's reminded him of his two o'clock with a Mr. Puckett. "Why don't you do your thinking down here in Webber?"

I bit my lip, sat down on one of the wobbly stools while the drama on Holly's soap opera mirrored my own, minus the mood lighting. "I can't do this, Brad."

"Can't do what?"

"You and me," I lowered my voice. "*Us.*"

He laughed. "What about us? I just called to catch up with an old friend."

I frowned into the phone. "Your timing is impeccable."

"Whaddya mean?"

"I've met someone."

I heard him get up and shut his office door. "You got a guy up there? So glad to hear it, Princess. You deserve the best."

"Don't call me that."

He huffed, his chair squeaking as he swiveled. And I imagined he was looking out across the cornfields, rubbing the bottom of his chin with a free hand. Perplexed. "Now I can't even take a trip down memory lane?"

"That road's been closed for over five months."

He chuckled, but beneath I sensed his uncertainty, his vulnerability, his inability to let me go despite his ego. Or maybe because of it. "Don't get worked up. I'm just paying a friendly call to a girl who holds a special place in my heart."

"Well stop being so friendly. I don't want to mess things up with Dylan."

"Dylan?" he laughed again. "What is he? Some frat boy?"

"No," I said, not sure why I was telling him anything. "He's a cop."

"A cop!" Another laugh. "You sure know how to pick 'em."

"I picked you, didn't I?"

Brad was silent, which was never a good sign. "You tell him about us?"

117

It was my turn to laugh. "What *about* us?"

"Jesus, J. When did you turn into such a ball-buster?"

I tapped my index finger against my forehead, then glanced at the television as a picture of Suzy Marsh interrupted the soap opera. She was pretty, with blonde hair and large eyes that could have been hazel.

Come to think of it...she looked an awful lot like Karen.

And me.

"I've gotta go," I whispered, my hands beginning to shake as I reached for the remote and turned up the volume.

"Why did you leave town?"

Foul play was not a factor in Marsh's death. The gunshot wound appears to be self-inflicted

"Don't call me again."

Marsh may have been despondent over a recent break-up.

"Let me make this right."

I drew a breath, my voice a wisp of what it had been. "You can't."

Chapter Sixteen

Salmon Fest soon arrived in all its glory—a blow-out resembling the Fourth of July only in the respect that it came in the middle of the summer and featured fireworks and a beer tent. In reality, it marked the beginning of the famous Lantern Creek Salmon Tournament; a pseudo rite-of-passage for all the young fishermen in Presque Isle County. Main Street was lined with blue and white canopies and cotton candy vendors, while the local barbershop quartet sang 'Lida Rose' up at the bandshell. The smell of French fries dripping in vinegar, funnel cakes, and axle grease met my nose as soon as I stepped outside.

Dylan had graciously offered to escort me to what was shaping up to be the social event of the season and I gladly accepted. Not only hadn't he gone AWOL after we'd slept together, but he'd also extended the loan on his Jeep while presenting me with a standing invitation to bunk at the lake house—something I'd taken him up on exactly three times.

And still no magic words.

I tried to shrug it off as he put an arm around my shoulder and led me towards the epicenter of Podunk entertainment.

"Something bothering you?"

Damn, he was sharp, but that's what made him good at tracking down drug addicts and wife beaters and people who shot teenage girls in the head.

Because I wasn't buying that crap about Suzy Marsh committing suicide.

"I'm wearing a new top today."

"I noticed."

"You said you liked me in blue," I offered as we passed a vendor selling elephant ears.

"I do," he stopped, asked if I wanted one and I shook my head while assessing his appearance. Nothing too fancy for Deputy Locke, but he sure looked handsome in a black short-sleeved button down and faded blue jeans.

Yes, Dylan was definitely a catch bigger than Old Granddaddy Salmon and so I decided to test the whole 'trust' theory by bringing something up I didn't want to talk about.

"Do you think Suzy Marsh looks like me?"

He stopped mid-stride.

"Not really."

I put my hand on his arm. "Tell me the truth."

He shrugged, but I could tell the subject bothered him. "There are a lot of pretty girls in Presque Isle County."

I smiled, content with his flattery in my blue scooped necked top, khaki skirt and brown sandals, my hair pulled back in a messy ponytail, watching as people swarmed around us, some oblivious to my presence and some blatantly interested in who he was with. I caught a few girls giving me the ol' Up and Down and felt my face turn four shades of red.

I wondered how many of the girls were exes, how many were wannabe-exes and how many just wanted to claw at my face for showing up with him. The thought that he'd had a romantic past apart from Karen and that some of those conquests might be alive and well and roaming the streets of Salmon Fest did not sit well with me.

"Want some?"

I turned to see him holding a cotton-candied finger inches from my face and shook my head, painfully aware of how public we'd become.

"What is it?" he asked again, his patience endearing.

I crossed my arms over my chest. "Everyone's looking at us."

He turned in the direction of my stare and waved to a group that had gathered near the entrance to the beer tent. "Lots of people come back to town for this."

"I noticed."

He chuckled. "Don't worry. I got all of these girls out of my system in high school."

"Don't tease."

"I can't help it. You're cute when you're jealous."

"I'm not jealous."

"Sure," he smiled. "Just like I'm not jealous of the guy with the full plate." I grimaced at the thought before a mock punch to his left shoulder shifted our attention. Dave stepped into view, followed shortly by Holly—who emerged like Aphrodite from the greasy steam of a corn dog kiosk.

"Hey, kids," Dave laughed. He was carrying a stuffed version of Sylvester the Cat and an extra-large Slushie, leaving Holly with only her designer purse and a look of pure adoration where her beau was concerned.

"Hey," Dylan returned the punch and the two were off and running, talking about the docks and how many throws it had taken to win Sylvester and what Holly had said when the weird barker down by the pony rides guessed heavy on her weight.

I turned to my roommate, curious myself and found that she couldn't wipe the smirk off her face. "You two certainly are the talk of the town."

"What do you mean?" I asked, unconsciously pulling down on my skirt. "Are people staring?"

Holly rolled her eyes, tapped Dave on the shoulder and he handed over the Slushie. "Sure, they are, but so *what?* I'd rub it in all their nasty little faces."

"*Holl.*"

"See that one over by the dunk tank? Green V-neck?" I followed her gaze and was saw a buxom girl with pale skin and long, red hair. "She's wanted him since freshman year. Got her chance once when we were all drunk at the senior camp-out, but he never went back for seconds."

I gave Holly a piteous look, one I hoped would shut her up, but she'd already visited the beer tent and could not be stopped. "Looks like she's gonna pull out your hair if you get too close." Turning her attention to another clump of vixens that had gathered near the bandshell, she said, "That one actually dated him for about a month. Thought they were gonna ride off into the sunset after graduation! Sur-*prrrise...* Stupid bimbo used to make fun of me in gym class. Said my boobs made it across the finish line before I did." She paused, took a gulp and then squinted in pain. "Who's laughing now, bitch?"

"How much did you drink?"

"I'm high on life, Squirt." She looked at me and laughed. "And to think my little roommate, the one I met through that guy I used to know who moved downstate would grow up and snag Dylan Locke. Never woulda guessed it, but hell—I'm riding this soul train 'til it hits a wall."

"Please stop," I begged, grateful that our dates were still engaged in manly conversation and had missed the gist of her outburst.

"All right," she conceded. "All I'm saying is it's good to see him out and about. The meathead missed Salmon Fest last year on account of the accident."

I reached out and gripped her arm. "You knew about Karen?"

She shrugged while taking a smaller, more cautious, sip. "Everyone knew. It was pretty friggin' obvious."

I stole another glance at the redhead and was relieved to see she'd moved on towards the Ferris Wheel. "Do you think they're all wondering why he's dating someone who looks so much like her?"

Holly stepped back, raised one eyebrow. "Now that you mention it, you do kinda bear a certain resemblance."

"Oh, geez," I said. "I bet they think I'm a clueless idiot."

Holly reached over, put an arm around my shoulder while touching her head to mine. "I wouldn't say clueless."

I frowned as our dates turned and rejoined the conversation.

"Wanna get something to drink?" Dylan asked, ever the chivalrous gentleman where my hydration was concerned.

I nodded. A beer sounded good, great, even, in light of Holly's monologue.

I hadn't taken more than ten steps when the carnival music went dead in my ears. I tried not to panic when I thought about all the girls watching us, just waiting for me to screw up, and scoped around for a place to sit. Adam had told me not to fight it, and I was going to take his advice.

I saw Dylan catch my eye, watched his lips form my name and heard nothing.

"I need to sit down," I said, hoping the words came out right. "My lunch didn't settle."

I watched them search for a seat.

"Go on," I instructed, my ears still numb. "I'll catch up."

I knew Dylan was reluctant, but then Dave gave him another punch and someone came up from behind to clap him on the shoulder and I was alone with a vision of Esther Ebersole in her white nightdress, combing her hair in front of a vanity mirror. Abraham appeared behind her, bent to kiss the soft curve of her neck and she put her hand to his face, turned in her chair and touched his lips with her own.

She spoke to him, told him she'd be to bed after she checked on the hired girl, her small feet making no sound on the wooden floor.

The back door was unlocked, and Esther opened it. Stepping outside into the autumn night, she made her way towards the barn where a lantern was burning in the stall of her husband's favorite gelding.

She stopped just short of the barn, looked inside and in that instant a man stepped from the shadows. A man whose face was lost in shadow. A man in a long riding coat and leather boots.

Jonas Younts.

Esther paused, looked back at the house and then continued on, her feet leaving dusty footprints. In an instant she was in the man's arms, her hands cupping his face as she covered it in kisses. They moved inward, toward the stall he'd lit with the lantern, his hands under her nightdress in an attempt to pull her bloomers down.

Before they could reach cover a noise from the house made them hesitate and Esther pulled away, the passion written plainly on her face. And beneath the passion was fear, then terror as Abraham strode into the barnyard, pistol in hand.

"Step away from my wife!"

Esther screamed as he raised the barrel, screamed as he pointed the weapon at Jonas Younts, and then jumped between them.

I felt her fall, felt her body in space and time and knew that she had been hit and that the wound was fatal. I felt all this even as something closed around my waist, keeping me from hitting the ground as a familiar voice said my name.

"Oh," I muttered, my eyes suddenly coming clear in the darkness, my body bent double over the rolling waves of the Big Lake.

I was on the breakwall, but how had I gotten out here? I'd never moved during a vision before.

"You okay?"

I blinked, images of Esther and Jonas still fresh when I saw his features suddenly materialize in the incandescent glow of Salmon Fest. Brown hair. Amber eyes. White shirt rolled at the sleeves—as they always were.

"Jamie?" I tried to stand up, tried to straighten my legs but found they would not work.

He eased me to a sitting position.

"What the hell're you doing out here?"

How I'd reached my current position without tumbling into the lake was nothing short of a miracle, as was Jamie's presence when I needed it most.

"I went for a walk."

"Shoulda stuck to the beach."

I nodded, unable to argue. "How did you know I was out here?"

"I followed you."

My heart did a chirrup. "Why?"

He smiled. "Why not?"

"Umm, Lots of reasons. Like I could break your neck, for one."

"Water under the bridge," he smiled that crooked grin and I laughed out loud, almost believing him. "Beer and the breakwall don't mix, didn't they teach you that in grade school?"

"Not downstate," I shook my head and tried to forget about the guy who was waiting for me on shore, the guy who would be pissed to know I was out here with Jamie Stoddard, vision or no vision.

"Thanks a lot," I said as I stood and began to pick my way back towards shore. "But I've gotta go."

"Always running away."

I turned back, was struck by the white of his shirt against the black water. "Jamie—"

"Maybe I'm not the bad guy."

I paused, disconcerted. "I never said you were."

"Yes, you did."

I turned toward the shore again, caught the sound of another person maneuvering the large boulders just in front of me and tried to focus. Soon Dylan came into sight, a frenzied speed to his movement as he spotted me.

"Justine!" he cried, pulling up short when he saw who stood behind me. "What the—"

"You should keep a better eye on your girl, Locke," Jamie said, his tone thick with underlying contempt. "I might have to start charging double."

Dylan looked to me.

"I came out here to clear my head," I began. "And tripped on the rocks. Jamie caught me."

"He what?"

"I caught her, Locke," Jamie offered. "Just penance for my last major fuck-up."

I saw Dylan tense, heard his breath catch and knew it took all his strength to keep from decking him right there. "Is that what you call it?" he finally asked, his body stiff with repressed rage.

Jamie's face shifted, his irrepressible calm shattered by a simple question. "You have a better idea?"

"Not my idea," Dylan paused, his face harder than I'd ever seen it. "Hers."

Jamie flinched. "What the fuck is that supposed to mean?"

"Karen knew you were on to us. Knew you wouldn't take it lying down and she was right, wasn't she?" I put my hand on Dylan's arm, tried to calm him but he jerked away. "Tell me you weren't thinking of me when you plowed her into that tree?"

Jamie grinned, but this time the gesture held no kindness. "I wasn't thinking of anything but wiping that smile off her face."

Dylan jerked forward, his hands twisted into fists. "Bastard," he hissed, swinging once, then twice as his rival moved from one rock to the next with the grace of a dancer on even footing.

"Keep swinging, Locke. You might put yourself in the water again and damned if I'll pull your ass out this time."

"Keep talking, Stoddard, and I just might take you with me."

Jamie laughed, his hubris high as Dylan lunged again, this time catching him on the side of the jaw. I tried to scamper out of the way, tried to let this be about two men duking it out but couldn't and so reached for Dylan's arm.

But he didn't stop, just pulled away so suddenly I lost my balance as a knife's edge of outcropped rock sliced the top of my hand.

Dylan turned, his anger dissolving as he knelt beside me, blood oozing from the cut. "Put pressure on it," he instructed. "The bleeding should stop."

"And if it doesn't?" Jamie asked. A simple question, but I tensed.

"It's only a scratch," I said, annoyed with them. "But you two need to cool down."

"Agreed," Jamie said, circling us as casually as he would a toddler in the grass. "Good catching up with you, Justine."

I looked away.

"Locke," he nodded, rubbing his jaw. "Glad we could clear the air. It's been a year in the making."

I heard Dylan mutter an expletive. "You lucked out tonight, Stoddard. Touch her again and I'll kill you."

Jamie's smile split his face. "Can't kill what's already dead."

* * *

Salmon Fest was pretty much a bust after the breakwall incident.

I tried to cajole Dylan, tried to make him understand why I'd ended up out there in the first place, but nothing seemed to satisfy him.

"At least the bleeding stopped," I offered.

He grunted something, still energized by his encounter with Jamie. "So, you take off half-blind and try to scale those rocks? Why didn't you tell me you weren't really sick? We could've sat it out somewhere until the vision passed."

"I don't know how I got out there." I looked down. "Holly doesn't know about my visions. Neither does Dave or all those girls who worship you and the last thing I need is for everyone to think you've hooked up with a psycho."

He stopped short. "That's what this is about? You're afraid of what everyone will think?"

I shrugged.

"Who the hell cares? You almost fell into Lake Huron!"

I looked down.

"When you didn't come to the beer tent, I asked around. One guy said he saw you walk towards the breakwall. I wouldn't have made it in time, would've had to fish you out of the water so don't pull this shit on me."

"I'm sorry."

"You keep saying that."

"I promise I'll tell you next time. I've already started locking the door and charging my phone and now I know that I need someone to help me stay put. It's not like I know what the hell I'm doing. I've never been this weird before."

Something in my speech must have moved him because he pulled me close and hugged me. "I'm serious, Justine. We're in this together or I'm out."

His words were like cold ice on a suntanned shoulder.

A moment passed before he spoke again, and in the interim, his voice softened into, "Wanna watch the fireworks?"

I glanced over my shoulder. "Dave and Holly?"

"Left awhile ago. Seems your roommate can't hold her liquor."

And so we wandered down the beach and away from the pulsating lights of Salmon Fest until we reached a cove whose only inhabitants included a man with a guitar, three girls and the campfire they had gathered around.

We stopped amongst an isolated copse of trees, strains of *Ain't No Sunshine* filling the silence between us. Sitting down on a blanket of dried moss, he put an arm around my shoulder.

We sat for a long time, listening to the guitar and the low voices of those assembled around it who were unaware of our presence as we sat hidden from view and in the company of darkness.

"I knew Karen all through school," he said and I turned, looked at him and knew he'd been waiting for this moment. "It didn't get serious until she started coming down to the docks when I worked Marine Patrol."

"When did Jamie find out?" I asked, hoping my question wasn't too forward, but he didn't seem to mind. In fact, he seemed relieved.

"He asked her point blank one night. She couldn't lie."

"Were you friends with him before?"

"We never got along."

"But," I began, wondering if I should tell him what I knew. "You went fishing together. He saved your life."

He let out a little sigh of contempt. "Is that what he told you? Whatever…I could have gotten out on my own. I was on the swim team."

"But you didn't get out on your own."

"What is this?" he asked, suddenly defensive. "Stoddard pulls his hero act on the breakwall and suddenly you're his biggest fan?"

I leaned away from him, suddenly uncomfortable with the contact. "I'm just trying to help you see the whole picture."

"He killed her. Plain and simple."

I sucked in my breath, "Dylan—"

"He told everyone who would listen how a deer ran into the road and he had to swerve. The other shoulder was clear, so how come he crosses the center line and rams her side of the car into the biggest cedar this side of the county line?"

"Maybe he didn't have a choice."

"He chose all right. He chose to take her out there knowing there wouldn't be any witnesses, he chose to make up that bullshit about the deer and he chose to come to her funeral with his head stitched up whining about how much he loved her when all I could do was sit there and listen."

I turned and touched his face, feeling his sorrow as surely as my own. "I'm sorry."

"A part of me knew what we were doing was wrong, but I never thought when I kissed her goodbye that day it would be the last time."

I tensed.

"J—"

"It's okay. I know how you felt. I read the letter."

"I shouldn't have said that—"

"We all have a past," I settled against him again, wanting him to comfort me but knowing he couldn't—not where Karen was concerned.

He seemed to appreciate my understanding because I felt his hands rubbing my arms, keeping me warm in the cool evening breeze.

"I don't want to talk about it anymore. Stoddard got off and there's nothing I can do about it. A wise person once told me to let it go."

I chuckled. "She sounds super intelligent."

"Strong, too. You should see her right hook."

"I have, come to think of it."

He laughed and the hippies sitting by the campfire turned, focused for a moment on the copse of trees we were hiding in.

I giggled too, but more quietly as he continued to rub my arms, our feet playing catch up while I closed my eyes and drifted off.

Dylan said nothing, just continued to stroke my bare skin until it had lured me into a place I'd never seen before.

An island in the middle of a marsh beyond Ocqueoc Falls.

I didn't know if such a place existed, or why it had come to me here on the beach at Salmon Fest when I saw Butler step from the forest. He was wearing cotton pants, a work shirt open at the collar and a vest made of leather. His long hair was tied back with a piece of rawhide, his black eyes unmoving as they took me in.

Moments later he knelt and traced something I'd seen before: a picture of a wheel with four spokes—something I could now place because Dylan had become my lover.

A tattoo on his back between his shoulder blades.

I'd asked him about it, wondering why he'd gotten it and if it had any significance, never realizing until this moment how it matched my necklace.

Adam's necklace...

I remembered his explanation now as I floated between the world I occupied with Dylan and this sacred space with Butler.

Got it in Florida on Spring Break. No idea why. Mom flipped out.

Just like my own mother had caved in when I found the necklace in her jewelry box.

Was it just a coincidence?

I knew better than that.

I'd always wondered what the intersected circle had meant, imagining it to be something holy and miraculous and transcendental and realized it was all three. Butler was drawing a medicine wheel and placing inside it the four totems that would safeguard the woman he loved and her descendants.

And marking those he had chosen to protect them.

Chapter Seventeen

"Thanks for letting me borrow the laptop," I scurried to keep up with Holly, computer pressed to my chest as we made our way towards Camp Menominee

She nodded quickly, double latte in one hand, car keys in the other as she hurried towards the dining hall. "Don't know why you needed to borrow it today."

I didn't know either, but ever since Salmon Fest I felt a sense of urgency, amplified by the fear that Dylan had somehow been chosen by Butler to protect me and that nothing I said would make him change course. Even if it meant sacrificing himself. I couldn't let that happen, not when I had the opportunity to find out what was happening.

"The internet's down at home and I wanted to see where you work and thought I could help with canoeing or something," I smiled, shifted the laptop. "Dad used to let me sit in back and steer."

Holly narrowed her eyes, pushed open the door with her hip. "I'll take that into consideration when the PowerPoint I'm supposed to finish doesn't get done in time for Family Fun Weekend. I need it back as soon as you're finished."

I nodded, the sound of chatter quickly filling my ears as we entered the large space where campers had gathered to devour eggs, bacon, and pancakes loaded with extra syrup.

"Dammit!" Holly muttered when she caught sight of their trays. "I told Jen to go easy on the fructose corn crack. Now we'll have kids spinning in circles during archery."

"Listen," I put a hand on her elbow, held her in place before she spun into the stratosphere. "I know this was last minute, but I'll make it up to you."

She smiled, "You'd better," then gave me a nudge towards the employee lounge.

Moments later I was at the end of a large wooden table with mismatched chairs, a *Birds of Northern Michigan* clock that chirped the hour just over my left shoulder. The windows to my right offered a view of Cade Lake and the pubescent band of girls who had decided to model their new swimsuits.

They stood in awkward circles, arms crossed low across their stomachs, shoulders hunched, the sun shining behind them and casting brilliance on the water. I was reminded of myself at the community pool, my crush doing backflips behind me, my flowered towel resting over my shoulders to guard them against the sun.

The lilting twitter of a robin reminded me that the clock was ticking and so I dove in, opened the laptop and began my search by looking up the four totems.

Elk—An animal of great strength, power, and stamina. One of its primary defenses is to outrun its predators.

Wolf—Defined by rules, ritual, and intuition. Protective of the pack, able to make quick and firm emotional attachments.

Raven—A messenger for the spiritual realm with the ability to shapeshift. Known to mimic the sounds of other animals.

Turtle—A symbol of longevity, survival, and clairaudience.

I thought of their attributes, thought about Butler and his love for Odessa and understood why he had chosen these totems.

He wanted my grandmother to live a long life surrounded by those who would protect her. He wanted her to be strong and wasn't above using a bit of magic to do that.

Which still didn't explain why she had chosen to lead a lynch mob against Jonas Younts.

And so, I searched again as a chickadee sang me past lunch hour, enduring the curious stares and mindless chatter of four counselors who had chosen to eat indoors.

It was almost one o'clock before I found something.

A letter from Odessa's brother to her mother, preserved on a website entitled *'Was Jonas Younts Framed?'* I scrolled down past a faded picture of Back Forty Farm and found the author—a male nerd in his prime—and wondered who else in Presque Isle County was thinking the same thing I was.

Dear Ma,

Dess is not herself. I do not mean that you should hurry home and waste that horse what is ready to drop, but I want you to know I can't think of a way to care for her.

Cal is sick, too, but Doc says not to worry, it is spread by eating those spotty melons what grows in the swamps.

Mrs. Karsten stopped by to tend to Cal and she and Dess has become friends even so that Dess wants to be godmother to her babe in arms.

She does things like that and I think I don't need to worry but then the other day she went and told fortunes for a lady in town what lost her husband in a house fire.

Then she tells me that I don't need to watch over her no more and she will prove it by telling fortunes for the ladies in church. I din't understand this but the other day she went ahead an' called them over while I was outside tendin' the hogs. She tells me the Injun what helped her plant the vegetable garden gave her the Sight.

I must admit, Ma—that I sinned and listened to what them gals was sayin' and some of it was true spot on. No way Dess could've known and now I wonders what that Injun has done to her.

I'm afraid that when she takes it into her head to do it again I won't catch her. Injun tells me not to fret because Dess is still the old gal we used to know and that I should not talk about things to the men in town.

Hurry home, Mother. I will buy you a new horse if Lolly cannot bear it.

Your boy,
Johnson

I sat back, thinking of the peculiar family Johnson, Odessa, Cal, and their Ma must have made, then scrolled down until I found another letter dated three weeks later.

Dear Ma,

Sorry to hear you cannot get away from Sister Nan. She always was one to keep company when they din't care to be kept.

I write to tell you that Dess has gotten herself into more trouble and that you should come as quick as you can. The Injun was made to move on and Dess cries day and night for him. I don't want this to worry you 'cause the Lutheran preacher still has hopes of giving Dess his last name even though he says she is damned to hell.

That pretty gal what moved into the Back Homestead with Ebersole was found dead four nights ago. Husband was kil'd too and now folks in town wants to lynch somebody.

Dess has talked to the sheriff and said she knows who we should go after. Said the Injun's medicine helps her see the killer and that Jonas Younts (that timber jack what came by and cut wood last spring) stole something what belonged to her and she'd be darned ('cuse my language) if he was going to get away with it.

I'm afraid she'll do something foolish for wantin' that Injun. Hurry home and tell Sister Nan you have a headache.

Your boy,
Johnson

Odessa had been angry at Jonas Younts for stealing something that belonged to her.

I scanned the list again, wondering if he had stolen the medicine bag and if so, why? Had he wanted to read omens? Form quick and lasting relationships? Run really fast? All of these things seemed trivial in light of what he had suffered at Esther's death and instinct told me it must have been something more he desired. Something that would earn Odessa Cook's eternal hatred.

"Squirt?"

I jumped, slammed the laptop shut and spun to face Holly.

She raised an eyebrow, a fresh latte firmly in hand as she swept the lounge for errant counselors. "Canoeing? Twenty minutes?"

"I can't," I stalled. "Mallard needs me to go over inventory."

"So, you're a watersports tease?"

"That's the word on the street."

She mumbled something meant to make me feel guilty, but I ignored her. I needed to get home to shower before my shift began at Huff's, although sometimes I wondered why I bothered.

"Thanks again," I handed her the laptop. "I found what I needed."

"You owe me," was her cryptic response, and so I shot her a thumbs up before exiting down a long hallway that bypassed the cafeteria. Halfway to the door, I slowed down next to a large display case, unable to understand why I would be drawn to it at a time like this.

I stood, slightly mesmerized while looking at ribbons from fishing contests past and pictures of campers who had since become grandparents. Leaning closer, I followed the chronology backward until I reached the oldest photographs.

I bent down, squinted into the reflection cast by a large window and saw a group of lumberjacks next to a clot of cut timber. Following their line to the left, I spotted a young man leaning casually on the upended handle of a wooden bucksaw. The slant of his shoulders told me all I needed as I noted his brown hair, strong forearms, and crooked smile.

Can't kill what's already dead...

And underneath the picture, a caption was written.

First groundbreaking at Cade Lake, summer 1889

I took a step backwards, tried to talk myself out of what I was seeing, but it was too late. And unless Jamie Stoddard had a twin he'd never mentioned this picture proved he was alive and well and sawing logs over a hundred years ago.

I moved away slowly, turned and almost smacked my head on the glass doors.

"Get a grip," I mumbled to myself, "Anyone could look like Jamie."

But something told me otherwise as I climbed into the Jeep and sped back towards the apartment, intent on getting some answers from Iris or Pam or whoever else I had to shake the crap out of.

Because it had suddenly become much more than just looking for my father.

I arrived home twenty minutes later and knocked on Iris' door—wondering why she hadn't invited me down for tea and crumpets and the abbreviated history of Lantern Creek.

I needed to know why I'd seen Jamie Stoddard in a picture that had been taken over a century ago, why he seemed to know my every move and why he seemed to be torn between killing me and protecting me.

After several minutes it became obvious that Iris was either hiding under her bed or simply not home.

I chose to believe the latter and so climbed the steps with a distracted air, not noticing the strange car parked in Holly's spot.

I'd already entered the kitchen when I sensed something was off. Joey didn't come out to greet me and the place had a strange smell, a smell I'd had on my own skin many times.

"Babe!"

I spun in a circle, fists clenched when I spotted him standing in the middle of the living room. "Brad?"

He took a step closer and I saw that his auburn hair had gotten longer, that he hadn't shaved in a day or two, but he still had the same dear face, boyish in its vice.

"What're you doing here?" I stammered while reaching back to grip the counter, cursing Holly for not locking the door…again. "That's not your car."

"It's a rental."

I couldn't answer, could only ask, "How did you find me?"

"Small town idiots always remember pretty strangers like you…for the right price." He smiled, and I was struck by his dimples, by the way his mouth moved when he spoke and realized I was starved for all things familiar. Which scared the hell out of me. "You look good, Princess. I could eat you up."

"I told you not to call me that," I muttered while smoothing my shirt.

"And you freaked me out big time." He circled the counter and I didn't know whether to send him packing or throw myself into his arms, hoping a little bit of his downstate sanity would rub off on me. "Is it true?"

"What," I took a quick breath. "Is what true?"

I saw his face harden. "The other guy."

I didn't answer.

He tried to smile, tried to laugh it off, but couldn't. "Why?"

"Are you serious?"

He took a step back, leaned against the counter. "I'm sorry," he shut his eyes, worked the bridge of his nose with two fingers. "Just come back home and we'll work it out."

I looked away. "Are you getting a divorce?"

"Not yet," he took a step towards me and cupped my shoulders, working the flesh under his thumbs as he'd worked other parts of me in the past. "But it's in the works."

"It is?" I asked, thinking of how happy this news would have made me last winter.

"I want you where I can keep an eye on you, Princess."

"You do?" I whispered, feeling my resolve slide away to a place where I didn't have to worry about dead ex-girlfriends or century-old lumberjacks.

"Of course," he said, his index finger seeking my chin. "I love you."

Nothing had ever sounded so good as I melted into Brad's embrace, my mouth seeking his if only to prove I'd chosen the right man, and in that instant, I felt a jolt of electricity that had nothing to do with attraction.

"God, I miss you," he whispered against my cheek, his hand on the waistband of my shorts in an effort to ease them over my hips. "Then you mention this other guy," he paused, drew back slightly so he could look into my eyes. "This asshole think he can satisfy you?"

I stiffened, my hands seeking his in an effort to stop their progress. "You need to leave."

He chuckled.

"I mean it, Brad."

He dipped to kiss the skin just beneath my earlobe. "I didn't drive three hundred miles just to turn around with my dick in my hand."

I put my palms up, pushed against him.

"Hey, now," he muttered, clearly annoyed.

I took a breath, closed my eyes and imagined myself as a woman who would have made her father proud had he been there to see it. "It's over."

"What?"

"You heard me."

"Don't get all worked up," he smiled, accustomed to getting what he wanted. "I just came to pay a friendly visit."

"So, you suck face with your friends?"

"Maybe," he bent his head again, nibbled at the other ear. "If she'll let me."

I clenched my teeth, imagined taking Brad's hands between my own and squeezing until his fingers popped open like wet summer sausages. Until he listened. Until he heard me.

I saw Dylan, saw the medicine wheel painted between his shoulder blades and realized I may have already blown it with the most decent guy I'd ever dated.

I quickly did a mental checklist of where he would be today.

Thursday afternoons meant patrol duty until six o'clock, which meant he might drive by and see the strange car parked outside the apartment. And if he walked upstairs and saw us now... I might as well have been naked with him in my bed.

"Get out."

I saw Brad shake his head, thought he might refuse and reached out to touch his shoulder, calling upon the totems Butler had given Odessa to control the anger I feared.

"What're you doing?"

I let my instincts guide me and tightened my grip.

"What the hell?"

I felt the fabric of his cotton shirt and beneath that his skin and muscle and bone, felt the beating of his heart and the rapid breath he drew while still uncertain of my affection.

"It's okay," I began, hearing his thoughts for the first time. "You can let me go."

He shook his head, his fear displayed, and an image of an old man flashed before me. A man confined to an empty house while rain, slate gray and the color of his eyes, beat against the side of a bay window.

I saw bedrooms once occupied by his sons, pictures of grandchildren who never came to visit and wondered at his regrets—the lover who thought of me on days like this.

Sadness pressed me to the floor, held me solid by the heels and left only fear in its wake. Fear of the empty house and the rain and the sounds that never came.

"Don't worry," I whispered, feeling his heartbeat slow, wishing I could erase every sorrow ever etched there. "That man isn't you."

"Yes, it is."

"You won't be alone if you take care of the people who love you."

He didn't answer, just waited until I chose to break contact and then stood looking at me, stunned.

"What did you do?"

I shook my head. "What you couldn't."

"I need to get home," he paused, swept his face with a shaking hand. "I need to see my wife and boys."

"Yes, you do."

He turned on his heel, made for the door and stopped just short of it.

"Is this it?" he asked.

"I think so."

"I think so, too."

How many times in life did something end so definitively? So abruptly?

"Take care of yourself," he said, and I couldn't speak, couldn't lay eyes on the face of the man I once thought could make me happy. I only knew that he was there one moment and that the next moment he wouldn't be. And I wondered if after enough time had passed it would seem as though he'd never been, as though we'd never been.

Our footprints washed smooth by the sea.

Chapter Eighteen

Mallard Brauski was not one to offer unsolicited fashion advice, and still, he found a way to insult me.

"I wouldn't go with green if I were you," he offered while lighting up. "Locke 'n Load'll think you puked on yourself."

"Aw, geez," I fretted, trying to remember what lay in my clothes hamper. "I don't think I have anything else that looks dressy casual."

"Dressy what?"

I rolled my eyes. "Forget it."

"He spring this on you sudden-like?"

I nodded. Dylan had hinted that he wanted me to meet his folks, but only yesterday had he given me a definitive timeline: six o'clock tonight to watch his sister play softball down by the bandshell.

And I was a nervous wreck.

"His Mom's got a stick shoved so far up her ass you'd think she was a popsicle," I tensed, "Umm...that sucks."

Mallard laughed, put a hand to the back of his head and gave a good scratch. "Got loads of money an' always spreadin' it around like it was fertilizer or something."

I didn't answer and he prattled on. "She's a looker, too. Took a run at her once when I caught her slumming down at the Cat Scratch Tavern but she didn't bite."

"Slumming?" I asked, my interest piqued. "Cat Scratch?"

"Some of the girls from her office took her to the bar in Posen for New Year's. Had one too many is all. Nothing wrong with it 'cept when the odds ain't in my favor."

I put my hands up, covered my ears. "In case you forgot I have to make a *good* impression on them tonight."

"Fuck that! You gettin' serious or something?"

"Like I'd tell you," I shot back.

He smirked, as if he knew something I didn't and said, "Hope you like us rednecks then 'cause Pretty Boy ain't never leavin' Presque Isle County."

I felt a smoldering ember of anxiety and fought to suppress it. Who cared if we never left Lantern Creek? I could settle down and make a career out of Three Fires, hang with my little brother and serve Polish sausage at every meal. No biggie. We could do Thanksgiving with his folks and Christmas with Mom—considering she would even speak to me again after I untangled this horrible mess I'd uncovered.

Mallard noticed my silence, reached out to ruffle the top of my head. "You're thinkin' too much."

I didn't have time to contemplate his sage advice as I grabbed my purse and bolted for the Jeep. One hour was not enough time to make the magic happen, not enough to put into makeup and hair and posture everything I wanted Dylan's folks to know about me.

Still, I wasn't opposed to trying and started by pulling out a short-sleeved white blouse. Casual cargo pants that hung low on my hips and my ever-present necklace completed the ensemble I felt sure would amaze them with its understated elegance.

Then there was the rest of me. I stood in front of the bathroom mirror, examining my hazel eyes and wavy blonde hair. Pretty was something I could live with…but *beautiful?*

Dylan had said as much but I still wasn't sold.

Flat iron in hand, I decided to straighten my hair. A bit of mascara and a touch of pink lip gloss completed my beauty regimen fifteen minutes ahead of schedule and so I sat and waited. And stewed, and thought about what Mallard had said and how Dylan would surely not invite me to a softball game with his parents if he wasn't serious about our future and didn't that include deciding on where to spend it together?

Joey jumped into my lap and I absentmindedly stroked his orange fur.

Footsteps on the staircase brought momentary panic, then a sense of relief as Dylan walked through the door, striking as ever in a blue T-shirt and khaki shorts. He even smelled good, like sun and sand and wind.

"Ready?" he asked, his tone clipped, and I wondered if he was anxious, too.

"Sure," I stood up, smoothed my pants.

Dylan's gaze swept me and I felt my chest go hot. "You look nice."

"Thanks," I smiled, wishing we had a moment to spare, a moment to tell each other what was weighing on our minds because I would start with Brad. His name lingered on my tongue, left a bad taste in my mouth as he put a hand on the small of my back and led me to the truck.

Moments later we were inside, his favorite classic rock station playing as he reached over and took my hand.

"Nervous?"

I nodded.

"Don't be." He squeezed. "They always like my girlfriends."

I frowned, wondering if that was supposed to make me feel better, then turned to look out the window as we rounded the bend towards Lakefield Park, a grassy field set back from the beach with a hotdog pavilion at one end and a bandshell at the other. Metal bleachers that were already half-full reminded me of my high school days, though I never had a date as hot as Dylan back then.

I tried to concentrate on the task at hand, tried to imagine what I would say to his mother and if I'd be able to get the picture of Mallard trying to seduce her over a chilled bottle of Pabst Blue Ribbon out of my head.

"Before we get out I need to tell you something."

I turned, my eyes large as though waiting for an unexpected blow and saw his face soften when he realized how worried I was.

"I looked through the report on Suzy Marsh's suicide."

"Oh?" I asked, wondering at the way people in law enforcement spent their free time.

"No one on the scene that night believed she killed herself. None of her friends remember her ever being depressed. Flaky, yes, but not depressed."

I didn't answer, just stared out the windshield at all the people who had gathered to watch the game.

"I think they ruled it suicide because they didn't have anything else to go on."

I continued to scan the crowd, caught between wondering where his parents might be and what he was getting at.

"You were right when you said she looked like you," he paused. "Like Karen."

My felt heart hitch, hating the way his fear spread to me like a contagious disease.

"I just want you to take extra precautions until we catch the guy who did this."

I frowned, his words making me feel like a concerned citizen talking to a detached cop. "You think there's a serial killer on the loose who has a thing for blondes? In that case you should arrest Jamie Stoddard, since he killed Karen, plain and simple."

He was silent for a moment, hurt by my words and how I'd thrown his own back at him.

Immediately I felt ashamed, and embarrassed, realizing that the stress of the past few weeks was beginning to take a toll and I needed to come clean by confessing to the kiss.

Right now.

"I'm sorry, Dylan."

He chuckled, "Thought you were going to stop saying that."

"I thought so, too. Listen—I need to tell you something. It's been bothering me and—"

He held his hand up, "Can it wait? My sister's coming over."

It sure as hell could, but I knew the longer I waited the more likely I would end up stalling or just hoping the whole thing would go away.

Which could happen since Brad was currently in Webber and likely to remain there.

Still, I needed him to trust me, and how could he if I never told him about kissing an ex-boyfriend in my apartment? But if I did tell him and he flipped out and dumped me…I looked out the window, suddenly nauseous and decided Dylan's little sister might have just saved my ass.

"Hey, Dyl," I heard her voice, sweet and high and cheerful, just as I'd expected, drifting through the driver's side door. "Thanks for coming."

"No problem," he leaned out and kissed her on the cheek and I glanced at her for the first time. She looked about twenty years old and was cute as a button in a red and white uniform, her long hair pulled back in a ponytail, her blue eyes sparkling when they saw me, the new girlfriend.

"Avery, this is Justine."

"Hi, Justine!" she reached in and shook my hand. "So nice to meet you. I've heard a lot of good things."

I looked at Dylan, who smiled and glanced away.

How cute… He'd told his sister about me… *Good things* about me.

"Nice to meet you, Avery," I smiled back, hoping that we could be friends, wondering if that would be possible if things went bad in a big way.

Cross that bridge when you come to it…

"Mom's running late," Avery continued, flipping her ponytail over her shoulder while giving her brother's arm a squeeze. "You never know who you're going to run into on the Lakefield Park bleachers."

"Yeah," Dylan chuckled. "Or the Cat Scratch Tavern."

Avery laughed, and I felt at ease, hoping her mother would be similar but knowing the chances were slim if she dressed to the nines for something like this.

"Gotta go!" Avery stepped back, "Stop down at the library sometime and see me, Justine."

"I will," I said quickly, realizing seconds later Dylan must have told her about the time I'd stalked him.

At least they didn't keep secrets.

Which was more than I could say for myself.

Moments later we were seated in the middle of the bleachers, Dylan's sister planted firmly at third base. I was struck again by how cute she was, how I'd felt when I saw them together in the truck and imagined what it would be like to see him with a girl he couldn't explain away with genetics.

The thought was enough to make me reconsider my stance on the "Brad Debacle," which made me feel like throwing up again.

As if on cue, he asked, "What were you going to say before Avery came up?"

"Hmmm," I began, stalling. "Can't remember."

"You said it was bothering you."

I fought frantically for a thought, any thought that would seem logical and locked in on the one thing I knew would throw him off. "When you said they liked all your girlfriends, did that mean Karen, too?"

He looked at me like I had a flock of penguins pouring tea on top of my head. "I never told them... I mean...they knew her from school and everything but... Are you worried they won't like you?"

"Yes!" I said quickly. "I am. And Avery said your mom really dresses up for these things and I don't really feel—"

"Mom would dress up to take a shit."

I laughed so loud the people around me turned.

"Don't worry. There's no reason she wouldn't like you."

Except for the fact that I'm a liar who has paranormal visions that cause me to wander around and almost fall off breakwalls, a married ex-lover who has a tendency to show up unannounced, an absentee father who has a second family stashed away at Three Fires Lodge, and a crazy grandmother who may have lynched an innocent man. But aside from that, Mrs. Locke—I'd be a perfect candidate for your son.

I felt another stomachache coming on, and so politely declined when Dylan asked if I wanted anything from the pavilion.

And as I waited for him to return I scanned the faces of the people sitting nearby. No one seemed interested in me, and yet a strange, prickly feeling sent the hairs on the back of my neck on end.

Then I saw him on the first set of risers behind home plate.

Adam...

Pam's red head bobbed beside him, as did Jamie's tousled brown one—his arm slung over my brother's shoulder.

I drew a sharp breath.

YOU DON'T LIKE HIM, DO YOU?

I didn't know how to answer.

HE SAVED MY LIFE ON THE BREAKWALL

I KNOW

BUT HE'S KEEPING SOMETHING FROM US. I SAW A PICTURE AT THE CAMP—

OF WHAT?

JAMIE STODDARD… I THINK HE WAS THERE ONE HUNDRED YEARS AGO

I caught sight of Dylan standing in line by the pavilion. Glancing my way, he gave a wave and I raised my hand in return.

THAT'S IMPOSSIBLE

I put a hand to my temple and rubbed as a headache began to build behind my eyes.

I KNOW WHAT I SAW

BUT THAT WOULD MEAN—

The sights and sounds of the game seemed to still around me as I tried to come to terms with this realization.

HE'S ALREADY DEAD

Pam turned, saw me sitting alone and waved me over. I shook my head and pointed to Dylan, who was weaving his way through the crowd as Jamie glanced up. His eyes stopped me cold, stopped my thoughts and left me wondering at the extent of his own powers.

Dylan was climbing the bleachers now, only feet away.

MAYBE IT'S THE OTHER WAY AROUND?

WHAT DO YOU MEAN?

MAYBE HE NEVER DIED AT ALL

Dylan sat down, hot dog in hand, his attention momentarily diverted by a Silver Escalade and the blonde woman stepping from it.

His mother, dressed in a cream silk blouse and pressed khaki slacks. Dylan turned, a flustered look on his face and said, "I need to go help Mom."

"Sure," I nodded. "I'll save your seat."

He took off at a fast pace as I remained on the bleachers, trying not to squirm and let the world know how uncomfortable I was when I felt the familiar fullness in my ears that told me a vision was coming. I closed my eyes, hoping I didn't stand up and take a nosedive over the bleachers and saw Butler running through the forest, Jonas Younts close behind. The next second Butler jumped over

142

a log, stumbled and fell as Jonas Younts closed the gap between them, his face displayed plainly for the first time.

The next instant, I was jolted back to the present as the cheers of the people nearby told me Dylan's sister had just tagged a girl at third.

I glanced towards Adam, my pulse catching in my throat because I'd seen the face of the man who'd been hung at Back Forty Farm, the same man who had overtaken Butler in the woods and watched as Esther Ebersole bled to death from a bullet fired by her husband.

A bullet that was meant for him.

I saw him leaning on an upended bucksaw, the face of the person who had saved me on the breakwall.

Jamie Stoddard and Jonas Younts were one and the same.

And I wasn't sure how long Adam and I could hide.

* * *

"Mom, this is Justine."

I started, forgetting where I was for the moment, then hopped from the bleachers and extended my hand to a slim woman standing beside Dylan. Her wheat-colored hair was swept back by a pair of Gucci sunglasses as she dazzled me with a peroxide-enhanced smile.

"So pleased to meet you."

I shook and didn't let go, perhaps to keep my wits about me before another vision swept me from her good graces forever.

"Thank you, Mrs. Locke."

"Call me Melinda."

Dylan put a hand on my shoulder, applied pressure, and I wasn't sure if he was trying to reassure me or get me to sit back down. I sat down.

"Did you save a place for Dad?"

The question held something I couldn't distinguish until I saw a woman in nurses' scrubs pushing a man in a wheelchair across the parking lot.

"That's him," Dylan offered, his hand never leaving my shoulder and in that touch, I felt his shame and anger and uncertainty. Turning to look, I caught him gazing towards the pavilion, unable to meet my eyes.

I couldn't ask, couldn't assume anyone would fill me in on why the man I'd seen standing in the photos was now unable to walk the few steps it took to reach the bleachers.

I tried to speak, pity and compassion rendering my tongue useless before Melinda said, "You're probably wondering what happened to my husband."

I nodded.

"You didn't tell her?" she turned to her son, readjusted her sunglasses and in that movement, I sensed her annoyance. "Michael's been ill for some time now." She glanced again to Dylan and I saw her lips tighten into a thin line. "He had a stroke and hasn't bounced back like we had hoped."

"I'm sorry," I said, feeling the inadequacy of my words.

"Don't be," his mother patted my hand. "Dylan should have told you."

I looked down, not daring a glance at my boyfriend and still, something told me there was more to the story.

"Practicing law is an impossibility for him now so we're trying to find someone to take over at the firm," she paused, put a finger just beneath her nose as though she might sneeze. "But we haven't found the right person."

"Mom," Dylan spoke for the first time, dropping beside me as I sat wedged between the two.

"What did I say?" she turned to me, shrugged her shoulders in a way that made me believe they'd had this conversation before. "I'm just expressing my opinion regarding the future of the firm your father worked his whole life to build."

"I'm not a lawyer," Dylan said, and I felt him pull away from me in the slightest, his whole body rigid on the metal bleachers. "Dad knew that when he hired John."

"John's not family," Melinda said quickly. "Your father—"

"Get off my back."

"If I were on your back you'd know it," she said, her tone reminding me of my own mother. Turning to me, she patted my hand and said, "He's always been so stubborn. We had a scholarship all lined up for him to study law at U of M and what do you think he does? Throws it away."

"I didn't throw it away, Mom," he said. "I was never a genius before you got it into your head to pay for law school."

"You had one semester left."

I saw him tense, saw his jaw muscles working in the way they always did when he was trying to keep his emotions in check. "Dad had a stroke."

His mother turned, leaned over me and I wished I could sink into the bleachers and let them go at it honestly.

"I was handling things."

"Don't remind me."

Melinda sighed and readjusted her sunglasses again. Dylan took this as his cue to stretch his legs and I was thankful for a breather of my own. After a minute had passed his mother flashed a brilliant smile.

"I apologize, Justine. We shouldn't air our dirty laundry in public."

"It's okay," I mumbled, wanting to stretch my legs myself and yet my affection for her son held me fast to my bleacher seat.

"Thank you for saying so." She turned back to the game. "Avery tells me you and Dylan are getting serious."

Avery had told her... That wouldn't have made her happy. Still, I was glad to hear third- hand that our relationship status was secure.

"Yeah," I agreed. "He's wonderful."

"He is," she smiled without turning her head. "But as I told you before, very stubborn."

I smiled, tried to steal a glance at the man in question but he'd already moved away to speak to his father's nurse. I saw him shove his hands in his pockets, rock back on his heels while his father's eyes followed the game.

"I don't know why he never told me," I found myself saying, wondering if I could trust this woman to give me an answer that wouldn't hurt me.

"My son is on a 'need to know' basis with practically everyone," she smiled again, gave me a sideways glance. "Maybe you can change that."

I didn't answer, just sat watching the game as she began asking questions that were obviously intended to assess my eligibility.

"What do you do for a living?"

I tried to stall, tried to think of something incredibly glamorous and came up with, "I tend bar with Mallard Brauski out at Huff's."

Her face crinkled at the corners. "Lucky girl."

I chuckled and felt like a fool. "Tips are good and I didn't really have time to scope out jobs in my profession."

She turned and I saw a reflection of myself in her sunglasses. "What is the scope of your profession?"

"I'm a journalist," I said, not bothering to mention how small the newspaper was and what sort of stories I covered.

"A journalist," she repeated, her Gucci's moving from left to right. "How interesting."

"I wrote for a newspaper downstate," I took a breath, glanced back at Dylan and knew he wouldn't be joining us anytime soon.

"In the city?"

I shook my head. "In a small town called Webber."

"I've never heard of it."

"You're not alone."

Melinda reached out, patted my knee. "Going back anytime soon?"

I gave her a puzzled look. Did she want to ship me off already? "Not if I can help it."

She laughed, patted me once more and I felt my ears filling up, felt my body flush with heat and fought with everything I had to stifle it. No way was I going into a trance with Dylan's mom sitting next to me, and so I gripped the bottom of the bleacher until it bit into my skin and felt the pain dull my senses.

Just then Melinda turned, a concerned scrunch to her tinted countenance. "My dear—"

"I'm okay," I mumbled, pressing harder. My ears began to ring, my body to shake.

"You certainly don't look like it," she turned, searching for Dylan.

"She just needs some food," he answered, and I had no idea how he'd gotten to me so quickly. "Low blood sugar. She didn't have lunch."

I heard his mother mumble a rebuke as we moved past her, Dylan's arm around my waist as he led me away from the crowd and back towards the parking lot.

"That was a close one," he said. "Mom would've freaked if you'd fallen over and crinkled her favorite slacks. "

I giggled, still woozy from being pulled out of the vision so quickly, felt myself being pressed into something hard and realized we were against the side of his truck.

"Can you talk?"

I took a breath, steadied myself and whispered, "Yeah."

"What was it?"

I shook my head, gave him a smile. "It wasn't anything."

"How?" he asked, "I looked up and thought you were going to topple over into Mom's lap."

I held up my hand, saw the red welt that just fit the groove of the bleacher seat. "I gripped the seat so hard that the pain stopped the vision."

He seemed confused, "You can stop it? With pain?"

"I think so," I mumbled, suddenly hopeful that this new part of my life could somehow be controlled. But did I want to stop the visions if they could give me the information I wanted, especially where Jamie Stoddard was concerned?

"That's good, J," he said.

Yep, being able to control my freaky ability was so much better than not having to deal with it at all.

"Hopefully this will all stop once I find my dad and get the hell out of this creepy town."

I felt him draw back.

"When you what?"

"Nothing," I said quickly, wishing another vision would wipe me out so he'd have no alternative but to bundle me up and take me home.

"Are you taking off after you find your dad?"

I looked at him, looked away, more miserable than I'd ever been.

"What if you don't find him?"

I glanced down, not sure how I felt about Lantern Creek minus the supernatural happenings. Although the scenery was nice.

"You know I can't leave town," he finally said.

"Why would I know that?" I asked, suddenly angry at him, at me—for assuming he would want to leave everything behind for a girl he couldn't say he loved.

"Things are complicated," he said slowly, thoughtfully and I wanted to hit him for using the same line twice. "Dad needs me."

"I know," I nodded, loving that he cared so much, hating that he cared so much. "You should be here. But Avery—"

"Needs to live her life."

"Your mom—"

His laughter startled me, and I could sense the sadness behind it. "Are you serious? All she cares about is that stupid firm and how much money she's losing every day because John isn't in the 'family.' Dad always took care of her," he stopped, put a hand to his forehead. "You'd think she'd return the favor."

"Doesn't she?" I asked, feeling like I was walking on eggshells, afraid of pushing too far.

"She has a nurse for that. Doesn't want to get her hands dirty."

"Maybe you're not giving her a chance—"

"Stop, Justine," he said, his voice firm and I did just that. Arguing wouldn't help, and I knew it was selfish to want him to go. But I wanted to be selfish, to wrap him up in my arms and keep him forever.

"I'm sorry," he whispered, pulling me into an embrace. "I should've told you about Dad right away but I kept hoping I'd get over it, get over you," he smiled in a way that made me want him. "But it doesn't look like that's going to happen anytime soon."

"Are you trying to sweet talk me?" I closed my eyes, leaned into his chest.

"Is it working?"

I smiled, nodded against his shirt.

"Stay here with me," he said, his arms tightening in the slightest and I wondered if it would be okay to dream that I could start over here.

I smiled, ready with a request of my own. "Introduce me to your father."

He kissed the top of my head. "You've got a deal."

Chapter Nineteen

"Beautiful day."

I started and looked up to see Pam standing over me as I stretched my legs outside of Cabin Three. Twisting my hair over my left shoulder, I noted the way it curled in the heat.

"Daydreaming?" she asked.

"Just thinking that summer is more than half over."

"What are your plans?" She asked, sitting down beside me.

"Not sure," I put a hand up and shaded my eyes against the sun.

"Seems like you might have an incentive to stay."

I looked down at my feet and grinned.

"Your father would be happy."

I gazed past her and towards the lake, my heart jumping in the slightest. I wanted to argue, to tell her she had no right to mention him, but the time for that had passed. "You think so?"

"I know it," she leaned her head back, closed her eyes. "His mother would be, too."

"His mother?" I repeated. Never in my life had anyone mentioned my paternal grandparents—or lack thereof. Dad had told me they died of sickness before I was born. Mom never wanted to talk about them at all.

And I'd kept my mouth shut, content with occasional visits from Grandpa Greer on my mother's side, wondering why something I'd never had in the first place seemed to be missing.

"Haven't you figured it out, yet?" Pam asked.

Something in her eyes told me all I needed to know, what I'd secretly suspected since the moment she'd mouthed the words "Take him" during our bar fight.

"Iris?"

Pam didn't answer, just bent over to pat Rocky.

"But I thought *you* were her daughter."

"You thought wrong."

"You told me wrong."

"You weren't ready. She wasn't ready," Pam began, a calmness to her I'd never seen before. "She couldn't get close for the same reason Robert had to get away. They wanted to protect you."

Protect me? Suddenly everyone wanted to do that.

"From what?"

She dropped her voice, as though she didn't want to say the words but knew she had to. "Red Rover."

I felt like someone had jabbed me with a hot poker. Sitting upright, I turned to her and touched her arm, hoping she could finish what her son had started.

"Adam—"

"Told me about him," she shook her head, pressed her lips together and looked up at the sky. "I think he told you, too."

"What?" I asked, playing dumb. "You know that's not possible."

"Is it?"

"Yes," I said, my words dying on my tongue. It was useless, and I was only hurting myself by not letting her help me. "Do you hear him, too?"

She paused, unnerved by our conversation. I, on the other hand, felt grateful that someone was acknowledging something. Anything.

"I thought so. A long time ago—"

"How," I began, wanting to understand but knowing I couldn't put the pieces together with a journalist's logic.

"It was wishful thinking," she said. "But now I know—"

"He talks to me."

"Yes," she said. "When Adam was young, he used to draw pictures of a man without a face."

"Red Rover?" I asked

She nodded. "When I asked him who Red Rover was, he wrote 'The Bad Man.'"

"Geez, Pam," I felt gooseflesh rising on my arms and quickly rubbed them. "I think this…Red Rover might have broken into my apartment."

"He knows about you two. And now that you're together it makes it easier for him to find you."

I looked at her, incredulous, then pulled my feet in and hugged my knees. "How do you know this?"

"Robert," she said, and in that one word a million assumptions strung together like a pearl necklace, broke and shattered.

"Dad knew? How could he? I don't understand—" I asked all at once, my mind a jumble as a cool breeze blew in from the lake and across my neck, stirring the water.

"Your father was a Cook and that name comes with a price to pay up here. I knew it, too—and when Adam was born I wasn't surprised when he left us."

"Why would he leave you? Why would he leave *me*?" I asked, the last question breaking free from my body with a sort of forced tension.

"It's easier for Red Rover to find you when you're together. Your power, your medicine, leaves a trace behind that he can sense and now it grows stronger. Robert never wanted you to know about your brother, never wanted to visit this kind of pain on you—"

I stood up, turned in a circle and gripped the railing of the porch. "What does he know about pain? Growing up without a father—why didn't he stay and *fight* for us?"

She shook her head, her own shoulders hunched, and I knew the conversation was just as awful for her as it was for me. "I wish I knew, Justine. Robert wanted to protect us, and he thought he could do that by leaving. I knew Red Rover had something to do with the story about Odessa and the Indian. I knew it was some sort of spirit sent here to hurt Robert's children, but I thought if I didn't believe in it…if I just kept quiet it would never find us."

"And do you feel safe, Pam? Out here in the woods with Red Rover wandering around at night?"

She looked up, her face a contorted mask of hurt and I regretted my words, regretted that I'd awakened my brother's nightmares in her memory. Maybe if I'd stayed home and ignored the picture I'd seen in the paper, everyone would be safe. Dylan, Adam, Pam, Iris…

But no one was safe. Not even a girl who could tackle three roughnecks without so much as a scratch.

I touched my necklace.

"I'm sorry, Pam. I don't understand any of this and I just want—"

"I know what you want. I wish I could give it to you."

I sat down beside her again, put a careful arm around her shoulders to let her know we were on the same side, despite everything. I waited, to see if she would accept the gesture and to my surprise, she laid her head on my shoulder and began to weep.

"I'm so afraid, Justine. Please know I never meant to hurt you or your mother. Please—"

"I know—"

"Things keep happening. Adam's restless in the night—I hear noises outside and God help me, I want to protect him, but I don't think I can. I don't think I was *meant* to."

I leaned in, touched her head to my own. "Why don't you run? Take Adam and get out of here?"

She pulled away, looked into my eyes. "Why don't you?"

I drew back.

"Because you know he'd find you."

She was right. I'd been drawn to Lantern Creek by the picture I'd seen in the newspaper, drawn to Dylan and Adam the first moment I'd met them, drawn to the photograph at Camp Menominee and the lighthouse and the tree that had caught fire but never burned at Back Forty Farm.

I stood up and dusted my hands on the butt of my jeans.

"I'm going to see my grandmother."

* * *

Iris stood in her garden surrounded by coneflowers and daylilies, wearing a blouse that caught fire in the sunlight, her hair tucked beneath the hat she'd been wearing the day we first met.

I slid from the Jeep and walked the few steps between us.

"Iris?"

She raised her eyes.

"Justine." And something in my thoughts must have told her everything because she laid her trowel aside, pushed her hat from the crown of her head so she could embrace me, her thin arms reaching around my back.

I couldn't speak for several minutes as she held me, whispering words that somehow helped to mend what had been broken years before.

"How did you know?" she asked.

It took me a moment to answer, "I think I always did."

"Of course," she smiled, her eyes dancing in the same way my father's had. "You can feel it."

I smiled.

"I'm sorry," she pulled back and held me at arm's length, the sun casting shadows between us. "I should never have left you alone with your mother."

I looked away. "No, you shouldn't have." No anger. No sadness. Simply a statement expressing fact.

And my grandmother did not take the blame upon herself, which I admired and someday hoped to emulate. "It wasn't your fault, Justine. She was so angry at Robert. So hurt by the way he handled things that at first I couldn't blame her."

"Iris—"

"Can you come inside?"

I nodded, followed her into the apartment and took a seat at her tiny kitchen table while she peeled off her gloves. Moments later she pulled two glasses from the cupboard and began pouring lemonade.

"I'm not sure what your mother told you."

I reached for a glass, took a sip. "Not much."

"Your father's heart was always bigger than his brain," she began while slipping into the seat opposite me, her fingers working the red fabric of her gingham tablecloth. "Never able to look ahead and see what was coming down the pike."

I took another sip. "You mean Pam?"

Iris sighed. "He fell hard and quick. Before long she was pregnant, and he didn't know what to tell your mother."

I looked down, fingered the same square of gingham. "But he did tell her, didn't he?"

Iris nodded, then glanced at me. "You grew up so pretty, Muffet."

I smiled, my heart in a place it had never been before.

"I gave you that nickname the first time you spilled your milk. Said a spider must have crawled up and scared you."

I felt a tingle in my nose. "I don't remember you."

"That's how I wanted it."

I swallowed again, took another quick sip.

"I thought staying away would make it better—would break the tie you had to this place and the things that happened here."

"It didn't."

She sighed, "We hoped nothing would come of my grandfather's stories but then you cut your knee climbing that silo—got that scar and Robert knew he had to act fast."

I looked up, found her face framed in sadness. "What stories?"

Iris got up from her place and wandered to the window to look outside at a world splashed in sunlight. Bending over, she worked the latch and opened our conversation to the birdsong that spilled through the screen.

"Calvert Cook," she began, her back to me as I held my glass. "Knew the Shaman well."

"Butler?" I whispered.

"He loved Odessa very much. Wanted a veil of protection to cover her and Cal should anything ever happen to him, but the medicine was too powerful, too alluring, and it attracted the attention of a young man who wanted to cheat death."

"Jonas Younts?" I asked, and Iris turned.

"You know?"

I nodded.

"When Jonas left Back Forty Farm the night of the murders, he went to Odessa's house and stole the medicine bag. Then he tracked the Shaman down, forced him to perform black magic in order to get what he wanted."

I frowned. "What was that?"

"Esther Ebersole."

"I don't understand."

"He'd heard the men in town talking about how the Shaman could resurrect a body. Odessa's dimwitted brother Johnson swore he'd seen it done to one of their barn cats and Jonas thought—"

"That he could bring her back to life."

Iris nodded. "He must have been crazy with grief. But something went wrong and it turned him into an unnatural creature."

"Iris—"

"Something that would never die."

"What happened to Butler?" I asked, my heart racing to beat the band, my palms beginning to sweat.

"He was never heard from again."

"Do you think Jonas killed him?"

She shook her head. "They never found a body. Grandpa Cal told me Odessa looked day and night for him."

My mind went to a dark place, imagining for a moment what I would do if Dylan vanished without a trace.

"You're very strong, Justine," she said.

"No, I'm not."

"Grandpa told me the girl with the scar on her knee would put an end to it all."

"Anyone could have a scar."

"He said her brother would speak with his mind instead of his mouth." She paused, looked at me long and hard. "Does he?"

"Stop trying to convince me I'm something I'm not."

"Don't punish yourself for Robert's decision." She covered my hand with her own. "He left because he loved you, because he wanted to face your enemy so you wouldn't have to."

I swallowed, thinking again about Pam and her speech on the deck of Cabin Three. "I don't have any enemies, Iris."

"I would beg to differ."

My comeback died in my throat as I stared into the lemonade- bits of pulp floating as freely as an amoeba in a Petri dish. "You're scaring me."

"You need to be."

"Fighting a group of roughnecks is one thing. Tackling some sort of immortal monster disguised as my handyman is not in my job description."

"Then go."

I tried to laugh, tried to take another sip of lemonade but the taste made me sick. No way was I going to clean up the mess that Jonas Younts and Butler had stirred up. This was their problem, and if I drove fast enough I could probably make it to Grand Rapids by dinnertime.

"You want to leave us all behind? Then do it."

"I don't—" I began, but found my resolve weakening as I thought of the person who'd been killing girls who looked like me. A person who could have let me fall into Lake Huron but didn't.

Iris came closer, the birdsong at her right shoulder as she splayed both hands on the red gingham. "You want answers? Close your eyes and make it happen."

"I can't control it."

She pounded her fist on the table. "You can!"

I started, my eyes wide and then did as I was told. I thought about the yellow liquid wavering in the glass before me, thought about Pam and Rocky sitting on the steps of Cabin Three—and Dylan, his back exposed to the sun as the medicine wheel rotated in a shimmer of radiance.

I saw Jonas Younts sink to his knees, Esther Ebersole in his arms as Abraham took a step closer and aimed the pistol for a second shot. The next instant Abraham's body jerked forward as though spun on an imaginary axis. He stumbled, gripping his stomach as fluid oozed from a gaping wound in his abdomen.

I saw Jonas cry out, saw Abraham fall at his feet as another shot split his head in two.

I was just turning to run when a second figure emerged from the shadow of Abraham Ebersole's barn. A large man with wide strides, a shotgun clasped firmly in his hand as he closed the distance between himself and a grief-stricken Jonas Younts.

"What do you see?" I heard Iris ask as if from a great distance.

"I thought Jonas was Red Rover but...there are two of them."

She drew a sharp breath. "What does the other one look like?"

I squinted, tried to look at the man, but his hat was low and his chin covered in whiskers. He pulled Jonas up by the scruff of his neck and tossed him towards the house.

Jonas yowled in pain, scrambled towards the front porch as the large man heaved the body of Abraham Ebersole over his left shoulder and made for the house. Moments later he returned for Esther.

"He's staging a scene," I said, my hands slippery on the wet glass between my fingers. "He wants to make it look like they were killed inside the house, that the man who did it had a grudge against Abraham for cheating him out of that gelding."

I waited a moment, then moved—my feet leaving no marks as the barnyard melted into a forest scene.

"Look closely," I heard Iris say. "Tell me who he is."

"It's dark," I managed. "They're chasing Butler."

"Stay with it," Iris was at my side, supporting me. "Just a bit longer."

I heard her, felt her bony fingers grip my shoulder as the large man overtook Butler and began beating him around the face and shoulders, dragging him back towards Ocqueoc Falls.

I followed, until I came to the island in the marsh where the circle had been drawn. A snakeskin was deposited in the center. A fire was lit and lock of long, dark hair I assumed was Esther's held against the licking flames. Butler was hoisted to his feet as the large man pointed the shotgun at his head, demanding the resurrection be performed or Odessa and Cal would pay for it.

I watched as Butler took the medicine bag in his hands, shook out the totems and began putting them inside the wheel while Jonas and his mysterious companion looked on.

And then he looked up, saw me standing in the shadows and shifted his aim. I dropped to my belly as blood rushed through my ears and eyes and nose—a surge of adrenaline propelling me through the underbrush on all fours.

He'd seen me, in my own time and place and I didn't know how it was possible, but it meant Iris was right and Adam and I had one hell of an enemy.

"Justine!" I heard Iris cry. "You need to come back now."

I was aware of that. But damned if I knew how.

"He killed Abraham." She stopped short, began shaking me. "He'll kill you, too."

I didn't need her to paint a picture as I lay on my stomach surrounded by ferns and a mishmash of pulpy wood and mud. I felt myself sinking, felt myself suffocating in the soft earth that cradled the Falls. I thought of Dylan and what would happen if I didn't make it back.

A picture of him weaving his way through the bleachers, hot dog in hand, came to my mind. And my hands, gripping the sharp metal beneath my seat until my hand exploded in pain.

Pain!

I searched for something to jam into my leg, grasped a piece of bark and felt it come apart in my hands.

"Justine," Iris cried. "Think about something in the room, something concrete."

I tried to imagine the glass of lemonade and how cool it felt between my fingers but all I could see was the earth and sky in a continuous loop and the water rushing up to greet me in a frothy foam.

A shotgun blast rang out. A small tree splintered beside me.

"Stop!" I heard Jonas yell. "Leave her be!"

The large man did not answer. He shot again and this time the shell embedded itself in the earth I'd rolled over two seconds before.

I heard the click, knew he was out of ammunition as I looked up into his darkened face, the butt end of the shotgun raised high to crush my skull. I grimaced, the strength I needed suddenly materializing as I reached up and took hold of the end. One twist and the gun was free and flying through the air.

I heard him grunt and the next instant he was upon me, his heavy hands around my throat as I fought to pry them apart.

"Too tight?" he smiled, his breath rank and foul.

I gasped, flashes of light exploding behind my eyelids.

He laughed while turning to glance at my writhing legs and the long, white scar that lanced my left kneecap. "Nice to meet you, Muffet."

I gasped again, the only air I had left as I felt a searing pain swipe at my cheeks. I touched my face, saw my grandmother standing over me and realized she had just slapped me.

Hard.

"That was a close one."

I blinked, touched my cheek again.

"Now he knows who you are."

"Iris—" I began, my hands going to my throat in an effort to rub the memory of his hands away. "Is he going to kill me?"

"He'll try."

"What do I do now?"

She sank into the chair opposite.

"Kill him first."

Chapter Twenty

Twenty-four hours had gone by since the incident in Iris' kitchen, hours that I passed in a state of almost complete paranoia compounded by trying to figure out how someone could almost kill me in a vision. The same person who'd glimpsed my scar and called me by my pet name.

I was debating how to break the news to Dylan when he dropped by for a surprise visit while I was cleaning Cabin Five.

"Oh, hey," I smiled while pushing my hair behind my ear, suddenly bashful. "What're you doing here?"

He tried to smile but couldn't. "It's Dad."

I tossed my dust rag on the counter and crossed the distance between us. His arms closed around me as he buried his face in my hair.

"We thought he'd be better by now," he mumbled. "And now Mom's talking about getting rid of the nurse and putting him in a home."

I pulled away, looked into his eyes. "I'm so sorry."

He shrugged, and in that simple gesture, I sensed his vulnerability, his embarrassment at having tracked me down in the middle of my workday. "You think I'd be used to her passive aggressive bullshit by now. This is all because of what happened at the game."

I reached up, touched his face and asked, "What can I do?"

He tried to smile again and succeeded. "Make him better."

I closed my eyes, put my forehead against his, grateful I hadn't told him anything about Brad or Jonas or Red Rover yet, wanting to protect him for as long as I possibly could.

"There is something you can do," he said, tracing my jaw with his thumb and I looked at him, suddenly desperate for a physical release of my own. I brought his lips to mine and in an instant he had me around the waist, pulling me against him.

Moments later I was leading him to the sectional couch, my own troubled thoughts driving my desire.

"Where's Pam?" he asked.

"Stuck at the front desk." I smiled against his mouth, tracing his bottom lip with my tongue. "Shouldn't be done with paperwork for an hour."

He splayed his hands on my back, lowered me to the cushions. "Which is fifty-two minutes more than I need."

I giggled, loving his humor even as my body began to ache with the need to possess him.

His fingers found a bare expanse of my hip. Working downward, he had my shorts unbuttoned before I could draw a pleasured breath.

"God, you're beautiful," he whispered, and I felt his hand slide under my T-shirt and unclasp my bra. The next moment his lips were feathering the soft shell of my ear, leaving it only to travel down my throat to my breasts, where I felt my nipples pucker inside of his warm mouth.

I heard someone moaning and realized it was me. I reached up, grasped the wooden arm of the couch, and turned my head to the side.

He was kissing my stomach now, my belly button, my hipbones, tracing lazy circles with his tongue and I felt my fingers curl against the couch, soft against the flush of my palms.

Moments later he returned to my side, put his arms up as I yanked his shirt off. His pants came next, and before a minute had passed he was naked beside me.

I reached up to touch his chest, to smooth my fingers over his tanned flesh.

"Feel better?" I asked, my heart pounding in my ears.

"Much," he smiled, and I hooked my arms under his while resting my heels in the soft hollow just behind his bent knees.

I've had the same dream since I was a kid...

Had it included a picture of us making love in Cabin Five while the sunshine fell into a welcoming lap of water outside the picture window?

Did it include anything beyond the summer? Next week?

Tonight?

When it was over I kissed his ribcage, his collarbone, then rose up on my elbows and looked into his eyes.

"We'd better get going," he smiled, "my eight minutes are up."

I giggled, sat up and allowed him to help me back into my bra. Even this simple gesture was filled with kindness as his hands brushed over my shoulders, adjusting the straps, bending his head to kiss where he had touched and in my heart. I wanted to repay him in some small way for what he had given me.

The next moment, I was removing my necklace, placing it around his neck as though it would help in some way. I wasn't sure how he would take it, what he would think it meant.

"Why would you give this to me?" he asked. "It's from your dad."

I smiled, reaching up to touch it, the silver so beautiful against his tanned skin. "I don't know. It just feels right."

"Are you sure?"

I leaned closer, kissed his lips lightly. "You said you liked it."

"I do," he replied, shifting his weight on the couch, his elbow grazing the coffee table where I had laid my purse.

The next second, he upended it, the contents spilling onto the area rug.

At once Dylan knelt to help me pick up, his fingers going still as he came across a business card that had fallen from some random pocket I hadn't checked in months—a memento from the first time I'd interviewed Brad.

"What's this?" he asked, flicking it between his index and middle finger.

I felt my face go hot and hugged my shoulders, wishing I'd thrown the stupid thing away the moment he'd given it to me. "It's nothing."

"You sure?"

I didn't answer, just reached out and took the card and stuffed it back in my purse.

Dylan stood slowly, his eyes never leaving mine. "A friend of mine owns a shop downtown. Said a guy was in there last week asking about you." He let the sentence die, looked at me for a beat before saying, "He left the same card."

I felt like I'd been dumped in an ice bath.

"He said you were looking to buy car insurance."

"Dylan—"

"Let me guess," he said. "The guy with the full plate?"

I cleared my throat, bent over to retrieve his shirt and handed it to him.

He took it in one hand, pulled it over his head but didn't speak, didn't smile, just stood and waited.

"We were together for a while, but it never went anywhere," I paused. "He was married."

I sensed his disappointment, his displeasure, and wilted beneath it.

"I'm not proud of it," I said.

He would not meet my eyes. "Why was he in town?"

I couldn't answer and so I reached up, my fingers glazing his collarbone and for the first time felt the intensity of the love he'd been unable to verbalize and knew I had to tell the truth.

"He called a few weeks ago and I broke it off," I whispered, the complexity of his emotions making speech difficult. "He didn't take it well."

His heart was beating quickly. His muscles tight. And still, he waited.

"He wanted me to go back to Webber with him."

"Woah," he put up a hand, backed away. "Are you serious?"

I nodded, frightened now.

"Why did it take a business card for you to come clean?"

"I tried to at the softball game, but Avery came up and then—"

"I asked you what was bothering you. You lied to me."

I glanced away, hurt by his words but grateful he was talking. "I wanted to forget it—pretend it never happened and I know it was wrong and I should have told you."

"Yeah," he ran a hand over his hair, capped his head with it. "Makes me wonder what else you're hiding."

I looked down, deep shame staining my cheeks as I pushed my hair back again in what was becoming a nervous gesture.

"Did he try something?"

I looked into his eyes, saw the anger and frustration and knew I had to tell the truth or risk losing him forever.

"Yes."

His jaw tightened, the lips that had given me such pleasure minutes before a thin line of disgust. And I wondered if he would rip the necklace off and throw it back in my face.

But he didn't.

"Did you kiss him?"

I swallowed, my face anguished, and Dylan didn't approach me or take me into his arms to comfort me as he had in the past.

"Yes," I managed to choke out. "But then I told him to leave."

"After you kissed him?"

"He kissed me!" I cried, terrified by how fast my heart was beating, by what I would do to make him stay. "And I hated it."

"Then why didn't you tell me?"

I opened my mouth to argue. Shut it again. Out of excuses.

"You obviously don't trust me."

"No," I begged, tears welling up over my eyelids. "I do…I love you—"

He stood silently for a moment, then turned on his heel while muttering, "I've gotta get out of here."

"No," I cried while jumping to my feet. "Please don't leave."

He didn't stop, but I caught him on the bottom step of the porch.

"Are you—?" I felt like vomiting. "Are you breaking up with me?"

Could he even? Tattoos and scars and intertwined destinies considered?

"I need some time," he looked up, his eyes filled with grim resolve. "And I need some space."

"What does that mean?" I asked, my mind flashing to Holly and her melodramatic 'He Turns Girls Into Zombies' story. Mission accomplished, Locke.

"Don't call me."

I gripped the railing as he turned his back and strode off down the gravel road that led to the main lodge. Seconds later he climbed into his truck and slammed the door, roaring away in a show of masculine fury I felt certain Pam would want to know about.

I closed my eyes, tried to breathe, tried to convince myself that this was only temporary and that a couple of nights alone in the lake house would provide him with all the "time" and "space" needed.

Dazed, I turned in a half circle and stared at Cabin Five, Rocky's mellow bawl announcing the approach of the woman my father hadn't seen coming down the pike.

His heart was always bigger than his brain...

Maybe we were more alike than I thought.

* * *

I'm not sure how I made it home that afternoon, the road seemed to bend in places it never had before as I drove back to my apartment.

Passing the quarry at a steady seventy, I began my post-apocalyptic strategy.

Should I lie low, drown my sorrows in a bucket of fried chicken, or dig out the Heap lest Dylan come looking for his car keys?

Memories of the morning I'd awoken to his sweet note struck me like a fist. I pulled off the road as tears that came from a deeper place than his rejection poured freely over my cheeks.

Would he even miss me if I ran his Jeep into a tree? Or would he consider it a reprieve from a sentence he'd unwittingly volunteered for when he stepped into that tattoo parlor?

I imagined the scene, saw him stepping casually from his cruiser, his smooth strides turning to jagged bounds as he recognized my vehicle. Would he cry out, collapse in the street or simply gather me in his arms, whispering all the while about how he'd been a horse's ass and would I please forgive him?

A primal urge to carry out my awful plan was outweighed only by the resolve to get home to my cat, my bed, and my pajamas. I couldn't make things better if I killed myself, and that dying-in-your-lover's-arms bit was only romantic in old movies. In reality, I was certain it wouldn't go so smoothly.

The more likely scenario was that I wouldn't die, just wind up a vegetable with a closed-head injury after which he'd turn to one of the Salmon Fest Bimbos for comfort, which would eventually result in marriage and the conception of their two golden children—Blake and Brooke. I was sure to get a pity visit from the carefree quartet whenever they vacationed close to my nursing home and had nothing better to do.

Five minutes later I pulled into my driveway and ran upstairs to an empty apartment. I took my cell phone out, looked at voicemail again just to make sure I hadn't missed a repentance call, and realized he wasn't going to crack anytime in the immediate future.

But I just might.

Moments later I stumbled to bed without changing into those coveted pajamas. Sleep did me no favors.

I tossed and turned in the sticky darkness, groped for my pillow, and thought it was him lying beside me as he had that afternoon in Cabin Five.

My racing heart woke me hours later, followed shortly by a ringing cell phone and Holly's chirpy voice.

"She's in bed. I don't know…" A long pause. "Maybe they had a fight or something…" Another pause followed by some giggling. "You kept me out too late, buster."

I moaned, sunlight piercing the shade on my window as Joey jumped from my bed to the floor.

"Shut up!" Holly continued, her conversation bringing her to my bedroom door. "Oh, I think I woke her up." Then a whisper. "Tell him she's okay, I guess."

I sat up in bed, disgusted by my appearance as Holly stuck her head in and frowned. "Sleeping Beauty, you ain't!"

"Thanks," I croaked while swinging my legs off the side of the bed, fresh despair at facing a whole day without Dylan settling like a wet blanket.

"What the heck happened?"

I scratched the back of my head. "Dylan's mad."

"So?" she shrugged. "He'll get over it."

I felt my bottom lip pucker and tried to cover it with a pout. "He said not to call."

Holly sighed, her eyes sympathetic in the settling light. "Is that why you're still in bed at four o'clock in the afternoon?"

I looked away.

"And does it have something to do with why you're wearing the same clothes I saw you in yesterday?"

"Maybe," I mumbled while rolling over to glance at my bedside bureau and the cell phone I'd so carelessly tossed aside.

"Get out of bed. It's not as bad as you think."

I looked up.

"That was Dave on the phone."

"Dave?" I echoed, desperate for any scrap of information. "What'd he say?"

"Just that Dylan's so mopey he backed out on that stupid basketball game they play every Thursday night and he's never done that." She smiled, came to the side of my bed, and patted my back. "So that's a good sign."

I sighed. "It is?"

"Sure." She smiled again, sat down and shoved the blankets aside. "He's not used to getting his heart broken. Except for Karen, of course."

I winced.

"Sorry."

"Don't be," I mumbled, annoyed by her optimism. "If you'll excuse me now, I need to get some shut eye."

"Oh, no you don't," she shook a playful finger at me, one I was tempted to bite off if it got too close. "Lethargy is a sign of depression and I'm not going to see you throw your youth away. So you have a few minor skeletons in your closet? So *what*?"

I sighed, rolled over and took my blankets with me. "Did I tell you one of those skeletons showed up at our apartment? That he asked around town for me and that's how Dylan found out?"

"Brad?" she gasped, her voice ripe with a type of tension only an activities director at a summer camp can produce. "He actually drove all the way up here just to see you?"

I nodded. "Now you see why I need to get some shut eye. Maybe when I wake up this will all be over and Dave can have his ball boy back."

Holly raised an eyebrow. "Did you...you know...*do* it?"

"Have sex?" I groaned while burrowing deeper into my covers. "No...but I did kiss him and that was enough to send Dylan off the deep end," I sighed, peeked out at her. "Did I tell you he said not to call?"

"Yep."

"I can't do it, Holl."

She shook her head, patted the bump that was my butt. "Give him some time to cool off, Squirt. He'll come around."

"You think so?"

"Sure," she cooed, clucking me under the chin. "It was just a harmless kiss."

I laid back down, cuddled into my blankets, as she got up and shut the door. Minutes crept by, followed by hours until another day had played itself out. Rolling over, I glanced at the digital clock and reached for my cell phone.

"Flats?" Mallard answered on the second ring. "Where the fuck are ya?"

I coughed, then tried to sniffle. "I'm sick."

He cursed, rattled on about his old lady needing her oil changed.

"It came on all of a sudden and then I fell asleep and then—"

"Save your breath." He spat, and when he spoke again I could almost hear the smirk in his voice. "I'll think of some way you can pay me back."

I coughed again, hung up before he could elaborate, and stared at the wall, wondering what to do with myself, wondering what Dylan was doing with himself and who he might be doing it with.

The phone was so close, so tempting with all those little numbers just begging to be dialed. One combination of which would lead to his voice and an end to this suffering.

Don't call...

He'd made it quite clear that he didn't want to hear from me, and I could honor his wishes for the time being if what I had in mind would work.

Closing my eyes, I tried to clear my head of all negative thoughts and imagined the lake house. Iris had told me I could control my visions. I just had to figure out how to do it.

At first, nothing happened and I was stuck staring at the ceiling. I tried to talk myself into a better state of mind, tried to convince myself that I needed to do this only to assure myself Dylan wasn't drowning his sorrow in booze and cheap women.

Still, nothing came.

I closed my eyes, slowed my mind to a crawl and seconds later the lake house came into view. Walking to the front door, I was tempted to knock but walked through it instead.

No one was on the ground floor and there was no sign that he had been home at any time during the day. I continued my search, caution rearing its ugly head as I approached the steps to his bedroom.

No noise was a good sign and so I ascended the staircase.

The bed was neatly made and so I tiptoed around the room looking for clues to his whereabouts. No keys on the bedside table meant he'd taken the truck somewhere. No wet towels in the bathroom meant he'd stayed somewhere else last night.

I was just considering my options when a shadow crossed the open doorway. Startled, I fought the urge to drop to my belly before remembering that Dylan couldn't see me because I was in some sort of parallel dimension, one I was hanging onto by the skin of my teeth because any disruption seemed destined to send me back to where I came from.

I followed the figure through the hallway and down the stairs.

"Muffet?"

Spinning, I backed up against the wall as my father materialized before me, his golden hair tied back in a low ponytail. His face was soft, his smile genuine as he crossed the distance between us.

"Dad?" I whispered, my hand extending of its own accord.

"Get out of here."

I shook my head, my eyes going wide. "I have to find Dylan."

He seemed displeased as he reached out and grasped my arm tightly, his fingers bearing none of the gentleness I remembered from childhood. "Red Rover's here."

"What?" I asked. "Where?"

"He senses you," He stopped, glanced over his shoulder at the front door. "Can see you."

"Why now?" I asked, remembering how Iris had described Jonas Younts as an unnatural creature. The more time I spent wedged between this world and the one I'd inhabited for twenty-two years, the more I understood her word choice.

"I called you here to end it. I tried to do it for you years ago, but you and your brother are stronger than I ever was."

I felt a stab of fear. "What happened to you?"

My dad took a step back and I had to check myself from throwing myself into his arms like I did when I was a little girl. When he had told me he wished the broken bird would die.

"Nothing."

"What do you mean, nothing? Where the hell have you been for the past ten years? Where are you *now?*"

"I'm right here."

I ran a hand over my face, frustrated to be arguing with my dad at a time like this. *If* this was even Dad.

"How do I know it's really you?"

"You don't know."

The voice came from behind and I spun, saw the large man who had killed Abraham Ebersole and thought of my brother, wishing he was with me.

167

"He can't help you." His voice was raspy, with a strange sort of accent that seemed a mishmash of Minnesota and Arkansas. And he had read my mind, here in this waking vision and I had no idea if I was awake or dreaming.

"You ain't dreamin', Muffet," he said, a sort of satisfaction in his tone and I turned, looking for my father, but he was gone.

"Who are you?" I finally asked, my own voice tremulous and I fought to stop it. No way did I want this asshole to think I was weak, or worse yet…afraid.

He smiled, his teeth as rotten as I remembered. "The Bad Man."

I drew back, stared into the shadowed face of Red Rover and was struck by something. His eyes—large and black and dead—were familiar.

"I'm gonna cut you, Muffet." He came forward, grabbed my wrist. "An' once you start bleedin' no one can stop it."

I froze, my mind hovering on Dylan as my pulse came into my ears in a crimson rage. Rushing through veins and arteries, it reached a crescendo at my temples.

I stared into his eyes, saw hatred pooled like stagnant water and struck out with my fist.

Muscle, bone, and skin seemed to fold as my knuckles sunk into his abdomen. I heard something pop, heard him groan and realized I'd hit my mark.

"Bitch!" he growled, his hand releasing me and, at that moment I darted away, making for the front door of the lake house as he lumbered behind.

Think of something in the room…something concrete…

Iris' words came back and I tried to remember. What was in my bedroom? Nothing but blankets I couldn't feel and a cell phone I couldn't reach and a roommate who had probably taken off with her boyfriend again.

I opened my mouth, screamed her name as Red Rover lunged forward, fingers splayed, and found an ankle. Down I went, knocking a picture off the wall and slicing my arm. I heard my attacker laugh, felt his fist travel from my ankle to my calf as he flipped me onto my back.

Once again, I drew back my fist but this time he caught it in his own, squeezing until I thought he'd crush every bone in my hand.

I cried out, tried to grasp the covers of my bed, but everything was sliding away like water through splayed fingertips and so I reared up, brought my knee to his chin where it made contact with a shattering return.

He howled, his hands reaching for the hurt as I slid from beneath him and scrambled towards the lawn. Darkness swallowed me while the humid air smothered me, making my progress slow as I limped toward what I hoped was help, my knee a throbbing mass of agony.

"Better hope I don't catch you, Muffet."

I didn't stop, just hopped on my good leg while reaching blindly for something I couldn't define. Flexing my fingers, I came up with a fistful of Joey's tail.

I pulled hard, felt my cat come off the bed and land on my stomach. Another sharp tug and his claws were out and I was back in my bed, surrounded by a sea of blankets and a digital clock that read 11:32 p.m.

I gasped, sucking in air, sweat bathing me in a thin sheen as I tried to sit up. Too shaky to move just yet, I pulled my shirt up and examined my belly-button. Joey had done a number on my stomach, but that was okay considering I still held a handful of orange fur.

I tried laying back down, tried calming myself but couldn't for the pain in my knee.

Pain that had followed me back.

I thought of Dylan and why Red Rover had been in his house and fought to suppress my terror. Then I pulled my arm from beneath the sheet.

In the low light, I saw a deep cut that had just begun to ooze blood.

Blood I wasn't sure I could stop.

Chapter Twenty-One

"Holl!" I cried as I stumbled to my feet. Tossing the sheets aside, I put weight on my knee and felt it give way.

"Holly Lou Marchand!"

No reply, and so I hopped down the hallway, intent on getting some pressure on a wound I wasn't sure would heal. Seconds later I made it to Holly's bedroom door. Her pink seashell nightlight illuminated a foot sticking out from beneath her comforter like a bone in a collard patch.

She was out like a light and I didn't have time to wake her.

I just made it to the bathroom sink when my knee gave out completely. Collapsing to the floor, I grabbed a towel and pressed it to my arm.

And waited.

At first it didn't seem to be working as the blood began to soak through the turquoise terrycloth. So, this was how it was going to end? On my bathroom floor with Dylan mad at me and Holly asleep in the next room.

Maybe they would write a story about my bravery, but I doubted it.

I winced, pressed harder and felt it slow.

"Holy friggin' Moses!"

I gasped, my grip sliding on the towel as my roommate entered the bathroom.

"Shit! Shit! *Shit!*" her hands fluttered like two chicken wings. Dropping to her knees, she yanked the towel back in place. "What's going on? Are you hurt? Did someone stab you?"

"Yeah," I managed. "But I think I'm okay."

"Then why the hell are you bleeding?" She paused, rocked back on her heels while slumping against the toilet. "Why the hell am I on the bathroom floor when I have to pee?" She stopped, looked down. "Maybe I already did."

I didn't know what to say but knew I had to start somewhere. Shifting positions so the towel was wedged between me and the toilet, I put my head between my legs to stop the shaking, the nausea, and began to tell my story—slowly at first. And as the drama unfolded, Holly slid into a half-sprawl beside me.

After it was over I sat in silence, the towel and dried blood stuck to the side of my arm, exhausted but afraid to sleep for fear of what I would find there.

"So, your grandma gave you some sort of special powers?"

I nodded.

"And now some crazy guy named after a kiddie game I used to play in second grade has come after you?"

I laughed, but even that took more oxygen than I could afford.

"Sounds nuts if you ask me."

I didn't know what to say, how to convince her that what had happened had really happened aside from the fact that I would never cut myself for shits and giggles.

"But I believe you, Squirt." She reached out and touched the top of my head. "And right now, we need to get you to the hospital."

"Not yet," I shook my head. "The blood is starting to stop."

"Do you want me to call Dylan?"

I nodded, my eyes filling with tears because she'd offered what I couldn't ask for.

"Dave'll do it," she reached out, squeezed my hand. "I don't have to tell him why."

"He wouldn't believe you anyway."

"Don't bet on it. I try my best not to date assholes."

I giggled, surprising myself with the sound.

"Wait here. I'll be back in a jiff."

Like I was going anywhere with a bum knee and a bloody towel stuck to the side of my arm.

If only he could see me now. I closed my eyes, fantasized for a moment that Dylan knew I was crippled and was at this very moment racing towards the apartment, hell-bent on kicking someone's ass. I imagined him bursting through the door and rushing to the bathroom where he would gather me into his arms and carry me to the yellow La-Z-Boy.

After that I was a little confused as to whether we talked about our fight or had passionate make-up sex on the blue shag. I was leaning toward the latter when Holly re-entered the bathroom, a frown on her face.

"Holl?"

She shook her head, smiled. "Dave talked to him this morning. Said he sounded fine."

I scowled. "Fine?"

"Well, not 'fine' in the actual sense of the word, but pretty darn good…" she paused, "Considering."

I pressed my lips together. "Tell me," I ordered, my eyes searching hers.

"Dave called when he bailed on their basketball game. Said he wasn't feeling up to it but they were supposed to meet up afterwards."

"And he didn't show?"

"Not exactly," she blew out her breath. "He could have just been late. Dave had an early shift, so he couldn't really wait around all night."

I tried to steady my breath, tried to still my shaking hands while pushing to my feet. One quick jerk and divorce proceedings with the turquoise bath towel were finalized. Ten hops and I was in the living room searching for my keys.

"Sit down before you kill yourself."

"I can't," I said. "Something's wrong."

"Nothing's wrong. He just needs time to cool off."

"What aren't you telling me?"

She looked away, twisted a strand of hair.

"I'm calling his cell."

"Oh, Squirt," she mumbled, but it was too late. I'd already found my phone and began punching numbers in, numbers I'd dialed a million times and it felt good and right, like coming home to warm food on the table.

Three rings and someone picked up.

"Hello?"

I didn't recognize the voice as Avery's but wasn't going to make the same mistake twice.

"Who is this?"

"Chelsea."

Chelsea? Who the hell was Chelsea? I looked up, my eyes searching for Holly's but she'd slunk off into the kitchen.

"Where's Dylan?" I demanded.

She laughed, pulled the phone away and covered the mouth piece. A muffled conversation that lasted several seconds followed and in the garble, I thought I heard his voice.

"Can I take a message?"

I bit my lip, fury starting its slow boil. How dare this person, this *"Chelsea,"* tell me I couldn't talk to Dylan?

I gritted my teeth and grunted, "Put him on the goddamn phone."

"He stepped outside for a smoke. Can I tell him who called?"

A smoke? Since when did Mr. *I'm So Fit I Could Survive on a Turnip* start smoking?

"Tell him it's Justine."

She laughed. "I'll tell him you called but it's going to be a late night."

"Great," I played along, "If he's up, tell him I'll swing by later and get my underwear."

Silence, followed by a hasty hang-up that made me feel a tiny bit better. But not much.

Hopping in a circle, I faced my roommate. She looked guilty, looked compassionate, looked anywhere but into my eyes.

"Did you know about her?" I paused, a throb welling in my throat that matched the pain in my kneecap.

She sighed, came to the counter, and leaned over on her elbows. "They met tonight for drinks over in Onaway but Dave had to leave early."

I hopped her way, balanced myself on one of our wobbly stools. "And when he left Dylan was hitting on someone?"

So much for taking a little time to cool down.

"Someone was hitting on him, but he kept blowing her off." She stopped. "At least he was then."

I tried not to cry, thinking of how quickly things could change from bad to worse and why I'd bothered to fight so hard for my life when it was perfectly obvious Dylan didn't give a shit.

Luckily my roommate wasn't one to dwell on the past. "You need a doctor."

I wanted to argue but couldn't, not when my arm pulsated like a discotheque and my knee felt as though it would never again support anything close to my current weight.

I slid from the stool and hobbled towards the door. "I think you're right."

Chapter Twenty-Two

My long-anticipated trip to the E.R. was profitable only in the sense that I came away with a prescription that could make me some fast cash on the streets and a knee brace that made me look like an all-star athlete.

And while my situation couldn't have sucked more, wondering whether Dylan was sleeping with some slut named Chelsea was a lot better than knowing Red Rover had killed him.

I was pondering my next move in the La-Z-Boy, my knee elevated at a perfect thirty-degree angle when the phone rang. For a split second my heart prepared for the dismount it had been dreading since the day before yesterday—the moment he told me the separation would be permanent and not to call him again. Ever.

I reached out, pushed the button that would connect me to the speaker I prayed had finally come to his senses and croaked out, "Hello?"

"Do you have a cold?"

"Well," I coughed, "As a matter of fact—"

"I'm worried about you," My mother interrupted. "Is something wrong?"

I felt my face go slack. She was worried? Concerned? Called of her own accord with no ulterior motives? "Never felt better."

She waited before answering—another oddity—and I gathered it, held it tightly because I didn't know what it meant or where it would lead us.

"I had a bad feeling," she paused again and, in the background, I caught the sound of silence and realized she wasn't multi-tasking. "I can't explain it."

"Bad feeling?" I echoed, trying to sound nonchalant. "About what?"

She drew a breath and I waited, my pain meds not quite dulling the edges as I'd hoped and when she spoke I felt my insides slide as if made of jelly.

"Something I should have told you a long time ago."

I bit my cheek. Never in my life had she voluntarily offered up valuable information.

"Dad?" I asked, letting the word be the cord that connected us.

"Yes."

I nodded even though she couldn't see, still unable to speak as the TV droned on, an undercurrent of white noise that just matched the jumble in my head.

"I knew eventually you would find your way to that place," she said, her sharp tone under wraps for the first time in recent memory.

"That makes one of us."

I heard her stifle a nervous laugh, realized she was in unfamiliar territory and decided to give her the break Dad had asked me to so many years ago.

"I know about Butler."

"You do?" She seemed relieved. And troubled. "How?"

"Iris told me."

Had I hurt her? "Oh?"

"And my brother."

She sighed. Nothing close to self-pity, just a simple acknowledgment of the truth and her inability to change it.

"Robert wasn't perfect."

"I never thought he was."

She laughed. "Yes, you did."

"I was eleven when he left. What did you expect?"

"Justine—"

"Don't take that away from me."

"I don't intend to," she began, her voice low and soft and full of something potent. "You're a grown woman and you deserve to know why I never treated you like one."

Another silence filled by the lonely childhood that had come between us. I wanted to forgive her for not getting over it and moving on, for crying at night and leaving me to fend for myself. It was only natural when you loved someone that much to grieve their betrayal.

But she had betrayed me, too.

"I wanted to keep you with me forever—and I knew what was coming...ever since that day you cut your knee."

I sat up in the La-Z-Boy, shifted my weight so my knee was straight, traced the white line running down the center of it with the tip of my index finger, and remembered the moment Dylan had kissed it.

"Robert went crazy after that...talking about the Shaman and Calvert Cook, going over the stories he'd heard as a little boy from Iris—stories about you and your brother."

"Mom—" I felt her pain, wanted her to stop and go on forever at the same time.

"Calvert said a brother and a sister would kill the monster Butler created and we hoped." She paused. "We thought as long as we never had another child you would be safe."

I put my fingertips to my hairline, undone by how much my parents had loved me. "Why did he have an affair? If he knew—"

"I asked him that same question and he always told me he didn't know," she took a deep breath. "I was very angry for a long time, even before he had the affair and, in a way, I can understand why he did it. I was cold...unfeeling...but I wanted a different life."

"Don't," I whispered, my pity for her plain in my voice. "It's no excuse."

"I know, Justine, but as time went on I began to realize everything happened for a reason. If he hadn't met Pam we wouldn't have Adam and the two of you wouldn't have your shot at ending this once and for all."

I scrunched up my face, unsure I'd heard her right. "Are you saying you think I can do this?"

"I'm saying I *know* you can."

"Mom," I whispered, undone by her faith in me. Unprepared for it.

"Your dad left us that day at the pool and drove up there, went into the woods behind Back Forty Farm and was never seen again."

I thought of Butler, and of Odessa, searching the long, northern nights for him and wondered if every Cook woman was destined to walk alone.

"Jonas Younts—"

"Must have known he was coming. Robert wasn't prepared, he had no idea what it would take to undo the black magic Butler had been forced to perform. He only had a handful of stories from his mother and the belief that a father's love could conquer everything." My mother paused, and in the gap, I heard her steady herself again. "I begged him not to go, Justine. I asked him to wait until you were older, out of high school and he told me it couldn't wait. His dreams had gotten worse and now there was another baby. He knew his children were in danger if Jonas Younts found out about them."

I shook my head. "It's not Jonas we need to be afraid of, Mom."

"What do you mean?"

"There's another one, the one I used to draw with my crayons—"

"The man with no face?"

"Yes."

"Did he hurt you?"

I took a breath, stalling for time because the last thing I wanted was for her to drive up here and meddle in something that could get her killed. "No…but he knows about me and Adam."

"I'm coming up there."

I bit my lip, ecstatic that she cared, but terrified she would mess something up and I would be trapped in this nightmare forever.

"Please," I whispered, tears pouring over my cheeks now, tears I swatted with an impatient hand. "You have to let me do this."

"You have no idea what you're dealing with."

"Yes, I do," I lied, "Iris has been helping me, and Adam and Dylan."

I stopped cold, wondering if I could really add his name to that list when she asked, "Dylan?"

I hobbled to the window, gripped the sill and looked outside.

"Is he tall?" she asked. "With blond hair?"

I felt my fingers tighten. "Yes."

"And blue eyes that sometimes change color."

"Mom—"

"And a wheel between his shoulder blades." She stopped, searched for the word. "A tattoo?"

"My God—" I said.

"Robert said he would watch over you."

I closed my eyes, all the nerve endings and bone and ligaments that kept me upright and moving and carrying on a respectable pace liquefying in an instant. I couldn't stand, couldn't sit and so I propped myself in the window sill and placed my forehead against the glass.

"A part of me was afraid he wouldn't find you in time."

"He did, Mom," I whispered, my hands quivering. "And I screwed it up and now he won't talk to me."

"You need him, Justine," she insisted. "The reversal calls for blood. *Your* blood."

I closed my eyes, the late afternoon sun burning the side of my neck.

"Once it starts you won't be able to stop it."

I tried to stay calm even as my chest ignited, remembering the dream he had told me about as I laid in his arms. "But Dylan can."

"You have to find him. Do what you can to make it right."

"I don't know where to find him," I began, my pulse doing a chin-up in my chest.

"Then you'd better start looking."

Chapter Twenty-Three

I didn't want to bartend at Huff's, didn't want to pour shots when Dylan's whereabouts were in question and still I figured an evening in the company of Mallard and his rowdy regulars was safer than sitting at home waiting for Red Rover to finish me off. I'd tried his cell phone again, hoping that he would answer and tell me Chelsea was a thing of the past, but it had gone straight to voicemail.

And damned if I was going to leave a message.

Three hours into my shift and I still felt lousy. My only relief came when I devised a plan to go driving around Presque Isle County after closing time, looking for the silver truck that would solve all my problems.

Don't call...

He didn't know about Dad's prediction or the fact that he was supposed to stop me from bleeding to death. All he knew was that he'd had some weird dreams about a girl that looked like me and that I kissed another guy and didn't tell him about it. Chances are he wouldn't talk to me even if I did locate his truck.

I must have looked pretty depressed because even Mallard kept his distance at first before circling for seconds as though barmaid baiting was a recreational sport.

"How come you're hobblin' around?" He glanced at my brace while shaking out his pack for a fresh smoke. "Spend some time on your knees last night?"

I didn't dignify his innuendo with an answer but continued to serve drink after drink to my smattering of regulars as Garth Brooks followed Shania Twain followed The Goose Girl Polka on our dilapidated jukebox. It wasn't long until the place was empty. I was just about to try Dylan's cell phone again when the doors opened and two girls walked in.

The first girl was pleasantly plump and plain, her V-neck blouse demure and matronly, but the second girl...

Mallard's jaw dropped so low a semi-truck could have driven through with clearance.

She smiled, revealing perfect teeth while settling on Shaw's barstool.

"Holy shit," Mallard panted under his breath. "That ol' fucker'd keel over if he knew that ass was on his seat."

I made a face, then limped over and asked them for their orders. The first girl asked for a wine cooler, smiled at me in a nice way and looked to her gorgeous friend. The second girl pulled her hair over a tanned shoulder, nicely displayed in a black tube top.

"Fuzzy navel."

I turned toward the tier of liquor bottles, thinking that if everyone had a drink that described them, a fuzzy navel would be hers.

She seemed out-of-place in Huff's but not in her own skin. A confidence only the crème de la crème possessed oozed from her pores as sweat did from mine. She opened her purse, a leather number that cost more than my four years of college and drew out a tube of pink lip gloss.

She applied it to her lips, smacked them together, and waited for her drink.

I grabbed the peach Schnapps, reached for a carton of orange juice, and wondered why they had come to this bar alone and if the Supermodel could possibly be waiting for her equally attractive boyfriend.

Which reminded me of Dylan. Which reminded me of Mom.

You need him, Justine...

In more ways than one...and so I ventured toward the till when Mallard wasn't watching, grabbed my cell phone and hit his number.

His ringtone—the University of Michigan fight song—jolted me. I spun, half-expecting to see him in the doorway before I realized what was happening.

Dylan's wasn't answering his cell phone because the hottie with the expensive purse had gotten her mitts on it.

I watched her fishing for the phone in her purse, watched her gaze shift to me as a sort of horrid understanding steeped her elfin features.

She didn't bother to answer, just grabbed her friend by the wrist, threw a five-dollar bill on the counter and got up to leave.

No way was I letting that bitch out the door.

Moving with the speed Butler had given me, I blocked her escape before she knew what was happening.

We stood looking at each other for a moment, my hazel eyes holding her translucent ones with every bit of hubris I could muster. She wrinkled her nose, pursed her lips, obviously not used to someone standing between her and something she wanted.

"Hey," her friend said, still trying to be nice. "Oh, uh, hey...what're you doing?"

I smiled, my super-strength just percolating beneath the surface as I imagined pulling her glossy hair out by the roots. Mallard must have read my thoughts because in an instant he'd put himself between us, the picture of old-fashioned chivalry in a white muscle shirt.

"What the fuck's goin' on?"

"That's what I'd like to know," Chelsea sniffed, her eyes widening in a show of annoyance.

"Why do you have my boyfriend's cell phone?"

She smirked, her mannerisms suggestive of someone who rarely bothered with other women. "He left it at my place last night. We're meeting up so he can get it back."

I lunged at her, knocking her buddy to the floor and it took all of Mallard's strength to hold me back.

"Let me guess, you're Justine?" Chelsea continued, a bit ruffled by my display but still under the assumption that Mallard could protect her. She didn't even glance at her friend, who lay sprawled on the floor like the kid from *A Christmas Story.*

I tensed again, my loyalty to Mallard the only thing keeping me in check.

"Dylan filled me in. Said he told you to get lost."

"Get lost?" I repeated as her friend pulled herself up off the floor and tiptoed towards the door.

"Said you had a hard time taking the hint." Chelsea smiled again. "Which probably explains all your daddy issues."

It took a moment for her words to register, but when they did I reached over, took a fistful of Mallard's shirt and pinned him against the wall. "Still think he's got your back, bitch?"

"Flats," he croaked, the collar of his shirt choking him, "Keep a lid on it!"

I took a step towards Chelsea, grabbed her wrist and squeezed.

"Shit!" she cried, terrified now. "What're you, some kind of *freak?*"

"You could say that," I hissed. "And unless you tell me how you got that phone I'm going to squeeze your wrist until your hand pops like a pimple."

Her green eyes widened, her little white teeth grinding against each other as she fought the pain. I looked to Mallard, found him transfixed and let go of his shirt. He didn't move, just backed up against the wall, hands splayed, a strange sort of admiration shining in his dark eyes.

"All right," Chelsea gasped, her polished veneer cracking at last. "We were having some drinks and I was hitting on him and he—" She stopped, winced. "He wasn't interested."

"Then what?"

"I was pissed. I'll admit it. I'm not used to getting blown off and then," she stopped again, tried to breathe. "He got a call and left so fast he forgot the phone on the bar."

"So you stole it?"

"Yes." She winced, her top lip curling like a horse going for a carrot. "I hoped maybe he'd come looking for it. He mentioned something about this place and that's why we came here." She turned, remembering her friend. "Katie? Katie!"

"Did he say where he was going?"

"No."

My mind, usually so panicked during times of stress, became still and in that instant, I knew what I needed to do. I reached out, touched Chelsea in the same way I had Brad and read her thoughts.

Images of Dylan in the orange T-shirt I'd handed to him after our tryst in Cabin Five came rushing so fast I had to fight for control or be swept away. He looked tired, beaten down, and depressed, a fact I noted with a momentary twinge of satisfaction before surveying the dark interior of the bar.

Chelsea stood apart from the crowd across the room, another attractive girl at her side and for a moment it looked like they were discussing who would get dibs on Dylan. Moments later Chelsea sauntered over; a vision in a white halter top and designer jeans. Her long hair was pulled back in a braid and she wore silver earrings that dangled against the side of her neck.

Dylan looked up, nodded in a way that said she could sit down, and ordered two drinks.

I tensed, not sure I wanted to see the rest.

They talked, they laughed, his smile catching my heart and holding it in a tingly grip. Chelsea reached out a hand, laid it gently on Dylan's wrist as if to say she was interested. He looked at her, surprised, then pulled his hand away. Mortification contorted Chelsea's delicate features into an ugly mask.

I watched as he turned away from her, reaching for his phone to take a call. At once he seemed agitated, one hand reaching to cup the nape of his neck where he worked the skin there with intensity. The next moment he hung up, spun on his heel, and headed for the door—Chelsea, his cell phone, and a half-empty bottle of Coors Light forgotten.

"Dylan!" I called from behind, trying to catch a glimpse as he weaved between layers of darkness and smoke. I caught sight of his orange T-shirt, made a beeline for the parking lot and just glimpsed him climbing into his truck.

I called his name again, but he didn't hear. He simply turned towards Lantern Creek and roared away much as he had that terrible day at Three Fires. I tried to run, tried to chase him but knew it was useless and so I stood, my fingers boring into the flesh of Chelsea's shoulder before releasing her.

She blinked, turned to look at me as if she'd just woken from a twenty-year bender.

"What's going on?"

"Nothing," I answered. One glance at Mallard and I knew he wasn't going to rat me out. "You were just getting ready to leave."

"Was I?" she seemed content. "Okay. Where's Katie?"

I jerked my thumb towards the window and Mallard looked out, nodded and said, "She's waiting by the car. Looks scared as fuck. I sure hope she didn't call the cops."

"She didn't," Chelsea explained, a loopy grin on her face. "She's very silly."

Mallard gave me a look that said he was thinking of taking advantage of dear Chelsea in her altered state, but instead took her elbow and led her towards the front porch, where we watched as she stumbled toward her car.

Katie took her friend's hand, shoved her in the passenger seat while circling around front, watching us the whole time. Moments later she backed up cautiously and drove away at the mediocre speed I felt sure marked all her daily activities.

"Holy Mary Mother of God," Mallard spat, straightening his collar.

"I know how this looks."

"I ain't ever been bested by no one since Howie Duff kicked my ass in seventh grade." He chuckled and reached for a fresh smoke, and I saw his hands were shaking.

"I didn't mean to hurt you."

He laughed, tried to light his cigarette and put it down when he couldn't hold his lighter steady. "You gonna tell me you're Superman's second cousin or somethin'?"

"As a matter of fact—"

"Flats—"

"I need to leave."

"You ain't goin' nowhere."

I looked at him.

"If you don't wanna, I mean."

"I have to find Dylan. No one knows what happened to him after he left that bar," I muttered.

"So?"

"I think he went looking for me."

"Why?"

"He thinks I'm in trouble."

Mallard laughed, his voice wobbly. "Are ya?"

I stood up, grabbed my purse and hobbled towards the door. "Yes."

* * *

I wasn't sure how fast to push the Jeep, but eighty-eight seemed a respectable pace when my boyfriend was missing. Reaching for my cell phone, I called Dave.

"Hello?" he answered, drowsiness sweetening his voice.

"I need to ask you some questions."

"Ma?"

"No!" I snapped. "It's Justine and I need to know if you've heard from Dylan since you met for drinks."

"Uh," he stammered, still confused. "No."

"Any idea where he is?"

I heard him clear his throat, heard the squeak of the bed springs as he sat up. "There was a girl at the bar, but I don't think—"

"He's not with her."

"Oh," he spoke slowly. "I never thought—"

"I know you didn't. I just need to find him."

"I'll try his cell."

"He doesn't have it."

"Shit," there was apprehension now. "Do you think he's in trouble?"

I didn't want to think it, not when we'd left things so badly between us. "I don't know."

"I'll get dressed and meet you somewhere."

"No," I said. "I don't want you mixed up in this."

"You shouldn't be looking for him alone."

"Mallard's with me," I lied. "Tell Holly not to worry. It's probably nothing."

"Wait—"

I hung up, gripped the steering wheel, and tried to imagine where Dylan might have gone after he left the bar, but my mind was a mass of worry and regret.

I focused on his hair, his face and the feel of his lips against my skin. I thought about his fingers and toes and how he had a mole on his left hip, just below his beltline—anything to connect me with his physical being. But I felt something blocking me and realized it could be the person I feared most.

I bit my lip, chewed on the soft skin until blood came, thinking that would help clear my head before it was too late.

I'M ON IT, SIS

My chest tightened.

GET TO THE LODGE. I'M LETTING ROCKY OUT.

DO YOU SEE DYLAN?

A pause, and it seemed like an eternity, but I knew he was trying.

HE'S WHERE THE WILLOWS KISS

WHERE IS THAT?

I tried to still my mind, to quiet it enough to get a read on what Adam was trying to tell me. Willows usually grew next to water, but I hadn't been roaming around in the woods enough to notice if one had been making out with its mirror image.

I gripped the wheel, precious seconds floating away, lost forever while Dylan was in danger, lying next to some tree I couldn't see…dead maybe.

I took a slow breath, tried to steady the despair that engulfed me like a slow freeze from my toes up. If he was dead… Because of me…

WHERE DAD USED TO FISH

I was pushing the Jeep past ninety when I saw the sign for Three Fires. I slammed on the brakes and skidded to a halt on the side of the road. Moments later I was creeping up the long driveway, my tennis shoes making soft sounds on the gravel.

I paused, crouched amongst the trees as Pam's house came into view. I saw Rocky heave himself from his customary position at the front door and prayed he recognized my scent. Moments later he bounded down the steps, pushed his head beneath my hand as I tried to quiet him.

FOLLOW THE DOG

I felt my heart burst from its bony cage.

BUT—

GO!

I'd just made the tree line, Rocky at my heels, when the front door opened. Pam's voice, clear and full of business, called to her dog.

I stopped, crouched amongst the undergrowth as Rocky decided where to place his loyalty.

"I need you, boy."

Pam whistled and his ears perked. Head twisted towards his mistress, he began to wag again, took three bounds towards the house and then turned.

"Come on, boy."

Another whistle followed by the promise of a dog biscuit and still it wasn't enough to break our friendship. He knew he needed to follow me and for an instant I placed myself in the lead, running wild through a field as the pack fell in behind.

185

Moments later I was racing towards the Jeep—Ocqueoc Falls was only a short distance away and I had to hurry, had to fly with wings I didn't possess and as I opened the door to the Jeep, opened myself to the idea that I could do the impossible as Rocky nudged my leg and jumped up beside me.

I didn't have time to praise him as I sped down the highway, my hands shaking so badly I could hardly grip the wheel. Five minutes later we were parked at the Ocqueoc Falls trailhead. I scanned the asphalt, squinted for a glimpse and saw Dylan's truck.

Two bounds and I was out of the Jeep and running toward it, prayers I didn't know I remembered tumbling from my lips as I yanked the driver's side door open.

I didn't call Dylan's name. I didn't want to listen to the silence I knew would greet me and so I did the next best thing—I started snooping for something Rocky could use.

I opened his glove box and saw the gun he usually kept there was missing. Grabbing a small flashlight, I bent down and reached under his seat. My fingers touched something smooth and I grasped it, pulled and found a Snickers wrapper and the string of green beads Mom had given me for Christmas. I held the jewelry, felt it slide between my fingers and had no memory of the last time I'd worn it or how it wound up under Dylan's seat, but it didn't matter, I kept digging, sure I'd find something with his scent on it.

Two minutes into my search and I found what I'd been looking for. A red T-shirt, one he'd worn during a basketball game down at the pavilion. He'd taken it off, had changed into a clean one right in the truck. I remembered the moment vividly: his sweaty face, the smell of hot dogs drifting down from the park, the way his body looked under my hungry gaze.

Before offering it to Rocky, I held it to my own nose, smelling the wind and water and sun and, beneath everything else, *him. Only* him. I buried my face in it, imagining it was his skin I was rubbing my lips against, his scent filling my senses and knew if I let myself go there for even a second, I wouldn't be able to pull back.

I knew I was going to have to enter the woods now, knew I was going to have to push myself past the breaking point with a slashed-up arm and bum knee.

But I had no choice. Dylan would have done the same for me and it made me wonder what the caller had said to him to make him forget his cell phone and ditch Chelsea.

Rocky lifted his nose in the air a couple of times, ready to get on with what he thought of as a great adventure, and I had to give up the shirt in order to grant his wish.

"Here, boy," I dropped it on the ground as he pawed at it like a chicken scratching dirt. Moments later he took off at a rolling gait.

I had just enough time to grab the shirt before I lost him completely.

The night was moonless, the forest black as pitch. I heard animals stirring as we passed by. Raccoon and possum scurrying beneath the brush, barred owls *who-whooing* from some high branch, their wings parting the heavy air. I followed the dog in front of me as best I could, the sound of the Falls slowly gathering in my ears until their rhythm became steady as a backbeat.

Moments later my mindless feet found water.

Rocky came up from behind and nudged me with his head. I gave him the shirt again. A low bark and I knew he'd found the scent. I gripped the flashlight, trying my best not to lose the black dog in the darkness.

He whimpered, sprinted ahead, and then turned to see if I was following. Of course, I was following. I had no idea which way was up or down or east or west.

RED ROVER SEES YOU

I skidded to a halt. Looked over my shoulder.

HE WANTS TO HURT YOU

I held my breath, released it, and called for Rocky. In an instant, he was beside me and I tightened up, sprinted forward into the blackness as his playful yips turned aggressive. Haunches tight, head low to the ground he took off at a speed I had to fight to keep up with.

"Dylan!" I cried, feeling him now that Rocky had led me this far.

An answer. Mumbled.

"Dylan!" I screamed, Rocky's tail just in sight as he wove around trees and over stumps, the river to our left and the whole dark world falling down on us.

"Justine?"

The voice was as sweet as anything I'd tasted or touched or smelled.

"I'm here," I choked, relief sweeping my body like a soft rain. Three more steps and Dylan came into view, his arm smeared with a dark liquid I could only assume was blood, his foot resting at an odd angle. Rocky was jumping in circles around him, very pleased with himself and I wanted to kiss his furry neck but knew that would have to wait.

"Oh, Dylan," I whispered as I sank to my knees, my arms reaching for him to assure myself I wasn't dreaming. "What are you doing out here?"

"What do you think I'm doing out here?" his voice was raspy, his question absurd as his arms closed around my back. "I'm looking for you!"

"What do you mean?" I asked, slipping my arm under his in an attempt to lift him off the ground.

"Twisted my ankle when I took a nosedive over that stump. I lost my flashlight. And my gun."

"Dylan—" I began, confused.

"You called me—said you were out at the Falls and then the line went dead."

"Why would I be out at the Falls in the middle of the night?"

"That's what I was going to ask you."

And in that moment it came to me.

Red Rover wanted us out here.

Together.

"You said you wouldn't be bothering me anymore," Dylan continued. "I thought…after our fight—"

I shook my head, locked my knees and stood up. "It wasn't me."

He took a small step forward and winced. "I think I know your voice."

"Do you?" I asked, my mind fluttering like a bird about to take flight. A bird known to mimic the sounds of others.

"Who was it then?" he asked, his hand tightening on my shoulder.

"Red Rover."

"Who the hell is Red Rover?"

Rocky's head, an ever-reliable link to reality, found its way under my hand, his tongue wet against my palm. One sharp bark and I was on task.

"The man who murdered Abraham Ebersole and tried to cover it up. The same man who killed Butler and then went after Karen and Suzy Marsh."

"Karen died in a car crash," he reminded me. "Suzy Marsh killed herself."

"You said you didn't believe that."

"They closed the case."

"Doesn't matter," I said as I pushed forward, my knee screaming in protest. "Because he's after us now."

"Justine," he rasped, his breathing shallow and I wondered how much blood he'd lost and if he was starting to go into shock. "I can't…"

"We have to move."

"Who is he?"

"I don't know," I answered as we stumbled along, Rocky beside me, guiding me, leading me through the forest as night sounds slurred together in a fluid symphony. "But Jamie Stoddard and Red Rover are connected in some way."

"What does this have to do with me?" he managed, his voice labored, and I felt him lean into me for support and wished I could pick him up and carry him without destroying his pride and what was left of my kneecap.

"He lured you out here to get to me. I don't understand why he didn't kill you when he had the chance."

"Screw him," he muttered, and I quickened my pace, sparkles of darkness forming a veil across my eyes. My pulse snagged on itself, the feel of Dylan's arm coming undone as the earth slipped from beneath my tennis shoes.

"I kept hearing things in the woods so I shot off some rounds to scare whatever it was off," he continued. "Then I heard your voice and so I took off running, tripped over that stump, and hit my head on a rock."

"What happened to your arm?"

"I don't know," he said. "I must have been out for awhile, because when I woke up it was bleeding."

"Shit," I cursed, my fear as close as my own skin. "I think he already tried."

"To what?"

"Kill you," I gasped, barely able to keep us both on our feet.

HE'S ON THE OTHER SIDE OF THE RIVER

I started, saw nothing but the thin beam of my flashlight and the wet woods it illuminated.

GET TO IRIS

"Can you lean on me and try to run?"

"Yeah, but…why didn't he kill me? What stopped him?"

"I don't know. And I don't care. I'm just glad you're alive."

I felt his body tighten, knew his movements as only a lover could and braced myself as he took off at a shuffling run. As we ran, I felt him holding me, felt myself holding him and knew that if either one fell the other would die in this dark wood.

"I'm sorry," his voice was at my ear. "For getting mad at you. I shouldn't—" He staggered, tried to move faster. "I had no right."

"You had every right," I returned. "I should have trusted you."

Rocky's bark drew our attention and I glanced to the river. On the other side, just through the trees, I saw a man walking at the same pace, his eyes shining like dark flames.

I pushed forward, the trailhead not far when I heard him wading across the water.

"Hurry," I breathed. "He's coming."

"Leave me," Dylan whispered, and I was reminded of every cheesy movie I'd ever been forced to sit through. "I'm slowing you down."

"Tell me something I don't know."

"You're the important one, not me."

"Stop it!" I hissed. "I barely made it through two days without you. Why would I leave you out here to die in the woods?"

He tried to comply, tried to move beyond the pain in his ankle and I listened as the night sounds suddenly ceased. Red Rover was near, his large arms and hands dripping water as he climbed the sloping bank a few yards behind us.

I bent low, heaved my body forward with all the strength I had and felt Dylan's feet leave the ground. We flew across the uneven terrain, the trailhead finally in sight.

A branch crackled beneath a heavy boot and my heart did a somersault. Rocky heard it, growled and darted off to circle behind. I heard him bark, saw his dark form leap at something and took the last chance we would ever be given.

"*Run!*"

Dylan heaved himself forward and came up against the side of the truck. Scrambling for leverage, I yanked the door open, heard Rocky howling and shut my heart to the sound.

"Justine!" Dylan cried, tossing me the keys. "Get in!"

I listened for the dog, was greeted with silence and jumped inside. Seconds later I was fumbling for the ignition when Red Rover stepped from the forest just in front of us, the brim of his hat sheltering the face he'd never had.

"Start it up!" Dylan yelled. "Lock the doors."

One turn of the key and it wouldn't start, and so I called upon my grandmother, mother, father…everyone who had ever owed me a favor to suddenly jumpstart the truck so we wouldn't end up on the front page of the *Lectern*.

Another crank and the diesel roared to life.

Red Rover was now at the hood, his large hands clasped together as he raised them over his head, ready to bash the front end like a sledgehammer.

"Go!"

I slammed on the gas as the truck lurched forward and Red Rover was thrown into the windshield. Glass splintered but didn't break as he slid the length of dented metal and dropped into darkness.

"Is he dead?" Dylan whispered.

"Not a chance."

"Can you drive?"

I nodded, put the truck in reverse and hit the gas.

We were halfway across the parking lot when I saw Red Rover stand and step forward.

GET TO IRIS

Fifteen minutes later we were at her door.

Chapter Twenty-Four

"Iris!" I screamed, well aware we might wake the neighborhood, Dylan slumped against me.

A light appeared behind the paisley curtain she used for privacy on the nights her granddaughter came looking for protection from a homicidal maniac.

"Iris!" I screamed again and was rewarded with someone unlocking the door. Moments later her eyes were staring at us from the small opening between the door frame and house.

Dylan grasped the edge, ready to break her small chain if she refused us entrance, but she didn't. She merely stepped aside as we stumbled into her kitchen.

"Are you hurt?" she asked.

I nodded towards Dylan while helping him to a chair. "I think he broke his ankle."

She hurried to her freezer, filled a Ziploc baggie with ice and wrapped it in a dishtowel.

"Thanks," Dylan said while pressing it to his ankle, relief untwisting his features before they settled on my knee.

"What's that?" he nodded at my brace.

I shook my head, unwilling to heap more shit onto an enormous pile.

"And your arm?"

"Nothing," I said.

"Tell me," he ordered. "Now."

Iris stood watching us, her green eyes darting between.

"Red Rover came after me in a vision," I paused. "I didn't think it was possible, I thought I was safe but...obviously not."

"You mean like Freddy Krueger shit?"

I stood, trying to answer as best I could. "Maybe...I think...I don't know. I was really normal in Webber, I swear. Nothing exciting *ever* happened."

"He attacked you," Dylan paused, and I could tell he was thinking hard on something. "And you still came after me?"

I wanted to tell him I loved him, but the words died on my tongue as Iris stepped between us and laid a hand on my shoulder. "She's a tough cookie, Mr. Locke. But strength will only get her so far."

I looked across the table at Dylan while sinking into the opposite chair, my adrenaline still pumping like a piston. Turning to my grandmother, I asked, "Mind locking the front door before the huge bastard who almost killed us breaks it down?"

She raised an eyebrow, unmoved by my sarcasm. "Red Rover?"

I nodded. "He used my voice to trick Dylan," I glanced in his direction. "I don't understand why he didn't kill him out there."

My grandmother leaned against the counter and crossed her arms across her flannel nightgown.

"I do."

She pointed at my necklace and Dylan looked down, somewhat surprised that it still hung there.

"You mean—"

"It protects you. Protects him."

"It looks like my tattoo," Dylan began, his fingers stroking the silver circle as I had in the past. "But why me? I don't understand. I just met her."

"Have you?" Iris asked. "Go back in your thoughts."

I looked at him, saw his confusion and thought back myself, to the moment I'd stumbled across the website at Camp Menominee. Johnson Cook's words floating by like bits of autumn leaves on the air.

"I've never met her," he paused, a small smile reaching his lips. "Believe me, I'd remember."

I thought of Odessa in the vegetable garden, Butler by her side as their fingers touched, the dirt beneath her nails showing me how my people had always worked the earth. The next moment Odessa leaned back as someone blotted out the sun and Butler stood, rubbed his hands on his canvas pants and then tipped his wide-brimmed hat.

A woman was there. Slim and pretty and holding a baby, her smile telling me that she cared about these people when so many others did not.

Mrs. Karsten stopped by to tend to Cal and she and Dess has become friends even so that Dess wants to be godmother to her babe in arms.

"Dylan," I asked. "What was your mother's maiden name."

He seemed puzzled. "Villareal. She wasn't from around here. Or least her Dad wasn't. Grandma Karsten owned a big farm out past Posen."

"Karsten," I repeated, the knowledge exciting me. "Odessa and your grandmother were friends. She even became godmother to her babe in arms."

"Babe in what?" he asked. "How do you know this? Should I even ask?"

I smiled. "When Grandpa Cal got sick a woman named Mrs. Karsten came to tend to him."

"You're marked, Dylan," Iris said. "Unfortunately, the medicine is limited to the necklace so you're out of luck when she takes it back."

"I'm not taking it back," I spoke up, my fear swelling in my throat. "I can take care of myself."

"Like hell. You're as banged up as me."

"Stop," I held my hand up, wanting him to think before he gave it back. "Where did Dad get this?"

Iris sighed, rubbed her arms as if a sudden chill had taken hold in August, perhaps relieved to be telling the story after a lifetime of secrets.

"Grandpa Cal had them made. One for the girl with the scar on her knee, one for the boy who could speak with his mind. Silver to open your mind to the powers you possess, the medicine wheel to protect you as you journey through life's four stages. He blessed them himself with a ritual Butler taught him."

"Ritual?" I asked.

"The Brave Dance," Iris explained. "An Ojibwa warrior would perform it before battle when he called his animal spirits to guide and protect him. Grandpa knew you would need it."

"Woah," Dylan put a hand up, and I knew the third degree was going to start soon. "What do you mean by that?"

Iris turned and opened the refrigerator, always ready to fill our stomachs in times of stress. "Just what I said. Butler screwed up and granted eternal life to a couple of jerks and you're going to take it back from them."

Dylan didn't answer at first, which I saw as a very bad sign. I dared a glance and wondered how long it would take him to run from me and my crazy destiny if he hadn't been icing his ankle.

"A couple of jerks?"

Iris nodded. "Jonas Younts and Red Rover forced Butler to perform a resurrection ceremony in the hopes of bringing Esther Ebersole back to life. But you can't force black magic on a man who doesn't know how to perform it. And so a mistake was made that you and my granddaughter need to fix."

"So, you're telling me," he began slowly—another bad sign. "That we're supposed to fight that thing we saw in the woods?"

"You look surprised, Deputy Locke."

He did not appreciate her humor. "She ran right over him with my truck and he didn't even break a fingernail."

"There's a way to kill him," Iris explained while pulling out a jar of pickles and setting it on the table. "But I've only got the basics."

"The basics?" Dylan echoed, and I leaned over, placed my hand on his to calm him down.

"I don't get it," I said. "If Butler died in the woods how did Grandpa Cal know how to make the necklaces?"

Iris chuckled, then unscrewed the cap and took a pickle for herself. "Does a Shaman ever really die, Justine?"

I shrugged, defeated. "I don't know."

"In body, yes—we all do. But his spirit was different than yours or mine. His spirit lingered. And still does."

"So, you're saying the dead guy has all the information we need to stop these two from killing us?" Dylan asked, and I could sense his anger, his powerlessness—something he never handled well—and hoped he would give Iris a chance to explain.

"That's exactly what I'm saying," she shot back, sensing his hostility. "It would have been too risky to write it down so Butler gave what he learned to the boy who couldn't speak."

"Adam!" I said suddenly, surprising myself. "I'm the only one who can hear him."

"What better way to protect a secret?"

I touched my forehead, suddenly alive with the thought. "But he's never said anything… I don't understand—"

"The spirit of the Shaman comes when it's needed. Your brother will know when the time is right."

"And if he doesn't?" Dylan asked, his anger breaking free. "Are we supposed to challenge these two to a fist fight and hope he comes up with a suggestion?"

My grandmother looked at me. "You really should have talked about this before tonight."

I glanced across the table, my annoyance shifting. "I haven't seen him for the last two days."

He seemed annoyed as well. Beyond, actually. "I just needed some time to cool off. Although a phone call telling me you'd been sliced and diced would have been appreciated."

I narrowed my eyes. "Would've been happy to if you hadn't left your cell phone with some slut named Chelsea."

His seemed shocked at first, then his brows came together as though trying to remember something that had happened years before. "Was that her name?"

"Yeah," I snapped. "And for not knowing her name she sure knew a lot about my daddy issues."

Dylan shook his head, rubbed at his temple with his left hand and I saw how long his hair had gotten in the last two days, how it was thick and golden and starting to curl around his ears and hated how I could still want him at a time like this.

"I had a lot to drink. I don't remember everything I said."

"That doesn't make hearing it any easier."

"I'm sorry," he acknowledged. "I wasn't myself. I'm not myself without you."

I felt the color rise to my cheeks as Iris chuckled, a smile on her face that belied the situation. "First thing you need to do is find those totems."

I glanced at Dylan, my anger subsiding. "I thought Jonas Younts had them. He stole the medicine bag to bring Esther back to life."

Iris smiled. "Robert got a package in the mail the day before your mom took you down to the pool. The totems were inside."

"What?" I asked, unable to believe that the lost pieces of my life were forming such a fantastical puzzle. "Who would do that?"

"Who do you think?"

"Jamie Stoddard," I whispered, not realizing what I'd said until it was too late.

"What's he got to do with this?" Dylan asked, his tone defensive.

"Calm down," Iris reached out and touched his arm. "You have to put your anger aside or you're not going to be able to help her."

"Maybe I was never meant to help her."

I looked at him, unable to process what he'd just said.

"You have no choice, Dylan," my grandmother insisted, and I was grateful to her because speech wasn't something I was capable of at the moment.

"Everyone has a choice," he returned. "And if Stoddard's a part of this plan then I'm out."

"It's not like that," I just managed. "He never wanted to live forever. He just wanted Esther Ebersole back."

"Who is Esther Ebersole and what does she have to do with this?"

"Your tattoo," I changed the subject, not wanting to go into detail about Jamie's love life, a strange spark of hope forming where their rivalry was concerned. "When did you get it?"

"Junior year," he admitted

"Before or after Jamie pulled you out of the river?"

"Before," he said. "I mean...spring break had ended and we were fishing for trout after the thaw."

"Did Jamie know you had it?"

He looked at me sideways. "Probably. We had gym class together."

"That's it!" I banged the palm of my hand against my forehead. "He knew who you were that day on the riverbank—that you were chosen to protect me and he saved your life because of it."

Dylan looked down, a year of repressed rage slowly rising to the surface and spreading across his face. "So, I'm supposed to believe that Stoddard's a hero? That it was all part of an elaborate plan to kill the woman I loved?"

For the second time in five minutes, I felt breathless. The words came so easily to him when he spoke about her, and here I was, asking him to risk his life for me.

"J—" Dylan began, sensing his mistake.

"No one's holding you here, Dylan," I said. "Go if you want to."

"Justine—"

"Go."

I looked at his face, masked by pain and fury and heartbreak, his knuckles bloody, his ankle twisted and swollen and felt my strength grow with my words. The spirit or thing or God that was greater than me and had always been greater would take care of me as it always had, with or without Dylan.

"I'm not going anywhere."

"Good," I said. "Then shut up and get your head in the game." Turning to Iris I asked, "Where are the totems now?"

"I don't know," she said, genuinely alarmed for the first time. "Robert didn't take them when he went after Red Rover in the woods. He must have hidden them somewhere safe."

"I never got anything," I said, "All he left was that note."

"And the birthday card you told me about," Dylan offered, helpful now that I'd smacked him down. "The one with the orange kitten."

I remembered tearing it up, the pieces of paper falling like confetti all around me, settling in my hair like snow. And the present, just the color of my bedspread, my birthday still over a month away...

"The gift!" I stood, my chair toppling behind me. "I never opened it."

"You think Robert put the medicine bag in there?" Iris asked.

I thought about it...thought about all the times I had wanted to open it. How something stronger than myself had told me not to. Until now...

"I'm going to get it."

Dylan stood, the Ziploc sliding to the floor. "You're not going upstairs alone."

"I have to."

"No," he insisted, his face furrowed with fear. "Not without the necklace."

"You need it more than I do."

"J—"

"I need you here—alive and safe—or I don't stand a chance out there." I paused, my heart in my throat. "Or anywhere else."

He reached down, took my hand in his and I could see the pain he was in, physical and otherwise. "I keep thinking about my dream."

I glanced at Iris, and she stepped forward. "Grandpa told us to look for a girl with a scar on her knee and a boy who spoke with his mind. The boy would catch fire but never burn, and the girl…" she looked to me. "Her blood would put out the fire."

I heard Dylan draw in his breath. "That's where I come in?"

She nodded.

"What if I can't stop it?"

"You can," I assured him. "Jamie wouldn't have saved your life on the riverbank if he didn't think—"

"I can't let you risk your life on something I might not be able to do."

I put a hand on his. "It was meant to be."

He pressed his lips together, looked down.

"I'll help you."

"You'll be bleeding, Justine. What if I don't know what to do? What if—"

He stopped short, and I felt his despair. It would have been harder for me if our roles were reversed. If Dylan's life depended on me believing in something that would have seemed impossible the day before.

"I trust you," I said.

His smile was shaky. "That makes one of us."

* * *

I stole into the darkness that was the stairwell to my apartment and climbed the steps to my back door.

All was dark in the kitchen, the air buzzing with the same heaviness that came before a thunderstorm.

GET THE GIFT

WHERE IS RED ROVER?

A pause. I hoped like hell he was working to get me an answer.

ON HIS WAY

I took a breath, imagined how long it would take to walk the eleven miles from Ocqueoc Falls, and crept down the hallway. I felt something brush my bare ankle. A strangled scream and I was against the wall, arms splayed in an attempt to move around whatever had chosen to attack my pink toenails.

Joey.

A low purr and I gave him a little nudge, sending him on his way as I entered my bedroom. I didn't dare turn on the light for fear of what I would see, and so I made my way to my closet and began rummaging for my present.

As soon as I touched it I felt the familiar fullness in my ears, the sounds of a sleeping apartment dulled to nothing and knew I was about to get an answer when I needed it most.

I remembered Red Rover on the porch, peering in at me as I looked out the window, the purple package in his hand. I saw him draw back, his fingers wanting to rip into the package at that moment but something had stopped him.

Jamie…

I saw him on the porch behind the larger man, saw them arguing as Red Rover told him about the package.

Jamie was laughing, telling him it was just a stupid birthday present and to run because he'd heard me call the cops.

I glanced down, saw the package tucked under my arm, and rushed for the hallway.

I ran down the steps and fumbled for the doorknob. Moments later I was in the kitchen, my grandmother at the front window as I dropped into a chair.

"Got it."

"Good."

Dylan stood in the doorway. He seemed relieved but there was very little I could read beyond that and so I put the package on the table, touched the faded paper with a reverence I might have reserved for some holy document, and began to peel it from the box beneath. One layer down and the memories began to wash my heated brain. Dad coming home with a cooler of fish for Mom and me to eat, and later—asking what I wanted for my birthday as he fried the bluegill in our cast iron skillet.

My fingers wandered to the ribbon. One pull and it came away from the paper, another layer uncovered, and I suddenly felt naked, thinking about what would have changed had I opened it right away and found a doll or teddy bear. All these years wishing for a genie to pop out and grant me three wishes.

Maybe it had kept me going.

Or held me back.

A quick tug and I was lower, my fingernails sliding beneath the seam of the box. One movement and the product of a million childhood dreams would be exposed to a little girl who could never make it what she wanted.

The top of the box came open.

Dylan leaned forward, expectant, as I drew out a buckskin bag cinched at the top with rawhide and lined with red beads.

"The medicine bag!" I heard Iris gasp.

I held it in my hand, felt the heaviness of the totems inside and loosened the rawhide.

A small piece of jawbone tumbled out, three canines still attached. A black feather came next, followed by a fragment of shell and the tip of an antler. I spread all four on the tiny table, looked at them and felt the significance of what they represented and did not know if I should touch them.

"The snakeskin?" My grandmother asked. "Where is it?"

"Snakeskin?" I echoed. "I thought there were only four."

She shook her head. "When Butler performed the resurrection ritual it required a fifth totem—a snakeskin—to grant immortality." She looked between Dylan and me. "How do you think Jonas Younts survived the lynch mob?"

"But didn't Odessa know he had become immortal? She had the Sight—"

Iris shook her head. "Grandpa Cal said she was never the same after Butler vanished. A clear mind was needed for the medicine to work, and Jonas Younts took that from her when he murdered the man she loved."

"She's talking about Stoddard, isn't she?" Dylan spoke up, at last, his voice hard.

I nodded, watched as he got up and turned in a circle, clearly uncomfortable with being confined to such a small space.

"At this point, I just want to know what really happened to Karen."

Iris touched his shoulder again. "Find the snakeskin, reverse the resurrection, and you may just get your answer."

"That's a pretty tall order," I tried to joke, feeling like a laugh was about the only thing that would save me at that moment. "I mean, we have no idea where to start looking and that guy is probably about three miles from here if he hasn't already hitched a ride with someone who is not afraid to pick up large men after dark."

My grandmother and boyfriend did not laugh.

"You need the snakeskin. It binds everything together."

Dylan put his head in his hands, worked the nape of his neck in tiny circles. "Then why don't you help us find it?"

I sighed, knowing she couldn't, wondering if it was time to start talking to Adam when a thought struck. "Jamie must have hidden it," I said suddenly. "If he's really trying to help us, maybe we can find him and—"

"You're not going anywhere until you get some sleep," my grandmother insisted. "I'll call Pam. Jamie and Adam can come here."

"Justine," Dylan said, his voice stern, and I knew it was taking everything he had not to bang our heads together and call it good. "I don't think that's a good idea."

I shook my head, determined. "I can't think of another way."

"We have to try," Dylan countered. "And we have to keep moving. This is the first place Red Rover is going to look."

"The truck was on empty," I offered, exhaustion settling in. "The Jeep's still out at Ocqueoc."

Dylan turned to my grandmother. "Your car—"

"Keys are hanging by the front door," she crossed her arms. "But you both know it's time to stop running."

"Iris—" he began.

"You're as safe here as anyplace else."

"What you mean is he'll find us wherever we go," I said, the reality of what I was about to face settling in.

"We could buy some time," Dylan persisted. "Time to think—"

"Nothing to think about," Iris said. "It's time to get your brother and end this once and for all."

Chapter Twenty-Five

I couldn't sleep.

Not surprising…

Lying under a blanket on Iris' living room floor next to Dylan, I saw a light shining from beneath her bedroom door. I wondered if she was reading and what book she'd chosen for a night such as this.

ADAM?

Worth a try, anyway… maybe I could break the news about Rocky.

I waited a few minutes and tried again.

HEY, LITTLE BROTHER—YOU OUT THERE?

Nothing but Iris' grandfather clock ticking away the minutes of my life.

I COULD REALLY USE YOUR HELP RIGHT NOW.

A car off in the distance with a very loud muffler…and I wondered if this was Red Rover's ride.

ADAM, YOU HAD BETTER FUCKING ANSWER ME!

I heard Dylan turn, his breathing finally settling into something close to steady and envied his ability to sleep.

I laid on my back, my hands resting over my chest, listening to the sounds Lantern Creek made as it slept through another night—and wished to be someone other than myself.

I had just drifted off when I heard the voice. "Muffet?"

I flinched, felt Dylan stir and strained to see in the darkness.

It was Dad. Standing in the corner by the china hutch. He wore a canvas shirt open at the collar. His jeans were worn at the knee, frayed at the bottom, his hair pulled back in a low ponytail.

"It's time," my father said, coming closer as he kneeled beside me, one hand reaching out to touch my cheek, and I felt nothing but a cool softness where his flesh should have been.

"Where's the snakeskin?"

"Follow the bird."

"Where?"

"To a place that doesn't die."

I closed my eyes, remembered the breakfast nook and the soft snow that had gathered outside its windows, remembered my father filling the small space with the smell of his coffee and paints.

"I'm scared," I said suddenly, wanting all the comfort I'd missed in the last ten years. "I don't think I can do this."

He smiled, and I remembered how safe it made me feel.

"Autumn is a second spring, when every leaf is a flower."

"Dad—" I laughed, tears coming now. He loved that quote—used to say it when we were raking leaves into slippery mounds, our feet sliding sideways. The clouds splattering against the sky like purple grapes, when I knew that winter was near.

"Don't be afraid, Muffet."

"I can't help it."

"Listen to your brother."

I laughed again, "He won't answer me."

"He needs to rest."

"Dad, please—what do I do?"

"Be happy, Muffet."

I stared. He had asked me to do the one thing I couldn't—what had been impossible since that day at the community pool.

"I can't—"

"You can."

"You left us!" I said, my voice rising, the tears spilling freely now over my lids as I sought the refuge of my pillow. And still I saw him in the darkness, kneeling beside me, his eyes cast towards the floor.

"I left you long before that day. And I'm sorry."

I couldn't breathe, couldn't process what he had said but in the deepest parts of me, I knew he was right.

Only now I knew why.

"I wanted a Dad."

"I wanted to be one."

"Then why didn't you?"

He raised his eyes to mine. "Because I knew this day would come."

I clutched my pillow, knowing his heartache, his despair, his stoic acceptance of the child that would one day cut her knee on a rusty nail and prove her Grandpa Cal right. The old stories brought to life in a place he had hoped to escape them.

My mother furious.

She had given up other children for this.

But human intentions were no match for fate—and like it or not I would have to face mine in the morning.

I unburied my face, watched as my father dissolved into the darkness and realized I didn't hear the grandfather clock anymore.

Blinking, I felt certain I had fallen asleep and gave in to the dream.

Standing now, I wandered to the front door, which had become a large piece of whitewashed oak with notches cut into it, all measuring my height from the time I was old enough to stand. I put my hand on the metal knob and opened it.

The snow was falling outside but I was not cold. It brushed my bare feet as I entered our backyard. Passing Mom's garden, I saw the red bird just ahead in the tall branches of an evergreen.

I followed and wondered if she would scold me, but she never called for me. I walked, the bird in front, through a hushed winter forest, something from an enchanted fairy tale until the path widened and spilled onto Back Forty Farm.

The main house was there, just as I remembered from my vision, white with green shutters, the porch wrapping around it like a warm hug. A sweet house, a warm house, the type of place a child would love.

A woman in a worn gingham dress stood off to the right, a woman I recognized from the book about Back Forty Farm.

Odessa.

She came and stood beside me, began to walk with me towards the house and it seemed as though we had always been together, taking this path that neither one wanted.

"Grandmother," I ventured, looking at her and seeing my father in the shape of her face.

She nodded, her long hair hanging in a braid down her back, her shoulders straight and strong.

"Did you find Butler?" I asked, my mind fixated on her wanderings through the darkened woods.

She nodded again and smiled. "In time."

We were in front of the house now and I wanted her to climb the steps with me, but I knew she would have to remain where she was.

"The medicine is a great gift," she said, her hazel eyes gazing at something just beyond the house. "That comes with a price."

I wondered what she meant and if it had something to do with how she had changed after Butler's disappearance.

"Keep the heart that was given to you."

I smiled, thinking that my heart was something that had always gotten me into trouble.

Just like Dad.

And the woman standing before me.

"It will be a light in the darkness."

I reached out, took her hand and felt our fingers intertwine.

The next moment I was alone, and so I climbed the porch steps, the bird sweeping through the front door just as Esther Ebersole opened it.

"Come in," she spoke "The weather is just about to turn."

I entered her house, watched as the bird flew towards the kitchen and perched on top of a china hutch very much like the one in Iris' living room.

"Do you care for tea?"

I looked at her, her beauty like that of a doll left out in the cold and nodded.

"Cream or sugar?"

"Both, please."

I followed her to the stove, watched as she put a kettle on and retrieved two china cups from a shelf just over the wash basin.

"Please sit."

I obeyed, took a seat at a large oak table and folded my hands on top of each other.

"Do you know my Jonas?"

I nodded.

"He cares for Red Rover."

"Cares for him?"

"Fears for his soul."

I reached for the cup she sat in front of me. Took a small sip.

"Why should he?"

Esther sat down beside me, put a hand to her neck and smoothed her plaited braids. "He killed my husband, forced the Shaman to make bad medicine."

"Bad medicine?"

"Black magic has a price. Red Rover knows that."

"Esther—" I whispered. Understanding why he had fought so hard to destroy me.

"They are damned."

"And I'm all that stands between them and hell?"

I looked at her again, saw the word pained her, that she wanted Jonas with her in death just as she'd wanted him in life.

"So why don't you kill me?"

She raised her eyes to mine, her lovely blue eyes that seemed as pale as the moon on a sheet of water.

"I hope," she began, her hands shaking as she took the china cup. "I hope you can save him."

"Is that why you came to me at the lighthouse?" I asked, placing my hand over hers to still her. "Because you wanted my help?"

She pulled her hand back, stood and went to the wash basin as the bird flew from its perch atop the hutch and out an open window.

"Take this." She turned and held out her hand. I reached for it, saw something clasped in her palm and realized it was the cameo. "Give it to Jonas."

"Why don't you give it to him yourself?" I asked.

She smiled, her teeth white and straight and still something about it made me uneasy.

"I think you know why I can't."

"No," I stood, intent on finding the bird and the snakeskin and whatever else this crazy dream had to offer. "I don't."

She looked at me, not flinching. "I'm damned, Justine—just like the rest of them."

I took a step backward, the cameo still in my hand and grasped for the doorway.

"It's no sin to love someone."

"What did I love more than my pride? My vanity?"

"You loved Jonas!" I snapped, hardly believing I was arguing with her.

"Did I?" she asked, taking a step closer. "He was young and handsome and my husband was not. What did I love, Justine?"

"You loved him and he *still* loves you."

"Does he?" She smiled, her face wistful and I knew I had to leave before this place took hold of me forever.

A few misguided steps led me to the porch, the barnyard where Abraham had died to the west, the lavender field to the south as the red bird waited beneath an eave.

Three more steps and I was running towards the tree that caught fire but never burned as the red bird swooped into a low branch, perched there and began to sing.

I ran, tripped, and fell as my fingers sought the earth beneath the snow, digging.

"The ground is frozen."

I looked up. Saw Dylan standing beyond me on the edge of the forest and said, "I can get to it."

"After the thaw."

I looked at my fingers, saw that they were raw and bleeding and then stood up, walked to him as he turned and led me into the woods. Minutes later we entered a secret clearing where the snow had not fallen, a temperate valley bedded with pine needles and smelling of spring.

He knelt on the needles, took my hands in his and rubbed them. "You're so cold."

I felt warmth beginning in my fingers. "Please," I mumbled, dropping to my knees beside him. "Don't stop."

He pulled back for a moment, his eyes questioning, and then wrapped his arms around my waist, collapsing backwards so that I straddled him as the warmth continued to drip like candle wax down either leg.

I touched his face, the tips of my fingers leaving red marks on his forehead and cheeks and lips. The blood that was supposed to end all this, and he took a finger, kissed the tip of it and then drew it into his mouth.

I gasped, looked up into the trees, searching for my father or Esther or the bird—anything that would tell me where I was.

"Stay with me," he instructed, his hands moving beneath my shirt to cup my breasts. Moments later he was exposing my bare flesh to his heated gaze and I reached down, pulled his orange T-shirt over the top of his head, marveling again at his physical beauty until all I wanted was to meld completely with this man.

And so, I laid down on top of him, tracing the lines of his jaw and neck and collarbone with my tongue, my fingers sliding over the flesh of his lower abdomen until I found the waistband of his blue jeans. One snap and they were undone and he was shaking them off, the trees overhead swaying with a breeze we did not feel.

"What is this place?" I asked, my lips travelling over the ridged expanse of his rib cage and down to his belly button, where I felt him draw a staggered breath.

"I don't know," he answered, his voice catching as I moved lower, and lower still, wanting nothing more than to show him how much I loved him before the sun rose. "But it's always been here."

"Like us?" I asked, rising again as he eased my shorts down over my hips. Naked now, I looked down on him beneath me, looked again to the trees and knew we were alone.

"I think so," he said, his eyes catching and holding mine as he guided me, his movements gentle yet determined, as though sensing the urgency I did and the fear that tomorrow would come and it wouldn't be enough.

He wouldn't be enough.

"Will you come with me?" I whispered, my hands braced against his shoulders, my eyes closing softly while seeking a rhythm we had perfected, something no other lover could duplicate.

"Justine," he began, his breath coming faster, his hands against my hips, holding them steady. "I'm afraid."

I understood and said nothing as I rode the wave of pleasure his body gave me, remained silent as the parts of me that seemed strong and straight and honorable buckled. Collapsing on top of him, I kissed his shoulder, nibbled at the soft skin just below his jawline, wondering if the mark I left would reveal itself in the morning.

Or if I'd wake to nothing.

Chapter Twenty-Six

Muffled voices outside the front door startled me. I turned, stretched, then squinted as light, weak as the tea Esther had served me in my dreams, crawled through the curtains.

I squinted at the clock, saw that it was just past seven in the morning and cursed myself for not getting up earlier.

But the daylight made everything seem better, even the events of the night before blended until together they made an odd concoction consisting of equal parts dream and denial.

I rolled over and grabbed the medicine bag, half surprised that it hadn't been spirited away during the night. Iris' bedroom door was closed, and I wondered if she had called Jamie and Adam and if they were indeed on their way over here to figure everything out.

Turning over, I saw Dylan, still asleep beside me. He had indeed shed his shirt sometime in the middle of the night. A quick peek under the blanket convinced me I hadn't been dreaming and a warm tingle swept my body.

I lay back down, wondering if I should wake him when the voices came again, louder this time and with a hint of annoyance.

"The rent's to be paid up by three o'clock today or you and your friend can find yourselves another place to stay."

I heard the words clearly, threw back the covers and got dressed before scrambling to the kitchen window. Holly was standing outside, late for work as the irreverent Mr. Stoddard waved his arms like an angry schoolmaster.

"We'll have it, Mr. S," she tried to placate him. "Didn't realize we were late."

He mumbled something under his breath, dismissing her the next moment and I wondered if calling her would be too risky. Dylan's truck must have clued her in to our whereabouts, but beyond that, she must be worried, must be wondering where I was and why I'd suddenly gone AWOL when rent was due.

I was lost in mindless thought when I saw Mr. Stoddard approach the door, his greedy eyes zeroing in on me, the other half of his problem.

One quick knock. Soft at first, followed by a more insistent, "You in there?"

I glanced back at the still-sleeping Dylan and chained the door before opening it.

"Mr. S, what a pleasant surprise."

"Whatchya doin' down here?" he smirked, and I could see the wheels in his head turning. "Keepin' the ol' lady company?"

I nodded, the chain still between us, the medicine bag still in my hand. "I fell asleep on her couch."

"Ah," he nodded. "Rent was due first of the week."

"Sorry," I fished in my pockets for some cash, felt my fingers brush something solid and realized it was the cameo.

My heart went cold.

"I think I have some money upstairs."

"I'll wait while you git it."

I shook my head. "I kinda need to stay close to Iris for awhile."

"Fine," he shrugged, taking a step back from the door. "But you and Hot Lips up there had better be squared away by three o'clock."

I bit back a smile, wanting nothing more than to shut him and his crazy, inane requests out of my life forever. "Shouldn't be a problem."

"I'll be back later," he moved away, his eyes still on me and in that instant, I saw that he had been painting, that the yellow speckles my father had worn on his forearms now matched the ones on my landlord. His shirt, a crew neck that had once been white, bore a faded logo.

REDDING—GROVER HARDWARE.

The paint had splattered across the DING and bled into the G, leaving only...

My grip on the door frame tightened as I scrambled to slam it shut, but not before my landlord braced his weight against it, his black eyes watching from the small space in between.

"Hello, Muffet."

He cares for Red Rover... Now I knew why.

"Scream an' you're dead."

I fought the urge to tell him he was full of bullshit, but my mind was spinning too quickly for comebacks. And he had a gun. Not the shotgun of my nightmares, but a 9mm revolver he'd pushed through the crack in the door and pointed straight at my head.

Dylan's gun.

"Think you can come outside now?" He asked, his fingers working the chain until he found its origin, pulling it loose from its casing like a knife slicing through warm butter. "Or should I send ya to meet that whore my boy was screwing?"

"She saved his life," I spat, still straining against his massive weight.

"*Ruined* is more like." He smirked, and I saw his tongue move across his teeth, which were stained and yellow and starting to show their true age. "Now gather them things up so we can git this over with. It's been a long time coming."

When I didn't move he pulled back the slide and I saw Dylan stir, saw his eyes flicker open as a storm of terror overtook me.

One bullet to end his life and then mine would be worthless.

"Move it."

The next moment he pulled me out the door and across the driveway, my feet tangling as he dragged me towards the red pickup he'd been leaning against when I first met him.

Back when he was just an asshole who hated my cat.

Moments later I was behind the wheel, the gun pressed to the side of my neck.

"Drive."

I hesitated, pulled at my bottom lip with my teeth as I threw the truck in gear. One glance over my shoulder told me Dylan had either fallen back asleep or was formulating a plan that did not involve rushing from the apartment in a hail of gunfire. Either way, there was a good possibility I would never see him again and the thought struck me like a stone between the eyes, making them water.

I saw him open the medicine bag, saw him shake it as if to make sure he'd gotten everything in his Happy Meal and when he looked back up his face was red with rage. "Where's the snakeskin?"

I took a moment to collect myself before saying, "I don't know what you're talking about."

He leaned closer, his breath fanning the hair on the side of my face as we pulled out of the driveway and headed toward the center of town. "I think you do."

"The others are there," I said, wondering how long I could stall him before he tired of me and put a bullet in my head. "What does it matter?"

He chuckled, convinced for the moment that I really was an idiot. "I need to burn 'em all up so I don't wake up in the morning with a new passel of Cook whelps to worry about."

"You mean so you can live forever."

"Mayhap," he said. "Why do you think I bought that piece o' shit house from your granny? To keep my eye on the mother hen until the chicks came back to the coop."

I swallowed, unnerved by the fact that he'd been watching Iris. "You didn't know where we were?"

"That Injun's magic was strong, kept you hidden until you and your baby brother got close again. That's when things started to git a whole lot clearer."

I swallowed, realizing that when Dad said we were stronger together, it also meant more dangerous.

"So, you started killing people who looked like me, hoping you would get the right one eventually?" I asked, wanting to hurt him so badly I could hardly see the road in front of me. I imagined how it would feel to put my fist through his gut—then remembered the gun.

I was strong but not immortal.

He had the market on that.

"Couldn't be helped. I guess my boy was a little tore up about the one, but he'll get over it."

"You killed Karen?" I asked, wanting him to answer for Dylan as well as myself.

"It was an accident, Muffet," he grinned.

"No, it wasn't," I said. "Jamie was helping her escape and you *did* something...something to cause the accident."

Mr. Stoddard shook his head, readjusted his hold on the gun.

"I shoulda known he was soft a long time ago when he went after that medicine bag. I told him to hand it over, but he kept sayin' there was a way to bring that whore he loved back to life. Said if I din't help him do it he was gonna put a bullet in his own head."

I grimaced, remembering Esther's beauty and how it could drive a man like Jonas to contemplate suicide.

"What makes you think I know where the snakeskin is?"

"Your Pa talk to you much?" He dropped the gun, traced the scar on my kneecap with the barrel. "How 'bout that witch went by the name Odessa?"

I swallowed, wishing I had a moment to think.

"Ol' Bob Cook got his hands on that bag when my boy wasn't lookin' so I 'spect he might have told you where the snakeskin is."

"He didn't," I answered, my fingers squeezing the steering wheel. "He left home when I was eleven and I haven't seen him since."

"Guess I don't need ya then," he said while raising the gun to my temple.

"No!" I cried, sweat pooling beneath my shirt and under my arms. "I can take you to where it is."

"Thought so," he smiled again, leaned back against his seat as I came to the 23 turnoff. "Your Pa wasn't able to tell me much at first either."

"Fuck you," I whispered, tears stinging my eyes as I swung left onto the highway, the forest encroaching at once, smothering us, and I wanted to scream, wanted to tell him to go ahead and kill me because no way in hell was I going to hand over the snakeskin once I'd found it.

And no way was this asshole going to get away with murdering my Dad.

"Your Pa was a fighter, Muffet. I'll tell ya that. Real strong, too. And I have to say that Law Dog you been screwing had some spunk. Good thing his gun was empty when I found it. Woulda cut him up into little pieces if it hadn't been for that charm 'round his neck. Got as close as that arm o' his and it got to me. But I'm gettin' stronger every day. Won't happen again."

"You've got a way with words, Mr. S." I glanced his way. "If that's your real name."

He rubbed his nose, adjusted his weight on the seat beside me and I heard his fat settle.

"Now what makes you think I'd play anyone false," he chuckled, tapped the seat between us with his gun. "I used to be a preacher in this town."

"Preacher?" I echoed, a misplaced memory surfacing along with my terror as the sign for Three Fires appeared to my left.

"Had 'ol River Run Lutheran for a spell back when I went by the name o' Henry Younts. Took the piss an vinegar outta most o' the lumberjacks what thought they didn't need no fire and brimstone."

"And what do you think of everlasting damnation?" I asked, turning to glance at him. He was staring ahead, his florid features softening in the light.

"I think you need to stop askin' so many questions."

I obeyed while turning my attention back to the road and felt my left thigh vibrate. Looking down, I knew it was the cell phone I'd jammed into my pocket the night before.

"Go on an' answer it," Mr. Stoddard instructed. "But you best behave or I'll take that blessed kneecap as a souvenir."

I looked at him for a moment, dazed, and then fished my phone out and held it to my ear.

"Hello?" I spoke, waiting for a voice and the next moment Dylan's was there.

"Are you with him?"

I gripped the wheel, "Sure am. How're you?"

"Not so hot," a short pause followed by, "Did he hurt you?"

I felt the bridge of my nose tingle, imagined how I would feel if our roles were reversed and almost lost it. "I'm good."

"He doesn't know where the snakeskin is, does he?"

Damn, he was smart and incredibly honorable, and hot and...

"I don't think so," I answered. "I'm running to the bank to get it."

"He'll kill you once he finds it."

I tried to laugh. "No kidding! You can pay me back later."

"Don't panic," his tone was steady—all cop. "I'll find you."

"I know you will," I said, my voice softening.

"Justine—"

"Gotta run. You're the best, you know that?"

"Don't," he began, his own voice unraveling.

The next instant he was gone, our connection lost and with it went all sense of composure, all hope for a future in California or Hoboken or Lantern Creek but I had to hold it together, had to act like the phone call had been from Holly even if Mr. Stoddard knew different.

HE DOESN'T

His voice shook me to my core, giving me hope.

TAKE HIM TO BACK FORTY FARM

ADAM—

I'M ON MY WAY

* * *

The late summer wind was cold, so brisk it stole my breath before I could give it away. I stepped from the red pickup, the ruins of Esther and Abraham Ebersole's house before us. I listened as my landlord's boots shuffled beside me, trying to imagine how many times they had travelled this road.

The one that led to everyone's beginning.

I thought of Dylan, wanting him to find me and wanting him to stay as far away as possible. And yet I needed him if I was ever going to stop this monster once and for all.

We walked in silence, a strange sense of calm descending where panic should have been.

I walked and thought of Esther, her cameo still in my pocket, and Abraham and Jonas and Odessa. I thought of Mr. Henry Younts, the Lutheran preacher turned immortal vigilante and spoke.

"Did you love her?"

"Hmmm," he grunted. "Who're you speakin' of?"

"Odessa," I continued, my feet taking me to the front porch of Back Forty Farm and up the steps, where I paused before opening the door, the red bird just beneath the eaves as it had always been. I thought of the letter I'd read that day at Camp Menominee and knew I had to play my cards carefully.

"I know Johnson and his ma wanted you to marry her."

He stopped, looked at me and for an instant, I saw the man he had once been— proud and simple and unable to understand why she had chosen Butler over him.

"Johnny was a fool and his ma not far behind."

I reached for the doorknob, which was ready to come away with my hand, and looked into his black eyes. "But it must have been painful for you to lose her, after everything with Cal."

He grunted again, blew a breath out. "I stood by her all right. Took her side when folks called her a whore for havin' that boy outta wedlock. An' me a preacher, ready to give her my last name."

I turned the knob, felt the door give way and shifted my weight away from him.

"An' what does she do but spit on it like it wasn't no better than those fleas what lived on her Injun."

"So, you had reason to hate him, to kill him—"

Red Rover turned, his eyes on me again and I did not see Henry Younts, only the wicked creature Butler's bad medicine had created. "Reason enough to bury him where he'll never be found."

The next second the door gave way and I moved, striking him in the jaw as he lost his grip on the gun. Next up was his big toe and I stomped on it, felt his bones crunch as I dove for the medicine bag.

"Bitch!" I heard him curse as he caught a fistful of hair. Slamming my head against the doorjamb, I saw stars.

Twisting in his grasp, I brought my good knee into his groin as he pulled, taking a clot of blonde hair with him but releasing the rest of me.

The next second, I was scrambling for the second floor while shoving the gun into the waistband of my shorts, the medicine bag in my hand. A quick glance behind told me he had no intention of following but seemed content to wait at the bottom of the staircase, his voice rising upwards like a death knell.

"That smarted a bit, Muffet. You've got a mean right hook."

"I appreciate that, Mr. Younts."

"That gun ain't gonna do you no good so why don't you jest come back down."

"Why don't you come up?"

"Mayhap I will. Take the sass outta ya." One step followed by another followed by a creak that told me he'd reached the seventh step, and I scampered for the southernmost bedroom, ran to the window and looked out at the oak ablaze in the morning sun—a red bird in its branches.

A place that doesn't die...

And I realized that the same thing that had kept the tree frozen in time had also been keeping Jonas and his father alive.

I remembered my dream, how my fingertips had bled while I dug beneath the tree for something I couldn't name.

The snakeskin.

And I had a pretty good idea who had hidden it here.

I felt a weight lifted and began to search the room for anything that might give me an advantage and realized the only way out was down.

"I'm comin', Muffet," he called, at the top of the stairs now. "An' when I ketch you, Law Dog ain't gonna like what he sees."

I gripped the frame, swung my legs out, and dropped onto the roof. Still, the ground was a good twelve feet below and a broken leg wasn't something I could afford with a lunatic on my tail.

I dashed to the edge, felt his presence behind me, and didn't look back. I jumped, my cell phone taking flight, my body curling into a position I'd seen Joey nail a hundred times. I landed with a roll, my legs folding beneath me and still my knee held out without the brace to support it.

Looking up, I saw Red Rover at the window, watching. The next instant, he disappeared, and I got to my feet, racing for the tree and the spot I remembered from my dream. Moments later I was on my hands and knees, digging as fast as I could.

I felt my hands burning, my fingers catch fire as blood appeared on the tips and still I glanced behind, ready to shoot with the useless gun if he dared to show his face.

But he didn't.

A few seconds later I came upon a small piece of burlap. Snatching it to my chest, I stood up and limped across the lavender field and towards the forest.

Once inside the tree line, I looked back at the house. All was silent, still— like a picture my father may have painted.

I wondered where Henry Younts was and why he was waiting now that I had everything he had ever wanted in my hands.

I stood for a moment, then took a step deeper into the forest. Another step and I remembered the clearing from my dream—the temperate valley that smelled of pine and springtime. It was there, I knew it—just beyond where the red bird had perched in the high branch of a maple tree while Dylan and I made love below.

I moved again, one hand on the barrel of the 9mm. I could only remember shooting a gun once before when Brad had insisted I go to the range with him. He wanted me to be prepared in case a weirdo tried to rape me in the newspaper parking lot—never stopping to consider that weirdo might be him.

I remembered the sequence: pull back the slide, load the chamber, safety off, and squeeze the trigger. Brad had taught me never to close both eyes when I looked through the sights. My peripheral vision was an edge, he said, and that's where the weirdos always came from. Even though it had made me dizzy, I shot that day with both eyes open, my elbows bent to absorb the kick, and I'd hit my mark.

I could do it again.

Moving on through the woods, I saw the river to the west and followed its progress, watching for the bird as it swooped in front of me, Odessa's words reminding me to rely on more than just my eyes.

I made my way towards Ocqueoc Falls as the light withered and still I felt like I was ahead of Red Rover.

Until I saw Karen.

I stopped, unable to believe what I was seeing.

She stood in the forest in the clothes she had died in, khaki pants and a white top smeared with blood. The left side of her face had been crushed, but not enough to dull our resemblance.

HE SENT HER HERE TO MESS WITH YOUR HEAD

I took a step backwards, my legs wet noodles.

HE'S DOING A DAMN GOOD JOB

Karen came closer and I noticed how her good eye watched me like a lioness stalking a gazelle. I saw her slender fingers clench and unclench, dark liquid staining her knuckles, oozing between them as though she'd been picking blackberries.

I pulled the gun from the waistband of my jeans and flipped off the safety.

"Get out of here," I ordered, the feel of the gun empowering.

SHE'S NOT REAL

I wanted to tell him to shut up because from where I stood, she looked pretty fucking real.

"Give the medicine bag to me," she reached out that stained hand, smiled, and I fought the insane urge to drop the deerskin pouch and run like hell.

Instead, I put my finger on the trigger and said, "Come and get it."

She smiled again, worse than any ghoul from my nightmares, and lunged at me.

I squeezed off a shot that hit her in the shoulder, propelling her sideways but not dropping her. Another shot found her neck, the flesh exploding in a spray of red mush.

And still, she staggered forward.

I knew I had about eight rounds left and aimed for her kneecaps.

The first one missed her altogether. The second hit her just below the thigh as she came closer, her fingers reaching for me as I stumbled backwards—falling.

I cursed, trying to get my bearings when I heard a loud bark. Looking up, I caught sight of a black lab zipping through the trees in a mad beeline for what appeared to be me.

"Rocky!" I screeched as she lunged again, the smell of putrefaction making me retch, her black fingers finding my ankle and twisting.

Seconds later the dog leapt into the air and came down with her neck in its mouth, tearing at flesh and bone, breaking her arms into little pieces. I looked away, not wanting to see what would happen to that decaying body.

But Adam was right. She wasn't real, and before I knew it Rocky was tearing at dirt and air instead of her, until what was left of Karen disintegrated like ash in the wind before vanishing altogether.

I sat watching, my breath coming in terrible pants before sliding the gun back into my waistband.

"Shit," I ran the back of my hand over my mouth and started to shake.

I was in disbelief one minute, sobbing the next, the medicine bag still in my hand. Seconds later I took hold of Rocky's fur and buried my head in the softness.

"Good boy," I whispered, and moments later felt his head on my shoulder. "I'm glad you're okay."

The forest seemed to breathe with me and then I heard it.

SAME HERE

I opened my eyes and saw Adam standing beside us.

"How did you get here?" I asked, forgetting for the moment that he wouldn't answer in a typical way.

I FOLLOWED THE DOG

"But Red Rover killed him in the woods," I touched Rocky again, unable to believe he'd survived, speaking aloud to my brother for the first time. And it felt so good to not have to hide it anymore.

ROCKY SAYS YOU SHOULD HAVE MORE FAITH IN HIM

"Rocky says—" I began, struggling to my feet. "Should I even ask?"

WE ALL HAVE OUR GIFTS

"And one of yours is talking to animals?"

ROCKY ISN'T JUST ANY ANIMAL. HE'S MY PROTECTOR. LIKE DYLAN IS TO YOU.

Like Dylan… I knew I couldn't let my thoughts linger on him or I would lose all the courage I'd gathered in the last half hour. And still I wondered if he had been able to trace the phone to the farmhouse and if he was on his way here because sooner or later I was going to have to cut myself.

"So, what happens next?" I asked, my eyes scanning the woods for Henry Younts, Dylan, Jamie Stoddard, Esther, the red bird…anything.

WE NEED TO GET TO THE FALLS

"Where Butler performed the first ritual?" I asked, "I saw it in a dream. It's an island—"

I KNOW WHERE IT IS

I reached for my brother, pulling him along as Rocky circled behind, looking for Henry Younts. And I was glad he was.

"I'm scared, Adam," I said, "What if—

WE CAN DO THIS

I looked down at him, his dark curls just reaching my shoulder, and ruffled the top of his head.

"You're something, you know that?"

YOU SHOULD TALK

I just managed to smile as we passed the trailhead for Ocqueoc Falls. Stopping, I bent a branch backwards, one I seemed to remember swiping Dylan in the face the night before, hoping it would help him find us. The next minute we were running down the path, the next minute veering off into the wilderness until we came to the place in my dream—a small island in the middle of a marsh.

I stopped, wondering how we were going to get to it and when we did if it would support our weight or sink to the bottom of the river.

One jump told me Adam was into the quick and easy route, and so I followed, my toes just reaching the spongy edge.

Once on solid ground, I opened my mind to my brother's and saw what was waiting inside, what my father had given him when he couldn't do anything else. I took out the medicine bag and used my finger to draw the wheel with four spokes, the same mark Dylan had between his shoulder blades, then sat back on my haunches and watched my brother as he gathered wet earth with his hands.

PUT THE TOTEMS INSIDE

I reached for the bag, drew out the antler, jawbone, shell, and feather. Placing one inside each quadrant, I saved the snakeskin for last, carefully pushing it into the hub with the tip of my finger.

NOW FOR THE FIRE

I watched him gather more mud, work it with his hands again in a way that seemed karmic, and after some time had passed I saw the mass begin to glow, spark, and catch fire until Adam's hands were nothing but a ball of flames.

And while I should have screamed or carried on or thrown a bucket of water on him I had to admit I'd seen stranger things in the last twenty minutes and so sat back and waited while he set fire to the wheel I'd drawn.

"How long will it burn?" I asked, the totems inside beginning to wither and curl as his own hands rematerialized without so much as a blister.

UNTIL YOU PUT IT OUT

I looked towards the trail, the realization stealing my air and all the while I thought of Dylan, wondering if he would get here in time or if we should wait.

But there was no time. My whole life had been leading up to this moment and I had to believe that the powers that had entrusted me with the gift would also lead Dylan where he needed to go.

YOU NEED TO USE THIS

I watched as Adam reached into the back pocket of his jeans and pulled out a hunting knife with a white bone handle—something I would have admired under different circumstances.

"Did this belong to Butler?"

Adam nodded, his face pinched and I knew he was wondering the same thing I was.

WHERE IS HE?

"He's coming."

WE CAN'T START WITHOUT HIM

"We have to," I glanced towards the forest. "Red Rover's coming."

I CAN'T STOP IT. YOU'LL BLEED TO DEATH.

"He'll be here!"

Adam sat back, watching the flames and I closed my eyes, willing Dylan to find me as I drew the blade across my left wrist.

Pain—at once sharp and aching spread up to my elbow and I bit my lip to stifle my screams. I dropped the knife as the blood came quickly, running down my palm and to the end of my fingertips where it met the hungry fire.

WE NEED MORE

I didn't understand at first, not until I saw him pick up the knife and take my right wrist in his hand. He hesitated, his face a mixture of terror and resignation.

"Do it," I whispered, already feeling weak. "I can't."

He drew the blade quickly and this time I couldn't stop the screams that radiated through the forest, alerting Red Rover to our location.

FOLLOW THE FIRE

I did as he told me, and as I followed the outline the flames began to sputter and die, my blood killing what water should have.

STAY WITH IT

I heard him but couldn't answer because the blood was coming faster, rolling off the edge of my fingernails and down past my elbows and filling up my ears and twisting my stomach and I knew—

"Justine!"

I looked up, saw Dylan running through the woods as fast as his bad ankle would carry him and almost forgot what I was doing. I tried to stand, my pulse pounding in my arms as Red Rover stepped from his hiding place and into Dylan's path.

I opened my mouth, tried to scream, and found I was too weak.

HELP HIM, ADAM!

One nod and Rocky was off, charging his old nemesis as he jumped at his throat, his teeth sinking into meaty flesh. I heard the preacher howl, heard him curse as he tried to get hold of the dog with his enormous hands. Three wild grasps and he had Rocky by the head, flinging him into the underbrush while turning his attention to Dylan, who had just reached the water's edge.

"You ain't goin' nowhere, Law Dog," he growled, pieces of flesh hanging where his chin had once been. One lunge and he knocked Dylan to the ground. I saw him rip at the necklace, tearing the talisman off while throwing it into the underbrush.

He was right about getting stronger, and now Dylan didn't stand a chance.

I was beginning to see spots, my skin chilled as I slid into a seated position, Adam supporting me, holding me—a quarter of the circle still burning.

FINISH IT

The next second Dylan had broken free and was struggling to his feet. He swung at Red Rover, his fist connecting with the latter's gut in a way that seemed as useless as the gun I'd thrown aside.

And then I began to pray—something I hadn't done since the day Mom had handed me that piece of paper over the front seat of our brown Pontiac.

I prayed for Dylan to live, for Red Rover to lose his grip and sink into the earth, for my blood to put out the fire. I prayed that Iris and I would share another glass of lemonade and that Mom would someday teach my daughter the difference between a Black-Eyed Susan and a Coneflower.

I prayed that Pam would be able to sleep at night and that my brother would grow into a strong young man who would come over to my house for afternoon barbecues.

I prayed that I would live to see a second spring come to this forest. That I would dream every night of Dad and his silver canoe.

I prayed all these things in my brother's arms, my blood flowing down my hands when a sound startled me. Footsteps—measured and deliberate—made me turn as a third figure emerged from the woods and took hold of Red Rover by the scruff of the neck.

It only took a moment for Dylan to get free—and when he did he wasted no time.

"It's over, Pa," I heard the familiar voice through my stupor and fought to continue, the circle extinguished as I moved to the hub.

"After all I done for you?" Henry spat at his son and I crawled on, Adam at my side, the earth rocking up to cradle me. "This is how you pay me back?"

"I never wanted any of this," Jamie Stoddard spoke, his form and face reminding me of an angel in these last moments as Dylan jumped the water. "I only wanted Esther."

"Too late for that," his father said, and I wondered if it was ever too late for anything.

And then Dylan was there, shoving Adam aside as he scooped me into his arms.

"Stay with me," his words were firm. "I'll get you through this."

I smiled, very calm. Very cold. "I trust you."

He put pressure on my wrists and at first, it felt lovely, warm and exhilarating. I smiled again, turned my face into his chest and let his heartbeat lull me to sleep. Because that was all I wanted.

"Look at me," Dylan ordered, his tone losing some of its strength, its certainty. "Open your eyes."

I wanted to, but the blood was still coming and his fingers were starting to slide as he fought for a grip, fought for us and I knew he would have to take it from here. That I would have to let him.

"Please don't leave me," he whispered, his face close to my ear and I couldn't make my mouth open, couldn't reassure him in the tiniest bit as he rocked me, whispering the words I'd been waiting for.

"I love you."

And then nothing.

Chapter Twenty-Seven

I didn't die—but the light at the end of the tunnel did make a cameo appearance in the form of a fluorescent bulb just above my hospital bed.

I ran my tongue along the roof of my mouth and drew a dry breath. One wiggle of my fingers told me my wrists had been stitched up. One furrow of my forehead said I had one hell of a goose egg where Red Rover had slammed me into that door frame.

I parted my lips, tried to lick them and opened my eyes. At first, I saw nothing but a bedside tray littered with the things I'd had in my pockets. Next to that was my cell phone and a bouquet of wildflowers with an unopened card that read simply: "Flats."

I chuckled, my throat raw and wondered what the doctors had been up to. "Justine?"

I blinked hard, saw my mom seated in a mauve chair, Pam to her left, and thought maybe I'd been wrong about the dying part.

"Thank God," my mother said while pushing to her feet, coming to my bedside, and taking my hand in hers.

"How did I get here?" I asked, confused.

"Dylan called an ambulance. They met him at the trailhead."

I tried to lift my hands and found them cocooned in gauze. I glanced at Pam.

"We had to tell them something," she said. "Not the truth, of course."

"We said you'd been depressed over a break-up," Mom offered, and I didn't know whether to be offended or laugh my head off. Yes...the nurses would be sure to handle me with tender loving care, the pathetic girl who had slit her wrists over a man.

Another glance at Pam and she pressed her lips together, patted my hand, careful not to disturb the gauze.

"Pam and I were catching up," Mom added, as though she and my father's mistress, side by side and together was as ordinary as spending the night in intensive care.

"Adam?" I croaked out, hating the sound of my voice.

Pam got up, came to my bedside. "He's in the waiting room. Has been since they brought you in."

I frowned, thinking of what my loved ones had been through while I'd been in la-la land. "I'm sorry."

"Don't be," Pam said. "I'm so glad we have you two back, safe and sound."

"Although it was touch and go with you for awhile," Mom offered, her tone unsure and I fought the urge to apologize again.

"Rocky?" I asked them.

"Is fine," Pam smoothed my hair from my forehead and I instinctively glanced towards Mom. She smiled, something of the woman I'd seen in the wedding album still there after all these years.

"How much did you two know?"

"I knew about as much as Pam did. Robert—" A slight pause and I wondered if his name was still a tender spot between them. "He didn't want us to worry." Then, to Pam, "Did he?"

"No," she answered.

Mom looked down, perhaps embarrassed, perhaps relieved or distressed or still in mourning for the man who had married her in the country chapel, just as Pam might be for the lover that had found her in his silver canoe.

"I'll leave you two alone," Pam offered, stepping towards the door and I knew she was leaving to check on Adam.

Once upon a time, being alone with my mother would have terrified me, but now I found a strange peace as she pulled the mauve chair to my bedside.

"I met Dylan."

I looked up, my face hopeful, "Is he okay?"

"A little banged up but it doesn't hurt the eyes much."

I blushed, thinking about what he'd said in the woods, wondering if it would change anything between us.

"Where is he?"

"He went home to shower and change," my mother paused, pleased with something and I could hardly imagine it had anything to do with me. "He slept here all night, you know," she motioned towards the chair Pam had just vacated. "In that."

"Mom..."

"You did good, Muffet."

I felt my eyes water, wondering why her opinion mattered so much and realized it always had, from the time she'd charged full steam into single motherhood to the awkward dance we'd done ever since.

"Your father would be proud."

I looked away, unable to answer as she reached out again, squeezing my shoulder.

"You loved him so much...*more.*" She paused. "Maybe I was jealous. I never understood it, never heard the things you did or saw the things you seemed to see."

"Mom—"

"But I guess I didn't want to get close to something I could lose."

I closed my eyes, wishing away her words and at the same time holding them close.

"I should have been there when you were afraid—when you needed someone to comfort you," she stopped, and I thought I heard her voice catch. "To tuck you in at night."

I turned my head, the tears flowing now as I thought back on an eleven-year-old used to her father's goodnight kisses climbing the steps alone, a mother at the bottom telling her to set her alarm clock so she wouldn't miss the bus.

"We can't go back and change the past."

"I know," she nodded, her face marked with a type of happiness I'd never seen before. "But I'd still like to change the future."

I looked at her, tall and slim and still pretty, her blonde hair the same color as mine and saw myself in her for the first time.

"You can start now," I smiled, tugging at the covers on the side of my bed, throwing them back in a way that said she could straighten them, pull them up to my chin, and kiss my cheek before turning out the light.

And she did.

Chapter Twenty-Eight

The old man was sitting by my bed—waiting before I even opened my eyes and I saw his face, remembered it from somewhere beyond the moment and knew he was a friend.

I sat up and he smiled, his amber eyes crinkling at the corners before I was able to remember. His gray hair had a startling effect, as did the clothes that seemed to come from another era.

"Jamie?" I asked, and he nodded, his face a mixture of resignation and relief. "How can you be here? I thought—"

"That I was dead?"

"Yes," I said, guilt causing me to look down and fiddle with my gauze.

"Takes a bit longer than a day to undo a hundred years," He got up, walked with a shuffling step to the window and pushed aside the curtain with a finger. "And besides, I wanted to thank you while I still had the chance."

I didn't want to ask him but knew I had to. "Your father?"

He put his hands in his pockets, leaned against the window. "He's gone."

"And my father?" I asked, looking past him.

He shook his head, his kindness displayed plainly now, and I wondered if it had been hard for him to pretend to be something he wasn't. Or if he'd been fighting the darkness that had consumed Henry Younts. "Pa and him met up in the woods and—" He paused, unable, or unwilling, to continue.

"My father is dead, isn't he?"

Jamie looked up at me and for a moment I thought he might tell me it was all a cruel joke and Robert Cook was waiting down at the diner in the corner booth, ready to share a coke and cheeseburger. And even though I could have imagined a thousand things I would rather be doing with Dad, the thought of sharing a simple meal hurt the most.

"I saw his picture in the newspaper downstate," I said. "That's why I came. During your big snowfall. In the hardware store—"

The old man held up a hand and I stopped. "I think he wanted you to see. Only you. To get you here. But he's gone, Justine. Forever."

His words left me reeling, even though I'd known if Dad had been alive he would have fought to protect his children.

"Where did Henry Younts…leave him?" I asked, wanting that much at least.

"Pa never told me. I never wanted to know. It was the same way with Butler."

"Jamie—" I began, my eyes welling up with tears, thoughts of Dad and his paints and his strong arms putting me in the crook of that hollow tree swirling like a fog suddenly lifted with sunlight.

"He was a Cook. And because of that a little bit of the man who loved Odessa lives in you and always will."

"Don't—" I began, too weak for grief this strong. "Not now…"

Jamie nodded, came towards me and touched my arm. "Just know that he loved you and your Mother very much. He never wanted to hurt you. Or leave you."

I wiped at the tears, "I know that now. Thanks to you. And I'm sorry…for what happened to you and Esther. Maybe I'm even sorry for what happened to Henry Younts."

"Don't be." He stepped back from the bed, darkness blurring his features and I wondered if that was how he wanted it. "You did what needed to be done. What should have been done if things hadn't gotten so"—he paused, searching—"out of hand."

"He loved Odessa."

"No more than his pride."

I waited, then realized he was trying to make sense of the man he'd shared so many lifetimes with and gave him a moment.

"I did my best to help you," he stood looking down at me, an old man who would soon get the answers he sought. "Even when I thought Pa might find out."

"Karen?" I asked, wondering what had happened on that dusty road in the black Jetta.

He nodded, ready to talk as well. "I got close to her on purpose until Pa said it was time to end it and I just couldn't…kill her like that. So, I took off, thinking we could run away or I could take her somewhere but he came out of the woods, stood in front of the car with his shotgun and I had to swerve… I *had* to, Justine— or he would have killed her on the spot."

"And when you saw my scar that day at Three Fires—"

He touched his forehead. "I knew Pa had made a mistake. But the images came to him in bits and pieces. He couldn't see clearly until you and Adam were together. He was like a predator stalking his prey and the scent was stronger. And I started to feel myself turning," he paused. "Becoming more like him. But I fought it, Justine. You have to know that. I fought it with all I had—"

"Jamie—"

"I should have tried harder to save her, to save Suzy Marsh, to save *you*."

I smiled at him, grateful. "You did more than enough."

He looked away, back towards the summer day dying slowly outside our window. "But was it enough? Do you think—to see Esther again?"

I looked over at the bedside tray—at the things that had been taken from my pockets and saw the cameo amongst the clutter of insignificance. Reaching out, I took it and brought it into the light where he had to bend close to see. At once his face changed, and he held out his hand asking to hold it and I placed it in the center of his palm, folded his fingers around it.

"From her?" He could hardly ask, his eyes going soft at the memory. "She was wearing this the night we met. At the barn dance, in Millersburg."

"She's in a good place," I said, knowing it was true. "And she's waiting for you."

He opened his hand, looked down on the cameo. "And I've been so long getting around to it. She must be pretty mad by now."

"Tell her you had to wait on me."

His laughter swept the room before tapering into a gentle cough I knew would get worse as time wore on and I wondered where he would go and how he would spend his last days and with whom.

"Thank you for this." Then, sensing my thoughts, "I'd best be moving on before someone catches wind I'm not your Uncle Rex from Indiana."

I smiled, watching as he worked the cameo between his fingers before sliding it into his pocket, and I reached out to him, my arms open as he stepped into them, bending as best he could, and felt like it had always been meant to be.

We stayed that way for several seconds before I felt someone enter the room, someone I'd been waiting for since the beginning and I wanted to hold onto this moment before he slipped away forever.

But I did let go as Jamie stood upright, Dylan just inside the doorway.

"Didn't mean to interrupt," Dylan began, not recognizing the elderly fellow who'd been embracing his girlfriend.

"Was just leaving," Jamie spoke, his voice very much the same and I saw Dylan pause, focus on the eyes before taking a cautious step backwards.

"Stoddard."

A slight nod of acknowledgment. "Locke."

An awkward silence descended, one in which all of our unspoken thoughts seemed to gather in the air.

"Thank you," Dylan finally said. "For what you did out there."

The old man nodded, dropped his hand to the pocket where I knew he would touch the cameo again. And again, when the darkness came for good.

"I loved Karen." A slight pause. "And a part of me was glad she found you," he stopped again, coughed into his fist. "If she had been who I thought she was, done what she was meant to do…it would have hurt her to see me like this."

I looked at Dylan and admired the courage it took for him to listen.

"Believe me when I say I never meant to hurt her."

"I do."

"The accident—"

"Doesn't matter anymore."

The old man turned towards the door. "I suppose you're right."

And with that simple statement, Jamie Stoddard walked out the door and down the long, paneled hallway and I was left with a heaviness that would mark his place in my life for a long time to come.

"J?" Dylan's voice reminded me of where I was, how much I'd missed him, and I turned, found him sitting on the side of my bed and began to cry because I was so happy.

He bent over, cupped the side of my face and kissed my forehead. "Please don't."

"I can't."

"It's over, baby."

"I know," I sobbed, and as I bawled he did the best thing a boyfriend could do—he crawled into bed and held me.

And so, we remained as he told me about how he had traced my cell phone to the farmhouse, how he had heard the gunshots coming from the woods and had taken off at a dead run, certain that Red Rover had killed me.

"Did I forget to tell you I know how to shoot?" I teased.

He smiled in return. "You might have."

"I was afraid you weren't going to get there in time," I confessed. "I broke that branch at the Ocqueoc trailhead."

"I saw it. But you shouldn't have started without me."

"I had to. Red Rover was right behind."

"I know, but—"

"You stopped the bleeding," I reminded him.

"Barely," he caught hold of my right hand, squeezed gently. "When you passed out I thought"—a quick shake of his head—"I don't want to think about what I thought. I carried you that way up to the trailhead."

"It's okay."

"No, it's not. I've never seen someone lose that much blood and live to tell about it."

"I did," I turned his face to mine. "Thanks to you."

He didn't move at first, just looked at me as he had the night he'd let my name dangle between us like a chime in the breeze. "Just don't ask me to do it again."

I felt my chest go hot and wondered if I would ever tire of being in love with him.

"I heard what you said."

He closed his eyes, a slight smile making his lips that much more appealing. "I wasn't sure if you did. But I meant it just the same."

One inch closer and his mouth closed over mine, a feeling of completion making me heavy and lightheaded. Moments later he broke contact, sank back into his position with I could only assume was weariness and asked, "What do we do now?"

I knew he wanted to know if I could stay in Lantern Creek—and I fought hard not to mention a cute bungalow in New England, the novel I hoped to write someday, and his job with the local athletic department.

"I can't leave," he said.

"Can't?" I asked. "Or won't?"

I felt him tense up, draw back. "Dad's sick."

"I know."

"I need to help Mom and Avery."

"You need to make your own life."

"I have. And it's here."

"That's great," I said.

"But not good enough."

"No," I began, hoping a subtle change of subject would put us back on track. "I think it's good you became a cop when you couldn't be a lawyer."

The look on his face told me I couldn't have shoved my foot any further down my throat.

"Dylan—"

"It's okay," He laughed it off. "Going to law school was never my thing."

I paused, began picking at the gauze around my wrists again. "What is your thing?"

He looked at me, unsure if this line of questioning could be trusted. "Isn't it obvious?"

"No," I persisted, wanting him to open up. "I mean the thing you would do if you knew you couldn't screw it up."

He shrugged, as though what he wanted wasn't worth telling. "I don't know…I guess I always kind of wanted to be a history teacher."

I smiled, loving the image, feeling the warmness in my chest that meant it was right. "Why didn't you?"

He chuckled, "Have you met my mother?"

"Once."

He smiled. "Then you get it."

I touched the side of his bruised face, pictured him grading papers at a cluttered desk, pushing a pair of reading glasses up from the bridge of his nose, students waiting outside to ask him about an upcoming test and it seemed as natural as anything I'd ever seen him do.

"You can do it, Dyl—*we* can do it."

"No, I can't."

"But you had a scholarship."

"For sports," he corrected, his tone telling me the last place he wanted to be discussing his educational future this was in my hospital bed. "I can't hack it, J. Wasn't making the grades before Dad had his stroke so like it or not I'm never going to be anything but a hick cop and the woman I marry has got to be okay with that." I felt him watching me and shrunk under the gravity of his statement.

"Is that a proposal?" I asked, then wished I hadn't.

"Is that an answer?" he shot back.

"Dylan—" I began, miserable with the turn our conversation had taken.

"We came together for a reason," he said, his voice resigned. "And now it's over."

"It was more than that."

"Was it?" he asked. "Can we really go back to being a normal couple after all the shit we've seen?"

I felt my hands start to shake, the hands that were bandaged from thumb to forearm and wished for an instant that I'd died in the woods. "Why are you doing this?"

He put his head down, touched my gauze. "I know there's so much more you want to do, so much more you deserve."

I slumped back against the pillows, wishing we'd been content to snuggle and kiss and keep our big mouths shut. "I want *you!*"

"Then you get Lantern Creek and Three Fires Lodge and tending bar with Mallard Brauski as part of the package."

I looked away, my heart broken. "You make it sound so glamorous."

"I'm not trying to make it sound like anything other than what it is."

"I can find a better job."

"Where?" he demanded. "You're talented, J. I read some of the stuff you keep in your journal. Sooner or later you'd get sick of this place and you'd hate me for making you stay."

"Don't do this," I whispered. "You wanted me to stay—"

"I did," he agreed. "But it's pretty obvious you don't."

"I never said that."

"I can't let you plug yourself into a life meant for someone else."

I bit my lip, stunned. "You mean Karen?"

He didn't answer. The silence was potent and full and wet and heavy and I felt my throat clogging. "You wanted this with her?"

He didn't argue and at once I felt him draw closer, felt his face against the side of my own.

"Come downstate with me," I urged, reaching out to touch his arm. "Try school again. Do something for yourself."

"I can't."

"Dylan—"

"I'm sorry," he whispered, his fingers in my hair, pushing it back from my forehead.

"So am I," I said, the poignancy of the evening somehow spoiled as I thought about our bungalow and the ocean birds gathered above it, light pouring over me from a southern window we would never get to see.

Chapter Twenty-Nine

I came home on Wednesday morning and spent most of the afternoon waiting for my life to go back to normal. Holly was there with bells on, ready to cheer me with stories about what she'd done in my absence, the least of which was sprucing up the apartment for my grand return.

I looked around, sniffed the air, and had to admit she'd done a good job.

Clean litter box or no, it didn't take long for my melancholy to return.

"So, what are you and Dave gonna do?"

She didn't answer at first and I wondered if she knew about Dylan and the proposal he'd yet to extend to the girl who'd better get used to living in a crappy town with a hick cop.

"I was gonna talk to you about that."

I couldn't hide my surprise. "You were?"

She smiled, her excitement barely under wraps. "He asked me to move in!"

I felt a lead weight settle in my stomach and sat down on one of our wobbly stools as she placed a plate of spaghetti in front of me.

"The bigwigs at camp offered me a job through the winter. With the extra money we'll be able to buy off his house and..." she paused, blushing for the first time. "Who knows?"

"Oh, Holl," I said, rolling a bunch of noodles around my fork, happy she'd gotten the ending I'd wanted. And jealous. "That's great."

"Yep!" she squeaked, clapping her hands. "Once I move in you and Dylan can come over on Friday nights and play euchre!"

Ah, the sweet domestic bliss of it all. "That'd be swell."

"He has a hot tub, too. Ooo, la la."

I shook my head. "Hot tubs give me a rash."

One glance at me and she knew something was off.

"You're moving in with him, right? I never would've said yes but Dave was sure Dylan was getting ready to ask you."

I smiled.

"You're gonna say yes, right, because if you even *think* about turning the meathead down I'm calling Jen Reddy and—"

"Stop, Holly."

She paused, really seeing my misery for the first time, and came around to my side of the bar. "What's going on?"

I looked down, still miserable. "I want to go downstate. He doesn't."

She grimaced like she'd gotten an ice cream headache. "So, you're just going to break up with him because of a stupid thing like that? Can't you just *pretend* you like it here in Lantern Creek?"

"I do like it—"

"No, you don't," she shook her head, not angry, just pleased with herself for being so intuitive. "You just came up here to find your dad and now that you saved the world from that Preacher turned 'Walking Dead' extra you're gonna bail on us. I get it."

"My Dad died here," I said—not angry either. "No...let me rephrase that-he was *murdered* here."

"Squirt—"

"Oh, and his mistress would end up being my boss for the next twenty years, and if I get tired of that I could tend bar with Mallard Brauski, maybe work my way up into the upper tiers of tavern management and sling cocktails on band night."

"Come on—there are other jobs—"

"Not at the newspaper. I'd have to figure something else out."

Holly laughed, put her arm around my shoulder and touched her head to mine. "All right, already. We have the list of cons. So, what are the pros?"

I smiled, looked up at her. "Well, *you* of course."

"That goes without saying."

"And Adam. I mean, it would be great to have a brother."

"Sure...and you can't beat the scenery."

I laughed, thinking the same thing she was. "He doesn't want me to stay."

"He'd go nuts without you."

"You think so?" I asked, knowing full well I'd go nuts without him.

"I know it. And the last thing Dave needs is a depressed buddy so please give it a shot up here."

"He wanted this life with Karen, not me."

She grimaced again, this time in pity. "That's not true. I saw them together. It wasn't like the two of you are. Sure, they had to hide it but still...he loves you, Squirt. Really and truly loves you."

"Sometimes that's not enough."

She let out a little huff, defeated, and decided to change the subject. "I can't believe what friggin' happened out there."

"Neither did the hospital. They put me on a suicide watch."

She shook her head. "Word on the street is that that Mr. S was poaching on state lands and had a hunting accident."

I cleared my throat, my thoughts flying to all the things Jamie hadn't told me.

"And that his son took a job in Florida."

"Now that I can see."

Holly laughed, and I was reminded of my first night in Lantern Creek when I'd gone looking for ghosts at the Presque Isle Lighthouse and found Dylan instead.

I thought back on that moment of first meeting and wondered if it looked anything like the barn dance Jamie had spoken of, a moment of lantern light and swirling skirts and Esther Ebersole's cameo brooch.

Had they loved each other at first sight? Or had their feelings grown over time like Odessa and Butler's did while planting the vegetable garden?

"I need to go," I said to Holly while pushing to my feet. "Take a drive and clear my head."

"You okay?" she asked, genuinely concerned.

"Not really," I replied. "But happiness is overrated."

Moments later I'd changed into long pants and tennis shoes. Grabbing the keys to the Jeep, I headed for the door as the sun began its slow descent into the western forest.

I drove in silence to Back Forty Farm, a feeling of calm holding me in a warm grip, and when I got there I began walking towards the lavender field. Stopping just short of the oak tree, I saw that the leaves were starting to wither and curl and knew it was dying.

And that death was just the beginning.

HEY, SIS

I smiled, happy I could still hear him. Happier yet that I could speak to him without having to hide it.

"How did you know I was out here?"

YOU SERIOUS?

I didn't look at him, knew he and Rocky were standing just over my shoulder and put out my hand, which he took with care. Turning towards the road, I knew it must have taken him at least a half hour to walk here.

"Your mom know where you are?"

He smiled. **I'VE BEEN KNOWN TO SNEAK OUT**

I returned his smile, thinking that Pam probably knew more than we gave her credit for.

"Where do you think Dad is?"

My brother didn't answer and so I looked at him, saw his eyes scanning the forest and after a moment they came to rest on something, and so I followed his gaze, amazed at how the colors had changed in so short a time. But autumn came early to the northern woods and had transformed three hickory trees into a cluster of yellow paintbrushes.

I smiled again, my prayers about a second spring coming to these woods realized and I knew if my father could have chosen a place to be buried, this would be it.

Adam's hands sought the necklace from around his neck. The next moment he was placing something in my hands.

I looked down, saw my own necklace and almost wept.

"How did you find this?"

I LOOKED FOR IT

I laughed, tears of joy mixing with my grief as we held them in our hands before making our way to the woods. We stopped beneath the hickory trees and knelt, our hands digging in the soft earth, making a place for the silver necklaces that fell from our fingertips.

And in this way, we buried our father, taking all the best he had given us and laying it to rest in a place of beauty, words of thankfulness skipping like a stone from my brother's mind to my own as we imagined the man we'd never known—the man who had gone into the woods and never returned.

We sat until the moon began its climb and hung from the oak tree's grasp like a glass orb, and I wondered what sort of life had been made in the house it shadowed. And at what cost.

One touch to the shoulder and I knew it was time to go.

I stood, looking at the brother I loved more than I ever imagined, and turned toward home.

* * *

That night I dreamt of Butler, saw him gathering earth and carrying it to the yellow wood where we had buried the necklaces. Once there, he knelt, drew a circle and touched the center of it. Standing once again, he turned to look at me and I felt his reverence for this place, his gratitude for what I had done for him.

I saw him straighten his shoulders and realized he was quite tall, saw him turn his back to me and walk away into the night and I hoped his life with Odessa was as happy as I imagined Jonas and Esther's would be.

Which reminded me of my own romantic troubles as I sat up in bed.

I looked at Dylan lying beside me and wondered if Holly was right about how much he loved me.

Because I wasn't sure he wanted me to stay. Because it would have been easier to stay if he'd wanted to go.

Knowing sleep was futile, I got out of bed.

"Justine?" he asked, more alert to my movements now than ever before and I bent over, kissed his bare shoulder while wondering if he would pull me down—ask me to make love—but he didn't.

And I wasn't sure I wanted that, either.

So, I walked down the hallway and sat curled up in the La-Z-Boy, wondering where I would be tomorrow when Holly moved out and if Joey would have a proper place to hang his scratching post. I sat as the clock ticked off an hour, then another as my boyfriend slumbered on.

Or so I thought.

"What're you doing?" he asked. I swiveled and saw him standing beside me, all sleepy eyes and messy hair, my favorite boxer shorts hanging low on his hips and wondered why he had to look so hot at a time like this.

"Just thinking," I sat upright, pulled my knees to my chest and rested my chin on top of them.

"About what?" He came and sat cross-legged on the shag, his blue eyes resting on me in a way that seemed resigned.

"Tomorrow's my birthday," I said. Not wanting a pity party or a cake with presents but wanting to acknowledge something that was real and beyond our troubles.

"I didn't know—"

"It's okay," I said. "We had other things on our mind."

He laughed softly. "We did. And we do. And you need to tell me what you're really thinking about."

"You know," I answered, absentmindedly picking at my gauze, wondering what would have happened if he hadn't stopped the bleeding; if everything had ended then and there.

He nodded but didn't look at me. "You're going to go."

"I don't know what to do."

He glanced up, his eyes hopeful and I hated him for it.

"I want you to come with me."

"Justine—"

"I want you to *want* to go."

He shook his head. "That doesn't make sense."

"It does to me."

He looked away again, didn't try to explain because he'd already done that in the hospital. "So, what now?"

I turned my cheek into my knee. "You get the life you wanted."

"What's that supposed to mean?"

"I don't fit here anymore. It's done."

"I knew you were going to say that."

I didn't argue. I had no strength for it. "You were right."

No howls of despair or pleas to the contrary from Deputy Locke, and I hated him for that, too—hated the way he could let me leave town without a fight when he'd almost died for me in the woods beyond Ocqueoc Falls.

"When?" he asked, and I felt my throat closing on itself, picked at the gauze again and wanted to rip it off, open the wound.

"Holly moves out tomorrow. I guess I will, too."

"Some birthday."

"It won't be the first time."

He cleared his throat, his eyes still down. "I'll be at work."

I swallowed, unable to hide my despair. "I'll leave the Jeep at the lake house."

He shook his head. "You're not driving the Heap."

If his words were meant to sway me with chivalry, they did just the opposite. "Don't worry about it, Dylan. I'm not your problem anymore."

He didn't react visibly to my words, but something in the way his shoulders tightened told me I'd hurt him. "I'm sorry if I made you feel that way."

I sat, rubbing my cheek against my knee as tears welled over my eyelids, wanting to tell him I didn't mean it and wanting him to feel the same pain I was. And so, I said nothing.

"Hang onto the Jeep until you get to where you need to go. It doesn't matter to me," he stopped, cleared his throat and I wanted to curl up in his lap and hold him close so I would remember what he felt like on the lonely nights to come. "You matter more. You've always mattered more and I'm sorry I can't make you believe that."

"Don't," I got out of the chair, went to him on the floor as he folded his arms around me, rocking me as he had at the Falls, his face against my forehead and I felt something touch my skin, something wet and realized he was crying, too. "I meant it when I said this was enough."

He pressed his mouth to my temple in a quick kiss, arms tightening as they had the night I'd jumped out of Jamie's truck in the pink flip flops he'd dared me to walk home in. And I wondered if I would have done things differently knowing what I did now, taken another road to another town or simply stayed put, always missing the place he had filled in my heart but never knowing why.

"No," he finally answered. "It wasn't."

Chapter Thirty

"Anyone know where I can get a good burger?"

I waited, my hand on the screen door as I surveyed the dark interior of the bar I'd come to love and spotted Mallard's white muscle shirt at the end of it, Iris seated on the stool just in front of him.

"Well if it ain't the ugliest barmaid this side of the forty-fifth," Mallard shouted. "Pam said you might be comin' 'round to say goodbye."

I nodded, tried to be brave and smile and act like my heart wasn't breaking when just that morning I'd walked away from the love of my life for reasons only my feminine pride could answer.

"I'm all packed," I chirped, daring a glance at Iris, wondering where she had been in the last few days and why she hadn't dropped by or sent flowers or cooked me supper. Mallard just ambled to the screen door and glanced at the Jeep.

"You keepin' the wheels?"

"Uh-huh."

"Put out for it?"

I wanted to smack him across the back of the head for asking such a question in front of my grandmother.

"None of your damn business."

He swung the door open, pushed past me while saying, "Just gonna check under the hood to see if she's sound." Then, over his shoulder, "Fix her up a plate, Iris."

I'd never seen my grandmother take orders from anyone and was mildly surprised when she got off of her stool and went around back. Moments later the smell of sizzling hamburger met my nostrils, making my mouth water.

"Where you off to now?" she asked, her back still to me.

"Not sure," I spoke above the sizzle, disappointed we wouldn't be sharing that glass of lemonade after all.

"Doesn't sound like such a nice place."

"It could be," I answered, thinking of the whole, wide world spread before me—the open road and the places it would take me.

"What does your Mom think of this?" Iris asked.

I shrugged. "She's okay with it."

"Well, miracles never cease."

"I beg to differ."

"Happy Birthday, by the way."

You know?" I asked. Of course she did.

"Been keeping track of them for a while now."

I looked away, unable to meet her eyes. "Thank you."

"Too bad you have to leave today."

I sat back on my stool and thought about Dylan.

True to his word, he had left my apartment at 7:30 to work a double shift, kissing me as though it were any other day and I'd stood at the kitchen window, sobbing as he pulled out of the driveway before finally pulling myself together and packing up my things.

"I can't say it's the best burger I've ever fried up, but it'll have to do."

"Thanks," I managed as she spun on her heel, setting the food down in front of me.

"You still have that big cat of yours?"

I nodded, wondering why she was beating around the bush at a time like this.

"He like the open road as much as you?"

I shrugged. Joey liked me, but not necessarily the cat carrier I'd stuffed him into.

"What do you say he stays with me—just until you get settled."

I felt my eyes widen and sat my burger down, took a small sip of Coke.

"Gives me an excuse to check in with you now and again." She paused, her green eyes meeting mine for the first time. "If that's alright."

I nodded, tried to pick up my burger but found my hands were shaking. My grandmother circled the bar, sat down beside me. "I'm sorry I didn't come sooner."

I looked at her.

"And I don't just mean the last few days."

I swallowed past the love clogging my throat.

"You're going to be fine. You're a Cook."

"I know," I said, trying to believe it.

"The end is sometimes just the beginning."

I looked up at her, wondering if she knew something I didn't when Mallard came swaggering back inside. "Checked your oil, Flats" he bragged, his smile wide and bright. "Might want to put a quart in when you get to wherever the hell you're going."

"Mind grabbing my cat," I said while rising to my feet. "Grandma here seems to think she can take better care of him than I can."

He glanced at Iris, scratched the back of his head and then did as I asked, and I found that letting go of Joey was easier than I thought because he was in good hands. Because I knew I would see him again.

Which couldn't be said for the other man in my life.

Five minutes later we were standing at the bottom of the porch, and I was hugging Iris, then Mallard as he ruffled the top of my head. "Stay outta trouble."

I couldn't answer, just climbed into the Jeep and backed out of the parking lot before I changed my mind and made a career out of the place.

Which wouldn't be half bad considering the location and clientele and opportunity for advancement. It was just a short drive from the lake house and we could make it work, especially while Dylan was in school and I had to support us.

I shut my mind to that thought, pulled out onto 23 and headed north towards Cheboygan with my load a little lighter and my heart a lot heavier, and glanced at the dashboard clock.

6:17 p.m.

Dylan would be breaking for supper about now, probably running up to the little diner at Hammond Bay—and if that were the case we might possibly pass on this lonely stretch of road.

I touched my cell phone, almost called him to meet up for coffee and then thought better of it because Lord knew where a small conversation could lead with our hearts still raw and tender and discombobulated and—

I glanced back at the road, saw something on the shoulder—something tall, with bronzed skin and dark hair. He stood looking at me and I realized who he was, what he was, as he stepped in front of my Jeep.

"Shit!" I screeched as I swerved across the center lane, grateful that the road was empty and I wouldn't have to add a new car to my list of necessities.

Three hundred and sixty degrees later I was sitting on the opposite side of the road with my heart in my eyeballs. A quick glance out my rearview mirror told me the Shaman had vanished just as steam began to pour from beneath the hood.

Does a Shaman ever really die?

"Dammit, Butler," I cursed while grabbing for the purple package that had landed in my lap—an open package I now kept because I understood its true meaning.

I looked at it and thought of the orange kitten in the party hat, the way I had torn it up—and the medicine bag, hidden inside. I wondered how my father had known the card would make me angry enough to tuck the present away.

But Dad knew everything…

243

Except how to say goodbye.

I looked at the box again, wondering why Butler had stepped into the road, knowing I would be forced to swerve, knowing the package would end up in my lap. Knowing it was my birthday.

Three months ago I would have written the whole thing off as a hallucinatory coincidence—but now I knew there was no such thing.

I looked at the box again, opened the top and saw something I had missed the night we found the medicine bag—a small note with five words printed on the outside in the neat, block letters I recognized.

To the Man You Love

At first, I couldn't believe what I was seeing, couldn't believe I was holding it after all this time.

My father had thought of everything, and a part of me wanted to rip it open, read every last line, but I knew that wasn't what Robert Cook had intended when he'd written it.

I thought of the man I'd kissed goodbye that very morning and knew he was the one I wanted to spend the rest of my life with, the one I wanted to father my children and the man I hoped would carry my cameo in his pocket, touching it from time to time when his thoughts darkened and I was no longer there to comfort him.

I thought of Dylan Locke and his fear of falling short.

Going long.

Jumping without a net.

And knew I didn't want to live if I couldn't fly.

Unfortunately, modern technology paired with horrible reception didn't agree with me.

"Dammit!" I cursed again, throwing my cell phone over my shoulder as I slumped against the driver's seat. Five minutes passed, then ten without a single passing car.

I glanced down at my feet, was mildly surprised to see the pink flip-flops and laughed to myself, knowing I would have walked a thousand miles to reach him, my heart lighting the way.

Opening the door, I offered a prayer to the God of small domestic pets that Joey was safe and sound and probably finishing up the leftover hamburger at Huff's and stepped out onto 23.

Four paces and I saw a police cruiser approaching, six and his lights went on. Twelve and I knew miracles could happen.

He came to stop about twenty feet behind the Jeep, stepped out and closed the distance between us in a few brisk steps.

"J?"

"Yes," I nodded as if his sudden appearance hadn't shaken me to the core.

"What happened?" He asked, and I saw in him the same thing I'd just recognized in myself.

"There was someone," I began. "At the side of the road. I think it was Butler."

He nodded his head, used to these things by now and asked the requisite, "You okay?"

"I think so…but Dylan," I touched his arm, brought the letter from my back pocket and placed it in his hand. "This was inside my birthday present and I don't know how we missed it and I think it was meant for you," I felt my cheeks go hot. "I know it was."

He turned it over in his hands, looked at what was written, and I saw his eyes widen as he glanced at me. "Your Dad wrote this?"

I nodded.

"Did you read it?"

I shook my head.

"Do you think I should?" he asked, uncomfortable and I felt my hope dying as quickly as it had appeared. "It's kind of special."

"And you're *not*?" I snapped. "How can you honestly stand there and act like you didn't save my life a week ago? That you didn't tell me you loved me, wanted to be with me?"

"Justine," one hand up, to calm the excited woman and I had to fight the urge to stomp on his toe and see if the superpowers were gone for good.

"Just read the damn letter," I whispered, "Throw it away if you want but stop acting like what we had didn't mean anything to you."

He looked down at the envelope in his hands, turned it over a couple of times before fingering the outside edge. "I'm not acting like nothing ever happened. I tried your cell when I got a call that someone had broken down out here. I thought it might be you—thought you might need help—"

I narrowed my eyes. "How could anyone have *called* you? No one's been by in the last twenty minutes which was why I was *walking* to town."

He glanced down and I saw his jaw loosen into the smile I adored. "In those shoes?"

I fought the urge to laugh but looked away instead as he circled to the front of the Jeep and popped the hood. After a few seconds he stepped away and scratched the back of his head.

"Loose radiator cap," he said matter-of-factly. "Was someone messing with the engine today?"

"No," I answered, a picture of Mallard's wide, bright smile playing through my mind—and Iris, suddenly so willing to fry me up the worst burger in town. "I stopped by Huff's to see Iris—"

"And Mallard checked your oil?"

I nodded.

"Did they know I was working today?"

"Have you seen the new police scanner next to the till?"

He chuckled, leaned back against the side of the Jeep. "Guess we need all the help we can get."

I smiled, the tension between us gone as he opened the letter, read the words my father had written so long ago. And when he had finished he folded it up, placed it in his front pocket and looked down on me through Robert Cook's eyes.

And I couldn't have imagined how wonderful it would feel.

"What did it say?"

He shook his head, his words measured. "That's between me and him."

I looked down, loving the sound of what he'd just said as he put an arm across my shoulder, turning me into his chest while resting his chin on top of my head. "I shouldn't have mentioned Karen—shouldn't have doubted what we had," he paused. "What we have."

I didn't answer. Couldn't if I'd wanted to.

"You can't know how it feels to want something you're afraid you'll lose," he paused, and I felt his fingers tighten around my shoulder. "Something you've loved since the first time you saw her." He pulled away, tipped my chin with his index finger until our eyes met. "I'll go with you."

I closed my eyes, felt the loose ends of my life bind together at last.

"I'll stay."

He chuckled, emotion softening his voice. "You could have told me that yesterday."

"No, I couldn't."

He pressed his lips to my temple, full of what I was feeling. "What now?"

I smiled, thinking of a bungalow by the eastern sea. A table at the lake house where we could play euchre with Holly and Dave on Friday nights and knew it really didn't matter.

"Go get some cake and ice cream?"

He put his head back, laughed into the August sky and I knew that our ending had become the beginning—and that the beginning was everywhere.

Evening in the Yellow Wood

I asked my father a question once, a man who now slept peacefully beneath the evening in a yellow wood.

His answer had been so simple.

Be happy.

And I was.

The End

Acknowledgments

Thanks to all who encouraged me on my writing journey: my wonderful teachers Darryl Smith, Jacque Andersen, Stuart Dybek, and Arnie Johnston who made me believe I might be a good at this thing. My amazing reviewers Lynda Curnyn, Steph Post, and Alexia Gordon. Special thanks to Cindy Taylor for her beautiful pictures and the many friends who became an army of positivity: Hayla Britton, Sharon Bippus, Trudy Camp, Bethany Hagner, Christa Braden, Danielle Oliver, Doloris Clark, Debbie Yoder, Lori Barczak (giving you my chapters is still the best motivation) Penni Jones (can I ever thank you ENOUGH?), Margy Eickoff, Kathy Rabbers, Karrie Frederick, Lisa Melville, Heather Nordenbrock, Sara Doe and Shone Rhyner. Thanks to everyone at Pandamoon Publishing who gave this little story a chance (Cheri Champagne, I'm looking at YOU) as well as Zara and Allan Kramer and the wonderful group of publicists (Elgon Williams and Christine Gabriel) and amazing people I've had the pleasure of working with since I signed. Thanks to Rachel Schoenbauer and Heather Stewart for your excellent insight and to Don Kramer for your GORGEOUS cover. Thanks to Meg Bonney and Matt Coleman for your general awesomeness. And to everyone in my Epsilon class— thanks for keepin' it real at 9:15 on Thursday nights.

Thanks also to the people of Roger's City, Michigan for welcoming me as one of their own and for planting the seed of this story in my heart, and to Squirrel (aka Mallard) for encouraging me to "write the damn book" that would one day become *Evening in the Yellow Wood*.

Last but not least, I'd like to thank my family for their support. Ron and Rachel, you've always been my soft place to fall. Cyndi and Teresa, even though we live on opposite sides of the country, knowing you believed in me has kept me writing. Mom and Dad, I hope the creative writing degree has now paid off! Ana and Aubrey, I know I spent a lot of late nights writing this book but I hope at the end of the day you think your mom is kinda cool. Meg and Stone, I wouldn't be able to do what I do if you weren't the kids you are, and to my husband, Scott, I hope you know how much your support has meant to me, how your love has illuminated my life, and how I look forward to one day buying our cabin in the northern woods where I can write stories and you can wrangle horses. Love you more.

About the Author

Laura is a teacher who loves to write about her home state of Michigan. She has a B.A. in Creative Writing from Western Michigan University where she studied under Stuart Dybek, and she has had her short fiction and poetry published in *Chicken Soup for the Soul, Word Riot, Tonopalah Review, SaLit* and *SLAB: Sound and Literary Art Book.* "The Pursuit of Happiness," a short story she wrote while at WMU, was chosen as a finalist in the Trial Balloon Fiction Contest.

When not writing, Laura enjoys musical theatre, hiking, swimming, reading, and performing with her Celtic band, Si Bhaeg Si Mohr. She also enjoys spending time with her husband and children as well as her dog, two hamsters, two gerbils, ten chickens, two horses and eight (and counting) cats.

Laura loves to connect with readers on her blog: (Sea Legs on Land) laurakemp.author@blogspot.com, as well as on Facebook, Twitter @LKempWrites and Instagram lkempwrites.

Thank you for purchasing this copy of **Evening in the Yellow Wood**. If you enjoyed this book, please let the author know by posting a review.

pandamoon
publishing

Growing good ideas into great reads…one book at a time.

Visit www.pandamoonpublishing.com to learn about other works by our talented authors.

Mystery/Thriller/Suspense

- *A Flash of Red* by Sarah K. Stephens
- *Evening in the Yellow Wood* by Laura Kemp
- *Fate's Past* by Jason Huebinger
- *Graffiti Creek* by Matt Coleman
- *Juggling Kittens* by Matt Coleman
- *Killer Secrets* by Sherrie Orvik
- *Knights of the Shield* by Jeff Messick
- *Kricket* by Penni Jones
- *Looking into the Sun* by Todd Tavolazzi
- *On the Bricks Series Book 1: On the Bricks* by Penni Jones
- *Rogue Saga Series Book 1: Rogue Alliance* by Michelle Bellon
- *Southbound* by Jason Beem
- *The Juliet* by Laura Ellen Scott
- *The Last Detective* by Brian Cohn
- *The Moses Winter Mysteries Book 1: Made Safe* by Francis Sparks
- *The New Royal Mysteries Book 1: The Mean Bone in Her Body* by Laura Ellen Scott
- *The New Royal Mysteries Book 2: Crybaby Lane* by Laura Ellen Scott
- *The Ramadan Drummer* by Randolph Splitter
- *The Teratologist* by Ward Parker
- *The Unraveling of Brendan Meeks* by Brian Cohn
- *The Zeke Adams Series Book 1: Pariah* by Ward Parker
- *This Darkness Got to Give* by Dave Housley

Science Fiction/Fantasy

- *Becoming Thuperman* by Elgon Williams
- *Children of Colondona Book 1: The Wizard's Apprentice* by Alisse Lee Goldenberg
- *Children of Colondona Book 2: The Island of Mystics* by Alisse Lee Goldenberg
- *Chimera Catalyst* by Susan Kuchinskas
- *Dybbuk Scrolls Trilogy Book 1: The Song of Hadariah* by Alisse Lee Goldenberg
- *Dybbuk Scrolls Trilogy Book 2: The Song of Vengeance* by Alisse Lee Goldenberg
- *Dybbuk Scrolls Trilogy Book 3: The Song of War* by Alisse Lee Goldenberg
- *Everly Series Book 1: Everly* by Meg Bonney
- *.EXE Chronicles Book 1: Hello World* by Alexandra Tauber and Tiffany Rose
- *Fried Windows (In a Light White Sauce)* by Elgon Williams
- *Magehunter Saga Book 1: Magehunter* by Jeff Messick
- *Project 137* by Seth Augenstein
- *Revengers Series Book 1: Revengers* by David Valdes Greenwood
- *The Bath Salts Journals: Volume One* by Alisse Lee Goldenberg and An Tran
- *The Crimson Chronicles Book 1: Crimson Forest* by Christine Gabriel
- *The Crimson Chronicles Book 2: Crimson Moon* by Christine Gabriel
- *The Phaethon Series Book 1: Phaethon* by Rachel Sharp
- *The Sitnalta Series Book 1: Sitnalta* by Alisse Lee Goldenberg
- *The Sitnalta Series Book 2: The Kingdom Thief* by Alisse Lee Goldenberg
- *The Sitnalta Series Book 3: The City of Arches* by Alisse Lee Goldenberg
- *The Sitnalta Series Book 4: The Hedgewitch's Charm* by Alisse Lee Goldenberg
- *The Sitnalta Series Book 5: The False Princess* by Alisse Lee Goldenberg
- *The Wolfcat Chronicles Book 1: Wolfcat 1* by Elgon Williams

Women's Fiction

- *Beautiful Secret* by Dana Faletti
- *The Long Way Home* by Regina West
- *The Mason Siblings Series Book 1: Love's Misadventure* by Cheri Champagne
- *The Mason Siblings Series Book 2: The Trouble with Love* by Cheri Champagne
- *The Mason Siblings Series Book 3: Love and Deceit* by Cheri Champagne
- *The Mason Siblings Series Book 4: Final Battle for Love* by Cheri Champagne
- *The Seductive Spies Series Book 1: The Thespian Spy* by Cheri Champagne
- *The Seductive Spy Series Book 2: The Seamstress and the Spy* by Cheri Champagne
- *The Shape of the Atmosphere* by Jessica Dainty
- *The To-Hell-And-Back Club Book 1: The To-Hell-And-Back Club* by Jill Hannah Anderson
- *The To-Hell-And-Back Club Book 2: Crazy Little Town Called Love* by Jill Hannah Anderson

Book Club Questions

1. What was your general impression of the story? Did it hook you right away or did it take some time to get into it?

2. What was your favorite quote or passage?

3. Who was your favorite character? Why?

4. What made the setting of the story unique? Could this story have taken place anywhere and had the same effect on the reader?

5. What were the major themes of the book?

6. If the character of Karen hadn't been killed in the car accident, how might the story have changed?

7. How did the character of Jamie transform throughout the story? How did your opinion of him change?

8. How did you like the ending of the book? Is there anything you would have done differently?

9. Did the book change your opinion or perspective of anything?

10. If the book was made into a movie, who would you want to see play the parts?

CPSIA information can be obtained
at www.ICGtesting.com
Printed in the USA
LVHW081207230121
677114LV00031B/2186